BEFORE THE RUINS

Jim Hohenbary

Before the Ruins

Jim Hohenbary

BLUEBERRY
LANE BOOKS

NEW YORK

To Mom and Dad

*Thank you for, among other things, letting me stay up past
my bedtime to watch Dracula.*

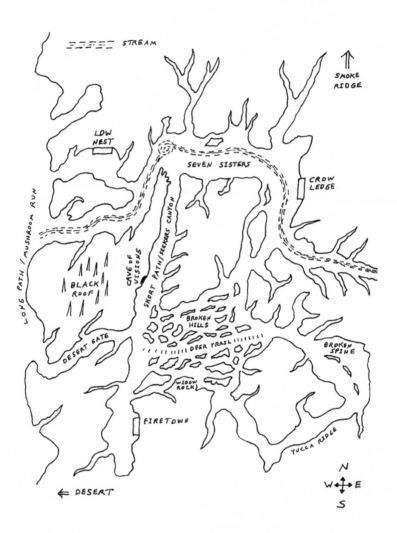

CONTENTS

"When Richard Wetherill, rancher and early explorer of the "Four Corners" region, inquired among the Navajo regarding the cliff dwellings he had found, he was told that those long-deserted structures belonged to the *Anasazi*. The word was translated roughly as *the ancient enemy*. While some now suggest that *the old ones who are strangers* might interpret the word more accurately, the term has still been commonly used to describe those early inhabitants ever since. We are left to only imagine what connotations the Navajo might have originally intended when they first migrated into the region and encountered these iconic ruins of the American Southwest, abandoned abruptly and left vacant for generations . . ."

– From *Roadtrip History: the Southwest*
by Ben Grant (1973).

PROLOGUE

Edge of the Map

"MY BRETHREN SAY you can be trusted. I must sail this night. When the tide flows out. Can you serve me?" the vampire asked. He rested one hand across the pommel of his sword. He also stood close, hoping to intimidate the sailor that stood before him, hoping that fear might speed the transaction. The battens in the sails clanked against the masts. He wanted to use the coming weather to his advantage. It might help him lose the Knights of St. John.

The knights intended to kill him, and persistent as thirst, they were closing their net once again. Standing over the Qian River and looking toward the Great Eastern Sea, the vampire had nowhere else to run, and his brethren in Lin'An had refused to hide him. "The Mongols give the knights safe passage," one of them had explained. "The Khan even lends his own soldiers and horses. How can we risk open conflict?"

"Power will tolerate all that sustains it," the vampire had nodded, quoting the Seventh Precept. He would have done the same thing. "Then I must leave your province by sea," he had told them, "Can you secure my passage?" His brethren, wishing for trouble to depart quickly, had directed him to meet this particular sailor.

"Where do you wish to go?" the sailor asked. He had already made a great deal of money taking "night passengers" up and down the coast. First the Song rulers, and now the Yuan officials, had turned a blind eye to the vampires. The demons paid well and demanded little more than discretion. And shelter from the sun.

The vampire smiled but did not show his teeth. "I wish to cross this ocean. To find its other shore." A few drops of rain splattered the pier.

CHAPTER 1

Arrows in Flight

Approximately 1287 A.D.
Somewhere in the American Southwest . . .

THE CHILL AIR of night still lingered despite the early morning sun. Makya loved how the light sliced to the floor of the canyon at this time of day. He wore no shirt and relished the coolness of the shadows. A necklace of knotted twine, dyed black, hung from his neck, matching the belt that fixed his breechcloth around his waist. Both were gifts from Sihu, his wife. The young warrior carried three spears, and a plain sack, still empty, hung from his belt. He swung the spears back and forth in one hand now, listening to the hum as they sliced the air. Makya was respected by his clan, the Morning Crows. Without equal in battle, he often led hunts and, when Hototo allowed it, raids against the rival clans. In fact, he already shared the status of war leader with Choovio, his elder brother. Many believed he might lead the Crows in future years.

He had chosen to hunt alone this morning. He wanted to find a Gila. Hototo, as spirit leader of the Morning Crows, had requested one. The knobby lizards, easily spotted by their orange and black skin, were scarce these days and tasted terrible; but their tough hide made a powerful balm for wounds. However, finding no promising tracks or holes, Makya had drifted to the margin of Morning Crow land. The boundary grew blurry and disputed here. He chose to walk in the soft sand, leaving the imprint of his sandals for the High Rocks warriors to find. He liked to test these borders, to remind them that the ground belonged to his people, that the nearby stream, finally flowing again, belonged to his people. He sought to breathe life into the Morning Crow right of ownership with each step. Despite all claims to the contrary.

And then Makya heard the snap of bowstrings high above his head, the wind abruptly perturbed. An arrow clattered sharply against the rocks behind him. Another caught his shin, its stone edge slicing to the bone with a downward trajectory that traced the path of its flight. Pain burned across his leg. He dropped to one knee and silently scanned the cliffs above him. Holding the spears to protect his head, he saw nothing. No motion broke the line between the sky and the rocky ledge. "Show your face!" he shouted. "Challenge me for real! Only cowards hide!" His voice slapped the canyon walls. No answer returned.

Makya plucked the arrows from the sand. He examined them. Hastily made. "No wonder they missed." He snapped both shafts, throwing the broken halves on the ground. The cut was deep but looked worse than it was. Using the tip of his spear, he cut a long strip of cloth from his sack, previously intended for the Gila, and tied it tightly around his wound. He began to trot quickly back toward Crow Ledge. Makya pushed the pain from his mind. However, blood still trickled down his leg, exertion keeping it fresh.

He felt certain that the High Rocks Clan had launched those arrows. He wondered if they had intended to kill him. Maybe they had just wanted to scare him. He shook his head. Why would the High Rocks Clan risk renewed conflict after last winter? Did they want to get thrashed again? It seemed that their renewed ties with the larger Ash Owl Clan were making the High Rocks Clan bold, making them eager to pick new fights. Even so, Makya felt certain that the Morning Crows needed to answer such attempts at intimidation. That they must not fear their own borders.

Makya resolved to tell Hototo right away. As leader of the Morning Crows, the shaman would want to know. But the young warrior felt his resolve slowly fade as he imagined the path such a conversation might take. Hototo would surely scold him for drifting too close to High Rocks land once again, especially since Choovio had not yet returned from his hunt in the mountains. Makya feared that Hototo might not even let him retaliate this time. "Not after last winter," Makya panted.

~ B ~

"Will the High Rocks Clan find us here? Will they shoot us?" little Kaya asked. As a daughter of the Morning Crow clan, she had learned to ask such questions. However, she did not really seem nervous. Her mother smiled.

"No, we are much closer to the Ash Owl Clan here."

"Will the Ash Owls find us?"

"I think we are safe. But you are smart to avoid them," Pavati gently praised her daughter as the morning sun warmed their skin. "What did I teach you?"

"When we see *two* braids . . . we run the other way!" Kaya recited as she struggled to situate the tumpline across her scalp. The leather strap slipped first forward then back, but she finally found the point of balance, just past her forehead. The young girl cautiously removed her hands. The firewood settled firmly against her bare back. Kaya turned slowly toward Pavati.

"Mom . . . look," she said.

Pavati clapped her hands softly. "You did it. What a big helper you are!" she said with an enthusiastic whisper. Kaya smiled proudly. Like her mother, she wore only a skirt for daily labor. And like all the Morning Crows, she knotted her hair as a single braid. Kaya had swept it over the front of her left shoulder to protect it from the bundle of sticks that now rested across her back. Two small feathers, black and iridescent, hung from the tip.

"We don't like the Ash Owls, do we?" Kaya said.

Pavati shook her head and frowned. The Ash Owls had made an orphan of her husband. His younger brother bore that burden too. Choovio and Makya had just been kids, not much older than Kaya was currently. "No, we don't like them," she agreed.

Pavati would never trust the Ash Owls, no matter how quiet they had been lately. She furtively scanned the horizon. However, she still felt relatively safe near Ash Owl territory. It was far smarter than going near High Rocks land these days. She kept her voice down. "You can tell your dad that you brought lots of wood home," she added.

"Will he come home soon? Can he cook on my fire tonight?" Kaya asked.

"The sheep move further into the mountains this time of year. We will eat with Makya and Sihu tonight. Dad will return home in a few days."

"Yes!" Kaya said softly. She took a small skip with her feet. Her firewood clattered but did not fall.

Pavati stooped to add more wood to her own load. "Should we try between those rocks?" she whispered to Kaya. Choovio would lay with Pavati by the dying coals when he returned to Crow Ledge. He would hold her as the night cooled. Pavati could almost feel his skin pressed against her own, his breath falling warm against her neck. A good shiver ran through her.

~ B ~

Old Chu'Si watched from the corner of her eye as two High Rocks warriors returned home to Low Nest. As matriarch of the clan, she paid attention when young men returned in an excited state.

"Did you see him jump? Hah! And he says we are cowards!" Wik said with a laugh.

"I think you almost hit him. Will he try to pay us back?" Nuk replied. He stole a glance over his shoulder.

"I hope he does!" Wik growled. He brandished his bow for emphasis. The two High Rocks warriors were just returning home. Their voices broke onto the terrace where Old Chu'Si worked. She deftly carved thin strips of flesh from large yellow pumpkins, hanging them to dry for the hard winter season. Seeing that both men carried bows, she shook her head and frowned.

"What have they done?" she asked herself. The old matriarch feared that they were trying to provoke the Morning Crows again. She wanted to march after them and break their arrows over her knee. Crack the bows over their heads. "Or maybe not . . . maybe not," she sighed. She could no longer chastise the young warriors. In fact, her authority counted for little now that Chayton led her clan. And every failed attempt eroded her authority. She thought it better to preserve what respect she still enjoyed.

Old Chu'Si had already been fuming at Chayton this morning. He had sent the women of the High Rocks Clan to gather yucca once again. Even her granddaughters had gone. "Nobody cares what the matriarch thinks. Chayton thinks ripe squash will prepare itself. Why does he need so much rope anyway?"

She wished that she could still hike to where the good yucca grew. Unfortunately, they had exhausted the nearby fields. That only made her angrier. She scooped the seeds into a rough bowl and added several that clung to her breechcloth. She then carried them to the tiny spring at the back of Low Nest. The sacred water had started to trickle again this year. However, the matriarch could not explain their good fortune. After years of fruitless supplication, her clan had not performed the rain ceremony since Chayton had forbidden it, and she did not understand why the spirits would still choose to smile upon her clan. "Maybe the Ash Owls have brought the rain. We are just in its path," she mused. She had never really been that impressed with the Ash Owl spirit leader. "But maybe I should I give Kotori more credit."

She washed the seeds with a small ladle of cool water, rubbing the slime from their shells. They would rot before planting if not cleaned well. She drank the water from the bowl, thick with the taste of raw squash. She would store them in one of the harvest jars, cache them after they dried. Cha'Akmongwi, the former spirit leader, had blessed those jars before his death. Chayton would have smashed them if he had known. He had banned all things associated with Cha'Akmongwi. Even the true name of her clan. She thought again of the Morning Crows. Hototo was a snake, coiled under his rock and waiting to strike, but even he still honored the spirits in the proper way. She could not say the same for Low Nest.

"High Rocks!" she scoffed. She slowly rubbed her back. "And more pumpkins still ripe in the field. What path do we follow?"

~ B ~

Makya reached the top of the ladder only to find Shuman standing before him. She loomed over him, more or less blocking his ability to step off the top rung. "How did you hurt your leg?" she asked. The matriarch of the Morning Crows, Shuman looked like a tree with deep roots, tall and proud but wizened by years of hard wind. "You are getting blood on my tallest ladder," she added.

"Can I climb up?" Makya asked. He had hoped to avoid this. Shuman stepped back and waited for Makya to plant both feet behind the front wall of Crow Ledge. She gave him no more space than necessary.

"I saw you coming from Seven Sisters Canyon. How did you hurt your leg?" she repeated.

"I was hunting Gila for Hototo."

"Usually not very dangerous . . . or very tall. How did the creature reach your shin?" Shuman asked. The matriarch wore a necklace of Gila claws and tapped it with her thumb. Her bright eyes were narrow with suspicion. The creases at the corners of her mouth were even deeper than usual.

Makya shook his head and smiled. "No. I did not find one today."

"Yes, I know. And I certainly know what the fangs of a weapon look like. Even little nibbles like that one. I have had far too much practice. Where were you?" Shuman asked. "Were you cutting across High Rocks land again?"

"I was not far from Seven Sisters. But I walked on Morning Crow land the whole time. The High Rocks Clan was—"

"I have told you. Hototo has told you. Give the High Rocks Clan a wide berth. Especially after this winter! And especially since they have made friends with the Ash Owls! You need to stay away from Low Nest!" Shuman snapped.

"I was only hunting . . . using land that we claim as our own," Makya protested calmly. He would not raise his voice against the matriarch. His leg hurt worse now.

"Was this really Morning Crow land? That boundary moves every time Hototo mentions it. You will trip over their pumpkin vines soon."

"I promise . . . definitely our land."

Shuman pursed her lips with concern. And as Makya waited for her to choose her next words, he gently leaned his three spears against the wall behind him. He saw Shuman follow the motion with her eyes. It only took one spear to kill a Gila.

"But you still provoke them by your actions," she finally replied. "You risk another ugly incident each time you walk in that direction. Our land or not."

"They want to scare us from our border. How can we allow that? They shoot arrows from the shadows and hide."

"But you give them the target. Even while your brother hunts far from Crow Ledge with many of our warriors," Shuman insisted. "What if you lead the Morning Crows one day? You must discern good risk from bad. We are blind to prudence when we treat all risk the same."

9

"They surprised me. I was not looking for them."

Shuman looked more frustrated than angry now. She sounded a kinder tone. "You are a good husband to Sihu. But when you risk your life without real need, you also risk her happiness. Do you realize that?"

"I did not mean . . ." Makya faltered. How could he disagree when Shuman brought his wife into the argument? Sihu was also her only granddaughter.

"I tell you again, Makya. Leave those sleeping bats alone. Nothing but grief comes from waking them."

~ B ~

"Why are you blocking my light?" Tocho asked. The war leader of the Ash Owl Clan smiled as he looked up and saw Len standing before him, one of his best scouts.

"I found these at the edge of High Rocks land this morning," Len said. He held out two broken arrows. "Some dry blood on the ground. It tracked toward Seven Sisters."

Tocho had just pulled free a portion of pale clay. He had worked it quickly into a rope, ensuring an even thickness along its length. However, he draped it carefully across his thigh and washed his fingers in the cup of dirty water he kept at his side. He took the arrows from Len and turned them over in his hands. Len stepped to one side so that his war leader could examine them. "Did the High Rocks Clan say anything?" Tocho asked.

Len shook his head. "I found these as I was headed back. But no, they did not mention any fighting . . . sloppy arrows. Can you imagine our Ash Owls making those?"

Tocho nodded. He thought for a moment and then handed the arrows back to Len. "Hard to tell what happened. Could have just been hunting. Should I ask Ahote to help you scout further?"

Len shrugged. "Ahote is checking traps near Broken Spine today."

"Maybe we should just leave it alone. If the High Rocks Clan does not seem worried. What about your errand?" Tocho asked.

"Chayton says that Kotori can, of course, lead the wedding ceremony. He insists, though, that our spirit leader not attempt any other ceremonies when he comes to Low Nest," Len said. He shook his head in disgust. "Do we even want such an ally?"

"Should I have sent another messenger?" Tocho asked. While he knew that some of his men disliked the High Rocks Clan more than others, he was surprised that Len would express such feelings to him. After all, they both knew that the Ash Owl Clan leader himself had suggested Len for the task.

"No need. I was tactful and smiled often."

"This wedding is an important step forward between our two clans. We need to build goodwill when we can."

"I understand that. But needing to ask permission for our own shaman to attend . . . does that not anger you?" Len protested.

"We know that Chayton hates all shamans, so the High Rocks Clan makes their concession by allowing Kotori to perform the ceremony. And we make ours by seeking permission."

Len gave a quick nod, gently chastened. "I will let you work. I just wanted to let you know." He gestured toward the damp clay that Tocho had draped across his leg. As Len turned and walked back toward the canyon, he snapped off the arrowheads and tossed the shafts onto the nearest cooking fire.

~ B ~

Ahote was running out of light. However, he could still make out the tracks from two sets of feet, the Morning Crow woman and child he had seen that morning. "What brought you all the way out here?" he whispered. Ahote thought it brazen to gather wood on Ash Owl land, but he had not bothered them.

11

He had simply watched from his rocky ledge and let them pass. "They always want to push!" Ahote added.

The Ash Owl hunter squatted to peer beneath a brushy juniper tree. He had come to check animal traps. "Nothing," he sighed. The trigger twig was still set, still baited. Its morsel of cactus fruit looked much less succulent than it had that morning. He fished another bit of fruit from his dry gourd and carefully reset the trap. His odds were better at night anyway. Most animals hid while the sun was strong. And in the morning, that noisy girl had probably spooked every animal in the vicinity.

On the other hand, none of his traps had worked last night or today. He was discouraged. Ahote was good at trapping. He knew many ways to construct them. He had even worked with Tocho to devise a deer trap last year; but Istaqa, the clan leader, had forbidden its use, telling him that it could catch men by accident, killing them as it would kill the deer. "Deer Trail runs close to Morning Crow land. You know they trespass. What if you caught one of their hunters?" Istaqa had asked.

In fact, Ahote often saw footprints pointing back toward Crow Ledge. He did not really care, though. They did not poach his traps, not in recent years anyway. "Could we just mark the rocks around it?" Ahote had suggested.

"Salt is expensive bait," Istaqa had added. Kotori, spirit leader of the Ash Owls, had agreed with Istaqa, suggesting that it would not honor the spirit of the deer, would not show respect if they hunted without effort.

"Maybe an insult to trap deer like timid mice," Kotori had warned.

Ahote had dropped the idea. He had no wish to dishonor his quarry. He had several pieces of fruit left. He set several of them like a trail. More bait would strengthen the scent and cover more of his smell. He popped the last red bite into his mouth. It tasted sweet and intense. He adjusted a few thorny sticks to encourage the right approach for the rabbits he hoped to entice.

Ahote intended to hunt west of Firetown next time, perhaps setting his traps beyond Desert Gate. The High Rocks Clan had reported recent success there. Ahote also wondered if he should speak with Kotori about his failed traps. Perhaps the spirit leader could intercede on his behalf or tell him what must be done. "Making the trap still requires effort. Why does that not count?" he asked. The quiet trail offered no answer.

~ *B* ~

The vampire took long strides across the desert scrub, brushing past low shrubs that seemed to defy the barren soil. Tufts of grass spotted the ground, dusty green in the gathering dusk, and a cool breeze blew at his back. It stirred the dry leaves. He loved these twilight hours. The stars were only just beginning to bloom, and more blue than slate yet, the sky still bore the memory of daylight. He had walked this path for many nights, unsure of his direction; but now he saw that a low rampart of mountains was emerging slowly on the eastern horizon. He kept them ahead and to his left.

Was he still hunted by the Order of Saint John? The vampire did not know. They had broken the old pact. They had shattered all remnants of the *Pax Secretum*. Sworn to his murder, they had chased him to the eastern shores of Asia, forced his flight across the ocean. He had sailed toward the lethal sunrise, toward the rumor of kingdoms and kin beyond uncharted waters. But the knights had still followed him, the same great current taking them both, the same fierce wind driving them ashore.

The vampire thought of the last emaciated sailor that had stumbled ashore so many months ago. "Spare me!" the man had begged. That crew had served him well. However, the immutable logic of hunger had won the night, even as moonlit surf had washed over his boots, even as flecks of blood had spattered bright across the ebbing foam.

Hunger also smoked in his veins now, his craving for blood growing hotter with each passing night. And although there were plenty of humans in this vast new land, the vampire had not seen them for weeks. Not since the desert had started growing under his feet.

The night sky slowly matured. Insects buzzed and snapped around him. A lizard startled and shot into the brushy ditch. Listening only to his thoughts and the steady crunch of red silt under his boots, he did not hear the lizard, not really. A long sword, forged from the finest Toledo steel, clanked gently at his side. A small bag, battered and stitched, shifted at his other hip. His heavy cloak, the tanned skin of wolves, muffled both and swirled behind his heels.

Massive rocks, like the naked hearts of mountains long gone, the ruins of time itself, dotted the plain. They would hide him well from the sun if he could reach them before dawn. The vampire hoped that this harsh desert had finally forced the knights to turn back. Or killed the last of them. He thought that his hunger was a fair price to pay if that was the case, but they had proved relentless. He dared not slow his pace.

CHAPTER 2

Lines of Demarcation

THE HORIZON WAS losing its grip on the dark once again. The stars were washing out, a sure sign of the coming sun. Dark formations of rock broke the plain. Flat like altars, the vampire thought. But the vampire judged that they were too far to chance before dawn. He stopped and looked for shelter. He longed to find an unsuspecting human, that first surge of blood filling his mouth, hot and tasting of iron. He longed to feel his veins quicken with life. But it would have to wait. He smiled hard. "Curse the dawn," he said.

The vampire stood in the bend of a dry stream, deep and narrow like a gutter through the desert. He took his sword from his hip and began to gouge the earth. He dug into the eroded flank of the channel. Thin roots snapped as he worked. The vampire quickly ripped a makeshift tomb in the embankment and, after walking his eyes over the horizon to ensure that he was alone, he crawled inside. A morning bird cackled softly in the distance. He pulled his cloak up and over his head like a burial shroud. He was safe from the sun for another day. Unless he was discovered.

The vampire did not sheath his sword. He kept the handle beneath his palm, ready to turn and slash. Although it was a great indignity for his kind to hide in the dirt like a common snake, and although it made him vulnerable, he almost liked it. His freedom had waxed as his pride had waned. There were no more alliances, no more fortunes, and no more friends, but he had seen more of the dark world than any vampire he had ever met.

The vampire inhaled the tang of dirt all around him. A little moisture still remained in the soil he had exposed. It reminded him of his long passage across the ocean and the stale air below deck, the earthy smell that had permeated the hull. The creaking mast still played in the back of his ears. All these months later, he could still feel the interminable rush of the current beneath the hull, the rising and falling of the waves.

He felt certain that others of his kind had landed on these shores before him. Rumors had persisted for years regarding vampire lords sailing toward the rising sun. Some had sought to explore. Others had fled. But none had returned. "Where are they?" the vampire asked. He longed to find another that could speak his language. He sank quickly into sleep as fire burned across the sky.

~ *B* ~

"Damn it. Not like this," Jerome sighed. The morning sun had erupted over the serrated eastern horizon, a line of distant mountains. Its light flooded the desert plain now, but Allain did not stir. And Jerome knew the ineffable sight of an empty shell. He had seen enough death to know it well. Jerome rose quickly and stepped to where his friend had bedded for the night. He knelt there, pressing his palm against the dead knight's brow to make sure. No heat remained. The cold night had stolen it while Jerome had slept, his vigilance overcome by exhaustion. Allain was gone. The Knights of Saint John had dwindled to one; and the oath they had sworn, to exterminate every last vampire in the White Rose enclave, now rested solely on his tired shoulders.

His friend had died in pain. His teeth were clenched, even as his dead eyes were fixed upon the charred bones of the night's fire. Jerome swept back the filthy blond hair of his friend and closed the eyes gently. He looked once more at the bite that had killed him, the horrifying mass of tight-swollen flesh at the bend of his left arm, blackish purple. The tourniquet had failed. Jerome exhaled.

Allain had stumbled, slipped as he climbed a steep embankment, startled an unseen rattlesnake that lay curled in the gravel. Incredibly fast and coldly irrevocable, it had been nothing more than a cruel accident. "Or was it a serpent charmed by the devil?" Jerome said, completing his thought aloud.

Jerome straightened and backed away from the corpse. He surveyed the desert plain before him. His eyes were hard. He thought it looked like a vast cemetery, its eruptions of reddish stone marking the graves of forgotten monsters. It felt just as empty; it wore the same burden of silence.

~ B ~

Makya straddled the retaining wall at the front of Crow Ledge. One of his legs dangled over the canyon floor. Sihu, as she prepared turkey stew over the fire, had asked him to mend several broken sandals for their young boys, and Makya had almost completed that task. He hunched forward, tying a new strap, braided from yucca leaves, into the ragged sole. At that moment, he wished his fingers were smaller. The repair was less sturdy than a new sandal would be. "But the boys will . . . outgrow them tomorrow," he whispered as he tightened the knot.

Makya stopped. He saw Hototo walking toward him, a large leather pouch in his hand. "Let me examine your wound again."

Makya nodded. He set the sandals behind him and laid his injured leg across the wall. Hototo had punished him three days ago for venturing too close to Low Nest, and Makya did not want to anger him further. The shaman would probably not stay angry for long, especially since he understood the threat posed by the High Rocks Clan, but Makya still detected a certain lingering hardness in his eyes.

"Too dark inside. We have the sun to help us here," Hototo said, quickly removing the poultice he had applied last night and

17

wiping the injury clean. He leaned forward and smelled the wound.

"What do you hope to smell?" Makya asked.

"Poison," Hototo said. He took another deep breath, his nose almost touching the gash, "The warriors at Low Nest are dirty. Not clean like us. They could foul an arrow just by touching it."

"What do you smell?"

"Nothing. The poultice is overwhelming." He brought his eyes close now. He looked carefully, pressing his finger gently on one side of the gash and then the other. "It has started to grow angry. Do you see that red glow? That anger will spread like rotting grain if we do nothing."

"I understand," Makya said. He knew that Hototo was a talented healer. Even better than the healers at Smoke Ridge.

Hototo pulled a small knife from his pouch, shiny and black, smooth as still water between the nap marks. Its handle was wrapped in very thin strips of leather. The strips were dyed bright red, as though to echo the purpose of the blade. "The Smoke Clan told me that this knife came from far away," Hototo said. He had never seen anything so sharp. He had once considered mounting it on a spear. "Hold still. This will hurt," he added as he gently pushed the gash open with practiced fingers. And then, using his free hand, Hototo carefully drew the knife through the wound, making the cut slightly longer and deeper. "I still need a Gila. Do you remember that?" Hototo asked. The blade stung. Makya inhaled sharply.

"I can search again tomorrow. But I have looked all across Morning Crow territory. The Gilas have vanished. Have we killed them all?" he asked. His voice sounded tight.

"The spirits would never allow that. I have seen Gilas swim. Perhaps they will follow the rain back onto our land. Now brace yourself." The callused hands of the shaman squeezed hard from both sides of the calf. It deformed the shape of the gash and brought blood to the surface, where it welled up inside the incision.

"This helps to purge the anger in the wound," Hototo said.

Makya clenched his jaw. "I will look upstream tomorrow."

Hototo now started one hand at the ankle and the other at the knee, pressing hard to force fresh blood toward the wound. He then squeezed from the sides of the calf once again, pushing the gash open to discharge the blood. Makya did not protest. The young warrior stared into the tall stands of corn below Crow Ledge. They rustled softly in the canyon breeze. A small cloud cast its shadow across the outer third of the field. Hototo worked his hands across the leg five more times.

Finally, Hototo had finished the bloodletting. "I think that is enough," he said. Makya exhaled. A bead of sweat trickled down the small of his back. He watched as Hototo lifted a small gray jar from his pouch. It smelled strongly of sagebrush as the lid was removed. The shaman quickly smeared another poultice with the pale green paste and wrapped it tightly around the injured shin. His eyes looked warmer now.

"Curse those High Rocks warriors," he said softly as he cleaned his knife. "I will check again in several days. But leave the poultice in place until then. Keep it dry."

Makya rose to his feet. Although pain bit into his leg, he did not show it. "I will wipe up this blood. Before it gets sticky," the young warrior said. A small puddle had formed, glistening red atop the stone wall.

~ B ~

The vampire had once been locked inside a wooden box clad with iron. Tortured. Spikes had stabbed at his naked body from all directions, holding him fast in tormented stillness, allowing no angle to force an escape. It also allowed no sleep. No shift of posture. "A coffin fit for the devil himself! No rest for the wicked!" they had jeered. This memory stirred him now.

His cloak, blocking the direct sunlight, also absorbed its rays. It had begun to radiate heat, telling him of the danger on the other side. All the while, his makeshift coffin held him fast as the summer sun burnt across the sky.

But this trial would end. He knew that this prison door would swing open with dusk. Unlike the fools who had tortured him, the sun had no intentions, no malice to persist for endless days, no desire to weigh his freedom in gold. Well, his brethren had paid that ransom, and then they had repaid the crime. Tenfold.

A bold scorpion crawled under his cloak. When he moved his leg, it stung his shin. He felt the immediate pain, but the poison fell into barren veins and would not harm him. The scorpion crawled up his thigh. He let it come and then smashed its hard carapace with the cross-guard of his sword. The heat outside continued to climb. He closed his eyes and drifted back into his sleep.

~ B ~

Tocho stirred the dark paint with the tip of his brush. He was eager to complete his bowl, now dry enough to decorate. Among the finest potters in the Ash Owl Clan, his mother had taught him many years ago. He would present this bowl to the High Rocks Clan at the wedding, when Chosovi married Kwahu, a respected High Rocks warrior. A goodwill gesture to the rival clan, the gift would mean even more since Tocho led the Ash Owl warriors. The first wedding between the clans in many years, it was especially important since Chosovi was the younger sister of Istaqa, the Ash Owl clan leader.

Tocho brooded as he worked, recalling the distaste that Len had expressed. The war leader had heard many churlish remarks about Low Nest over the years. Who had not insulted them from time to time? Tocho also knew that the wedding had its detractors. But if Len felt strongly enough to speak his concern, how many more warriors grumbled in secret? Tocho reflected that one rash act could ruin everything.

He hoped it would not come to that. He was actually looking forward to working with the High Rocks Clan. He wanted an ally to help deter the spiteful Morning Crows. "Hototo," he scoffed. The name was stained with grief. The shaman, arrogant enough to serve as both spirit leader and clan leader for the Crows, had stung the Ash Owls too many times over the years. Tocho winced at the memory of Gathering Rock. He still bore scars from that cruel ambush. He recalled the arrow that had struck his shoulder blade. The bone still ached on the coldest of days.

Tocho recalled how the High Rocks warriors had clashed with the Morning Crows last winter. Even in defeat, that series of bloody scuffles had revealed a newly invigorated High Rocks Clan. "Fearless and well trained now. The High Rocks warriors have improved since we fought them last," Len himself had marveled.

Of course, Tocho also worried that the High Rocks warriors might prove too fierce, an unpredictable ally. They seemed too eager to challenge every trespass. It could draw the Ash Owls into fights not their own. "Lot of flames from not much tinder," he mused. However, the war leader still preferred a hot-tempered friend to a hot-tempered foe. And Istaqa believed that an Ash Owl alliance with the High Rocks Clan might actually help tame both Hototo and Chayton. Tocho hoped his clan leader was correct.

Chosovi would marry Kwahu soon. Tocho was eager to complete his work. The large bowl flared wide at the top. Good for sharing but difficult to construct. He leaned close to mark the first lines, both braids sliding gently over his bare shoulders, biting his lip as he concentrated. The dexterity to follow the curve and judge its symmetry also made him a great hunter and warrior. He would paint the pale surface, both inside and out, with a black pattern of celebration. He would incorporate designs from both of the clans. A bold music of triangles and bars, a visual cadence, already danced in the back of his mind.

~ *B* ~

Soon the air would shimmer with heat. Jerome had spent the morning sitting in the dirt. He reclined against the nearest boulder and stared at his boots. He knew that he lacked the time or reserves of strength to properly bury Allain. He also knew that he was losing time. However, he had already lost the trail of the vampire, and another hour would make no difference. His chest felt both hollowed out and filled with cinders. His fallen friend had connected him to his distant home. And now nothing did. With an impassable ocean mocking any possibility of retreat, only his oath remained.

Allain's clothes and armor were no better than his own. Jerome took only the stocky crossbow that they had passed back and forth for endless miles. Heavy burden that it was, he could not relinquish the chance to kill the vampire from a distance, especially now that he was alone.

Jerome also took his friend's water skin, not quite empty, and the ration of smoked meat that Allain had not been able to stomach, the final remnant of their last horse. Allain had removed his gloves in the night. Jerome examined them. Also finding them no better than his own, he draped them over the closed eyes of his friend. Whether burial shroud or blindfold, he did not know. And finally, he scooped up the reddish soil with both hands. Jerome sprinkled it across the body of his friend, a symbolic gesture.

"If a sip of wine and dry cracker . . ." Jerome stopped himself. He wiped the dust from his hands and looked off into the horizon once more. He continued. "You thought we'd go no further than Constantinople. You thought we might turn back after the plains of Pagan. Yet here we are. I declare this whole land your tomb. Let the years and miles bury us both then. Amen."

He took another handful of dry earth and let it fall across his friend, taking special care to let the grains fall upon the exposed part of his cheek and into his hair, which seemed important for some reason. Jerome turned away and gathered his own gear, his weapons. The vampire would not like this open plain. He would head for those mountains, seek the shadows. He always did. And he would press forward, always looking for new victims, hunting for new blood.

Before he departed, Jerome returned to the corpse. The bite was still exposed. One more scoop of sand quickly covered the ugly discoloration. He squatted down and whispered. "Allain, I take your oath and add it to my own. And so rest in peace," he said. Of course, he had said those words many times before. Allain had too. But the chain had now reached its last link; and as Jerome walked away from his friend, the silent husk that remained, he refused to glance back.

~ B ~

Hototo heard laughter on the terrace below his room. Three floors down. He rose stiffly and looked out his window. He blinked in the bright sun, now falling toward the horizon, and as his eyes adjusted, saw Makya and Choovio. The two brothers held ears of corn against their own ears and bobbed up and down. They flicked their tongues like lizards. Hototo could not imagine why. But several children had gathered and giggled now at the sight. Hototo smiled. He was glad to see that Choovio had returned. He enjoyed seeing Makya and Choovio so relaxed. They both accepted much responsibility within the clan. They had grown up with it. Sons of Saya, the former clan leader, the burden of leadership trailed them like a shadow.

He shook his head and smiled. The Spear of the Morning Crows would almost certainly pass to one of them when he could no longer lead. "But which one?" he whispered. Both were highly respected by the Morning Crows. His two strong hands. Choovio was older and more restrained, the obvious choice. Makya was bold and full of energy, the most talented warrior. He loved them both like sons. Hototo had actually helped raise them after the Ash Owls had killed Saya.

He would have insights to share when the time came. But of course, Shuman would ultimately choose. "Choovio," Hototo whispered. He knew she would prefer Choovio. Shuman loved Makya as well but she feared his reckless nature. Too rash and impulsive. After all, the young warrior had sparked a bloody clash with the High Rocks Clan last winter. "Over a turkey," the shaman sighed. And still Makya seemed determined to provoke them. Hototo balled his fist. He imagined what might have transpired if that arrow had done more than just graze the shin.

"Fire knows how to climb a stick. But I prefer the climbing vine. Do you believe Makya can learn that lesson?" Shuman had asked. Hototo thought it a beautiful notion. However, he worried that Shuman did not fully grasp the High Rocks threat. Did she appreciate the depths of their impiety under Chayton? Perhaps Makya was wise to push against them. The Morning Crows might need brash leadership one day. Makya possessed that spark.

Hototo moved away from the window and slowly stretched. His hips were sore again. He would have to choke down another batch of yucca root tea. "Blaah," he grimaced. Although he disliked its taste, he would gladly suffer it to avoid showing pain. Any sign of weakness could erode his authority. And the shaman estimated that he might need that authority soon enough. If the Morning Crows clashed with the High Rocks Clan again, Hototo feared that the Ash Owls, vultures that they were, would now join the fight.

~ B ~

The vampire knew the advent of dusk. He could feel his body quicken with the strength imbued by the night. His mind flowed into the shadows. He rose deftly from his tiny catacomb, rolling smoothly into a ready stance. The vampire kept the edge of his cloak wrapped in his fist. He felt no stiffness or cramping from his time in the ground, and he never would. The hardships of aging—he had left those privations behind.

He stood still and scanned the horizon. An orange hue still anchored the western sky. A purplish hue tinged the foliage. But no human figures broke the plain. No thin ripple of voices floated to his ears. And he smelled no sign of the knights, none of the faint odor of sweat and sour clothes that had so often dogged him. Their camp smoke and charred game were still gone from the wind tonight. The vampire smiled and pressed forward.

While age could not touch him, the hardships of the moment could still bedevil him. The sting on his leg smarted; and although fresh blood would heal him, the vampire saw no immediate hope for relief. In fact, hunger had kept his pace sharp for days. He wanted to reach the distant peaks. Men made homes around the long feet of mountains, even in the shadows of inhospitable peaks. He did not like this desert anyway. Too much exposed terrain. The knights who chased him could spot him from miles away here. He felt like a mouse in the shadow of wings. And shelter was a constant concern. He could always spend the day curled under his cloak if he had no alternative. "But shields are not hiding places," he muttered.

~ B ~

"You must have told Hototo?" Choovio asked.

Makya nodded slowly.

"Good. He needs to know when Low Nest provokes us. Was he angry?" Choovio asked. He could not help smiling at his younger brother.

Makya shrugged. He sat beside the trickling stream with Choovio and Pavati. All three of them dangled their feet into the cool water. They stirred the reddish silt and watched it slowly fade into the current.

"Tell him what Hototo said. It was not that bad!" Pavati said. She smiled too, but her eyes were kind. She wore a ribbon of blue cloth in her braid. It accentuated the dark shine of her hair. She moved as one with her husband this morning, grateful that Choovio had finally returned. She ran her toes back and forth across the top of his foot in the water.

"Not really yelling. Hototo mainly just warned me to stay away from High Rocks land. Well, actually he told me to stay out of Seven Sisters Canyon completely. The word 'forbid' may have been used."

"And he was calm like that?" Choovio asked.

"Like flashes of lightning inside a dark cloud. Nothing hitting the ground but . . ."

Choovio laughed. "Like when Hototo caught us smashing pumpkins?"

"How did I miss that?" Pavati asked.

Makya smiled. "We were just kids. Honani had the idea. He told us anything would bounce if it struck the ground hard enough. Even pumpkins. I think we only dropped five or six of them."

"Oh, Honani had the idea . . . that explains a lot. And Hototo did not punish you for that?" Pavati followed up.

"We were so little. Hototo grabbed us by the braids and just dropped us in front of our father. Our dad was killed later that year actually. But Hototo did not make a sound on that occasion. I think he just walked away and left us to tell what we had done," Makya said. He smiled at the memory.

"But why do you think Hototo was so calm *this* time?" Choovio asked.

"Shuman had already yelled at me. He might have thought her scolding was enough. And Hototo also asked me for precise details. He knows that the threat from the High Rocks Clan continues to grow. But he did make me empty all the fire pits in Crow Ledge." Makya held his fingers to his nose and inhaled. "My hands still smell like ash."

"What did Shuman say?" Pavati asked.

"She lectured me about leadership again. Why does she do that? Everybody knows she will choose you to lead the Morning Crows. The favorite," Makya gestured toward Choovio and rolled his eyes.

"Well . . . have you seen my latest scar?" Choovio replied. He tilted his shoulder forward to show the small mark on his back. Shaped like a wishbone. Still ragged and pinkish. Makya winced.

"I know. I know. That should not have happened. But I am not wrong about the High Rocks Clan. Push or be pushed when it comes to them. And anyway . . . Shuman *already* liked you better."

"I am very likeable. But you see all that Hototo does. What he bears. Do you still wish to lead the Morning Crows?" Choovio asked.

Makya shrugged again. "I think you would lead us well. But I think I would too."

"Can I tell you something? Shuman shares similar advice with me. Maybe the race is not yet settled after all. She once told me that, when the time comes to choose a new leader, an easy decision is like having only one arrow to your name. I think she meant that wise matriarchs want many prepared to lead."

"Please. You are the elder son. I will not change her mind," Makya said. A sadder note had crept into his voice. The two brothers both stared into the stream. They watched the sun dapple its surface. Their discussion promised no further benefit, at least not this morning, and they were content to let the water carry away its potential for conflict.

"I am glad the arrow only grazed your leg," Choovio finally replied.

"Of course!" Pavati echoed.

"If you had been killed . . . Hototo would have assigned you twice as many chores," Choovio teased. He also firmly poked his brother in the shoulder.

~ B ~

"Well . . . God favors the lucky," Jerome said. He stood in the bend of a dry stream, the body of Allain now two days behind him. Sweat trickled under his matted gray hair. In the late morning sun, he stared at the eroded flank of the wash, still in shadow beneath the gentle overhang of its earthen bank. An empty gash had been sliced through the soil, too deep and square at both ends to reflect natural patterns of erosion. Long enough for a tall man. "Or a devil," Jerome murmured.

He touched the broken whiskers of several roots that hung from its ceiling. He saw that crumbs, hard clumps of dirt, had been broken out and swept into the streambed. Fanned out to make them less visible. He plucked a broken root from the dirt around his feet, worked it between his fingers. He smelled it slowly. Mostly dried out but not entirely baked. Not yet.

He frowned. "Maybe two days behind. I knew it."

He squeezed a little water into his mouth, warm and stale on his tongue. Little remained. His thirst was not yet quenched, but the sun would soon reach its withering apex. He peered into the hole once more. He knew that the most brutal part of the day was coming, and this seemed an ideal place to take cover. The crossbow rode heavily across his back. He lifted it from his shoulder and leaned it against the embankment.

The knight now took out his sword and dug into the crevice with its sturdy blade. Once he had enlarged the hole for more clearance, he climbed stiffly inside, laying the crossbow over his feet. Jerome smiled as he felt the cool earth against his arms. It felt good to rest his aching joints. He closed his eyes, perfectly safe as the sun watched his back.

He was hungry too and considered what to do about it. He had seen dog-wolves, scruffy and small, prowling this desert in the moonlight, heard them howling in the distance. Jerome thought that he might try to kill one for dinner tonight, once the sun had finally retreated. Once their nocturnal chorus began.

~ B ~

Another week had passed. No sign of the Knights of St. John. Although the vampire wanted to interpret this as good news, he could not let down his guard. The knights might still follow, even if they were too far behind for the vampire to catch their scent. To sense nothing proved nothing. He kept a brisk pace.

The vampire had lost them before. He felt sure that he had. But they had always picked up his trail eventually. How they had found him in Pagan, amid its welter of temples, he still did not understand. The vampire wondered if God was helping them, if they tracked him by signs and visions. "Seems unfair," he whispered. Hunger still seethed under his skin. His veins felt like anger lost in the dark. Hot coals beneath the cold ash. He wanted to feel the pop of an artery between his teeth. He wanted to feed until he could no longer swallow.

The vampire kept his brisk pace. He had walked along the banks of a wide wash and come across the muddy demise of a narrow stream. He was now following it back toward its source. It only trickled for the moment. He walked, still moving east, toward cliffs that rose before him, rough time-hewn layers of red and slate. Good shelter.

The plain and its hills were yielding, exchanging the lonely pariahs of rock and earth that had littered the desert plateau for a more intricate upheaval of the landscape. Stubborn trees clung to slopes now, short and gnarled; but the wood smelled strong and fragrant. The vampire often lost sight of the mountains these past few days. He followed the lower elevations when he could, the terrain of shadows.

If there was a pattern to the land, he could not see it from his point of view. He imagined himself like an ant exploring Rome. He knew of no map for this land and did not care to make one. He was only passing through. The memory of Rome reminded him of the great Flavian Amphitheatre. They called its bones the Colosseum now. And they buried bodies there. Even the peasants. "An ordinary cemetery," he muttered. It was nothing glorious anymore. Lions no longer roared from their holding pens. Steel blades no longer rang one against the other. The midnight spectacles had fallen silent. The smell of blood no longer filled the arena. The vampire shook his head. He mourned the path of history.

And then the vampire stopped and knelt down. He breathed sharply and then again. The smell of humans on the path ahead. It was faint. It was also different, the odor of unfamiliar plants in their sweat. He examined the ground before him. He saw five partial footprints in the reddish dirt. However, they were inscrutable. He could not follow them. Their owners had moved with utmost care. "Clever men," the vampire noted.

He circled the area slowly now. The vampire sniffed the air with predatory skill. He stopped twice to pluck leaves from a ubiquitous local shrub. The leaves were small and silver in the clear night. He rubbed them between his fingers to release the smell of sage and cleanse his nose. Closing the loop, he breathed deep once more and held the air in his lungs. Humans had definitely passed this way in the heat of the day. There were two lines of scent, one faint and one more recent, two different paths.

The cliffs broke in several directions. He followed the stronger scent. Unsurprisingly, it ran parallel to the thin seasonal stream he had followed for miles. It was taking him toward the wider canyon. Good. The babble of water might cover the sound of his approach. His boots moved more quickly as his heart turned the easy mark from prey to hunter.

The night waned, though. "Curse the dawn," he said. The vampire sought shelter as he reached the rocky shoulders of the canyon. Plenty of hiding places. He approached several large slabs of sandstone. The tops were dark and flat where they had cleaved from the cliff above. Almost black. They faced the sky, more or less. They were scarred with lighter lines that caught his eye. He picked his way slowly along their perimeter.

The crude figures of two horned men with very large hands, and several blocky animals were scratched into the surface of the rock. "Deer or sheep maybe?" the vampire guessed. He ran his finger gently through the lines. He also saw some squares filled with dots and marks that looked like claws. Further up the slope. He did not know what the pictures meant, but he liked them. It was like finding a fence—lines of demarcation—the hands that made them certainly waiting ahead.

CHAPTER 3

The Enemy Stranger

T HE STARS GREW brighter as the western light faded below the horizon. Like a rising celestial tide. The vampire slipped quietly from the tight crevice where he had passed the day. He scouted the scent again before pressing further into the network of canyons. A running line of bluffs and cliffs broke the sky above him and cast deep shadows across the ground. He moved among the few small trees that lined the stream. The stream, its vitality not yet robbed by the open desert, flowed a little more strongly here. This landscape suited him better. It felt a little more like his home.

The human smell grew sharper now. The scent trail dissolved into many, even though he saw few footprints. Despite the hunger that raced through his veins, he moved slowly. He intended to hunt carefully. He knew nothing of the people who lived in this hard land. "Strong blood and weak weapons," he said hopefully. He could always hope. He also hoped that they did not carry the crucifix. Although he winced at the thought, he doubted it. Few but the Knights of St. John had brandished the cross since he had fled Constantinople and passed through the Sultanate of Konya. He had hoped the Seljuq rulers there would turn the Christian knights away at the border. But the *Fahreddin* had helped the knights instead. The vampire shrugged. "The enemy of my enemy is still my enemy!" he lamented.

The vampire knelt to examine some black stains in the dirt. They were bright to his keen eyes. He sniffed the dirt between his fingers. Rabbit blood and the remnants of a trap. The canyon branched in several directions as he moved forward. He scouted several of those corridors. They were also marked with

figures.   More   impish   stick   men   with   bows   and   a
disproportionate bird adorned one. They were scratched into
the rock and nearly white. Another rock revealed a man holding
a small spear in each hand. Several lines meandered near the
head in irregular patterns. Two spirals dominated the face of yet
another flat stone. Larger than the other markings, the vampire
was impressed by their symmetry.

However, he quickly returned to the widest floor of the
canyon, to the banks of his modest stream, the kind of place
where men might camp or gather. He began to smell smoke in
the distance too. It was laced with the smell of meat and savory
plants, but the vampire did not consider whether it smelled good
or bad. It was not blood.

Humans were definitely close now. He closed his cloak
tight around his shoulders and pressed forward with a long
stride.

~ B ~

Makya slept next to Sihu and his two sons. His status
among the Morning Crows afforded his family a window at the
front of Crow Ledge, and the light of the moon slanted into their
small sleeping quarters. A vivid nightmare gripped Makya. He
moaned but could not speak. Utter darkness. The sound of
wolves. Claws grated on rock as they climbed the canyon wall.
They lunged silently into Crow Ledge. Hackles bristled on the
back of necks. Padded paws slapped across the sills of windows.
They were creeping close to the mats where his family slept.
Eyes ashine, even with the moon at their backs. Hot breath
against his neck. Makya struggled but could not move. His
fingers refused to close around his knife; he could not lift it from
the floor. It kept slipping from his grip.

He started awake, panting as though he had climbed a great
distance. He was sweating and cold. He had rolled almost
entirely off his bedding. His left palm was braced against the

33

front wall. He pulled his hand back toward him. And as he flexed his wrist, his arm ached as though he had relieved it from great exertion. He stared up toward the window. It looked no different than any other night, but Makya still half expected a wolf to thrust its head through the opening and bare its fangs.

Makya moved back onto his bedding. He sought to shake loose from his dream. He told himself that it was nothing. "Honani has the watch tonight," he whispered. He tried to relax, feeling certain that Honani would not watch idly as wolves raced across the terrace and lunged into their rooms. "How would they get up here?" he added. He knew that wolves could not climb the face of the cliff.

~ B ~

The canyon curved gently. As the vampire turned the corner, he saw stand after stand of an unfamiliar plant, all evenly spaced, more or less, and about the same height. "Crops," he whispered. His parched heart raced to see further proof of humans nearby. As a rule, men did not walk far to tend their fields. These crops were not quite shoulder high. "Like short bamboo," he added. But he also saw tasseled pods on the stalks. Squash vines covered the ground around those taller plants. Their blossoms were bright among the dark leaves, and he could see a number of gourds, green but flecked with yellow, growing amid the leaves.

The vampire bent low and retreated. Despite the hunger aching in his veins, he wanted to get a better look before he pressed onward. He had not seen houses yet but he knew they would stand nearby. He wanted to see if he could spot them from a cautious distance.

The vampire hurried to the far wall of the canyon and kept his distance. The side of the cliff was not sheer there. It sloped upward in weathered layers of rock and reddish earth. He climbed the blind side of the tall outcropping. A few stunted trees, if you could even call them that, curled from the slope. But he saw large stumps too; many trees had been cut down. Although he was an excellent climber, the vampire still stepped carefully and with utmost quiet as he moved across the smooth contours of eroded stone.

~ B ~

Time crawled for Honani. His chin tipped slowly toward his chest. Like sand seeping through a crevice, the sensation of sleep was gathering in the back of his mind. He shook his head and pushed his eyes wide open. That scattered the sand for the moment. Through the small window of the sentry room, he scanned the canyon once more. He sighed to himself, adjusted the thin blanket across his shoulders. "Quiet as usual."

Honani thought about the sentries at Low Nest and Firetown. Perhaps they were all fighting sleep together, each one sitting alone and wishing for company. "Could we all keep watch together?" he murmured. After all, the Morning Crows had no intention of attacking the other two clans. Maybe the other clans felt the same way.

He closed one eye. He then switched and closed the other eye. He repeated this game multiple times, watching as the window, and the canyon in its frame, jumped slightly from one side to the other. Honani wondered if straight lines really existed. "Just two eyes willing to compromise?" he whispered. He still held one eye shut and let the other eyelid close as well. He felt the sand rising again, more quickly this time. It felt good. He could hear his own breathing. It sounded far away. Like the sound of wind passing over a sheltered canyon full of shade.

~ B ~

As the vampire crested the hill and crept through the brush, still gripping his scabbard to keep it from clanking, he saw an

unexpected sight.   Across the canyon and across the small
stream, he saw an entire town constructed within the living rock.
It filled an oblong concavity in the sheer cliff, an improvised
castle hung like a tapestry.   The eye of the waxing moon lit it
brightly. He simply gaped. He had seen nothing quite like it.

For some reason, it reminded him of villages he had seen in
the Aegean, so many years before, crowded together and
hugging the cliffs that overlooked the sea.   The memory
surprised him. He could still remember the sun against those
white plaster walls, the red tile roofing, the blue sky beyond the
mast, the motion of dazzled waves beneath him. He did not
often remember the sun. Not so vividly. He reluctantly shook
the image from his mind. "Very clever," he whispered.

Maybe two or three stories above the canyon floor—it was
difficult to judge from a distance—and built into the steep slope
of the rocky cliff, a stone wall fronted the settlement. He could
not imagine how they had anchored it. Beyond that wall he saw
a series of open courtyards in tight constellation, mostly humble
in size.   Low ridges of stone masonry divided them.   Small
repeated stacks of firewood and distinct piles of pottery further
delineated one from another. They blended into a long, uneven
crescent directly behind the rampart. Slightly raised, an upper
terrace also opened back toward the cliff, providing another
cluster of courtyards flanked by stone walls. Ladders peeked
from holes in the center of the larger courts. The vampire
guessed, admiringly, that the floors were also ceilings, that rooms
lay behind the initial wall.

Behind and around the courtyards, multiple levels rose
toward the ceiling of the cavern, and in some places, gave the
impression of stacked blocks. The walls of the structure formed
a complex interplay of towers and terraces. It vaguely reminded
the vampire of the monumental boulders piled along the canyon
floor. Like the design had been suggested by the landscape itself.
The structure was larger and more elaborate along the right side
of the terrace where the cavern rose higher and recessed more

deeply. The vampire saw that ladders leaned between the levels as well. "Maybe two hundred people?" he guessed.

The walls that rose above the courtyards were punctuated by occasional windows, some little more than slits in the stone, and doorways with high thresholds. Several of them, special for reasons the vampire could not discern, were cut into the shape of a stocky letter T. It reminded him of a Tau Cross. But the design was not consecrated with Christian intentions. It had no power to hurt him. Rows of exposed timbers jutted from many walls. The vampire saw that they served as beams between floors. He also saw that strips hung from some of those logs. Likely food hung there to dry. More pottery stood against several walls on the roof levels. Several dozen turkeys dozed in a small pen.

The crops that he had seen before dotted the entire canyon floor around the town. The stream cut its path through the cultivated land. A few thin irrigation channels radiated from its edges, and the vampire saw that the farmers used a system of simple stone gates to regulate the flow of water. At one point along its bank, a few trees had been preserved. Compared to the massive trunks that the vampire had seen in the jungles of India, wreathed in vines and racing to reach the light, these seemed small and alone. However, they were still larger than any plant he had seen in many miles, and no crops were planted in the clearing that radiated beneath their shade.

In the tallest tower of the fortress, he counted four levels above the courtyard. The walls, coated with white plaster, shone in the moonlight. Some were painted with geometric designs. Adorned with wandering black lines and triangular stripes, they were kin with the rock art he had seen before but more refined. Most of the windows were dark, but two flickered dimly, the light of small fires dying inside. Reddish light, the product of embers, also gently lit the entrance to one of the holes in the floor. Nobody stirred. The vampire turned back. He followed the path of his ascent back down into the canyon. He stepped quickly but forced himself to move quietly. He wanted to get closer. He wanted to hunt.

~ B ~

Makya saw that his wife and sons were still asleep. They breathed softly beside him. Deep and unhurried breaths. "Those baskets . . . over there . . . not those," Sihu moaned. She was dreaming. Honani had raised no alarm. Makya strained his hearing now. He heard nothing but normal night noises: the chirring of insects, the wind along the stream. The smoke of his dream had cleared, but the young warrior still felt uneasy. He had started to sense some presence in the canyon below. He could not explain it. It was an itch at the edge of his perception. Like hearing the silent hole where a scream should have been. He felt the hair stiffen along the back of his neck.

"No blood," Makya muttered without thinking. He did not even bother to look out the small square window. He rolled quickly to his feet and grabbed two spears. He slipped out of his room, allowing Sihu to sleep, and climbed out onto the nearest roof. He felt the silent scream get louder as he moved into the cool moonlit air that joined Crow Ledge to the encompassing night.

~ B ~

His descent from the far side of the canyon now complete, the vampire climbed a small hillock on the other bank of the stream. He studied the facade. Although he saw no doors or windows on the canyon floor, and no inviting steps or ladders that led from the ground to the structures above, he finally spied some shallow notches that rose across the steep face of the rock on one side, forming a narrow path for entry. "Easy to defend," he breathed. "Difficult to assault." His eyes drifted upward. The sheer cliff above the town was black with patina, the work of cascading rain and constant wind; and from where he stood, the interplay of patina and raw stone looked almost ornate. Looking up from the floor of the canyon, it reminded him of two giant wings draped above the town.

The vampire recalled another rocky citadel, a wicked monastery that he had once attacked with his brethren, carved into the rim of an unfriendly mountain, more fort than temple. Those unclean monks had killed first, without permission from the local ruler and in flagrant disavowal of the pact, an early sign of the troubles to come.

In fact, the monastery had expected the vampire and his brethren to retaliate, and when that attack came, the monks had defended themselves like rabid animals. However, as strict ascetics, the monks had rejected even the crucifix as a form of idolatry. The fools had not used the cross to bar their doors and windows. They had placed no rood behind the altar. And the monks had paid the price. Their purity had destroyed them.

Torches flared in his memory. The vampire could still smell burning tar. He recalled how it sizzled as it splattered his skin. The monks had dug narrow tunnels deep into the cliff, forced the vampires into close quarters. The passages had not been wide enough to wield swords. Not even tall enough to stand erect. He could still hear the screams in the dark, the sound of iron-tipped staves as they punched into armor, feet scrambling over stone floors suddenly slick with blood.

The vampire returned his mind to the canyon. He knew that many men and women slept inside; he could feel their pulse at this distance. It throbbed like the sound of cicadas in the summer forest, and his appetite sparked like rage now, hunger and murder fired into the original sin of the vampire race. It had been so many nights since he had fed. And so many nights before that. But he forced himself to focus and return to cold clarity. His kind did not last long if they could not control their passions.

~ *B* ~

As Makya stepped to the edge of the roof and looked across the canyon, his unease converged powerfully with what he saw. He startled. The figure on the hill was tall and gaunt, skin pale like the moon, black hair drawn back tightly behind his neck and tied into a knot. His sharp nose and black eyes reminded Makya of a bird. His dusty clothes were strange too. They hid much of his skin, even his hands. As though it were the heart of winter. A full cloak hung down his back. And then he brandished a terrible knife. It was longer than an arrow. Its blade shone beneath the moon like the scales of a fish. Like nothing Makya had ever seen. The stranger turned it slowly back and forth, the gentle motion filled with malice.

For one moment, Makya struggled to understand what he saw. And then he recalled several tales from Hototo, whispered tales that were rarely told. Makya felt his body vibrate with fear. He pushed his panic down and eased away from the edge of the roof. He finally shouted for help. "Enemy stranger! Enemy stranger! Enemy stranger!" His people had no other name for these rare demons.

Makya heard many people scramble to their feet inside, startled by the alarm in his voice. Quick to action, Choovio joined him first on the roof, shaking the sleep from his head. He clutched a knife in his hand. "There! Do you see him?" Makya asked.

His older brother nodded. "Who is the sentry tonight?" he whispered. Honani stumbled out into the night only a couple of breaths later. His bleary eyes were wide with confusion. Choovio shot him a disapproving glance.

They shouted at the demon as more warriors gathered. "Haaa! Haaa! Get away! Get out of here!" But to no avail. The demon only stared. He only stood there, fouling their home with undead eyes, challenging them with his long blade.

"Like being watched by the new moon," Choovio whispered to his brother.

"Sihu, hand out the bows!" Makya called.

~ B ~

The vampire jolted with surprise. A lean, muscular man had just emerged atop the first level and near the tallest tower. He stepped through the small doorway and, swift and silent, moved to the edge of the roof, two primitive spears at his side. His skin was dark, and his black hair was pulled back into a single braid. Probably handsome to his people, he wore no shirt, just a plain necklace and some cloth across his hips. An ornate pattern of lines, not unlike the walls behind him, had been woven into the fabric.

The vampire stood motionless and let his gaze fall dead against the canyon wall, hoping to avoid eye contact. But it was too late. The young warrior swept his eyes across the canyon and startled; he saw the vampire standing at the top of the hill. "Damn," the vampire said. He was appalled at his careless approach. They had caught him standing in plain sight. He quickly adjusted. After fixing his stare upon the young man, he unsheathed his sword. He turned the blade slowly to show the moonlit glint of steel. An intense moment of silence passed between them, and then, still staring back with wide eyes, the young man backed across the roof. A few steps from the wall, he shouted the alarm. While the vampire did not know the words, the tone was unmistakable.

The vampire stood firm, determined to sow fear before his departure. More young men spilled out into the moonlight, also sporting single braids and similar dress. The first several rallied on the roof. Others had emerged onto the central terrace and moved quickly to the front wall to spot him. They pointed across the small stream and shouted. The vampire only stared with grim concentration, still moving his sword gently to catch the light. He knew the effect of silence. And then he saw gestures exchanged, men forming into distinct groups and reaching back for weapons. He saw bows and arrows passing through doorways. "Here they come," he said to himself.

He turned and scrambled down the hill. The vampire put his original approach, which also happened to be the intended path of his retreat, to his back at first, a feint to confuse their pursuit, before eventually dropping out of sight. No good chance to enter the town would come tonight. He would not even attempt to feed. Hungry or not, this circumstance was new and called for caution. And he had no wish to fight dozens of men, particularly men who could build such a fortress.

He recited the second of the Eight Precepts to temper his frustration as he doubled back. "Discipline thine appetite. Discipline thine appetite," he murmured as he sprinted away.

~ B ~

Hototo dreamed that he struggled to lift a green pumpkin of enormous size. He could not move it, his arms constantly slipping against the smooth ribs, slightly wet with morning dew. And now it was screaming. He could not see its mouth, could not see the source of the scream. He draped his body across it, trying to muffle the sound. And as the howl vibrated against his heart, he could finally understand. "Enemy stranger! Enemy stranger! Enemy stranger!" The words rattled with clarity inside his chest. He jolted awake. He heard Makya shouting those words several floors down. The dream dissolved.

Cold fear rushed through his limbs, but no stranger to the discipline of his own will, Hototo forced himself to rise and lunge stiffly to the small window. Makya stood on the roof several levels down. Although it was not his night to keep watch, the young war leader still held spears in his hand. "Where is Honani?" Hototo whispered. He heard many Crows moving now, the rattle of ladders in the rooms beneath him. His eyes

42

were hazy as he scanned the canyon, but they adjusted quickly. The shaman quickly spotted the demon.

Even more than the pale cast of his skin and the strange look of his clothes, Hototo felt the unsettling sensation of staring at any empty vessel. He had felt it before. "Muna," he whispered. The shaman felt an anxious fear, dormant for years, stir inside him. It pulled tight across his chest. He watched intently as the demon gently turned a colorless blade in the moonlight, a slow warning. It seemed impossibly long and thin for a knife. He had not seen such a weapon before. It held his gaze. "I have not prepared them. I have not . . ." Hototo trailed off.

And then the enemy stranger turned and sprinted away. His dark cloak came alive in the wind behind him. The demon moved in the direction of Firetown. Hototo thrust his head out the window. "Give chase! Give chase!" he shouted, more affirmation than command. He doubted that even Makya was fast enough to close the distance. But he understood that they had to make the effort.

The shaman turned from the window as men disappeared over the wall. He quickly grabbed what he needed to clear his mind and purify his kiva for the night ahead. He knew the location of every herb and powder. Even in the darkest corners of the small room. Supplies tucked under his arm, Hototo started swiftly down the ladder. His free hand brushed from rung to rung as his other hand ran loosely down the rail. As he reached the lower level, he jumped past the last several rungs and landed lightly. He saw that Kaya stood behind him, eyes wide in the unlit room.

She said nothing. In both hands, she clutched a new corn-husk doll. He could see that Kaya had sewn a small tunic for the doll, but he could not tell its color in the dark. He smiled and gently placed his hand across the top of her head. "Try to go back to sleep. Nothing to worry about," he assured.

CHAPTER 4

Revelations in the Dark

THE VAMPIRE RAN across the canyon, retracing his steps now. He sprinted at first, and then kept the easy pace of loping wolves for several more miles. The sound of the settlement behind him quickly dropped away. The vampire left no discernible trail. He had been hunted for years and he knew how to vanish into the landscape. His predations betrayed his location far more often than his feet. He needed to find refuge far from the men, and too much of the night had already passed. They would have the advantage of hunting him under the sun when he could no longer run, when he could not alter his hiding place. They always did. "Curse the dawn," he panted.

He turned to his left, down another corridor of stone. He had scouted these cliffs early in the night, an hour or two before he had decided to keep to the stream, and the vampire had seen a promising hole high in the rocky face of the western cliff.

~ B ~

Makya climbed quickly down the ladder into the primary ritual kiva of the Morning Crows. Fashioned of masonry stone, the circular room stood below the terrace and was the largest at Crow Ledge. Unlike some of the smaller kivas at Crow Ledge, a low bench, also built with stone, ran along the curved wall; but Sowingwa, respected elder of the Morning Crows, huddled with Hototo in the center of the room. Both men wore loose shirts with long sleeves. As the older men often did. Sowingwa talked with the shaman before a small fire. He nodded when Hototo replied, his braided hair the color of ash. He also rubbed his palm across his knee, as though it were injured; something he did often.

Hototo traced an idle circle in the dirt. His legs were crossed. He sat on piled coyote hides, which was unusual. "I think we are done," he said.

Sowingwa nodded and rose stiffly to depart. He stared at Makya, offering no greeting as they stepped toward the ladder. But Makya pressed forward.

"No sign of him, none we could follow in the dark at least. He just vanished," the young warrior reported. Hototo tossed a pinch of dark powder into the fire. Gold sparks skittered in the flame. He breathed in the smoke. Silence hung in the room. The spirit leader looked at Makya with sad eyes. His face looked older tonight as he stared up from his fire. Time and worry were beginning to erode deep lines into its hard surface.

"He'll return," Hototo finally said. "He craves human blood just as we thirst for water. Sit down," he added. Makya dropped to his knees to listen, the stance of respect inside the kiva. He had not heard Hototo mention enemy strangers in years. Makya had not even quite believed him before; he had not thought that Hototo lied, only that they were tales that did not need to be true.

"Are they human?" Makya asked.

"Cursed . . . demons," Hototo replied. "Demons," he repeated. He twitched his lips several times. He did not seem to know what to say next. Makya looked into the fire as he waited. The young warrior recalled hiding over the kiva portal with Choovio one night when they were very young, watching the smoke curl up toward the stars while they eavesdropped. Hototo had spoken then of enemy strangers, talked of how the Smoke Clan had once, many years ago, defeated three of them, a group of demons that had hunted as a pack. However, one of the boys had sneezed—Makya and Choovio still argued over which one—and Saya had caught them before they could hear more. The clan leader and annoyed father had sent them sternly to bed, and after that, all requests for more such tales had been rebuffed.

Makya broke the silence now. "How should we fight them?" he asked.

"We have only seen four or five here in the last three generations. None since your birth. I had hoped that we had destroyed them all. I had wanted to forget them," Hototo said. He fed some twigs to the tiny fire, prodded the coals. "But as the sibyl at Smoke Ridge once told me: the last rain assures you of the next rain, even though it knows nothing of the clouds to come."

"I was visited by evil wolves in my dream and when—"

"One of those strangers killed your mother," Hototo interrupted.

"How is that possible? I have always been told that she passed with my birth," Makya insisted.

"One and the same," Hototo nodded. "She was full with your life when an enemy stranger attacked her. Down by the old cottonwood tree and under the bright moon. Just like tonight."

Makya felt the blood rise in his cheeks. He felt like Hototo had slapped him across the face. "Why would the Morning Crows hide this from me?" Makya said.

"Saya and I were there. Nobody else knows the true story. Not even Shuman. And certainly not the old men." Hototo gestured gently to the ladder, clearly meaning Sowingwa.

"But you—" Makya began. Hototo flashed his open hands, bidding the young man to listen. Makya waited once more, showing the proper respect, even though his head exploded with questions. Hototo added another dash of powder to the fire. More sparks shot through the flames. The shaman inhaled and finally continued.

"I felt great fear among the animals that evening, and then the fox and rabbit hid together in my dreams. They huddled in the corn, trembling at the sound of something coming toward them. When I awoke, I felt that something was wrong, as though a carcass were rotting; but I could not name it so I climbed down, intending to sit among the trees. I wanted to rest along the stream and see what the water might tell me. I took my spear because I felt so anxious."

Hototo paused. He seemed to struggle and shook his head. "Your father said that Muna had left to cool herself that night. Her birth pangs had started. But only slowly so Saya let her go. When I came near the stream, I saw the demon over her. His teeth were deep in her neck. He held her wrist tight. I could hear him sucking her blood into his mouth. Her blood also ran into the stream. Like her shadow was dissolving. I was filled with terror when I saw him. But the demon was distracted by his greed. He did not hear my quick and careful steps. I brought my spear high and thrust it down between his shoulders. He snarled and twisted toward me as I drove the sharp stone into him. His fangs were bare and smeared with gore. But I killed him. Struck the heart. It is where an enemy stranger is most vulnerable."

"But my mother . . ."

"The spear stabbed her too. It sliced through the monster more easily than I had expected," Hototo said. His tired eyes glistened in the yellow light of the fire.

"You . . . you killed her?" Makya whispered.

"No. Muna had lost too much blood already. And better for her to die than live under that curse. And then I saw Saya jump to the ground from Crow Ledge. He rolled hard in the dust and stumbled to his feet; he sprinted to the edge of the water. He had seen it happen. I can still hear the dry crackle as I kicked the demon from my spear. Muna released you into the world before she passed—"

"You should have told me. You should have—" Makya said.

"Saya wanted to tell you after the rites of passage. But he was ambushed by the Ash Owl Clan. When the fighting between clans . . . he died too soon," Hototo said. Gray light drifted down through the entry hole at the top of the kiva now. Makya

47

said nothing for many long breaths. He felt his hatred renewed for the Ash Owl Clan. It flashed inside him like strands of hair passed over flame. They had killed his father. He felt hatred for the demon too. And then his anger flashed at Hototo.

"Then why did you not tell me after those rites? My father wished me to know. But you have kept this secret from me, would not have told me even now. Did you . . . did you hide this from the Morning Crows to avoid blame?" Makya blurted out, pointing his finger at the shaman. He regretted it instantly. Hototo bolted suddenly to his feet and stepped across the fire, scattering hot coals toward Makya. They stung his knees. The young warrior tumbled back over his ankles. He landed on his hands. Hototo stood directly over him now. His whole face flared with anger. And then, with reptilian speed, Hototo cuffed Makya hard with both hands, striking both sides of his head. Makya scrambled backwards. His ears rang with pain. He was stunned by the quickness and strength of the older man.

"You will show respect. You thank me poorly with your words," Hototo growled. Makya knew that his temper had crossed the line. Not only did Hototo lead the Morning Crows, he had also become a surrogate father after Saya had died. Makya had been disciplined many times before. He forced himself to swallow his pride. To swallow his anger.

"I am sorry," Makya said.

Hototo stared for another moment and then returned to his seat. The heat in the room slowly faded. However, when Hototo finally broke the silence, he spoke with the hot edge of command. "We did hide the circumstance of your birth, even from the matriarch, and so it shall remain. We wanted no cloud to darken your place among the Morning Crows . . . so that it would not taint your own mind. So that none might say that the shadow of an enemy stranger was upon you. And so it has been, Makya. And so it has been."

"I spoke without thinking. I know that you—"

"It took me the rest of that night to hide the shell of that demon; and then to properly bury your mother. I told Shuman, truthfully enough, that immediate burial was needed. She tended you while Saya helped me carry Muna to the Hill of Return."

"I did not realize–"

"Stand up," Hototo interrupted. "Your dream . . . it seems as though the enemy stranger disturbed your dreams. Perhaps the demon touched her womb in some manner," Hototo said.

Makya shook his head. He did not understand.

"Your dream warned you. You felt his presence. The demon that killed your mother might have touched your spirit. Not cursed but touched. You may have the power to sense his kind more than most. That might have saved us tonight."

"I felt him when I woke from my dream," Makya said.

"But every rope must have two ends. If he can also sense you . . . what if your presence also attracted him to Crow Ledge?" Hototo said. "We will hunt him this morning, while the sun blocks his path. The light will burn him. I have been told that it steals his strength even when he hides. But you will stay with the village. The risk is too great. You will guard Crow Ledge with the older men," he added.

"But I could help you," Makya objected. "I can find him and lead the warriors. You cannot expect–"

"I can expect. And I do expect," Hototo said with flat finality. He stared hard at Makya. "You are the fox. Listen to me. You must hide with the rabbits now. It was perhaps the meaning of my dream so many years ago. And if we must search near the High Rocks land, well, better that you are not seen with us." Hototo waved his hand toward the ladder. "Now . . . please find Honani and send him here immediately. That fool fell asleep on the watch tonight. He will be punished."

Makya nodded, struggling to digest what he had heard. His ears still rang from the blows. The meeting was over. He scaled the ladder as fast as he could, eager to leave the kiva. Although he was filled with turmoil, he took some comfort in the thought that Honani's upcoming meeting with Hototo might be even worse than his own.

~ B ~

The vampire judged that only the most skilled climbers could hope to reach the hole in the cliff above him. He knew that he could climb it. He had endless experience, nocturnal strength, and the courage of immortality to aid him.

He could tell that it ran deep into the rock, and with likely shade from the arc of the sun, it promised safe slumber. The sun was nearing the horizon. The sky had tinged blue at the eastern horizon as he pulled his knees into the cave, quickly brushing aside a pile of sticks. It opened into a level tunnel with a high ceiling. The walls angled sharply to his left and terminated past his view. Good. Good enough for staying perhaps. Finding new hiding places each night was risky. He began to explore.

The far wall of the cave ran about forty steps from the portal, the end of a crooked alley in the side of the cliff. His eyes were meant for the darkest night; even the tiny fraction of gray light that diffused around the corner, the forward shadow of the coming dawn, was sufficient. He saw the back of the cave almost immediately. The vampire stopped cold. He saw a ring of stones with cold ash and cinders in the middle, black stains on the ceiling above. Sprigs of herbs and roots were stacked neatly across a flat rock, and more flat rocks leaned against the wall. Paint tattooed the grotto wall. Handprints and concentric spirals floated among more horned figures and simple animals, not only black and white but also bright yellow and red. Thick torsos and thin limbs, they crowded the wall with a sense of motion, as though each figure had frozen as eyes had fallen upon them. The vampire took a long breath. This cave was known. The locals could visit here; they used this cave. The sun would sear across the cliffs behind him very soon. He was trapped until nightfall. "Curse the dawn!" he said again.

The vampire moved to the far corner of the cave and sat, frustrated, with his legs crossed, his back to the decorated wall. The pale gray tint of morning filled the mouth of the cave at the other end of the tunnel. He took another long breath, and then the vampire took a whetstone from the small bag at his waist. He began to pass it across his blade with slow authority as the day took its throne. This helped him focus and prepare his mind for another period of anxious waiting.

~ B ~

Hototo climbed stiffly from the kiva. Among the men and women who milled about Crow Ledge now, he saw that Shuman waited for him. As tall as most Crow Ledge men, the matriarch of the Morning Crows gripped a woven blanket across her wiry shoulders, shielding herself from the cool morning air, worry written into her thin face. She looked to the hill where the enemy stranger had stood. Although wrinkles ran from the corners of her eyes, she studied the scene with the acuity of an active hunter, many questions working behind her gaze.

"You must send word to the Ash Owls. Istaqa can help us fight this demon," she said. Lines pinched the corners of her mouth.

"No. I will ask them for nothing. Not while Istaqa leads them," Hototo said emphatically. The spirit leader still bristled from his quarrel with Makya and he had just loosed his ire against Honani. His temper was already short.

"We must warn them. We have that duty," Shuman said.

"What duty do we owe those killers? Would they do the same for us? It wouldn't surprise me if Kotori conjured this demon to afflict us," Hototo said.

"Haaa!" Shuman scoffed. "Kotori has not the magic to cure his own aching head," she said, mocking the shaman of the Ash Owls.

"Then he would make a poor ally," Hototo replied with a wry smile. "Shu . . . we must not look weak by asking our enemies for help. We can handle this alone," he said more seriously. Shuman folded her arms. She still looked across the stream.

"It would show our desire for good relations. We could use this moment to make peace again. We could finally visit friends. Just imagine. I have not talked with Mansi in many years. How long has it been?" she prodded.

"Like setting out corn for the rats. We will not embrace such people. Not while I lead the Morning Crows!" Hototo said. They locked eyes now. Sparks of anger passed silently between them.

"I think we need to warn them," Shuman repeated firmly.

"And mock those loved ones whom the Ash Owls have killed?" Hototo pushed back.

"And what of those that this demon has not yet killed?"

"They still live. The future is uncertain. But the past . . . memory is like the rock that shelters Crow Ledge."

"True. But these cliffs shed stones from their flanks all the time. Boulders larger than kivas even. Perhaps our quarrel with the Ash Owls could fall away like an old memory. Could hunting the enemy stranger together become the fresh memory that took its place?" she offered.

"How can the crimes of the Ash Owls grow into old memory when the slain are still absent from Crow Ledge? We still miss them. Makya and Choovio still miss their father. The dead cannot return." Hototo lifted his chin, daring Shuman to deny his point.

Shuman spun abruptly and walked toward the turkey pen. She fed them each morning. "You stubborn goat!" Shuman spat. She said it loud enough for Hototo to hear.

The turkeys were agitated when she reached the enclosure. As Shuman tossed corn at their feet, the birds, upset by the unusual commotion and perhaps sensing her anger, ran from the seed as it landed. They crowded the far corner of the pen with a frightened rush of flapping wings. "Ohhhh . . . do you think I have come for your heads this morning?" Shuman asked gently.

CHAPTER 5

Where the Enemy Lies

T HE SUN WASHED the canyon and dissolved the
morning dew. The young men of the clan, Hototo at
point, had left to hunt the enemy stranger. Makya had
stayed as commanded. He sat on the high roof and looked down
across Crow Ledge. Knowing that the enemy stranger could not
venture into the sunlight, Makya tapped his knife and his palm
against the roof to pass the time, building a complex beat. His
wife and sons had departed to gather wood with some other
women, Shuman included. "And perhaps some pine nuts from
the high ground," Sihu had told him.

"Just stay clear of the caves and ruins," Makya had told her.

He finally closed his eyes, seeing that many Morning Crows
worked below him. "Plenty of eyes," he assured himself. His
vigil only mattered at twilight if the men did not return. Makya
drifted toward sleep. He had not slept much last night. And the
sun was warm. He let his mind stretch into the canyon, his inner
eye soaring over the rocks and brush. He thought of the link
that Hototo had described and he wondered if he could feel it
now. His inner ear strained to hear the awful silence that had
swirled around the enemy stranger. "Where might you hide?"
he whispered. He felt nothing.

But then, at the moment when sleep took him, an image,
not quite a dream, flashed on the wall of his mind. He felt
himself frozen in his tracks as an eclipse turned the sky dark
purple. Cold and shivering on the floor of the canyon, he saw a
gash high on the face of the cliff. The enemy stranger rose from
the hole. The corona roared behind him, a ring of fire behind
the moon. The very rocks wanted to scream. But silence. He

waved Makya forward with the tip of his blade and smiled, fangs white against blood-dark lips.

Makya jerked awake, clutching his knife. The sun danced in the stream below, finally flowing again after years of drought. There was no eclipse. But the young warrior knew what he had seen. "He hides in the Cave of Visions," he said. Makya felt sick to his stomach. How dare that demon foul and defile the sacred cave! His hands began to shake. The hunting party was long gone. They had intended to first walk south toward the Ash Owl border. They would not return until dusk, or only pass the cave tomorrow if they then walked west along the edge of Ash Owl territory and then turned north into Seeker Canyon.

By that time the enemy stranger would have left the cave to become the hunter once again. The opportunity would be lost. Makya thought hard about what he should do. He knew that these demons were strong and wild under the moon, but he was also pretty sure that they were weaker now, not much stronger than mortals, according to the few tales he could recall. Makya felt confident that he could kill this enemy stranger and imagined himself dropping its body before Hototo. And yet, Hototo had warned him to stay. He paced back and forth across the roof.

~ B ~

Squatting along the muddy tail of a dissipating stream, Jerome stared at several footprints. They were baking hard, the wet ground receding. "Damn me twice. The heel of a boot," Jerome said. He walked up one bank of the stream and down the other but could not find a clear trail. He also saw several other prints, sandals on smaller feet than those of the vampire. They seemed to suggest several different directions but nothing certain.

Jerome thought about his options. He would prefer to follow the stream for his own comfort. And the owners of those sandals would probably make use of the stream too. This might certainly entice the vampire. But on the other edge of that same sword, Jerome was not that eager to meet the locals himself. Other knights had shown more skill with languages and hand gestures. They had shown more patience too. Jerome had learned to hate the Tower of Babel during his travels, the chaos of incomprehensible tongues that was its legacy. "Nimrod!" he sneered as he spat into the mud for emphasis. The knight massaged his thigh now. He could still feel a previous misunderstanding, the broken tip of an arrow, floating next to his femur.

Jerome also had to consider that the vampire was still trying to shake the Knights of St. John. No other reason for the devil to flee into the desert in the first place. "Water is life… but what does he care about water?" Jerome reasoned. He recalled his long ocean voyage and its many contradictions. The knights had fought unrelenting thirst while water lapped the hull. They had given thanks for the rain, parched tongues extended, as waves washed across the deck and wind ripped the sails. And finally, they had driven their leaking vessel against the rocky shore to save their lives. Even as they destroyed all hope of returning home. He could still feel the sound of splintering wood. It had vibrated through every bone.

"This land is beautiful!" Allain had exclaimed as they fought to push their horses, all jutting ribs and terrified spittle, into the azure surf. One of the horses had snapped its leg as the ship ran aground, a gruesome break. They had driven it ashore all the same, forcing it onto dry land like the rest. Jerome had drawn his sword quickly; he knew that panic and pain would taint the meat. However, he had stayed his hand until the poor beast had fought clear of the strand and secured dry land. Lousy meat was better than none at all. And the tide would come in quickly.

~ B ~

Using the gently curved notch along the edge of the stone, Old Chu'Si expertly stripped the blue kernels from the ear of corn, allowing them to fall into the concavity of her grinding well, worn deep from years of use. She set aside the tool and picked up her grinding stone. It fit perfectly inside the curve of the larger stone. And perfectly against her callused hands. She began to grind the corn into meal.

She knelt next to Lenmana. They were good friends; chores often brought them together. Their tanned arms and plain tunics were flecked with corn dust. Lenmana, some years younger, softly hummed a wedding song. Her cousin, Kwahu, would marry Chosovi from the Ash Owl Clan tomorrow; and Lenmana was happy for the couple. The High Rocks women had been working for days to prepare a suitable feast. In fact, women worked corn into meal all across the terrace of Low Nest this morning, creating a rasping music that filled the air, the methodical clack and shuffle of dancing stones.

Although Lenmana did not know the Ash Owls well, she was excited for Kwahu to move to Firetown. She had been there before and helped with new construction, her clan shaping and lifting stone after stone to repay their debt of corn several years back. Lenmana had badly smashed several fingers that summer, and the nail of her middle finger still refused to grow straight. But she still admired the scale of Firetown, the ambition of its design.

Old Chu'Si stopped. "A marriage between the clans makes more work," she said, catching her breath.

"Do you think it will feel tense tomorrow when the Ash Owls arrive?" Lenmana said.

"Yes. Our clans do not really know each other anymore. Even so, we might still find old friends among them.

"Do you think the Ash Owl matriarch will come?" Lenmana asked.

"Mansi has lost her sight. Or so I have heard. Still, I hope she might make the trip. We used to arrange many marriages between our two clans . . . before the fighting started. Before the Ash Owls turned against us." Old Chu'Si scooped fresh meal into the basket at her side.

"Chayton hopes to see more such weddings," Lenmana enthused. Old Chu'Si did not reply. She only clapped the dust from her hands and grabbed another ear of corn. "Why does Chayton himself still not marry?" Lenmana asked.

"He should marry the first snake that slithers through the canyon."

Lenmana shook her head but smiled. "That tongue of yours. He is going to hear you one of these days."

"I try to make sure he does. I tell him to cut that long hair. I ask him to consult with me. But does he listen?" Old Chu'Si replied.

"He needs to choose a wife. I would volunteer!" Lenmana joked.

"The young women might stop begging to do his chores if he claimed a wife!" Old Chu'Si said. "And would you toss away your husband so quickly? Lapu is one of the good ones!" she added.

"He is a good husband. I think Lapu would even help me grind corn if I asked him. He has been fermenting some good beer for the wedding these last few days. We just need to chill the jugs in the stream tonight. Takes a little trouble to anchor them. But the beer definitely tastes better cold."

"Then you should hang onto Lapu for sure," Old Chu'Si said.

"Well . . . maybe I could just use Chayton for the night. I could always throw him out the next morning. How about that?" Lenmana said with a wink.

The old matriarch could only shake her head in disapproval.

"Oh, of course not!" Lenmana assured. "But our clan grows stronger with each season. Even you must see that Chayton leads us well. His plans are bold."

Old Chu'Si just shrugged. She pressed her lips tight. She began to crack the hard kernels of corn once more. However, she wondered if she might even venture to Firetown herself after the wedding. Could she rekindle her old friendships? Could they dangle their feet together from the wall of Firetown? Could they once again lift up their fingers to trace rivers through the stars? She hoped that they could, that they might simply step over the intervening years and find familiar paths on the other side.

~ B ~

Makya walked down to the stream now. It was not unusual for him to carry weapons—he was an important hunter and warrior among the Morning Crows after all—and nobody took notice of them now. He gripped his bow and arrows in one hand, held four spears in the other. He sat down on the roots of the large cottonwood tree and stabbed the pebbled sand. A thin cloud of silt swirled into the shallow current and then vanished.

"How can I stay?" Makya asked himself. He told himself that no true Morning Crow would allow such demons to desecrate the Cave of Visions. He told himself that the opportunity to corner the enemy stranger might not come again. And maybe the spirit leader was wrong after all. Even wise leaders were fallible; Hototo had told him so many times. Maybe his mother could have been saved. Perhaps guilt or regret colored the vision of the shaman. The fox hiding with the rabbit could mean anything. That the fox could bring danger if he did not hunt. That all hunters must join the fight before fear swept the fields. That none of the warriors should have left Crow Ledge this morning. Or perhaps its portent had long passed. Such an old dream anyway. Makya gathered his spears and clinched his teeth. He imagined his absent mother bleeding at his feet, probably under this very tree, and his hatred for the enemy stranger burned hot. The demon that had disturbed his sleep last night, like a fresh fire coaxed from a recovered ember, merged in his mind with the one that had stolen his mother.

Not looking back, he left the canyon with a quick, disciplined trot. He knew that he could reach the cave while the sun stood high in the sky if he kept a strong pace and took the rough path over and through the Broken Hills. That route would intersect Seeker Canyon near the cave and keep him far south of High Rocks land too. And then he could face the enemy stranger at the nadir of its power. Makya keenly felt the breach of trust as he ran, but Hototo would forgive him, Makya thought, when he placed the enemy blade at his feet. When he rolled the bloody head of the demon across the floor of Crow Ledge. When the clan was made safe once more.

He thought again of the long knife that the demon had carried. Not even the Smoke Clan could build such an instrument. What power for the clan that wielded that weapon. The other clans would not stand before it. "It is . . . an oppor . . . tunity . . ." he panted to himself. Makya imagined that all murders would be avenged. That the Ash Owls would pay again and again for killing his father. He pushed himself to pick up the pace.

~ B ~

"This land is still beautiful," Allain had insisted later. Only days before his death. Jerome had joined him as they watched the desert dawn set fire to the eastern horizon. Warm colors had washed across the rocky ground and displaced the shadows. Like the hues of autumn in his beloved France.

Jerome shook his head now. "Why even think about it?" he asked himself. He studied the landscape ahead. A wall of reddish rock rose up in the distance like some sort of primeval Jericho for titans long deposed. However, Jerome saw two sizeable gaps, one to the left that was likely the source of the stream, and one to the right that seemed to drift toward slightly higher ground.

"Bastard would expect me to follow water. So then . . ." he trailed off. Jerome decided to follow the stream just until it ran swift and clear. Of course, he could drink muddy water here and now. He had done that many times. However, the risk of falling ill was greater. And a short walk promised the refreshment of real running water. Jerome imagined lowering his mouth into the current and drinking until he could swallow no more, until he felt the cool liquid backing up in his throat.

Jerome would also replenish his water skins and wash the dust from his face. However, he would then break away from the stream and head for the other break in the rocks. If the vampire assumed that Jerome would follow the stream, he might hope to lose the knight by choosing the other direction. "He knows the sandals point in both directions," Jerome said. Every knight knew that it was important to understand your enemy. But Jerome also felt that it was important to understand what your enemy believed about you. "Like seeing through both sides of the window at once," he declared. Jerome nodded to himself. He felt that he had made the right choice.

~ B ~

Choovio moved through the remnants of an abandoned pit house. Nobody had lived there for generations. Most of the Morning Crows, avoided the old dwellings as much as possible, not wishing to disturb the spirits that lingered there. However, the humble structures could easily serve as hiding places. Although holes had opened in the old roof, creating hazy columns of light in the first room, some unlit recesses remained. Choovio needed to inspect a smaller storage chamber at the rear of the dwelling. His men waited outside. None of them would have room to fight if they filled the cramped space.

Kele had told Choovio that the chamber was intact, which meant it was sheltered from the sunlight. Unlike the rest of his clan, Kele had a strange fondness for the ruins, which usually spooked his friends but made him indispensable today. His guidance had helped them inspect the old dwellings much more efficiently. "Kele . . . what were you doing in here in the first place?" Choovio whispered to himself. He stared through the opening. His inspection revealed nothing but black space. Barely taking a breath, he strained every sense as he crept through scattered trash, dried leaves, and broken pottery. Choovio fully expected the small room to reveal the demon, even though he sensed no foul presence. He thrust his spear through, hoping to bait a response. However, as he raked the spear across the empty air, a startled mouse bolted over the threshold and between his legs. He staggered backwards with an awkward leap. "Ssshhhh," he hissed through clenched teeth, still keeping eye contact with the dark portal. He was glad his friends hadn't seen him jump.

Choovio stepped back to the doorway. "Are you in there?" he whispered, still hoping to provoke a reaction, to draw the monster out. No answer. No sound at all. He took a deep breath and threw himself into the storage room. He landed on his shoulder and rolled into a balanced crouch, spear at the ready.

Choovio climbed back into the morning light moments later, slowing his breathing and letting the tension subside. At least momentarily. He saw the challenge with grim clarity. There were many more abandoned structures ahead, some uncomfortably close to Ash Owl land. In fact, the Ash Owls would probably view the Morning Crows as trespassing before the search was over. Especially since all his men carried weapons. And even if the Ash Owls had been friendly and blind, there were still countless places to hide in this land, only one of which would hold the monster. It reminded him of the old Morning Crow proverb: *You can only find water where it is.* Choovio felt a new appreciation for its odd wisdom.

Choovio wished Makya had been allowed to join them. Hototo always had his reasons, but his brother was an excellent warrior, perhaps the best among all the clans. The other warriors waited in a loose circle, allowing Choovio to collect himself. They let their muscles relax as well. Choovio brushed the dirt from his knees and shoulders. "Makya is probably sleeping the day away. How does he get so lucky?" he joked.

Honani agreed. "The old women have probably stuffed him full of corn cakes already." He was a trusted friend of both brothers, and the bright morning sun had quickly thawed any anger that might have lingered from his failure as sentry the night before.

"Where next?" Choovio asked. He looked toward Kele now.

Kele motioned further along the ridge. "I think there are two more shelters that way. I found an old granary too. It is well concealed. Hard to imagine an enemy stranger finding that one. Do you still want to check it?"

Choovio nodded. "We should assume that the demon is clever."

~ B ~

The vampire rested easily in the lotus position. His sword was drawn across his lap. He had returned his whetstone to its pouch. He opened his eyes as he heard scrum shifting near the bottom of the cliff. He had sensed an approaching pulse. However, the vampire had not heard actual steps until the visitor had started to climb. The stealth impressed him. He was able to hear, and smell, the Knights of St. John from near the horizon. But these warriors were different. No steel or horses that he could see. No apparent crucifix. But perhaps not to be taken lightly.

The vampire sensed that the visitor below was the same individual who had spotted him last night. "Twice startled . . .

once warned," he muttered. However, he did not have time to consider that fact for long. The young man scaled the cliff with impressive speed. He breathed deep but did not fight for air. He quickly reached the cave entrance. The vampire rose in one fluid moment. He grasped his sword tightly in his gloved hand, knowing that he was vulnerable now. He was thankful, and also surprised, that he only heard one climber. He waited in stillness. He would require the hunter to round the corner and press into the dark to find him. He recalled a proverb of his kind. "A shark must take its prey in the water," he said. The mouth of the cave, full of blinding light, would char his skin in an instant. And sustained exposure would cremate him. He winced at the memory of past burns.

CHAPTER 6

Lighting Fires

MAKYA STOOD AT the very mouth of the cave, one spear locked in the crook of his arm, legs tensed for battle. His other weapons lay at his feet. He calmed his lungs and listened. He could see nothing but increasing darkness as the cave curved away and into the cliff. He still felt the enemy stranger, that horrible silence. He knew that the creature waited at the rear of the tunnel. Sweat cooled on his skin. Makya waited for his eyes to adjust. It was not enough to clear the deep shadows. He knew that no sunlight reached the back of the cave, and he had no wish to fight blind.

Fortunately, the rituals that Hototo led here were always performed by firelight. The cave stored wood accordingly. Makya kept his eyes on the ragged edge of the dark and knelt carefully. His shins hung out over the precipice. He laid down his last spear quietly as he listened for any sign of movement in the dark. Lifting the dry brush and kindling that the demon had swept aside, he picked up a drill and bow. He doubted that the enemy stranger had seen them. Hototo always stored them beneath the kindling.

Makya also pulled free the fireboard and the palm guard placed beneath it. Sewn from many layers of tough leather, the first layer already burnt through, the palm guard protected his hand as he pressed down against the top of the drill. He spit into the leather to reduce the friction. The old fireboard was pocked with the blackened holes from previous visits. He quickly set tinder beneath the board; and then, looping the bowstring around the drill, began to work the bow with long strokes. Its string, braided from both leather and tough yucca fibers, began to spin the drill quickly against the fireboard. Sweat and dust gritted across his palms. He had done this many times; but knowing that the enemy stranger was close, only restrained by the sun, he struggled to execute. Each moment passed slowly. Like watching sap ooze down the bark of a pine tree. His arms strained to spin the drill faster, to hold it tightly against the board. He could feel the heat gathering against his palm. His eyes danced between the plank and the darkness as smoke finally began to curl from the board.

~ B ~

The vampire knew the sound of friction—the intruder was starting a fire—but he could only wait. While the dim light near the bend was no danger, it offered no advantage either. "Curse my roof," he said softly. He could feel the quick pulse of the young warrior now. The vampire squeezed the handle of his sword in matching time with the stroke of the bow.

He continued to wait. How long did it take? The vampire began to wonder if the warrior sought to lure him out. But he had no intention of taking the bait. The back of his mind drifted. He closed his eyes for just one moment. He recalled a bitter memory. The Order of St. John had caught his brethren at White Rose Castle, named for the dense thickets of pale roses that formed a thorny barrier around its walls, not so many years ago.

Many vampires had convened there to discuss the further deterioration of the old agreements. Unfortunately, one of them had been betrayed by a human servant. They were stunned when they heard the knights rushing into the castle, their armor clanking with every step, many feet upon the floor. The vampires reached their swords quickly, confident in their skill and numbers, even while the sun stole much of their strength. However, once the skirmish started, the knights only feigned retreat. More clever than usual, they lured the vampires into a trap, a high room chosen for its many entrances and proximity to sunlight. The bastards had brought mirrors, large and sturdy. They aimed each one into the room, directing sunlight where it did not belong, forcing his friends into the crossfire of screaming light. "Make for the wine cellar!" one of them had hissed as they scrambled to escape.

By accident of position and by protection from his cloak, the vampire had been able to retreat. But he saw many of his brethren burnt to ash as he turned away, heard howls of pain as he sprinted down the rough stone stairs and away from the massacre. An access tunnel, low and damp, had hid him until dusk. Tiny roots had wormed through its vaulted ceiling.

That night had marked the beginning of his exile, many friends gone forever. The vampire winced at the memory. His eyes shot open. The tang of smoke had finally hit his nostrils. Flames would soon follow.

~ B ~

Makya stalked slowly forward, spears and arrows cradled in his right hand, torch in his left, strung bow slung across his shoulder. Light painted the rough curve of the wall, but he could not yet see around the corner. "Like sticking my hand into a rattlesnake den," Makya thought. He stopped and lit another pile of kindling brush from his torch. He used his longest spear to push the flaring brush forward past the bend.

Makya held his breath, listening for even the softest step. He heard nothing, no motion at all. And then the demon barked a single word: "Come!" Makya jumped like a startled lizard as the voice struck him unexpectedly. Makya did not know the word. But he knew the tone, the note of command. He was glad the demon could not yet see his reaction. He hoped that was the case anyway. He left his thoughts, as past battles had taught him, and hurled his body around the corner. He kept himself low but raised the torch high, gaining his first line of sight toward the back of the cave. He saw the demon in the dim light. Unmoving at the end of the tunnel. The blade hung coldly from his gloved hand, its tip poised just above the dust. His cloak was drawn across his body with the other hand.

~ B ~

"Where has Makya gone? Have you seen him?" Shuman asked. The matriarch had already stacked her wood and asked several other Morning Crows the same question. Still holding her empty tumpline in her left hand, she stared at Sowingwa now.

Holding a basket of turkey feathers, Sowingwa shrugged. "Not since this morning. Do you want me to look for him?" he asked. He could easily guess her concerns. In fact, he had planned to spend the rest of the day fletching fresh arrows.

"Children saw him sitting down by the stream. But nobody has seen him since. I thought he might have told you his plans."

Sowingwa smiled a little. "He was a child the last time he cleared his plans with me. I would worry more if he wanted my blessing."

"I miss when Makya was a child, but his two boys have lately restored my memory. I will check with Pavati now. Excuse me."

Sowingwa nodded.

Shuman turned to climb the nearest ladder and then, stopping after several rungs, looked back over her shoulder. "Tell me if you learn where he has gone. The sun will set soon enough. And last night is not over."

~ B ~

Makya leaned his spears cautiously against the wall. He crossed his chest with his arrows. "Makya!" he said forcefully. He repeated the motion and said his name again. He wanted to throw the demon off balance and perhaps see how he reacted. He wanted another moment to study the coming battle.

The vampire smirked. He recalled a few others that had shared their names. He did not really understand that. Did they just fear the silence? Did they wish to reason with him? Did they think it made them his equal? Or perhaps they hoped to learn his name in return? He nodded and replied with mock courtesy. "Vampire." He tapped his sword against his cloak to illustrate. He would share nothing more.

Makya did not reply. He tossed his torch halfway down the tunnel instead. He needed to free his hands. Sparks skittered and died as the torch landed and flared again. The kindling pile blazed now too, setting dim shadows in motion. Ghostly patterns swam on the walls all around the vampire as the light played off the painted figures. The crackle of dry tinder and heavy breathing, the rush of courage, were the only sounds. Things would happen quickly now.

Makya saw that the vampire would make him close the distance. The flame of the torch, now in the dirt, would not last long. Makya knew that the fight must also end quickly. In fact, he knew that battles were short and intense if they were decisive. "Like rolling down a rocky hill," he thought. The death of his mother flashed in his mind again. He quickly notched his strung bow. He fired his first arrow at the enemy stranger without hesitation. "Die!" Makya yelled as he released the string.

The vampire ducked fully behind his cloak as the arrow left the bow. The finest ring mail was sewn inside its leather lining, and many victims had donated gold for its construction. It stopped the arrow but cost him another hole in the leather, more broken ringlets. He would have to patch it again. "That will cost you," the vampire snarled. Makya fired again. The second arrow fared no better. Although the arrows struck the cloak hard, stone points were no match for the tight pattern of steel. Five arrows were soon expended. Three lay on the ground. Two dangled from the cloak. Still the vampire did not advance. Seeing that the intruder had no more arrows, he swept his cloak behind him. "Come," he repeated.

Makya dropped the bow and grabbed his spears to charge. He gripped three in his left hand. He held the fourth spear, the shortest of them, high in his strong right hand. His elbow and wrist were level, just above the line of his shoulders, ready to thrust with all his weight behind it. He wore no armor at all. "Like a hoplite," the vampire thought with a flashing memory. He was very old and knew others older yet. He had been taught the style himself. Seeing the signature of technique, he felt his focus rise another degree.

Makya stole a quick glance back to the mouth of the cave, measuring the distance in his mind, and then closed the gap quickly. The vampire swung his blade up from the dirt, a slashing strike that was intended to surprise Makya, catch him under the chin in the grip of his own forward momentum. But Makya blocked the strike against his extra spears. The blade sliced through one spear cleanly but caught in the dense desert hardwood of the second and third. The force of the blow slapped the intact spears against his head. But it was not the kind of blow that could throw off an experienced warrior. Makya parried the sword up and out. He lunged and thrust his free spear at the level of the ribcage.

The vampire twisted forward and leaned right to easily avoid the strike. However, he had an instant to wonder as this first clash unfolded. The spear had missed him. But it would have missed him regardless. He had expected better execution, but there was no time for contemplation. Makya exploded forward once more, his spear arm thrusting completely past the vampire now. It was unexpected, the wrong move for a man with spears; and the vampire was forced to adjust.

Makya rammed his shoulder into the vampire, just below his ribs. The hard blow forced the vampire to throw his leg far back for balance. In the same moment, Makya let fall his extra spears and swung his left arm over the recoiling right arm of the vampire. He swung the stabbing spear behind the demon and grabbed it with his left hand.

The vampire snarled and twisted to his right, trying to break his sword arm free, but Makya locked the length of the stave behind the vampire, right across the small of the back, and lifted violently. He jerked the demon off his feet, slamming his head hard into the roof of the cave. He brought the vampire down and then did it again. The muffled thud of flesh against stone echoed. Makya then pivoted and charged back toward the mouth of the cave, still clutching the demon, holding him off the ground. Makya was astonished at how light, and how cold, the vampire was.

The vampire was stunned by the blinding pain that washed across his skull. And Makya, who showed impressive strength, still kept control of his sword arm. But the vampire quickly regained his wits. He hit Makya across his cheek with his free left fist, tight blows in quick succession.

Makya could not believe that such a thin creature, with leverage so compromised, could deal such hard blows. Red pain washed across his vision. His ears screamed. He twisted and slammed the vampire down, catching his skull once more against the wall as they landed. His spear snapped. But Makya locked hands behind the writhing vampire and kept his shoulder pressed just under the ribs of his opponent. The kindling fire burned beside them. Makya felt the heat against his thigh.

Makya quickly shoved away from the wall with his feet, throwing both himself and his foe forward. The vampire knew that the young warrior was wrestling them both closer to the light but could not yet regain his balance. In fact, the vampire could barely keep hold of his sword, now tangled in his cloak. "You will not!" the vampire hissed. He aimed more sharp blows with his free hand. However, each time the vampire punched, it cost him stability, allowing Makya to throw him another step closer to the mouth of the cave.

The vampire was still stronger and beginning to recover himself. With rising alarm, Makya felt the disparity in power. Even though he held the better position, his grip was starting to loosen. He still wrestled well, keeping the enemy stranger off balance for five more hard breaths. And then, as Makya pulled his knees forward, coiling for another push, the vampire seized the moment, finally breaking his other arm free. He let go his sword, a desperate act, and grabbed the braid of hair with both hands. The vampire pulled with all his strength, viciously snapping back the head of his adversary. It broke the failing grip behind his back and twisted Makya backwards over his legs. The vampire fought back to his feet with animal quickness, the cave entrance now behind him, too close for comfort but still obscured by the initial bend in the tunnel.

Before the vampire could stand, his escape slowed as he ripped himself free from his cloak, Makya rocked back onto his shoulders and threw a desperate kick. His heel smacked into the chest of the demon. Hard. The extra force sent the vampire tumbling back, and further toward the light. The vampire rolled heels over head and curled back to his feet with a frustrated bark. "Raaaaaa!" The mouth of the cave breathed hot air across the back of his neck now. Glancing over his shoulder, the vampire saw the wicked line, the boundary between shadow and direct sunlight. Painting the floor near the entrance, it might as well have been a lake of fire.

The blade of the enemy stranger lay in the dust. Straining every muscle to move with enough speed, Makya gained his own feet again and grasped its handle in time. He faced the vampire, breathing hard, and for one frozen instant, time stopped. "Come," the vampire growled once more.

Makya swung the sword fast and hard, lunging forward; but he was unskilled with the blade. The vampire saw it as he stepped aside from the blow. The vampire shifted his weight, ready to dodge the next strike and take back his sword, take back the advantage. But Makya, feeling his lack of skill with the weapon, took the vampire by surprise once again. Instead of slicing at his enemy, he tossed the blade toward the back of the cave. It clanged against the rocks. The old vampire, with so many battles in memory, still lost a moment as his eyes followed the sword out of sight in confused disbelief.

Makya hit him hard against the ribs once again, shoulder driving forward and toward the entrance. The vampire stumbled back but twisted and arched as he fell, using the momentum of the young warrior to throw him to the left. They crashed to the ground. Makya had landed on his stomach, half in sunlight and half in shadow. He tasted dirt and blood.

The vampire caught the wrist of the young warrior and hooked his calf, refusing to let him roll to safety. Makya worked his free arm and leg. He fought to claw free from the shadows. And then, in one swift instant, the vampire let loose his grip and spun to his feet. Makya lunged away from the shadows. However, the demon caught his ankles. Sunlight seared across the exposed wrists of the vampire, but he quickly dragged the prone warrior back into the shade.

The vampire dropped immediately across the exposed back of his intended prey. Makya fought to his knees and struggled to twist free once more. However, the vampire pulled back on the braid for a second time, bringing up the chin of the young warrior. He sank his fangs into the pulsing neck. He had not fed in so many days.

Even as Makya felt his neck pierced between cold lips, he hurled himself forward with desperate exertion, clawing back into the bright pool of sunlight with the vampire across his back. It burnt the vampire across the face, the acrid smell of burning flesh in an instant. He was forced to let go. He recoiled into the shadows with a shriek of pain, now blood smeared and scorched with burns.

Makya, wild with pain and fear, lunged into the daylight, throwing himself down over the face of the cliff with one rolling dive. He grabbed blindly to slow his momentum. Half falling and half scrambling, rocks and dirt sluiced to the bottom ahead of him. The ochre dust of the cliff clinging to his sweat, he sought traction, allowing the rocks to gash his chest and thighs.

It was not enough. He tumbled the last third of the descent, landing hard across the flat boulder at the bottom. Makya had fallen before, but never so far; he was going to pass out. But he smiled as he felt the warm sun across his skin. Like a defensive wall against the demon. Broken bones and lost blood quickly dragged him under.

~ B ~

Sihu, the young wife of Makya, sat on the front wall of Crow Ledge. Her bare feet dangled over the edge. She followed the stream with her eyes, as far as the landscape allowed, first one way and then another, searching anxiously for her husband. Several women pulled weeds among the squash vines below. Sowingwa disappeared into the kiva behind them, holding a small knife in his teeth. He was humming to himself.

"Hold still. You want me to braid your hair or not?" Pavati said, kneeling behind her. Pavati was tall for a Morning Crow woman, broad through the shoulders. She wore a long necklace of small white shells, dark red beans and pumpkin seeds. She had dyed the seeds blue and called it her *Corn Harvest* necklace for the pattern of colors.

"Why not just make the *Corn Harvest* necklace from actual corn?" Choovio had once asked her.

"You must think Crow Ledge was built for crows!" Pavati had replied.

"Where would Makya have gone? Do you think he climbed up to the high ground?" Sihu asked hopefully. Often praised for her sharp nose and bright eyes, so much like the crow, Sihu was shorter and thinner than Pavati. She was also shorter than Shuman, her grandmother.

"I heard he left with weapons. I'm sure he is fine," Pavati said lightly. She spent time with Sihu often. Shuman had once told them, both Sihu and Pavati, that the wives of brothers shared much, even when their tongues were still. Pavati recalled that wisdom now but questioned it. She did not think Choovio would leave if Hototo asked him to stay.

Sihu spoke with frustration in her voice. "Makya tests the patience of Hototo too often. Shuman as well. He will be punished again. If he has went down Seven Sisters . . . I wish he would learn from Choovio. Why would he leave?"

Pavati laughed lightly. "Your husband cannot sit on his hands. Hototo should have known that. Enemy strangers are no threat while the sun shines. Makya probably just went hunting."

"But still."

"No need to worry, Si-Si. Even if Hototo is angry when Makya returns, his anger will fade quickly. Do you remember how he screamed after the turkey incident last winter?"

"Too well. Makya said that Hototo kicked his fire across the floor of the kiva. Even the big logs."

"And yet it was over before night cooled the canyon. Do you remember? They were laughing again before Kaya fell asleep. Will you hand me that brush?" Pavati said.

~ B ~

The vampire retreated back into the deep shadows. Despite his wounds, he did not make a sound, listening carefully to the struggle down the face of the cliff. He heard Makya fall, wounded but alive. More or less. He spat in disgust and stalked quickly to the back of the cave. He lifted his sword from the dust. He saw some blood along one edge. It had nicked the human as they rolled. The vampire licked it clean. The grit from the cave floor made no difference. He wiped his sword once more with his glove and laid it across his knees.

His burns would heal swiftly with more fresh blood but they stung fiercely now. The top of his head throbbed too. He watched the embers of the discarded torch die. He had not taken enough blood to kill the young man. But he had drained him enough to turn him. "Farmers do not turn their sheep into farmhands," he whispered. He shook his head in slow frustration. He had violated the Fifth Precept. "Take no foe across the river," it exhorted. The vampire knew that he must finish the clever boy at dusk. The young warrior would be even more dangerous if he turned completely. Tendrils of smoke hung in the air. Almost like incense.

It reminded the vampire of the rich blood he had taken in the high Himalayas. He had tasted none richer. The memory calmed his frustration. He began to murmur to pull his focus from the pain, an Eastern mantra. The vampire had heard it many times as he had waited for prey. He did not know what it meant. But the technique still helped.

~ B ~

Ahote and Nalnish, both hunters from the Ash Owl Clan, lay across a warm ledge. Tattered cloaks covered them. They had repeatedly rubbed the reddish dust from the cliffs into the leather. It reduced their visibility and protected them from the sun while they watched for game. They had been hunting without success. But now they looked down into Broken Spine Canyon, disputed land, and watched as a very large group of Morning Crows conferred quietly below.

The canyon was wide and level. A thin ridge of rock, interrupted by wide fissures at several points, sliced across its floor. The broken spine. Both clans had taken wood from this land for years, to assert their claim over it, leaving little but immature brush and exposed soil. This added to the skeletal impression left by the spine itself. Like the disinterred back of some great stone beast.

The men below all carried weapons. One older man scratched lines in the dry soil with his spear. He gestured with authority. "I think that is Hototo, clan leader of the Morning Crows. You can tell by the black feathers on the neck of his spear. Do you think they have come to attack us?" Ahote said under his breath.

"Clan leaders do not lead raids," Nalnish said.

"He holds spears like the others. Wait," Ahote replied. They saw the men divide into two clusters. And then Hototo began walking, with one party, back toward Crow Ledge. "See. He returns now."

The other party remained, with a few more men than the group that departed. Pairs of scouts fanned out. But they did not push into Ash Owl territory. They only swept the perimeter of the canyon. "If they had fewer weapons, I would think they were searching for a lost child," Nalnish observed. Other men scavenged what wood they could find, even pulling several small trees from the cliffs. The two accidental sentinels watched in tense silence. Unseen.

"They are so exposed; they will need six sentries at once. Istaqa would never instruct us to camp there. Why camp on this land?" Ahote said.

Nalnish nodded. "Perhaps they provoke us. Maybe they have come to insist that Broken Spine belongs to them."

"See how much wood they waste. That fire will be huge. Are they scared of the dark?" Ahote asked.

"I think the Morning Crows have lost all their brave men and wise leaders."

"Foolish leaders are rash to the detriment of all. We must get word to Istaqa. You watch here. I will carry the message," Ahote said.

"I'm the faster runner. And you have better eyes. Let me go," Nalnish said. Ahote gave a quick nod. Nalnish lifted his body just barely and slipped quietly away from the ledge. "I will head down that shoulder of rock to stay out of view."

Ahote slid into the shade of a boulder and settled into his vigil. The sun just brushed the horizon. He wondered if corn would grow in Broken Spine Canyon.

~ *B* ~

"Should be dead," Makya groaned as he opened his eyes. He stared into the dark mouth of the Cave of Visions above him. Although he heard nothing, he still felt the demon above him. And with scalding regret, he realized that he should not have challenged the enemy stranger alone. "Fool!" he coughed softly. Pain stabbed his spine. Yes, Choovio had been too far away. However, others had remained at Crow Ledge. Even old Sowingwa might have made the difference. Makya saw now that options had existed.

He also noted the length of the shadows; the sun would fall quickly from the sky and set free the enemy stranger. He needed to escape. Makya forced himself to his feet, willing himself to rise and limp away. He focused his pride and training as a warrior to master the pain. He saw blood on the rocks but not very much, even though his arms and legs were lacerated in several places. The bones in his back felt smashed, and his neck burned like he had been stung by scorpions. His left arm also hung useless, fractured in two places in the final fall.

The setting sun hurt his eyes and burned his skin as he walked. The rocks glinted unusually bright. He worried that hitting his head had disturbed his vision. He followed Seeker Canyon due north, not the way he had come, only away from the monster and out of the sun. Easier to traverse than the Broken Hills. It would give him another path to Crow Ledge eventually. He would pass Four Toe Rock, eventually intersecting Seven Sisters Canyon. He covered his trail like a true son of the landscape. He broke off a branch to sweep any unavoidable footprints. "See if he can track a ghost," Makya said as he skirted a low shelf of flat rock, thankful that his wounds were not bleeding.

As the sun began to sink, every part of his body screamed with thirst, as though he were swimming in deep water and his body screamed for air. He knew that he had every reason to thirst, but the intensity alarmed him. And while his present path would eventually intersect the stream, it was contested water. Even though it was the same stream that ran past Crow Ledge, the High Rocks Clan claimed that it crossed their land once it left Seven Sisters Canyon. It did angle south, past the entrance to High Rocks Canyon itself, before gradually turning back toward the setting sun. It eventually dissipated into the open desert. Makya scoffed at that invisible line. "The spirits will judge them," he spat as he walked ahead.

He knew that High Rocks warriors might kill him on sight, even more likely now that pledges of alliance had passed between Chayton and Istaqa, but he did not care. He also knew that Hototo and Shuman would rage if they learned of his trespass. But thirst commanded him, just as the need for air rules the drowning man. "No need to tell them," Makya whispered.

~ B ~

The horizon glowed orange beneath some distant clouds. The clouds were dark and purple in the falling light, reminiscent of smoke from a failing brushfire. Cool wind swirled across the ledge now. Ahote tightened his plain cloak around his shoulders and resigned his heart to a long chilly night. His ribs ached, but he needed to wait until the black night was full before he shifted to sitting. The Morning Crow scouts had trickled back from all directions. The men turned their necks back and forth, looking out across the floor of the canyon as they talked.

Ahote watched the fire they had lit. It blazed high, as though they wished to celebrate. But as dusk slowly faded to night, the warriors took seats with their backs to the fire, spears across laps. It was not how men camped. As he watched them look out into the dark and dancing shadows, none of them talking, it gnawed at him. "What are they looking for?"

He regretted that Nalnish had not seen them act this way. Istaqa would hear an incomplete tale.

"Perhaps I should bring my own report?" Ahote murmured. "But what am I watching?"

~ B ~

Makya finally saw the stream as dusk settled. Last to fail in the worst years of drought, it was finally reborn this year. It gurgled along the base of the cliff, and then the wall of the canyon jutted sharply across its path. It gathered there into several deep pools as it changed directions. Black patina streaked the rocks above. Shrubs rioted to life around the plentiful water. A few small bats whirled above him, feasting on nocturnal insects. Makya knew that if he turned left and followed the stream around the bend, and then turned into the next canyon, the High Rocks Clan would eventually come into plain sight. They still called their home Low Nest, even after Chayton had seized power and forced the clan to change its name.

To his right Makya looked into Seven Sisters, the canyon that would lead him back to Crow Ledge. Makya moved forward carefully. He walked to his left, toward a wide breach in the foliage. The bank of the stream was shallow and rocky there, where temperamental flooding had scoured away the vegetation amid a field of boulders. Makya circled toward that beach. His senses tingled now. He could tell that he was not alone. And as his line of sight cleared the screen of riparian brush, he stopped and held his breath. The injured warrior saw that an older man blocked his path, crouching at the bank of one of the pools. His hair looked like a bowl, cut just above his ears. The High Rocks style.

Although Makya told himself to wait, to hide behind the bushes until the man cleared out, thirst clawed at his throat. It begged Makya to press forward. To remove the obstacle and drink, drink, drink. He thought now of the scar forming across his shin. The cowards who had attacked him very near this place. He felt anger boil up inside him.

CHAPTER 7

Thirst

THIRST SHOVED ALL prudence aside. It demanded that Makya move immediately. He crept quickly from the cover of one large rock to another. He was naturally quiet like the fox, and he knew that the noise of the water, and the rising darkness, would further mask his approach. As he ducked behind one last boulder, he grabbed a rock, heavy and jagged, with his right hand. With a few more quick strides, Makya was upon the High Rocks elder. He spun toward Makya, stunned with alarm, as Makya closed the last several steps.

His actions flowed into a single blurry moment. He saw the man drop some twine as he turned and gasped. The fibrous string held four clay jugs together. They popped loose into the current. Makya felt his body come alive with rage. He swung the rock upward with explosive speed and caught him where the jaw met the neck. He even surprised himself with the force of the blow. The smacking thud of stone tearing into meat merged with the ugly snap of bone. Blood bloomed from his neck as the force of the blow knocked his head and torso back into the water. His hands and feet quivered on the bank. Makya panted and dropped to his stomach nearby.

He winced at the pain of broken ribs as he slid his body forward to reach the deeper water. He drank directly from the stream, three big gulps. Cold and fresh. He expected to feel his thirst slake as the water did its work. Makya plunged his head into the pool and tried to wash away the taint of regret. The body lay upstream, one leg bent under, head nearly submerged. This was not the first warrior of the High Rocks Clan he had killed. Even near this stream. He thought of last winter and the situation with the stolen turkey. But this felt more selfish. "Hard days need bold action," he reasoned. He shook his head in the water.

But instead of feeling restored, he retched and gagged. Some of the water spewed from his mouth. "Too much too fast," Makya told himself. However, an ember of panic smoked in his brain. It tasted wrong. It tasted like ash. He took another gulp and waited. A few intense moments passed. Just as Makya calmed himself, he retched again, ejecting the water forcefully. Like stomping on a water skin. His throat felt leathery too.

Makya stirred the water with his hand. He wanted to stir away the vomit liquid, make sure it was fresh. He hoisted himself a little further into the stream. "Just take sips," he told himself. Blood from the old man drifted through the water like plumes of dark smoke beneath the surface. Makya did not see it. Or perhaps refused to acknowledge that he saw it. The blood stirred toward him, mixing with the current.

He sipped. The hint of blood, diluted as it was, tickled his tongue like fresh corn from a steaming husk. Like rare meat and thick beer, rich with corn pulp, after a day of hunting. It tasted like life. Makya kept his mouth in the cool water and took another quick sip. He did not gag this time. And he did not think. He only knew that the water tasted vital again. He twisted toward the current and sipped again. It tasted better yet; his body quickened. He closed his eyes and took a deeper drink. Then again. And again. He angled toward the corpse without thinking. Animal hunger, and some dark instinct newly born, nudged him, his lips in the flowing current, toward prey. His strength waxed with every sip.

Makya lifted his eyes. The neck of the man lay close now. He saw the dark plume, his face fully in it. Horror flared in his brain, an array of embers suddenly joining into the fire of realization. At the same time, almost like he watched another person, he felt his mouth gulp more bloody water, still eager. More warm than water. The sharp tang. He felt the pain of his injuries vanish. It tasted like the truth. Like spirits appearing in

83

the Cave of Visions. He felt his own sharp teeth sinking into the flesh.

~ B ~

Pimne and Chua walked through the failing light, brothers from the Ash Owl Clan. They wore special beads and new woven shirts instead of the usual breechcloth and hunting cloak. Their shirts were clean white and adorned with the red motif of Firetown. They carried a young deer, lashed to a stout stick. Blood still dripped, if slowly now, from the gash in its neck; tiny drops spattered with the steady bounce of the pole as they walked. A wedding present for tomorrow. Chosovi was a close friend and childhood playmate. And after she married Kwahu, a warrior of high standing within the High Rocks Clan, an abundance of roasted meat would help stir kindred feelings between the two clans.

"I don't know if this is smart," Pimne said.

"Chosovi and Kwahu are well met. Don't let anybody hear you question their match tomorrow. You know Tocho warned us about that," cautioned Chua.

"I mean this shortcut. Greedy Crow Canyon. What if they catch us?" Pimne replied.

"Who . . . the Morning Crows? They are granary mice. This deer is too heavy to walk all the way around their land. I hate the Long Path," Chua replied.

"I will tell them to kill you first then."

"Good to know. But this is the far edge of their ground. Nobody will know we took this route. Why would they be up here at dusk?"

"I don't know . . . maybe looking for lazy Ash Owls to ambush. They have been too quiet lately. You know the saying. *Not even a Morning Crow can trust a Morning Crow.* I would bet my sandals that they plan to make trouble soon. Especially with the wedding. It makes me nervous."

"Too heavy. Will take a long time in the roasting pit too," Chua repeated. "Too bad we caught him so far away. Finding a wedding present right next to the wedding would have been too easy," he laughed.

Sharing the carcass and not planning to linger, the two brothers did little to cover their trail. What would a stray footprint mean in the morning, or a few drops of blood, they thought.

~ B ~

The vampire stood at the base of the cliff. His face still stung with burning pain, and his skull still throbbed. His eyes scanned the ground. He could see where the young man had landed. He saw where Makya rose and walked. He saw blood spattered on rocks. But a few strides later, the footprints grew sparse. Then confused. Then nothing but a broken branch and inchoate disturbances near an outcropping of rock. The vampire nodded his approval. It took skill to vanish like that.

Blue still tinged the dusk, but the comfort of night was growing deeper. He felt his strength surge. Like newly worked steel growing cold.

"A lamed wolf looks for the pack," he said. Whether he could track him or not, the vampire thought that the boy, "Makya" he had called himself, would head back toward the fortress in the cliffs that he had seen last night. He could also smell the drift of faint smoke in the wind. But the smoke led in the wrong direction.

The vampire began retracing his steps from the night before. But he soon stopped. He saw that another trail had joined the path. Two men and drops of animal blood. He was pleased and eager to heal his injuries. The tracks were fresh and followed his current direction. They were also easy to follow. He pressed forward with a hunting stride now, sword and scabbard loose from his belt and clutched in his hand. His heavy cloak, last defense against the morning, billowed behind him.

He pushed forward until he heard two voices. He swept wide across the floor of the canyon to close the distance. Or perhaps even slip forward into an ambush position. He saw two strong men ahead of him, rather short and built like those he had seen before. They wore loose white shirts and longer skirts that hung to the knee. They hefted a small deer carcass between them, its legs tied across a staff. Hunger burned through every sinew; the smell of blood and sweat filled his nose.

He hesitated. He needed to find Makya. He could not let the bitten warrior escape him. However, he needed to feed too. He stirred the dirt with his finger. "Hunt for prey or hunt for tracks," he whispered. He tugged his gloves tight and gripped the handle of his sword. He glided across the canyon with a light step. He thought of the tiger taking chase, stretching its stride to accelerate in silence.

He had seen tigers before, and not just the doomed beasts that had bolted, full of torture and hunger, into the Amphitheater. He had seen majestic tigers in the moonlit forests of India, silver and sable, stalking the striate shadows. They too would choose immortality if given the chance. They chose to extend their lives with every kill. And the vampire felt kinship with them.

Two howls of confused terror rang out together across the canyon. And then one. Then ringing silence.

~ B ~

Hototo walked, deeply tired, toward the Morning Crow home, his men behind him. All windows were dark. All ladders were stowed off the ground. A cool wind rustled in the corn and through the small copse of cottonwood trees.

As he came close and the early night resolved into focus, Hototo saw that Sowingwa watched from the high roof. His old friend carried a bow and arrows in his lap. Shuman stood next to him, and not Makya. She wore a short necklace of shells, bright in the moonlight. The breeze flirted with her long hair. It was unbraided once again. Hototo felt that Shuman should set a better example by wearing her Morning Crow braid proudly. However, he could not deny how striking she looked when she let it loose. Like another woman entirely. He had never challenged her on the subject.

"What has happened here?" he said as he reached the base of Crow Ledge. Shuman looked down over the wall. She had come to meet them.

"Did Makya come and find you?" Shuman asked.

"No, I instructed him to stay and guard Crow Ledge. I told you that."

"Makya left this morning with weapons. Alone. He has still not returned," Shuman said. Hototo heard as much anger as concern.

"Foolish!" Hototo spat but caught himself. He clinched his fist hard. His warriors stood in silence behind him. They scanned the shadows behind them nervously. "Where did he go, Shu?"

"He said nothing. Two girls washing bowls at the stream saw his back as he left the canyon that way. I thought perhaps he followed you," she replied with a wave of her hand toward the south. "At least he did not walk toward Low Nest."

"We did not see him. Was he . . . I fear that he was charmed by that demon. We should not have left him."

"Where are the other men? I do not sense victory in your shoulders," Shuman asked.

"They hunt still. They will camp at the broken spine tonight."

"Ash Owl land," Shuman said crossly. "You should have sent runners to the other clans!"

"*Our* land," Hototo corrected. Shuman stared down at him with flat disgust. "We must not seek help from those who have shed our blood. We will defeat this demon alone," Hototo insisted. He turned to his men. "They would see our call for help as weakness. Or even as some sort of trick. What have they ever wanted but war with us? Except maybe to steal what is rightfully ours," he added.

"Surely not in the face of an enemy stranger," Shuman pushed. Her voice was gentle now.

"We can talk more of this tomorrow. Or perhaps Makya will return with good news," Hototo said hopefully. "But the dark is not safe."

Shuman handed down the sturdy ladder. "Hurry then," she said.

Hototo divided sentry duty as each man danced quickly up the ladder. Atop the roof he faced Shuman. Her lips were pressed tight together. "My heart is anxious," he confided.

"What will you feel when Makya returns?" she asked. Hototo shook his head. He had been egregiously disobeyed by his favorite stepson, and Shuman knew it.

~ B ~

Ahote walked toward the blazing fire. It burned an equal distance from the spine and the canyon wall, maximizing the line of sight on all sides. He had not yet reached the dim edge of its glow; but the Morning Crows still saw him, an approaching shadow in the dark. Warriors bolted from the ground, spears tense, their faces obscured by yellow light behind them. "Ready arrows!" one voice yelled.

"Wait! Just one man!" Ahote shouted back quickly. He lifted both hands above his head and froze. His legs flushed with panic. He knew that Nalnish would soon report the situation to Istaqa, giving the Ash Owls plenty of warning. Ahote could have, despite the chill and discomfort, simply continued his vigil in the cliffs. That would have been good enough. He suddenly feared he had gambled unwisely.

"Hold . . . hold," one of the Morning Crows said. "Nobody shoot!" he added.

The circle of warriors quickly uncoiled from around the fire to face Ahote. The Ash Owl warrior could hear the crackle and hiss of the fire in the moment of silence that followed. He took a few deliberate steps closer. The Morning Crows waited. Ahote finally stepped into the full light. They were close enough to talk now. "Why are you here? What kind of hunt requires a bonfire?" Ahote asked. He spoke loudly but carefully. His heart pounded in his chest. He had set aside his weapons before approaching the camp. He had no hope of defending himself if they were hostile. Better to demonstrate that his intentions were not violent.

'Who are you, Ash Owl?" the same man replied. "I am Choovio. We are Morning Crows."

"I am Ahote. None come with me. May we talk?" he asked.

~ B ~

Istaqa shook his head slowly as Nalnish told him about the worrisome gathering of Morning Crows at the broken spine. He was not afraid of them. His clan, the Ash Owls, was the largest. And his builders were skilled and clever. He felt certain that Firetown was impregnable. Nobody could scale its approach without paying steeply in blood. "Why would the Morning Crows strike now? We are all headed into harvest," the Ash Owl leader asked quietly.

"I do not know," Nalnish replied, still holding his dusty hunting cloak in the crook of his arm. He stood in the broad central courtyard of Firetown. Two small fires always burned there. They flanked the roof of the central kiva. Istaqa had instituted the practice years ago. He felt that it reinforced clan identity. It also sent the message that the Ash Owls could always find firewood; it asserted that their lands were rich and wide.

Nalnish felt anxious as he spoke. Istaqa was short but built like a stone wall. He looked like the powerful clan leader that he was. His broad shoulders and thick body attested to his strength. But he spoke softly. He forced the clan to listen if they wished to hear him. His two war leaders stood with Nalnish.

"We have not provoked them," Istaqa said.

"Perhaps our new alliance with the High Rocks Clan scares them. We make that kinship even stronger with the wedding that begins tomorrow," said Tocho. Istaqa valued his strategic mind even more than his artistic skill.

"We have shown no recent hostility. Conducted no raids," Istaqa replied. "And their harvest is full like our own. After many lean years."

"An alliance is hostile by its nature. Do you not agree?" Tocho replied. Istaqa nodded but recoiled inside. His dream was to unite the clans once more, nothing more. It had been that way before he was born. But the threads had unraveled. The clans had been hostile for many years. And the long drought had taken its toll.

"I agree that the outside of the cactus is the first part you see," Istaqa said. "What does Kwatoko say?" Kwatoko assisted Tocho in leading the warriors. He also served as chief architect for the Ash Owls when building needs arose. In fact, the drumbeat of construction had rarely slowed under Istaqa. Kwatoko did not like the Morning Crow Clan but he did not scheme against them either. He thought before he answered, just as he planned walls before he laid stones.

"I would fear us if I were them. And many of us will depart for the wedding at Low Nest tomorrow. Less men here to defend our home."

"Or easy to intercept as we travel," Tocho added.

"But they camped in full view . . . in the open space between our lands. Why did they not hide?" Nalnish said.

Tocho spoke again. "That is our land. An open threat perhaps. An attempt to warn us away from the wedding and sour our alliance?"

"Why do they care?" Nalnish asked.

"The High Rocks Clan is smaller. Hototo can act with impunity if we are not an ally to them. He can divert the stream into his crops again, hunt on their land, and steal more corn in the dark. But if we stand with them . . ." Tocho responded.

"Hototo is a mangy coyote," Istaqa nodded. His tired eyes smiled a little. They had been rivals for many years. He rolled a pinyon nut between his fingers.

Kwatoko spoke again. "Maybe they hope to draw us down from our walls. Invite open combat out there since they cannot hurt us here." He had improved the defensibility of Firetown during several building projects. He took pride in his work.

"They have sent no messenger. They have not asked to talk. And they carry their weapons. It does smell of brash leadership," Tocho said.

"And if we greet them . . . ask them what they want?" Nalnish asked. He stared into the canyon. The night looked darker as the flames danced behind him.

"Then we alert them and lose the advantage that you and Ahote have provided. What can they possibly want when they camp on our land with bows strung? Most likely to hurt us," Kwatoko replied.

Istaqa raised his palm. He felt unsettled. He did not want this. He wanted a quiet harvest. He wanted to honor the kindness of the rain. He wanted to see a successful wedding tomorrow. Tocho and Kwatoko chafed his instincts. But so much bad blood had passed between the clans. So much had been spilled. And Istaqa knew that the Morning Crows were dangerous. He could not ignore the risk. "They cannot hurt us here. But they could ambush us tomorrow. They could catch us with gifts in our hands. So attack them, walk to Low Nest unprotected, or lose the upper hand to communicate . . . what other options exist?"

"None," Tocho nodded.

"One at least," Istaqa said. Tocho stared at his feet. "We can wait. This night is still new. Perhaps Ahote will bring us more news. Kwatoko will post men to watch the approaches to Firetown. Tocho will plan options for safe travel tomorrow."

~ *B* ~

Lenmana, wife of Lapu, walked toward the stream from Low Nest. She carried more jugs to store in the cool water. They dangled together from a length of yucca twine. She could hear the beer sloshing inside. She and her husband had been asked to chill the fermented corn mash for the coming wedding. It would honor Kwahu and his bride to lavish hospitality on the Ash Owls when they arrived tomorrow. After all, the Ash Owls were accepting a High Rocks warrior into their clan as part of the ceremony.

As she stepped around a dense screen of young cottonwoods, Lenmana startled. Standing by the pool in the moonlight, perhaps an axe throw away, she saw the back of a disheveled warrior, dripping with water. She froze. Muscular and tall for his people, although not as tall as Chayton, or Sik, the High Rocks war leader, he wore his hair in the single braid of the Morning Crows. He was looking down into the water. She followed his gaze. A body lay on the rocky bank, bare leg twisted into the mud, head and torso still in the water. "La–" she gasped, barely more than a breath. But the warrior jerked his head even at that; the rest of the name died in her mouth. Their eyes met. The hair rose on her neck.

She saw his eyes in the moonlight. His gaze was cold like the eyes of a corpse. Her blood chilled. She wanted to scream, to run back to Low Nest and the safety of the High Rocks Clan, to fall to her knees and wail. But Lenmana only took one slow step back. She still clutched the rope in her hand. The man did not move. He carried no weapons. Was he the bait in some trap? Did other Morning Crows hide in the shadows?

Her breath quick with fear, she took another step back. Then another more quickly. The killer jerked his arm across his stomach, not quite forming a fist. She thought it looked almost like indecision. Had she surprised him? Her pulse raced even faster. She stepped back again. "Ahhh!" she let loose a sharp breath and glanced back as her calf poked into some prickly branches. Her eyes darted back to the warrior. He was already lunging. But away.

Lenmana watched as his feet tore into the loose rocks and mud and sprung away. His arms pumped. His stride stretched, quick and light. The warrior was as fast as a bolting animal. Unnaturally fast. As he retreated down Seven Sisters Canyon, toward Morning Crow land, Lenmana heard herself screaming, an anguished wail of alarm. The jugs of beer tumbled to the ground, several breaking as they struck the earth and each other. She felt the warm liquid gather around her feet. Her husband lay unmoving in the pool, his body only rocking slightly in the current.

~ *B* ~

The vampire heard, faint on the wind, a woman screaming in the far distance. Tools of the night, his ears were sharp like a blade for silk. His eyes were sharp too, carving every shadow into sharp relief. Blood burned in him now and filled him with the reckless fire of life. He felt strong, invincible, every cell thrumming with the hot spark of immortality. His face was flawless once more. The laceration on his scalp had vanished.

He decided to check out the sound, thinking that perhaps it had something to do with the young warrior he sought. He did not glance down as he stepped over the two dead hunters and their deer. However, he swept his cloak to the left, away from the bodies of his new victims. Letting his attire smear with the offal of his victims was a line that he did not allow himself to cross. He had seen plenty of ferals in the endless years, plenty of men who had forgotten themselves.

CHAPTER 8

The Enemy Familiar

MAKYA RAN AS hard as he could. He fled down Seven Sisters, sprinting east toward his home. He was amazed by the power in his legs. He had never run this fast before. Especially for this long. He breathed hard but felt little fatigue, navigating the terrain with ease. Before reaching Crow Ledge however, Makya veered into one of the many side galleries that branched from the main floor of the canyon. The alley he chose inclined steeply and was defined by piled rocks and cracks filled with stubborn brush. He chose a particularly rough slope, strewn with slab boulders, careful to leave no trail as he moved to higher ground. Makya had climbed this escarpment to hide when he was a child. He had lived on Morning Crow land his whole life and knew many good places to hide.

The night seemed sharper. The dark, though still present, had become transparent. He saw small lizards as they darted off his path, every scale distinct, even in the deep shadows under the cliff. Their black eyes shone bright with reflected light. And they were louder, the scrape of their tiny claws more distinct. In fact, every detail of the land around him hummed with clarity. The stars burned as though they might kindle the night sky.

One massive rock leaned into the side of the cliff. Makya found a wedge of open space where the two sides fit imperfectly. The front of the space was only a crevice. It would conceal him well but allow him an easy view down into the canyon, allow him to watch the Seven Sisters corridor. The back of the space was wider. He could still retreat quickly if need arose. He would watch for the demon. He still honored his charge to guard the Morning Crow community. But he also needed time to think.

Remorse chewed at his heart. He had failed to kill the demon and had likely sparked more High Rocks hostility. But he had not intended to kill that man. "Of course not," Makya told himself. He recalled the reaction of the woman, her terror making the whole incident feel even worse. Hototo would certainly punish him. Makya knew that. However, he accepted that fact with resolute calm, just as a falling man accepts the approaching ground. He clenched and unclenched his fist. He felt no pain in his arm, no pain anywhere.

In fact, his injuries were gone, and his body was fully restored. Fierce vitality had poured into his veins as he drank the blood of the dying man, and Makya had wanted it. He had lusted for more blood and less water. Until he had buried his mouth against the wound, tore the neck with his teeth to release more blood. He ran his finger across the sharp fangs in his mouth. He also felt drying blood at the corners of his mouth. He began to wipe it away. "How could this happen?" he whispered.

But Makya knew the answer. He knew that this was the way of enemy strangers. Fear and doubt flooded his heart, and he struggled to master the storm of emotions. Tears blurred his vision. However, he could summon great mental discipline. Hototo had taught him that. "Have I really changed?" he asked. He did not feel like a demon or monster. He still felt like Makya, only stronger and filled with power. He told himself that he did not need to fear this enemy stranger now. He would simply find him and destroy him. The demon would have no advantage and simply fall to the better warrior. Makya flushed with sudden pride. He could use his new strength and become the powerful protector of his clan.

But where was the demon now? He had surely left the Cave of Visions at sunset. Makya prudently waited and listened. He tried to stretch out into the edge of dreaming, hoping that he could sense the demon as before.

~ B ~

Chayton pulled his long hair and screamed. He stamped his foot. The intense leader of the High Rocks Clan, his foul temper in full display, swung his fist in the air. He turned on his heel, toward those that had followed him to the bend in the stream, many High Rocks warriors. "They must sacrifice for this! We will kill . . . every last Morning Crow!" he shouted. His voice rattled off the canyon walls.

Lenmana knelt nearby. She cried over the body of Lapu, his neck torn like an animal bite. She had dragged him out of the water. "He looked wrong. His eyes looked wrong," she moaned. Chayton did not attend her words. He thought she seemed hysterical.

The High Rocks Clan had no spirit leader. Chayton allowed no shaman at Low Nest. He had executed the last, making an example of the hapless Cha'Akmongwi.

"Shall we raid them?" Kwahu asked.

"No! We make war on them!" Chayton snapped. "All warriors here now. Weapons for every hand. And bring the new attack ladders!" he added. He looked from eye to eye with a fiery gaze. He saw angry assent. But also some questions. Kwahu looked at him, chin down slightly.

"He was not right. Monster . . ." Lenmana moaned behind them.

"Evil comes upon us. They seek to disrupt our friendship with Istaqa and the Ash Owls. To poison our joy as we prepare to celebrate," Chayton said more calmly. "We cannot let such acts stand," he added.

"We stand with you. Lapu must be avenged. They are murdering cowards!" Sik agreed. He led the warriors and hunters of the High Rocks Clan. He was tall and rugged. Only the High Rocks leader was taller. His blood burned hot most of the time.

Lenmana sobbed behind them. "Kill that Morning Crow bastard. Kill them all." She still lay prostrate over the cooling body of her husband.

Chayton continued. "And shall we give them time to enjoy this murder? Shall we allow them time to celebrate his death?"

Murmurs of disagreement rippled among the men. "They deserve no rest," Sik said, his jaw clenched. He spoke for his warriors.

"Then the time has come. We will not allow them even one more tranquil night," Chayton said. "We must return justice to them tonight. This night. We will reach them well before dawn. They will never expect such a quick response. And they will learn respect as they die!" His voice rose with sudden anger. He slammed his fist into his hand. The warriors nodded eagerly now. His confidence enthralled them. Chayton had come to the High Rocks Clan from across the mountain, an imposing stranger. He refused to braid or cut his hair. He refused to speak of his past. But he had also rescued the clan from disarray and ill fortune, helped them stave off disaster when they were most vulnerable. He spoke again.

"We must postpone the wedding; we will not celebrate in the shadow of grief. Your task, Kwahu, is to tell the Ash Owl Clan. Run tonight. Take the shortcut through Greedy Crow Canyon. You will postpone your wedding day until next half moon. You will tell our friends—"

"But I will fight—"

"No," Chayton shook his head. "You must deliver the message. I need you to alert our allies," he said. "And you must explain to Chosovi in person," he added. Chayton was brash but not cruel to his friends. Chayton needed to inform the Ash Owls, and Kwahu would not be focused for battle anyway. "Warriors gather here now," he called loudly. His order released them to action. "And somebody take that beer back to Low Nest," he added, waving his hand toward the jugs that still bobbed in the pool, caught in the swirling current.

~ B ~

Makya saw the warriors of the High Rocks Clan. They were small below his lookout, following the far side of the stream, and yet, he saw them with sharp clarity. He saw their short hair bounce as they moved, even as they passed among the trees. "They have hair like toddlers!" he scoffed. He was alarmed, though. They were marching toward his home at Crow Ledge, keeping a disciplined pace. A few carried bows. But most carried spears and war clubs, an innovation that Chayton had brought across the mountains, tools of close combat. So many men. Their ranks had swollen in recent years. They passed through his line of sight one after another. Had he sparked this attack? Makya knew that he could not excuse what he saw as just an accident of timing.

His heart skipped. He thought of his wife and kids. He saw them asleep in his mind. Nobody standing watch. What if Hototo had not yet returned? Hototo had instructed him to stand guard, to guard them this very night. He began to tremble at the shame of his error. He rose to follow them. He felt the strength in his body. His heart flooded with rage at the thought of these men. He would kill them all. He felt he could.

He braced behind the boulder, waiting for the end of the line. To his surprise, he saw three quartets of men pass last. Each group carried a long sturdy pole, hewn smooth but notched at intervals, crowned at each end with four sturdy wooden spikes. These crossed spikes, long and thick like axe handles, were wedged and lashed into place. The poles themselves were five men long, thicker than his arm. They were very straight. He guessed that they were distant pine trees. He had never seen anything like them. Makya watched as four warriors trotted to the back, relieving the last four men of their burden. A silent exchange.

He prepared to slip quickly down the hill, to follow once they moved ahead. However, Makya had lost his weapons in the Cave of Visions. And the men at the rear carried giant poles. He could not kill one without alerting three more. He would glide behind them, stalk for an opportunity.

But he froze. He saw the demon tracing the footsteps of the High Rocks warriors, his stride light and flowing like a practiced hunter, his dark cloak alive with the breeze of movement. Makya felt a bereft chill pass through him. The enemy stranger stopped and slowly scanned the canyon. Makya turned his limbs to stone. He did not even breathe. The demon resumed his path, abruptly following the Ash Owls once again.

Makya bowed his head and exhaled slowly. He knew that his duty had not changed. He crept slowly down the slope to follow. He kept to the opposite side of the stream. Makya wanted the demon to attack the High Rocks men. To create the chaos he needed. But as the canyon curved toward Crow Ledge, the enemy stranger still drifted well back. Makya felt his despair rising. He ran through reckless options in his head. Had the High Rocks Clan conspired with this enemy stranger?

But at the last moment, as the High Rocks warriors broke into a quicker trot, the demon veered right and climbed the steep cliff with fluid agility. The cliff slanted eventually toward the Morning Crow dwelling but on the opposing sandstone wall of the canyon. Makya pulled up short. He had not expected this. Had the demon finally seen him and moved to snare him? Or did he plan to watch the coming attack. Makya moved forward more slowly now. He scanned the moonlit escarpment to find the monster, keeping the canyon floor between them.

But then Makya startled. He heard the warning alarm. Two Morning Crow guards. "Crows awaken! To the wall! Bring your weapons!" He felt momentary relief; his people had spotted the attack. And then the alarm was drowned by the outcry of howls and yells, the chorus of the High Rocks Clan, now storming the base of Crow Ledge to exact tenfold revenge for his actions.

~ B ~

The vampire brushed away the loose rock and knelt in the rusty dirt, both knees down and ankles crossed under him. A hawk on its perch. Looking down across the canyon from his ledge, he saw the stronghold well. All fires were out. They could have seen him too in the bright moonlight. But they were not looking in his direction. He had sensed Makya several times. But the young warrior was not close. Just a shimmer in the noise. The vampire could not decipher his location. He hoped the coming battle would force the boy from hiding. Even better if it killed him.

Shouts shattered the nocturnal quiet. A volley of arrows forced back the guards at the corner of the dwelling, even as men and women issued from the dark doorways, stringing their own bows, struggling to place arrows. The attackers reached the base of the cliff, quickly climbing the steep talus slope that marked the lower part of the ascent. However, they stopped as they reached the true face of the cliff. Relatively smooth and nearly vertical, it posed a greater challenge. Some of them began to climb the rocks with nimble precision. The vampire admired their skill. Several used the slanting row of shallow toeholds that the vampire had noted before. They quickly attracted many defenders. Other attackers fanned out along the base. More arrows were exchanged. The vampire saw an arrow slice through the cheek of one defender. She did not retreat. "Rough neighborhood," the vampire smiled.

And then the siege poles reached the wall. They were handed up and thrust into place. Smooth and quick, a practiced move, to preserve momentum. The top spikes were lifted over the front wall and swung forward. The bottom spikes were longer and thicker. They were allowed to wedge into the top of the talus and find their natural crevice as the top spikes caught against the top of the wall. Angled forward, warriors instantly sprang up the poles, their hands and feet gripping expertly against the notched wood, even holding spears. The vampire had seen men climb palm trees in roughly the same way.

Due to the slant of the pole, the top spikes pointed down over the wall once stabilized, requiring defenders to lift them vertically to throw the poles off. "Clever men," the vampire said. The attackers ascended quickly. Although their weight on the poles made it more difficult, two of the poles were still shoved off as the defenders desperately fought to hold the wall. Men crashed against the ground. Several rolled back to their feet. An old woman, her hair not braided like the rest and wearing a necklace of shells, kneeling on the highest roof, shot down at the ground, pinning one of the attackers where he lay. The vampire heard them shout. He heard the impact of bodies and weapons, the clatter of arrows against the cliff; but the distance blunted its effect. And of course, the vampire felt no anxiety for the outcome. He scanned anxiously for the man he had fought in the cave instead. He did not see him.

And then, under the cover of several disciplined bows, and with the defenders covering too many points of attack, two men crested the remaining pole successfully. The attackers had their toehold. More men scaled the pole behind them and surged forward. One of the other poles was quickly restored near the first. A bottom spike snapped. They simply rotated the poll. More warriors crested the wall.

"Too few defenders," the vampire said. Where were all the men who had taunted him last night? As more attackers reached the terrace of the stronghold, the side of the cliff quickly exploded into ragged chaos. Knives and war clubs and fists. The reckless confusion of violence made worse by the veil of shade beneath the great cliff. The defenders gave ground, collapsed back toward the entrance to their homes. One wiry old man, his long braid tossing back and forth behind him, seemed to hold the fraying line of defense, spear in each hand. He handled them with surprising vigor. Many fought well, but the vampire particularly noted his skill and tenacity.

~ B ~

"Drive them back!" Hototo shouted. He swung the spears, now clutched together like an axe handle. He caught the High Rocks warrior hard across the jaw and stunned him. Then he swung the back end of the spears forward, slamming the shafts sideways into the chest of another man. He pushed forward, using the stumbling man as a shield. The falling man flailed, snapping the necklace that Hototo wore. A string of snail shells, they clattered underfoot as the Morning Crows surged forward beside the shaman, splitting the attackers like a wedge. With the *thwack* of stone against bone, Hototo saw a High Rocks man fall to his right, old Sowingwa dealing the blow with an axe, gray hair falling loose from its braid.

Hototo strained with all his might. His breath came rough. However, as the Morning Crow defenders overcame the leading edge of the attack, the High Rocks men that fell before them— dead men underfoot and downed men writhing to rise—stalled the change in momentum. Hototo kicked one of them in the neck before the man could rise from his knees. But the man swung both arms around his leg. Hototo punched hard to loosen him.

So many had gained the ledge in front of him now. They crowded the courtyard, a fierce throng of shadows in motion, and howled violence. Hototo heard Shuman scream from the roof. "They come behind you . . . behind you!" She had shot arrows down from her roost, but she had no more. She tossed rocks now.

The third siege pole had been established again. It was erected far from the other two. It grabbed the balcony where the women would grind corn during the day. Away from where the line of defense had formed. Hototo turned to see a warrior gain the ledge and tackle Pavati, the wife of Choovio, as she sought to pry loose the pole. Another warrior topped the pole right after. It was instantly heavy with climbers. Men and women turned to repel them, but there were not enough to spare.

The attackers regained the advantage. The High Rocks men caught their footing and pushed forward once again. Hototo saw Shuman scramble down, knife between her teeth. She had run out of rocks. He saw Sowingwa, his friend, stumble back now, tripping over dirty pots and bowls that had been stacked for cleaning from the evening meal, landing hard against his back. Sik, the High Rocks war leader, who could challenge even Makya and Choovio, had thrown him aside with impunity.

The clan was crumbling. Hototo had seen such moments before. But only from the other side. And the momentary glance backward cost him. The handle of a war club caught his shoulder. He staggered back, seeing red from pain, and swung his spear wildly in defense, only catching himself against his own people.

But as he struggled to right himself, the shaman heard a wild growl and startled shouts. As his vision cleared, he saw the High Rocks men whirling around, checking their own surge. He followed their gaze; a man, moving with remarkable speed, hurled himself onto the ledge. From a feral crouch, he lunged and landed amid the enemy. He exploded into the nearest High Rocks warrior, ripping the club from his hand as the man wilted beneath a vicious fist. "Makya!" Hototo gasped.

Makya swung the enemy club with incredible force, destroying the face of another attacker. He reversed it quickly and struck another warrior under the chin. He grabbed another by the neck with his free hand, twisted him off the ledge, his feet leaving the ground. The High Rocks men instinctively stumbled back, confused. Makya charged at them, hurling himself into their crowd, snarling viciously like an animal.

He was wrong to close the gap. Many of the High Rocks warriors converged on him, determined to overwhelm the threat. But as they locked with Makya, it turned their attention away from the other Morning Crows.

"Now! Now! Now!" Hototo yelled. They pressed the attack once more. Hototo stabbed hard into a ribcage and twisted past as the man swung his knife. They needed to break the High Rocks attack into chaos and soon. Hototo met the next attacker. His spear broke as he blocked the stroke from a heavy club. Another spear rushed past his shoulder and struck his attacker. It was Sihu, the wife of Makya. Morning Crow men and women charged forward, fury and hope in every strike now.

However, among the enemy crowd, Hototo saw Makya fall, multiple warriors driving him down, wrenching the club from his hand. "Push forward! Throw them!" he barked. His voice cracked with exhaustion. Fighters from both sides slipped in new blood. It smeared across the packed clay of the courtyard. Before he could shout again, Hototo heard a vicious hiss. And then screaming. A High Rocks warrior rolled away from Makya, clutching his neck. Makya tore himself loose, sharp fangs bare, and charged at Sik. Like the panther striking its prey from high ground. Throwing him back against the rampart, Makya tore at the neck of the High Rocks war leader too. Makya was loose now and savaged several more warriors as they closed with him, teeth like weapons.

Hototo stood in stunned disbelief as the battle carried past him. "No," he whispered, more breath than voice. He saw the sharp canines, dark with blood. He had seen fangs like that before.

~ B ~

The vampire locked his hands behind his head in dismay. "Makya!" he hissed. He saw bleeding men running, retreating across the canyon, some with hands clamped on necks. The scaling poles were abandoned in panic, toppled in the dirt. He saw Makya still standing. He shook his head in disgust. As the attackers retreated, he knew that dawn would break soon. The vampire slipped quickly to the canyon floor. He followed the same path as the retreating men.

He caught two fleeing men from behind; one had been bitten by Makya. His sword flashed. He took the head of that man in one clean stroke. He hit the other with the hilt, and then, catching the dazed man, took his blood, strong with the tang of fear and battle. The last prey of the night.

The vampire ran, filled with power and fully sated. He knew that Makya had bitten others as well, maybe as many as five; but the retreating warriors ran far ahead now, and the night was growing dangerously short. He finally turned aside. He did not wish to follow them home and risk detection; they had likely posted guards while they dared the attack. He stopped before a dirty hole in the rocks. Its narrow mouth was behind some shrubs, tucked into the back of a natural berm. He had scouted it before he saw the raid unfolding. The entrance was small but shaded and easy to hide. Easy to overlook.

He peered inside and found more space than he had hoped, enough to stretch his arms wide once he passed the initial hole. The vampire quickly slipped inside and then, turning toward the entrance, wedged a large rock tight against the narrow opening. He wrapped his cloak around him and closed his eyes. "Curse the dawn," he said. His hands were folded across his chest. He thought of burial and death. And of the woman that had taken him into the night forever.

"The king of cats does not wish for any court. Only more mice," she had told him. But she had walked him across the threshold anyway. He recalled moonlight across the small lake at her country villa. The gentle chill of her hand against his own, the coolness of her breath. He could still see the curve of her neck, pale and thin, beneath her sandy hair. The vibrant color of flowers bathed in torchlight. Feel the cold sting of her teeth.

"Stray cats breed," the vampire said. He smiled a little and closed his eyes. The sight of wounded men, their bites ragged like animal wounds but bleeding very little, fleeing across the desert without any notion of their future; she would have laughed in human sympathy.

~ B ~

"What have you done? What have you done?" Hototo yelled. The last of the High Rocks Clan still fled. A few tired victory shouts followed. His hands trembled. "What have you done?" he repeated. Makya stood before him now, blood smeared and exultant. He had many scrapes and several deep gashes, including a spear puncture on his thigh; flesh stood open high on his forehead, an axe wound perhaps. But they barely bled. Most of the blood was not his own. His wounds would heal with magical speed.

"We must thank the spirits," he said. "They have handed me the power to deliver us from our enemies. I was wrong to leave against your order. I know my error. But they have blessed me still," he said quickly.

Hototo wanted to strike him. "What has happened?" he insisted. He forced calm into his voice but he gripped his broken spear tightly. His own shoulder radiated with pain. Cuts on his legs and arms trickled blood. He was not a young warrior. It would take seasons to truly heal. Sihu stood three steps behind Hototo, eyes already brimming with tears. She waited, thankful that respect for Hototo demanded it, horrified to see her husband both wounded and changed. Sihu had seen that, although Makya sounded no different, an ineffable spark of life no longer burned in his eyes.

Makya told him what had happened. Hototo listened; he also saw the scene of horror unfolding around him in the gray light before dawn. Kids streamed onto the terrace in search of parents, some bleeding, some tending the wounded of the clan.

Pavati moaned with pain from an unseen injury. Her daughter, Kaya, wept over her. Another warrior listened for breath at the lips of his uncle. Sowingwa clutched his bleeding scalp as he leaned unsteadily against the wall. Shuman stabbed several fallen High Rocks warriors in the heart, twisting the spear as though she weeded corn with her digging stick. She still listened closely to Makya, watching him even as she moved through her grim task.

"This should not have happened!" Shuman interjected, her foot pressing down on the cheek of a dying man, pausing with her spear in the air.

"They had already built the ladders. They had practiced with them. You could see it," Makya retorted.

"You killed first. I warned you to stay away from Low Nest. Do you see now?" she said, bringing the spear down hard.

"They came to kill us in our home!" Makya replied. His temper was quickened after the battle. "Shall I just forget their violence this night? Shall I not–"

"Be quiet!" Hototo snapped. "I must conduct the ritual of passing for our dead. I must exhort their souls to return to the lower world and leave their grief in the dust. Salves must be prepared for the injured. We must bear away the High Rocks dead. And then, then I shall consider this. Until then . . . hide in your room. Go quickly and do not leave until I call upon you," the shaman said. "You *will* obey me now," Hototo added fiercely.

"Yes. Of course," Makya nodded. He pushed his anger back down. The rush of battle was passing. Makya felt suddenly tired and weak. The sunrise was coming. It tugged at his flesh. He saw more fully now the carnage around him. He heard Pavati slap her palm against the dirt in agony. He heard Kaya crying. His spirit trembled.

CHAPTER 9

Morning Follows Violence

ARRIVING FROM LOW Nest, Kwahu stood before Istaqa as the night dissolved into morning. They stood at the foot of the cliff beneath Firetown. Too many men were awake. Bows and arrows leaned against walls. Both Kwatoko and Tocho flanked Istaqa. They held spears but not anxiously. Kwahu saw that they looked tired. However, thoughts of his own situation claimed most of his concern.

Kwahu told them of the murder of Lapu, ambushed beside the stream, and of the postponed wedding between Chosovi and himself. He also told him that Chayton was attacking the Morning Crow Clan. Kwahu rubbed his eyes. They burned from lack of sleep. He looked wretched. Disappointment hung about his shoulders like a heavy cloak.

"When will this happen?" Istaqa asked. His face was tense, locked in rigid calm. He said nothing of the Morning Crow warriors camped just beyond his territory.

"It is done already," Kwahu responded.

"How many men did Chayton send?" Istaqa asked. He stared far into the canyon, looking past Kwahu. Kwatoko and Tocho stared down respectfully, leaned against their spears. They were there to listen and collect orders from Istaqa.

Kwahu hesitated. He was afraid to answer. He could tell that the powerful clan leader before him was displeased. Relations between the Ash Owls and the High Rocks Clan had only recently improved. He feared that Istaqa might completely cancel the wedding in anger. Or even kill the messenger.

"How many men?" Istaqa repeated. Not unkindly.

"All . . . all of them," Kwahu said. Istaqa jerked his gaze into close focus. He looked at Kwahu, his eyes round with genuine surprise. He said nothing. He could not find any words.

Tocho could not hold back. "But the Morning Crow warriors—"

"Wait," Istaqa said. His voice was an urgent whisper. He let the silence hang. He was angry and confused. But he was too disciplined to lose control. What Nalnish had seen might offer a strategic advantage. Istaqa did not wish to share the location of the Morning Crows with the High Rocks Clan, not until he knew more himself. Kwahu finally spoke.

"There is something else," he said nervously. His hands were shaking.

"I think I need to hear as much as you know," Istaqa said.

"I bring more dark news. I took the Short Path tonight, past Four Toe Rock."

"Morning Crow land," Istaqa said. He tipped his head for Kwahu to continue.

"Pimne and Chua are dead," Kwahu blurted out. Istaqa exhaled slowly. His face flexed like a strung bow. His eyes raged. Kwatoko turned away in grief. He stared at the wall that rose beside him.

"How did this happen?" Istaqa asked.

"They had killed a deer for my wedding. I mean for Chosovi and I. It still lay in the dirt between them. Untouched. They were slain and left for the vultures on Morning Crow land. I ran when I recognized them. They wore new shirts for . . ." Kwahu paused to control the intense emotions. ". . . I can show you where. I will help you retrieve them," he added.

Istaqa rubbed his eyes slowly with one hand. He clinched his other hand into a fist. He finally spoke.

"Thank you. You must tell Chosovi and comfort her first. This will stab her heart." He looked at Kwahu and smiled sadly. He gripped Kwahu by the arm.

Kwahu nodded.

"We had hoped to see her marry you today. Welcome you into the Ash Owl Clan. But we must weather this storm first. Kwatoko will find you some water," Istaqa said. He turned to Kwatoko. "And find him somewhere to rest until Chosovi awakes."

~ B ~

At first light, Ahote bid farewell to the Morning Crow warriors camped in Broken Spine. They had told him about the enemy stranger. He believed them. However, he knew that the rising sun would protect him now. He would circle away from his previous path and follow Yucca Ridge back to the Ash Owl settlement. It was longer and required an uphill hike, but the high ground kept him guarded by the sun. The main route cut through canyons full of shade. The cliffs of red rock held too many fissures and overhangs. There were also dens and caves where nocturnal creatures might hide. And he knew they did. Ahote thought of old storage pits and abandoned homes along the path. Yucca Ridge was safer. The message was vital.

Ahote and Choovio had talked during the night, keeping the bonfire to their back. They had not slept. The Morning Crows would turn and follow the edge of Ash Owl land west, as they had always intended, sweeping their border until it curved away from the Ash Owl settlement and headed north. That path north, known as Seeker Canyon to the Morning Crows, would take them past Black Roof, where their sacred Cave of Visions opened high on its steep eastern face. They would definitely need to check there. "You know the path I mean?" Choovio had asked.

Ahote only nodded, feeling some discomfort. That path was the shortest distance between Firetown and Low Nest. And because of that, both the Ash Owls and the High Rocks Clan called it Short Path rather than Seeker Canyon. Even worse, many of the Ash Owls also called it Greedy Crow Canyon. It was far from Crow Ledge and not often used by the Morning Crows. This made the Morning Crow claim of ownership a regular source of resentment. Ahote, less strident than many from Firetown, kept this to himself.

And then, eventually, the Morning Crows would turn back toward home at the corner of High Rocks territory. Heading east through Seven Sisters Canyon, they would strive to return to Crow Ledge before nightfall. Ahote would urge the Ash Owls to search their own territory and to warn their High Rocks allies. "Stay to the trails north of Widow Rock. We can search our own land," Ahote had warned.

"Too many warriors too close to Firetown otherwise," Choovio had agreed.

The next day the messengers from the two clans would meet, when the sun was high, at the site of their prior encampment. If the enemy stranger had not been destroyed, they would decide how to proceed.

Sweat ran from his hair as he climbed toward Yucca Ridge. Ahote recalled seeing Choovio, almost two years ago, in the last major skirmish between the two clans. Two hunting groups had clashed. Choovio and his brother were lethal. They were very fast. They had flanked his men, even against the terrain.

~ B ~

Sunlight marked a bright square across the floor of the room. "You are cold to touch. Like the dead," Sihu said. Her eyes were red and full of water. She sat in the middle of the sunlight, her slim back rigid. Dust motes marked the path from the window. Makya sat in the darkest corner of the room, back against the cool plaster. A small clay bowl of porridge, pounded corn with small bits of rabbit, sat at his feet. He could not eat it. He gagged when he tried to swallow.

"I am still the same. I am still your husband. This—"

"No," Sihu retorted. "My husband was warm. Like sunlight. How can I sleep next to you? How can my children lay next to the dead in the dark?"

Makya felt tired. His strength had waned with the rising sun. He stared at the bowl of food. It made him feel sick.

"Sihu . . . the spirits have helped us. They have given me the power of the enemy so that our enemies will not destroy us. But my heart is still mine."

"You have the curse of the enemy too. The spirits allow many things. They permit Pavati to lie dying while Choovio wanders far from Crow Ledge. While you are forced to seek shelter in the shadows."

"I am sorry," Makya said. He believed that Sihu was wrong. But he meant it. He wanted to comfort her. He wanted to swallow the porridge, show that it contented him, but he could not.

"My husband . . ." Sihu said more gently. She smiled weakly. "I fear you now. How can I not tremble when my husband grows fangs? But if your heart is not changed . . . then perhaps my fear will pass," she said, forcing out the words.

They let silence fill the room. The whole Morning Crow settlement was muted now. They could still hear corn pounded below. The clack of firewood re-stacked upon the ledge. Muffled flutes, the murmur of the sipapu song, stole from inside the Great Kiva. But few words were exchanged across Crow Ledge. Makya, even though he did not desire it, could also hear her blood as it pulsed through her body. He felt it. He would not tell Sihu that.

Sihu felt her sharpest stone knife beneath her thigh, tucked under the woven rug where she sat.

~ B ~

Kele squatted by the small stream, letting the cool water surround his aching hand. Although he had wanted to stay in

Broken Spine Canyon with Choovio, the shaman had asked for volunteers. "The demon could return to Crow Ledge while we search here. Who will come with me?" Hototo had asked. Kele had stepped forward. They had already explored most of the old pit houses after all. Those situated on Morning Crow land anyway.

"What if I had not come back?" Kele murmured. They had needed every defender to repel the High Rocks attack. The young Morning Crow had deflected the blow from a war club during the fighting. A dark bruise, swollen and tender, now defaced the back of his hand. But he did not think the bones were broken; he could still make and unmake a fist. His hand had diverted, rather than absorbed, the full force of the strike. Kele had fought well in the chaotic battle. That fact added a certain satisfaction to the throbbing pain.

Several years ago Hototo had told the Morning Crows that the clubs were unworthy weapons. "Chayton is an unworthy leader who disrespects the spirits. We must not imitate him. What battle has he won?" Hototo had added. Kele hoped that Hototo would reconsider after facing some of those clubs last night, after burying the dead and tending the wounded this morning. Kele gritted his teeth as he slowly curled and uncurled his fingers.

"If I made one . . . we could practice against them," he reasoned. Thinking of the damage the clubs could do, he rubbed the top of his head with his other hand. He felt the small and uneven hole, beneath the skin, at the top of his skull. He had fallen when he was a boy. His hand had slipped while climbing to Crow Ledge, even though he had climbed the same path countless times before. He had struck his head when he landed. And then Kele could remember nothing until he awoke three days later.

"Hototo has cut a hole in your skull to wake you. Do not touch your head!" his family had told him.

They had not expected his reply. "I want to see the old places. I want to see where our ancestors lived," he had told them. He had spent many spare moments sitting among the ruins of old abandoned pit houses in the years that followed. He had looked for signs of even older dwellings too. In fact, he still yearned to see ancient things. He wanted to visit places older than any story the Morning Crows could tell. Kele had fallen out of time for three days. And the backward horizon of time fascinated him now. He did not understand why. He did not understand what he wanted the past to tell him. He knew only that his accident, or perhaps the cure, had sparked this desire within him.

~ B ~

Chayton ducked his head through the dim doorway. He sucked the marrow from a rabbit bone. He had come to check on Sik, wounded by Makya the night before.

The war leader braced on his hands and knees and vomited water into his bowl in the corner. It splattered the walls.

"No better?" Chayton asked.

"Worse. This is an evil magic. Why can I not eat or drink?" Sik gasped. A plain blanket hung over the window, wedged into place with several small stones. Chayton squatted and gently gripped the injured warrior by the arm, expecting fever.

"Are you chilled? Your skin feels like the night air."

Sik shook his head. "I lost some blood maybe. I feel so tired now."

Chayton released his grip and straightened his legs. "We are making some medicine tea. Perhaps that will stay down."

"Why I am still so thirsty? Makya had sharp teeth. He bit me like he was a demon!" Sik said. Fear and frustration mingled in his voice. He gagged, bringing up a little more water. Beads of spittle stretched from his chin. His back and neck were blistered red from the morning sun. But the ugly gash under his jaw did not bleed.

We will bring the tea," Chayton assured. The talk of magic and demons annoyed him, but he chose to let it pass this time. It was not just his war leader. Two other warriors were also begging for water only to violently spew it moments later. They were also burnt, hiding from the morning sun that had scorched them as they retreated from Crow Ledge.

~ *B* ~

The sun climbed well above the cliffs now. The morning was beautiful; a few white clouds, still and lonely, hung from an immensely blue sky. Tocho led two small bands of Ash Owl warriors away from Firetown, following Kwahu to retrieve the bodies of Pimne and Chua from Short Path. He had left many warriors behind to guard Firetown. "Why did they not take the deer?" Tocho mused. None of the other warriors replied. He twisted his spear in his palm as he walked. Once his men gathered the dead, he would travel on with Kwahu and several others to Low Nest. "It seems vengeful. Maybe even desperate," he added. His men still did not answer. The sorrow of the moment had outrun their curiosity.

"Chayton must account for his actions," Istaqa had told Tocho back in Firetown. "If he has really attacked Crow Ledge, while all the Morning Crow warriors sat on our doorstep, we must learn the outcome. They have smashed the hive, but the bees were already loose."

Tocho had nodded.

Istaqa had shaken his head quietly. "Chayton surely hit them at their weakest. This random attack against the High Rocks man. Pimne and Chua dead."

"What do you think it means?" Tocho had asked.

"Chayton dared risk all his men. Perhaps he has better spies than we know. He must have seen the Morning Crows depart.

He knew they were weakly guarded and decided to attack. What would this mean? That he does not care about the opinion of his allies. That he does not care to warn us that the enemy comes our way . . . even though he sends his messenger."

"Then why do the Morning Crows camp?" Tocho had asked. He already knew that Chayton was rash. That was not news.

"Pimne and Chua killed. While Ahote and Nalnish watched the Morning Crows gather in strong numbers. Who killed them? Was anybody even killed at Low Nest last night?"

"You think Chayton has betrayed us? You think *he* killed Pimne and Chua? And then sent Kwahu to deceive us?"

"Two of our brothers dead. Kwahu invites our warriors to walk onto Morning Crow land to collect the bodies. While we know the Morning Crows wait at the edge of our land. Maybe Hototo, that old coyote, convinced the High Rocks Clan to stop fighting over that trickling stream and start warring together. Their dwellings are closer after all. Or maybe Chayton has no true allies. Has he tricked us both?" Istaqa had asked.

"He was not born here. His blood is not desert blood," Tocho had added in agreement. He casually resented the outsider. Chayton had deep and messy scars across his shoulder blades that he did not explain. He also refused to cut his hair, rejecting the custom of his adopted clan. Many felt that Istaqa should have annexed Low Nest and absorbed the High Rocks stragglers. But then Chayton had arrived at its nadir. Now they flourished again. "But why cancel the wedding then? He could more easily ambush us as we arrived to celebrate."

"I do not know," Istaqa had responded sincerely. "But assume we are watched as prey when you leave Firetown. Hototo may wish to trick both Firetown and Low Nest. Take fast men. We must return the bodies of Pimne and Chua from Greedy Crow Canyon and bury them properly. We must learn more regarding what Chayton has set in motion. Even if he works with our interests. We must prepare to crush the Morning

Crows if they attack. And we must not catch our feet in unseen traps."

Tocho recalled the last thing Istaqa had told him. He had gripped his arm. "Not us today. Not us."

Tocho had sent scouts ahead, instructed them to watch from the cliffs along Short Path for any activity, Morning Crow or High Rocks. He had also sent several men to Widow Rock. While the canyons and tributaries were complex beyond Widow Rock as they dissolved into the Broken Hills, it was an effective chokepoint. It allowed his men to watch the approach from Broken Spine Canyon to Firetown.

As they forged ahead, Kwahu said very little, staring ahead with impassive sobriety. He did not know the Ash Owl warriors all that well and brooded over his wedding. The death of Pimne and Chua had produced quiet tears when he told Chosovi. Just a few. That had been worse than open weeping. "Please bring them back to Firetown . . . before the animals find them," she had asked with a whisper.

Tocho watched Kwahu closely. Even though he liked him, even though he liked the marriage to Chosovi, he still worried. What if he did not know Kwahu well enough? What if they did not know Chayton well enough? What if the High Rocks Clan wanted the alliance even less than his own warriors? And yet, even as Tocho looked for some hint of guilt from Kwahu, Tocho also regretted that he could not yet present his gift to the High Rocks Clan. His wedding bowl had turned out well, perhaps his finest work. He had shown Chosovi as soon as he finished but he was eager for more people to admire it.

~ B ~

"Can you drive this curse from him?" Sihu asked, still seated stiffly in the patch of sunlight. Hototo stood in the doorway, bending forward to lean his head across the stone threshold. He looked at Makya. Makya stared back, eyes wide with curiosity. It had not crossed his mind that he might be healed.

Hototo turned his gaze back to Sihu and shook his head with a kind smile, the kind that only sad eyes can bring. Sad and alight with conflicting memories. "No. This is beyond me. Enemy strangers are not from our world. Not even from the land of our spirits. They do not rise from the lower world like our own souls."

"Where then?" Sihu asked.

"From the darkness. From . . . the abyss that all life rebuffs while it lives." He had discussed that very same question with other spirit leaders many years ago.

"Why do the spirits allow such demons among us? Why do they allow dead men to walk?" Sihu asked. Hototo felt the tension ripple across the room. He admired her blunt ferocity. He knew that Sihu would make an excellent matriarch for the Morning Crow Clan. Just like her grandmother, Shuman. He thought before he answered.

"The first spirits looked at the abyss all around them. They answered with light. The making of the world defied the abyss." He paused and added, "But the night reminds us that we must light fires even so. That they did not vanquish the abyss."

"Is my husband lost to the dark then? Is that what you—"

"I am right here. Having sharp teeth is not the same as being a wolf," Makya snapped. He had not expected her to reject him like this. He felt drained now. He was beginning to tally the cost. He wanted her support.

"Enough," Hototo said calmly but sternly. He was too tired and unsettled to enter their quarrel. Not yet. "I have come to take Makya north to visit the sibyl," he added. Both Makya and Sihu looked at each other, perhaps the first spark of connection between them since Makya had returned. Her spine stiffened slightly.

"Can the sibyl help where you cannot?" Sihu asked. She spoke coldly but, deep in her chest, she was terrified, the sudden blaze of small hope.

"One seeks the sibyl for wisdom more than magic. We must ask what this means for the Morning Crows. For you," Hototo said.

Sihu bowed her head. Her posture sank again. Hototo saw her jaw flex as she regained her composure.

"Still . . . the Smoke Clan possesses powerful magic. We will ask them when the time comes," he said. But he felt no hope as he spoke the words. Sihu stared at her knees now. "We must take many steps to reach them. We should leave now."

"No," Makya said flatly. "I cannot."

"Show him," Sihu demanded. Makya reached out his hand, his finger extended, and passed it quickly through the sunlight that slanted down to where Sihu sat. His lips tightened. Smoke danced up from his fingertip. The smell of burning flesh instantly crossed the room. When Makya pulled his hand back into his lap, Hototo could see blackened skin across his finger.

"That is unfortunate. Then we leave tonight at dusk," Hototo said curtly. He had expected that but was still disappointed to see it. He sought to hide his own emotions. He turned and walked quickly from the doorway.

~ B ~

Chayton walked to the largest kitchen room. It intersected the plaza at the front of Low Nest. He still sucked his rabbit bone, primarily to mask his own anxiety now. It was starting to disintegrate in his mouth. Several young girls worked dry corn into meal just outside the entrance, kneeling over their grinding stones. Another girl gutted a turkey, piling its offal into small bowls, dividing the organs by their intended use. Inside the room, Old Chu'Si, supervising the girls, pounded medicinal herbs with her own smooth grinding stone, smaller and more precise than the stones used to pulverize the corn. Heat radiated from an oven on the floor behind her.

"Will this tea help?"

"No," she said. She hated him. It was mutual. She did not look at him or rise from where she knelt.

"What is this sickness?" he asked.

"Now you care about what I know?"

"Answer me!" Chayton snapped. Chu'Si did not flinch. The young women outside stopped grinding corn. They stared at their hands.

"They were keeping an enemy stranger among them . . . wicked wicked wicked," she said.

"What does that mean?"

She paused. "Those men that cry out for water . . . they are dead. Like the warrior they fought."

"I do not give up on my High Rocks brothers," Chayton said. "Tell me how to save them."

She stopped her work and looked at Chayton finally. Her eyes met his. They were bright and unclouded, despite the difficult years. "You cannot save them," she said softly. "They are dead right now. Dead since last night. His curse has passed to them already," she added.

"Why can they not drink?"

Old Chu'Si set the pounding stone down. She rose to stand and face him now. She wiped sweat from her eyes with the back of her hand. The matriarch stood little higher than his ribs as she stepped close. She pointed her crooked fingers at the clan leader. "You listen to me. Nothing stops their thirst but human blood. Nothing but blood now. Only the night will welcome them. They have become enemy strangers. A kind of demon. That is what I know," she said with an angry whisper and wave of her hand.

"And if I give them blood, will tha—"

"Do not speak such words," she snapped. "Stab them in their hearts with your spear. Then bring Kotori from Firetown to prepare their souls. Do not let their souls linger here. And then, after Low Nest has been made pure, call upon our Ash Owl brothers to hunt the enemy stranger that hides at Crow Ledge. Do not even speak of other—"

"It was no stranger. Sik knew him. It was Makya, the younger one who leads their warriors. The one who brought us to grief last winter," Chayton said. He saw her eyes widen with surprise. "Hurry with that tea. I have no time for crazy ghost stories."

"You cannot allow these men to live at Low Nest. Panthers are not pets," she declared.

Chayton said nothing. He turned and dipped back out onto the plaza.

"Panthers must be killed," she said after him. But he heard the smack of stone against stone once again as he turned the corner, the women resuming their work.

"Ants between her ears," Chayton said. However, he was not smiling. He flung his rabbit bone through the air, sending it tumbling into High Rocks Canyon. He thought it sounded like the lies that the old shaman used to tell. "No time for White Bat nonsense," he scowled.

~ B ~

Istaqa stared up at the striated vault of stone that sheltered his city, soaring bands of red-orange ochre that arched over the terraced roofs of Firetown. He crossed his arms. "And you believe him?" he asked. They stood in the central courtyard, above the largest kiva.

"They were scared," Ahote said. "And they let me live."

"The wild plan of a trickster?"

"Last night . . . one of the Morning Crows . . . he said that the eyes of the enemy stranger chilled him, that they reflected the moonlight. His fear seemed real enough."

"So I should scatter the Ash Owls to hunt for this beast? Even as the Morning Crow storm darkens the sky all around?" Istaqa asked. He did not like the plan that Ahote had described. The hunter seemed to have given no thought to the wedding, no thought to how it might look to the High Rocks Clan.

"I saw no storm. I saw them leave. They walked west from Broken Spine Canyon. They took Deer Trail to sweep the southern edge of their land, but I told them to stay north of Widow Rock, and they agreed. They will return to Crow Ledge before nightfall."

Istaqa stared hard at Ahote. "They were headed all the way to Desert Gate?"

"Yes . . . but then they will turn toward Four Toe Rock. They will follow Short Path."

"Greedy Crow Canyon . . . they take every chance to claim that land," Istaqa said. The clan leader felt his stomach tighten. Tocho and his men were already headed there to retrieve the bodies of Pimne and Chua. But Istaqa did not share this concern with his tired warrior. Rumors had already started to skitter from room to room, like hungry mice, and Istaqa did not want to feed them. In fact, he had not even told Mansi that the wedding was postponed. She had been pleased to learn of the new alliance. The news would certainly upset the ailing Ash Owl matriarch.

"Yes," Ahote said. He wanted to deflect the issue of territory. "We must warn Chayton and search today. We must kill this demon."

"I have heard the tales around the fire. But I have never seen an enemy stranger. Many years ago we heard the rumor that Crow Ledge had killed one. Do you know who had supposedly defeated this monster?" Istaqa asked.

"No," Ahote said.

"Hototo. Young spirit leader for the Crows . . . alone. I wonder if that was even true."

Ahote said nothing. Istaqa gripped his shoulder.

"Nalnish is resting. Please rest as well. You have done well," he said. Istaqa gestured toward the sleeping quarters.

"Those men last night . . . they fear an enemy. They want our help," Ahote insisted.

Istaqa nodded. His brow was furrowed. He fervently hoped that Tocho could avoid the Morning Crows this morning. He needed them to come back to Firetown unscathed. The war leader had known to watch for trouble before he left. But it was still worrisome. Ahote hesitated but he saw that the discussion was ended. He turned and walked away.

Istaqa did not leave. The clan leader looked up once more. The vault above Firetown would kindle and glow when the late afternoon sun struck the stone. And soon enough Kotori would light the sacred fire in the central courtyard. When the shadows of the new moon were thick like clay. To honor the Ash Owl spirit and offer thanks for the harvest. Yellow light would dance against the reddish rock. The spirit of flame would shimmer all around them and lick the walls. Drums would fill those flames with sound. The great hollow logs would reverberate against every stone. Even through the high apartments that curved gracefully along the back wall and brushed the vault itself. Even through their bones. And the lower world, realm of spirits and ancestors, would wash against them like a dry spring renewed.

Istaqa looked back to the lower walls of Firetown. The flame motif, an undulating river of red and black layers that flowed in geometric lines across the white plaster walls, adorned much of the exterior facade now. He had instructed Tocho to execute the design ten years ago. They added fresh paint each year to keep it from fading. Even in tough times.

"All who visit . . . all who trade with us . . . they will remember the sight of Firetown," Istaqa had told the clan.

~ B ~

Kwahu led the Ash Owls forward. Tocho spotted the trail that Pimne and Chua had left, the deer dripping blood between two pairs of human tracks. He watched the path as they walked. The tracks led north, the shortest route to High Rocks land. "The tracks definitely move toward Short Path. Morning Crow land," he mused.

"Land they do not use. Greedy vultures," one of his warriors replied from behind.

The blood trail slowly diminished, but the footprints continued. "The Morning Crows only claim Short Path because it holds their sacred cave," Tocho said.

"Maybe we should just let them claim our home for their rites too," another warrior pushed back.

"I did not mean—"

"Let them find another hole in the rocks. They had no cause to murder Pimne and Chua," the warrior added angrily.

"Save your anger for the Morning Crows. I only consider what motivates them. What kind of war leader would spurn such knowledge?" Tocho asked.

The Ash Owl warriors, showing respect, did not reply.

CHAPTER 10

Arrows Finding Flesh

C HOOVIO AND HIS men broke into pairs, sweeping
through Seeker Canyon and its crooked branches,
gradually moving north toward the Cave of Visions.
They had cautiously avoided the approach to Firetown. They
had kept well north of Widow Rock as Ahote had warned,
cutting across the Broken Hills instead. The men drifted far
apart now as they searched the crags and shadows, every den and
shelf. However, they had seen nothing and slept little. Some
still hunted keenly. But others, jaded with the apparent futility
of the search, just moved through the shade.

Two young Morning Crow warriors, Lusio and Ayawamat,
stared up an embankment, wondering if the small ledge above
them merited the effort. It looked very shallow. "Your turn,"
Ayawamat said.

"Then we go back?" Lusio asked. They were south of Black
Roof. And the path they followed away from Seeker Canyon,
called Desert Gate, sloped unevenly uphill. The disarray of cliffs
and canyons would eventually give way to scrub desert if they
kept going.

The blue sky was plentiful over Desert Gate. Several hawks
drifted above them, silent, paying no heed to the two skinny
warriors below. Lusio and Ayawamat had decided to check the
north side of the Desert Gate corridor first, formed by the actual
southern flank of Black Roof. They would then cross over and
check the opposing side of the canyon as they turned back. They
needed to finish their sweep quickly in order to return to Seeker
Canyon and meet back with Choovio beneath the Cave of
Visions.

Lusio scrambled up the embankment. He picked his path well away from the shaded portion of the ledge, gripping the roots of a stubborn juniper that hung from the cliff to hoist himself up. He would then slide to the entrance, moving laterally from the high side. He would check any den the same way.

~ B ~

Two scouts from the Ash Owl Clan, Len and Nayavu, crawled along the top of Black Roof. Tocho had dispatched them to Black Roof before sunrise to keep watch over Short Path. They squinted into the morning sun. The rocks were already warm beneath them. They saw Morning Crow warriors beginning to gather below them now, from several directions, examining some large rocks and the surrounding area. "There are so many. Definitely looks like Greedy Crow Canyon now," Len whispered. Kwahu had told the Ash Owls that the bodies of Pimne and Chua lay further to the north, closer to High Rocks land, near Four Toe Rock. And Len and Nayavu had spotted their slain friends from the far northern edge of Black Roof— hunters and prey both horribly exposed to vultures—before doubling back to their current position.

"One of us should warn Tocho. Our warriors will come this way soon to collect the bodies. This could turn into an ambush!" Nayavu whispered back.

"What is the quickest way down without being seen?" Len asked.

"Use the . . . No. I will go. There are some erosion fissures behind us. Choked with stunted trees now. It will be fastest to climb down there and circle back."

Len nodded. "I will stay. I can try and signal if Tocho comes too quickly down Short Path."

Nayavu clasped Len by the shoulder and then took off, running low across the flat expanse. Some tracts of high ground were vast, supporting vegetation and life. Black Roof was not as large and mostly barren. Fire had claimed it many years ago. Nayavu, only a young child when it happened, still recalled the conflagration. He recalled seeing birds in retreat as the blaze took hold, the commotion of many wings, the first warning. Many people had come to watch from the canyon floor. Orange light had crackled and hissed on the rocks above, filling the night sky beneath an immense blot of gray-white smoke. He recalled the taste of smoke in the wind, fouling the air and scratching his throat for days after the flames had died.

And the charred trunks of trees stood now in lonely desolation around him, even years later, like an assembly of withered spirits. Like shadows impervious to the light. Even the Morning Crows disliked spending time on Black Roof. However, many trunks had vanished in recent years, fuel for cooking fires and for warmth. There were not so many left now. And at certain places, favored by the terrain, charcoal scuffed the rocks below Black Roof. Where thick logs were dropped to Greedy Crow Canyon for portage. Nayavu had hauled many logs to Firetown last year himself, his aching arms and shoulders smeared with soot. He saw more fresh stumps as he ran.

Len watched awhile longer, counting more Morning Crows as they arrived. If Tocho stumbled upon them, the Ash Owls would be in grave danger. Of course, that assumed the Morning Crows intended violence. But Len could not imagine what else they wanted. "Just too many men," Len said to himself. He was counting more than thirty warriors now, and they all had weapons at the ready. "Stay out of sight," he added. He was thinking of Nayavu.

~ B ~

Lusio stood at the top of the natural embankment. "This den is too shallow," he said. He looked down the rocky slope, marking the path back to Seeker Canyon. As he scanned the inlets and sloping cliffs along the sides of the canyon, he saw something glint sharply in the sun, a quick flash of light back behind the rocks. "Ahhh!" he gasped. He scrambled down to Ayawamat, scree falling behind him.

"What?" Ayawamat asked. His eyes were wide.

"Down there!" Lusio pointed with his spear. He jumped up and down. His necklace jangled around his neck.

"Shhh. We already checked that," Ayawamat replied.

"The other side. I saw . . ." Lusio stopped.

"What?" Ayawamat repeated.

"There! I think I saw it again!" Lusio shouted. He ran toward the sighting. Fear and excitement flooded his veins. Ayawamat picked up his bow and ran behind. But Lusio pulled ahead. He knew that, if he could kill the enemy stranger, his standing among the Morning Crow warriors would leap. Except for the trouble with the High Rocks Clan last winter, there had been few skirmishes over the past year or two—too few opportunities for the younger warriors to prove themselves.

"Wait! Lusio . . . wait!" Ayawamat hissed after him.

~ B ~

Choovio and most of his men stood below the Cave of Visions. A spatter of blood on the rocks. Dirt disturbed below. "The blood scatters from this point. Like a body dropped from the cave," Honani observed. Honani hoped to impress Choovio today. Both ears still felt tender from where Hototo had disciplined him for falling asleep on the watch.

"No blood trail leading away. Where is the body?" Choovio said.

"We have seen the trail of two hunters. Could one of them have found it? Or maybe one of them tried to climb to the cave and fell?" Honani guessed.

"But that trail keeps going in the direction of Seven Sisters. They did not stop here," Choovio said. The others nodded.

"We need to check inside the Cave of Visions," Choovio added with resolve.

"Enter without the spirit leader?" Honani asked.

"Good hiding place. Hototo would approve," Choovio replied. "Who will come with me? I need two volunteers," he added. But the focus changed before any volunteers could step forward. Two more Morning Crows were returning from their search. They were running with an urgent step. The group shifted as they stepped into the gathering.

"Look down. I am showing you my spear," Cheveyo panted.

"What do you mean? Why?" several warriors asked.

"Act interested," Cheveyo said. He pointed at its unremarkable stone edge, picked at its lashings. "Ash Owls on Morning Crow land. We saw them coming this way," he casually waved his hand to the south.

"Could you tell their purpose?" Choovio asked.

"They had weapons. It looked like a raiding party. One of the High Rocks Clan went with them too," Cheveyo added. "Somebody touch my spear and nod. We saw another one of those bastards spying from Black Roof. What should we do?" he asked.

"We could inspect my spear now," Honani joked.

"Good to see you awake this morning," Cheveyo shot back.

~ B ~

Lusio reached the spot where he had seen motion. His heart pounded. He slowed his breath. He had been to this place before with friends. Fallen rocks screened a large open space under the overhanging cliff. The floor sloped smoothly toward the back. Tall enough to stand near the front. Good shade and good shelter for waiting out the weather. Cool and dry. He had searched many such spaces in the last two days.

He slipped between the rocks with one swift step. He gasped. A strange man sat before him. He looked lean and old. Long gray hair obscured his weathered face, covered his entire jaw. His forehead was peeling and red; he was sweating. He wore a loose shirt of badly faded leather. His arms were bare. A shiny bowl, with a skirt of tiny rings hanging from one side, sat between his legs. Lusio did not know what it was. But he could see that it would reflect the sun. Most of all, he was stunned as he looked into the strange face. Blue eyes! The stranger had bright blue eyes!

"Well . . . hello there. Do you own this place?" the man asked. His voice was hoarse. An echo followed his words, returning from the stone ceiling above him. He smiled as he said it. Lusio did not understand him.

"Don't move!" the young Morning Crow yelled. His own voice bounced sharply. He had seen the enemy stranger two nights before. This stranger looked different: the beard, the gray hair. And the man had, except for his pale armpits, spent lots of time in the sun. But the clothes, the structure of his face, the long smooth blade: these were the same. Lusio wondered if there could be more than one type of enemy stranger. And this stranger smelled terrible. Lusio brandished his spear. The man did not seem to understand him either. He did not move, though. He did not even seem scared.

"Calm down, kid. Just sitting here."

Ayawamat leaped between the rocks. He saw Lusio, spear in defensive position, and then he saw the stranger, unlike any normal man he had ever seen. He pulled his notched bow and fired without saying a word. The man pulled away. But the shot grazed his cheek, high on his cheekbone. "Damn you," the man hissed. He jumped to his feet, knees bent beneath the low roof.

Lusio jolted into action as he saw the man rise. Fueled by the fear and excitement that had simmered since they left Crow Ledge, he charged the stranger. He held the spear high but gripped it overhand, ready to lunge and thrust. The long blade flashed upward, its polished edge scattering light that filtered past the screen of boulders. The man slapped the spear away with the flat of his blade. Lusio stumbled with the force of the strike but spun quickly. He charged again, giving himself no time to think, no time to let his fear catch up.

Another arrow whistled past and clattered across the rocks as Ayawamat moved to his right and shot around Lusio. "Too much," the stranger said. He struck down to parry the spear. The blow cantilevered Lusio forward. The stranger grabbed him by the braid as he brought the blade up hard and fast, hitting the young warrior across the throat. Blood splattered across the ground as he ripped the weapon clear. The stranger sat back hard against the sloping rock, letting Lusio collapse to his hands and knees. The blade clanged against the stone as the stranger let it loose. He twisted back, reaching behind him. Ayawamat struggled to place another arrow, his hands trembling. He saw Lusio slump forward. A pool of blood was forming beneath him. And then the blue-eyed man swung a weathered weapon forward. Ayawamat saw its curved bow and guessed its purpose. But only as the stranger squeezed its trigger.

The short arrow tore into the naked ribs of the young Morning Crow. High in the chest. Ayawamat dropped his own bow and stumbled frantically out into the sun. Crushing pain filled his entire chest. He ran as far as he could. "Help! Help me!" he gasped weakly. He dropped to his knees in the middle of the sunlit wash, Seeker Canyon just out of reach, blood spilling out from between his fingers, the arrow almost completely buried in the wound.

~ *B* ~

Nayavu took a deep breath. He had quickly scrambled down the southern face of Black Roof, scraping his arms and legs in the process. He had just started his run toward Short Path, hoping to intersect and then follow it south, at least until he connected with Tocho and the other warriors. But now he stood over a dying Morning Crow warrior instead, his single braid twisted in the sand behind his head. The slain man gurgled in agony. Choking on blood. His eyes had fallen out of focus.

Nayavu turned his head in all directions but saw nothing amiss. He dropped to his knees and gently pulled a bloody hand away from the wound to inspect it. He saw the tail of an arrow; its thick shaft buried deep, its feathers unfamiliar. "What kind of . . . crazy arrow?" Nayavu muttered. He continued to stare. He did not understand what had happened.

"Haaahh! Haaahh!" two men shouted in the distance. Nayavu looked up. Two more Morning Crows were running toward him now. They had seen him as they turned the corner from Short Path. Both men brandished spears.

Nayavu jerked his hands into the air and showed open palms. But his hand was smeared with blood, bright red in the noonday sun; and the body lay on the ground before him. And in such close proximity to Black Roof, he knew that the Morning Crows claimed the sand beneath his feet. Seeing how it looked and knowing that more Morning Crows waited under their Cave of Visions, Nayavu jumped clear of the sandy wash and started running.

Legs already warm from his prior exertion, he slanted to his right. He hoped to reach the edge of Short Path and turn south before they cut off his retreat. He needed to reach Tocho and the other Ash Owls coming from Firetown before the Morning Crows reached him.

They angled to intersect him, but Nayavu reached the canyon first. He saw their eyes lit with rage now. They had clearly seen the dying man at his feet and assumed the worst. He made the turn and sprinted ahead. "Stop him! Cut him off!" the warriors barked from behind. Nayavu saw that two more Morning Crows were scrambling down an embankment ahead of him. Their bows were strung. One of the men behind Nayavu whistled an alarm over his shoulder with two fingers between his lips. "More warriors are close," Nayavu thought. He dropped his own spear for the sake of speed. He pushed past them, still hugging the western side of the canyon. He ran hard for a good distance. But his lungs burned; his legs were filling with sand. He was fading now.

And then he finally heard an Ash Owl warning call ahead. One of his brothers, scouting ahead, had seen him coming, and Tocho and his men were close enough to warn. He pumped his legs harder. But he suddenly crumpled, pain biting his thigh, an arrow finding its mark. "He killed Ayawamat!" one of the Morning Crows shouted behind him.

"No . . . not me," he gasped loudly as he rolled to jerk the arrow from his thigh. Feet pounded closer. He rose to fight, drawing his knife and holding the bloody arrow in his other hand. But the spears closed at full speed. Nayavu was thrown backwards as they stabbed him, the impact exploding into his chest. As his skull hit the ground, he saw Tocho and his men turn the corner. They sprinted forward. "Not today!" Tocho yelled. The Ash Owl scout who had sounded the alarm lunged down the hillside to join the charge.

"For Pimne and Chua!" another shouted. The four Morning Crow warriors turned and fled.

"Get to Choovio! Head for the cave!" the Morning Crows shouted.

"Run them down!" Tocho yelled.

Nayavu lay in the dirt as the Ash Owls passed him to give chase. He thought of his wife and children. They seemed to call him back across the distance. To again watch the snow drift down, silently, just beyond the ledge of Firetown, the cold winter air against his skin, the warm fire at his back. He wanted to watch in silence as before.

~ B ~

Several arrows flew past the fleeing Morning Crows as they closed on the Cave of Visions. Narrow misses. "Where is Choovio?" one gasped. He was exhausted. They stopped and stumbled around to face the closing Ash Owls, driving hard for revenge.

The Morning Crows heard shouts from above. They were muffled by the distance. "Trap! Trap! Retreat!" They looked up and saw an Ash Owl standing at the top of Black Roof. He waved his arms wildly.

Tocho and his twelve men were close behind. "Rrraaahhh!" they screamed as they charged. If the Ash Owls saw or heard Len on the cliff far above, they did not heed him. They saw only the men who had dared to run down and kill Nayavu moments before. But as they hoisted their spears, panting themselves, arrows hissed past them in two directions. With a scream and echo, the Morning Crows exploded from behind the boulders and brush that lined this portion of the canyon. They sprinted down the narrow slopes from both sides of the wash.

Most of the Morning Crows had gathered by the time the alarm whistle and din of pursuit reached them. Choovio had quickly divided his men, pointing to the flanks of the canyon his men had just searched. "Vanish there. And then like two hands clapping!" He had snapped his hand together to convey the plan of attack.

The Ash Owls were instantly and seriously outnumbered as the Morning Crows spilled into view. "Retreat!" Tocho screamed. He heard arrows puncture flesh behind him. They whirled and began to move, but wounded men slowed the reversal, arrow wounds biting. The Morning Crows closed quickly from all directions. No escape routes. Tocho and his men collapsed into one another and sought to close ranks, spears out. Kwahu stood bravely with them. He had no choice. Chaotic shouting filled the canyon.

And then the Morning Crows smashed into both flanks. Dead sprint. Like two rows of teeth coming together. Some spears were deflected, jolting the air with a messy percussion, wood striking wood. But other spears found their mark. Some fighters were thrown off their feet. Tocho simply had too few men. The Ash Owls splintered into individual acts of desperation as warriors scrambled to fight free. Kwahu, desperate to live for his wedding, caught one Morning Crow hard with his club, smashing his wrist. He slipped past another one with a fierce shove. He brought his weapon high to strike again. However, he was tackled from behind. Dirt filled his mouth. He saw the knife that swept toward his throat.

Tocho twisted to avoid the thrust of an enemy spear, landing a hard punch with his fist, but then stumbled as two other warriors, locked in combat, crashed into his left leg. As he lunged into an open space, fighting to catch his balance, Tocho saw one of his friends crumple with a broken spear handle jutting from his gut. He saw three Morning Crows slam another Ash Owl into the dust. "Run! Run if you can!" he barked.

Len dropped his arms in horrified silence.

~ B ~

Kotori, the thin spirit leader of the Ash Owl Clan, nodded quickly. "Yes . . . yes . . ." He sat with his legs crossed on the floor of the most sacred kiva in Firetown. His kiva. He sat in front of the hearth shield, the large flat stone that diffused the flow of fresh air around the fire pit. Two long braids fell behind his narrow shoulders in the usual Ash Owl custom, but Kotori had also washed his hair with red dye. It showed well over the streaks of gray that pulled across his scalp. The fire motif embodied. A spray of small red feathers also hung from his neck this morning.

Kotori listened while Istaqa paced back and forth. It was an honor. While observant of rituals and rites, the clan leader rarely asked Kotori for diplomatic advice. He did not often ask for spiritual advice either. However, strange events were unfolding. Alo, the young spirit apprentice, knelt beside Kotori and stared at the ground respectfully. The boy held a small flute, his lesson interrupted.

Hands clasped behind his back, Istaqa recited the news from Kwahu, regarding the death of Pimne and Chua and the attack by the High Rocks Clan against Crow Ledge. He also shared the strange reports from Nalnish and Ahote, regarding the Morning Crows at their doorstep. He finished and knelt before Kotori. They had lit no fire today. A shaft of sunlight from the entrance above was sufficient. Istaqa saw that Kotori and Alo had recently whitewashed the circular wall. It felt like an impassive face now.

"I must visit with Mansi later and wish to respect your discretion. How much will you tell her?" Kotori asked.

"Only that trouble with the Morning Crows has delayed the wedding. She fights to catch her breath already. Rumors of demons can only make cruel nights worse."

"You are kind to lighten her burden," Kotori nodded.

"You must tell me the truth. Are they real . . . the enemy strangers . . . or are they like the spirits we worship?"

Alo glanced up at Istaqa in wide surprise. Had the clan leader just implied that the spirits were not real? Kotori sat motionless for a long moment, eyes closed. He exhaled slowly and fingered the bright feathers and beads that hung around his neck.

"We must not alarm my young pupil. We know the spirits are real. But I understand your question. The spirits are here. They come into us. We . . . call them forth with our art and dance. But they will not pluck an ear of corn or fit stone upon stone."

"Indeed," Istaqa replied. One corner of his mouth smiled, no teeth showing. Kotori smirked back. He nodded but only a little. At last he scooped up a handful of sand. He continued.

"But the enemy stranger: he could carry this sand wherever he would."

"You believe then?"

Kotori nodded. "I have rarely spoken these words before. But Hototo killed one many years ago. He bore its husk away for disposal and secretly asked me for advice. Real enough to kill. Teeth like a wolf. We burned the corpse together in Broken Spine Canyon."

"Do you give Alo nightmares with this story?" Istaqa joked.

"Hototo boasted that he killed the demon in single combat. And I know that he lies. But there were also older tales before that. And tales from other clans, including the Smoke Clan."

"So you think the Morning Crows tell the truth now?"

"You come to the difficult question," Kotori said. He looked up toward the strong timbers of the roof. A beautiful chamber. He closed his eyes again, thinking before he spoke.

"Your mentor needs time to think. What does the apprentice say?" Istaqa asked.

"I would let the demon kill them. We don't need the Morning Crows," Alo said nervously. He gripped his flute tightly now.

"Scorpions exist. But what if I tell you that I see one on your shoulder?" Kotori interjected, gesturing with his left hand.

"Do you?" Istaqa asked. He arched his brows.

"No," Kotori said. "But would a wise man refuse to look?"

"Only if I thought you wanted to slit my throat when I looked away," Istaqa said.

Kotori nodded. "So your task is to check your shoulder *and* watch the knife."

"Indeed. Thank you for your wisdom," Istaqa said. "Please prepare for Pimne and Chua. We must prepare their souls to travel back to the lower world. I have sent Tocho to retrieve the bodies."

"Yes. Of course," Kotori nodded. He bowed his head. He hated burying men he had birthed himself years before.

~ *B* ~

Len stumbled back from the top of the cliff, sick to his stomach. He had seen three men escape below. The chaos of limbs and bodies, as the Morning Crows had smashed his brothers from both sides, had initially allowed four Ash Owls to break free. They stumbled and crashed toward open space, parrying blows from Morning Crows as they went. Not to wage war in return, only to flee. Len saw them run. But then one had fallen, an axe landing viciously against his back. He tried to rise, but a second blow to the neck finished him. Some Morning Crows followed the surviving three. He did not think they would make it, not all of them. One limped as he ran. He could not clearly tell who from behind, maybe Tocho, but he saw the gash across the back of his thigh.

His hands were shaking. "How could they? How could they?" Len said. He had killed in battle but had never actually seen such a slaughter. He needed to warn Istaqa. He retreated across the desolate rock, aiming for the spot where Nayavu had descended. Nayavu had clearly not warned Tocho and his men. He feared the worst for his friend and told himself to move with caution.

Len had moved far from the edge of the cliff but still felt too exposed among the expanse of stumps. He swept wide, trotting quickly through the charred trees that still remained. He saw that some saplings had finally returned in the last several years. They had started to change the grim mood of the landscape. But they grew very slowly. It would take his whole life for Black Roof to heal. Or perhaps even longer.

Len finally found the ruts choked with brush. They were steep, but Nayavu had been right. The roots and branches would allow him to climb down easily and quickly enough. They would also help him stay out of sight. He could not tell how long the Morning Crows would stay on the battlefield. It was their sacred land. They would tend to their own wounded. Len began his descent. He took his time, watching for any signs of movement below. His trembling slowly faded as he focused on the labor of placing his feet, gripping the rough limbs, avoiding scrapes from the dense underbrush.

~ B ~

Jerome relaxed just a little. He heard the conflict move away. Another small miracle. God had preserved him once again. He unlatched the crossbow and listened. He heard a rising echo of shouts, rolling faint off the walls of the canyon.

"He's here alright," Jerome muttered. Violence followed the vampire like a shadow. "Or maybe he just finds it the way flies find garbage," Jerome added. The knight crawled from behind the rocks and looked out from under some low bushes. He scanned the canyon floor. No movement. Stepping carefully into the sunlight, wearing his helmet now and a vest of chain mail he had quickly unpacked after the fight, which he usually wore only at night, he walked to where the young warrior had died and worked the quarrel free from between the ribs. He scrubbed it clean in the sandy soil. He wiped the blood from his hands too. He thought of one of his fellow knights, killed by some crazy local at the edge of the jungle, clavicle completely snapped by an ornate blade, engraved like it was some sort of crown. Not even at the hands of the vampire.

Years had passed since then. So many days of hunger and thirst. Did the earth unfold forever like an endless tapestry? And now only he remained among his Order. It did not matter. He was still sworn before God to hunt this vampire and execute him. By holy decree. He felt again the heavy burden of his mission. "Vengeance for all," he muttered. He rubbed the gash on his cheek. Well, at least these locals did not appear to have steel.

Jerome thought about the other corpse under the sheltering rock, bleeding out. And this one at his feet. He wished he could trap the devil here. The scent of blood would call out like trumpets. The vampire might come to investigate. However, this blood would smell stale by dusk. Jerome knew that the vampire would not drink it. The undead only wanted blood that spilled fresh from the veins. And the locals would surely come looking for the bodies; Jerome had never seen a tribe that would leave their dead on the ground. He gathered his things carefully, taking time to clean his sword, and then dragged the other native out into the sunlight. "Need to get high and watch the canyon," he grunted. Jerome left the two bodies near each other but did not lay them side by side. He dropped their weapons near their hands.

Jerome doubted that the vampire knew he was here but he was alone now. And once the vampire discovered that, he would only have one chance.

"Not many pieces left on the chessboard . . . better make it count," he said.

~ *B* ~

The sun was falling toward the horizon, an orange and purple blaze through an embankment of gathering clouds. Len stood before Istaqa.

"I saw three men escape. I think Tocho might have gotten away. Did none of them arrive? Did Nayavu not return?" Len said. He forced himself to ask. He had feared that the Morning Crows might linger in Short Path as they attended to injuries. Thus, once he had reached the bottom of Black Roof, he had veered toward Long Path to avoid detection. He had not seen the final footsteps of his friend.

Istaqa could only shake his head slowly. His face was rigid with anger, his fists clenched. He wanted to strike Len just for bearing the news. He wanted to stick Hototo on a stake and impale him for all the clans to see. He wanted to destroy every Morning Crow. Reduce their homes to rubble.

"It looked like the whole Morning Crow Clan. They have no hearts. Do they revere nothing? How could they murder us while we seek only to bury our dead?" Len exclaimed in misery.

"Had Kwahu . . . had he returned to the High Rocks Clan or did he still travel with them?" Istaqa asked. He feared the answer.

"He was there. Kwahu was killed by the Morning Crows. I could spot him quickly from his short hair. He fought well but . . ." Len winced as he replied.

"Please find Kwatoko. He becomes our war leader now. Send him to me quickly," Istaqa said flatly. He took several deep breaths. His voice sounded like it had no connection to his soul. Only words departing the mouth. Len nodded curtly and hustled away to check the kivas for Kwatoko, thankful to have finished his report. He hoped that Istaqa would not resent him for the news he had brought. He hoped that dusk would arrive quickly to hide his face.

The setting sun hit the ceiling of Firetown, kindling the bands of ochre rock into the brilliant red-orange that gave the Ash Owl home its name. Istaqa took no notice now. He stared into the sunset, not seeing it but rather rehearsing his words. He would need to speak with Chosovi too. His heart hurt for her. His own sister! She had hoped, both for love and for the Ash Owls, to marry Kwahu on this day. But the High Rocks warrior was dead instead, his body butchered and discarded in Greedy Crow Canyon.

CHAPTER 11

Isolated

T HE SILENCE OF the setting sun, the silent accumulation of shadows across the land, the silence of the grave. Eyes open. The vampire pushed the stone away from his makeshift tomb. He pulled himself into the night and rolled onto his feet in one fluid motion, hand on his sword. He inhaled deeply and smelled the air. He smelled a cacophony of stale blood and sweat. But not from the conflict he had witnessed last night. Wrong direction. This was some new conflict. As the wind shifted, he smelled something else too, just at the edge of his senses. He tested the air again. He worked his fist against his open palm in frustration; he smelled the unwashed stench of the Order of St. John again for the first time in weeks. They were not dead after all. He briefly thought about fleeing the area. He had fed the night before after all. But he wondered if the knights might inadvertently help him suppress his new problem, the ferals now loose among the local population, untrained and unchecked, if he stayed in the area. "None may own the eternal night untaught," he said, reciting the First Precept.

Of course, he had recruited apprentice vampires before. But he could not cope with the language barrier here. He could make them undead; but he could not initiate them into the brotherhood, could not teach them the Eight Precepts. Those bleeders he had watched flee across the valley could only complicate his life. He was alone. He watched a tiny bat wheel and dart above him.

The vampire stepped smoothly down the berm that hid his hole in the rocks, walked lightly back to the canyon path he had left last night. He moved from rock to rock, not wanting to mark the sand with his boots. Looking west he saw the panicky retreat of the bleeding men from the night before, the blood spatter in their footsteps. But looking east, back toward the stone fortress, he saw fresh tracks atop the old, many men running quickly in the opposite direction. Had the men with short hair dared attack again? Or were these the men that had seemed absent from the battle he had witnessed last night? Perhaps they were finally returning. But from where?

His insight flashed. "They are hunting me. They probably checked that cave." The vampire shrugged. There was no reason to be surprised. He looked down the canyon in either direction. The wind, stronger than last night, had moisture in it. He shifted his cloak across his shoulders. He decided to follow the fresh tracks back toward the cliff dwelling once again. The vampire wanted to make sure of his hunch, wanted to become the hunter again. And he still needed to kill Makya. There was also some value in learning one section of this landscape particularly well. "Traps are mostly made out of familiarity. Who told me that?" he wondered.

~ B ~

Choovio stood before Shuman in exhausted disbelief. "To the Smoke Clan? For what reason? Why would Hototo take Makya there when the danger is here?" he asked. The cool wind swirled across Crow Ledge.

Choovio had seen the disturbed ground in Seven Sisters, the chaotic tracks of retreat toward Low Nest. The blood on the ground. They had hurried to Crow Ledge as quickly as possible. However, with sore feet and some wounded men, they had also found poor Lusio and Ayawamat and born the burden of their dead. To return to find Hototo and his brother gone, Choovio felt abandoned. Shuman gripped his arm. No fires burned outside; but as she stepped close, he clearly saw that she was bruised and cut, her cheek swollen.

"You must defend Crow Ledge until he returns," she said. She quickly told him all that had transpired while he was gone. His safe arrival, and the return of so many warriors, eased her burden. She trusted Choovio. She took comfort in the fact that Hototo had shown trust in him as well. After all, he had selected Choovio to hunt the enemy stranger. And Hototo had also abruptly departed for Smoke Ridge this evening. Shuman reasoned that the clan leader would not have left without full confidence in Choovio, without some surety that Choovio would soon return to protect Crow Ledge.

"Of all the foolish . . ." Choovio interjected. He stopped himself. "We saw his broken spears in the Cave of Visions. We saw where he landed," he added. As he listened, Choovio walked to the poles abandoned by the High Rocks Clan, now hauled onto Crow Ledge and sprawled along the front of the terrace. He ran his hand along the wood. These were clever inventions. He looked around. Weapons were piled, including some of the High Rocks clubs. A few interior fires were lit but shielded. He saw now that all angles of approach were watched by women and old men, tired but alert.

"Can you take me to Pavati now?" he said. He could find no other words. His own report, regarding the Ash Owls and the elusive enemy stranger, could wait a few moments. Shuman nodded. She knew the imperative of an injured wife. And the old matriarch guessed enough already. She saw lips tight with grim concern. They carried no token of victory over the demon, only a pile of Ash Owl spears and injuries that needed attention.

~ B ~

Ahote dreamed, exhausted from his vigil the night before. He stood high in the mountains. It also seemed like home. He had traveled there before but never climbed so high. He shivered with cold. Dark clouds, like a wall of swirling smoke, belched freezing mist. The ice crunched thick beneath his sandals. The wind stung his face. He had only seen the tree line from afar in waking life, but now he stood at its edge and stared up the rocky slope beyond. One last tree stood amid the worn boulders. Alone and halfway to the peak. Like an isolated sentinel. Three dark limbs broke up and out from its massy trunk, each twisted from years of harsh conditions. Ice coated its bark from root to twig. Thin shafts of sunlight broke the clouds and made the tree sparkle like the scales of many fish darting suddenly below the surface of the stream. He thought it very beautiful.

But then the clouds closed, and darkness gathered around the tree. Ahote could hear nothing, save sleet pelting the mountain. He knew that ice still gathered on its limbs. That they hung almost to the ground now. He wanted to free its branches, to shake loose the cold burden, and he strained to reach it. The dreaming warrior worked his feet more desperately. He could find no traction against the icy slope, could not close the distance. Ahote could only watch, unable to avert his eyes.

Crack! The splintering echo of the heaviest limb snapping under the weight of ice. He saw it fall, shards of ice scattering, pale wood exposed along the fracture. *Crack!* Another limb releasing its burden. *Cra-cra-crack!* Ahote wanted to scream. He fought to let out the sound, but his throat was closed.

"Wake up. Wake up," he heard Kwatoko say. "Istaqa has called for war council and wants us to gather."

He woke and stared at Kwatoko. Kwatoko looked troubled but smiled down at him. Night had fallen. Light from a cooking fire played against the wall from another room. His thin blanket lay crumpled below his feet. The tree still shivered at the back of his mind, its trunk now splintered. It felt unsettling, like a premonition of death. He wondered if the enemy stranger was approaching Firetown. But Ahote had no time to consider its meaning more closely. Kwatoko stood over him, nudging a sandal into his shoulder. Ahote nodded and pulled himself stiffly from his woven mat.

~ B ~

The moon was high in the night sky now. The wind was cold and slightly moist. The stars along the Western horizon were obscured by darkness, thunderheads advancing slowly, lightning flaring deep in their heart. Hard rain was coming.

Most of the High Rocks Clan slept, except for guards in the cliffs who watched the approach to Low Nest from all directions. However, Chayton paced along the roof. He had sent two tired warriors to bed, taken their watch. All slept with weapons at hand tonight. They had hurt the Morning Crows, but not enough. He felt sure that they must retaliate. How could they not? But he doubted that it would happen quickly. Hototo would bide his time. And Chayton had worries closer to home at the moment.

He had never seen an illness like this. Thirst still tortured his wounded warriors, those the Morning Crow had bitten, even though they could not drink or eat. Whatever they swallowed was still quickly and violently expelled, including the medicinal tea. The sun had burnt their skin much too quickly. Chayton feared that they were dying.

In fact, Old Chu'Si had insisted that they were already dead. He certainly did not believe that. She only wanted to incite fear, wanted to see him make mistakes. Erode his authority. It would not surprise Chayton if she had boiled her own hair to make that tea. Even so, three of his best warriors were still in trouble. Losing his war leader would deal a painful blow to the High Rocks Clan.

Chayton turned his mind to consider his own first days at Low Nest. They had called themselves the White Bats then. Hunters had found him injured and alone, trembling with fever. They had held good tea to his lips and heaped wood upon the fire. It had broken his fever. However, once his head had cleared, Chayton had seen great privation all around him: fetid rooms and dying crops, hostile neighbors and poor defenses. Starvation and violence had circled like vultures. Worse yet, Chayton had seen that the White Bats were at the mercy of a confused and tormented spirit leader. The fool had made every problem worse. "Cha'Akmongwi!" Chayton scoffed into the wind.

Despite those difficult conditions, the White Bats had continued to feed Chayton. They had allowed him to renew his strength, and he had worked and hunted in return. He had fought at their side until he was admired, quickly building both trust and gratitude. And then, finally, Chayton had done what was needed, what the White Bats could not bring themselves to do. He had sworn to suffer no more shamans.

At dusk, Chayton had moved all three ailing warriors into the ritual kiva. The room had gone unused without a spirit leader to conduct the traditional rites, and Chayton had used it for storage lately. Its location, at the western edge of the Low Nest structure, put some space between the sick men and the sleeping quarters, but the kiva was right below him now. He could hear their misery well. "My veins hurt!" Nuk groaned.

"Mine too!" Wik answered.

Sik groaned in agreement.

Chayton clenched his teeth now. He faced a terrible choice. He did not want to feed kindling to the noxious fire of false beliefs. He had no desire to affirm the prayers of spirit leaders. He refused to return to that. On the other hand, he could not let his warriors die without trying to save them. And he knew, given the strange nature of the illness, that only the ministrations of a healer would count as trying.

Chayton understood, all too well, that the executed spirit leader was both talisman and shadow for his own leadership. The persistent memory of those dark days kept his detractors quiet. However, his revolt had also usurped the authority of the matriarch. And the old woman still walked among them, still complained. Like a splinter buried deep in his hand and too difficult to remove. What if the contrast between light and dark began to fade? If the High Rocks Clan saw that he too could fail, those old resentments would surface quickly. Those that still remembered would find their voice, and their grievances would bleed like newly inflicted wounds if Chayton refused to summon a healer. He felt it in the unsettled eyes of his people. More than they said.

Chayton scuffed the dirt in frustration. He worked his grip back and forth around the handle of his war club. And finally he exhaled slowly, releasing the agony of his decision. He would swallow his pride, holding aside his convictions for the moment. He would summon Kotori from Firetown at first light. He did not know what else to do.

After all, Kotori was his ally now and well loved by the Ash Owls. The High Rocks Clan would embrace this decision. Chayton only hoped that allowing another sip would slake, rather than intensify, their thirst for a spirit leader. After all, he had also agreed to allow the wedding ceremony. He could feel his traction slipping, the slope growing steeper. "But what choice do I have?" he asked.

Unfortunately, many whispered that Hototo was more gifted than Kotori as a healer. Chayton found himself wishing that he could seek help from the Morning Crows instead. He could barely face that cruel thought, even alone under the stars.

~ *B* ~

"I trust you both. But how can we trust the Morning Crows? We know they like dirty tricks. Think of Hototo and the ambush at Gathering Rock," Kwatoko said. He winced at the memory.

"But last night seemed very strange, even for Hototo," Nalnish said.

"I know that Choovio was sincere. We share a common enemy right now," Ahote insisted. He stood against the wall. His face was already flush from arguing. Warriors filled the central kiva. They lined the stone bench that ran along the wall, and many more, those of lower standing, sat on the floor. "Today was a knot of snakes. It was an accidental fight between scared–"

"Tocho was not afraid of anything! And his spirit lies out there in the dark!" Pivane growled. His angular face looked even more harsh than usual. He gestured toward the roof. He craved war with the Morning Crows. Ahote turned on him.

"Not what I meant!" he raised his voice.

"We were retrieving our dead!" Pivane shot back. For the fifth time. Other young warriors nodded from the dirt floor, their jaws tight with hot emotion.

"I know. But how could they know that?" Ahote asked.

"Easy enough since they killed Pimne and Chua. It seems like they could have left the bodies to draw us out into Greedy Crow Canyon," Len said. He rose from the bench to address the group.

"My anger burns too. But the greater enemy must bring us together!" Ahote pleaded. He felt the argument slipping away. He could not change their minds; the Ash Owls would do nothing to stop the enemy stranger. Instead, they would attack those that hunted the demon. Ahote felt cold. Despite the rising heat in the room.

"I saw the enemy today. Choovio led them. He clearly lied to you. If they knew about the High Rocks wedding . . . maybe they wanted to trap us all. Maybe Pimne and Chua just happened to fall into their trap first. I was too young . . . but I have heard the story of Gathering Rock. How can we trust the Morning Crows?" Len retorted.

"That makes no sense. They would have just killed Ahote by the broken spine," Nalnish said. But Len pushed ahead.

"The enemy slaughtered good Ash Owl men today. They caught us in the shadow of Black Roof and murdered us. Pure and simple murder. How can that bring the two clans together for any purpose?" Len said.

"Never!" Pivane interjected.

"But we need to talk with Choovio again. We need to find out what he knows. I will accept the risk of going myself. I would not risk any—" Ahote said, making one last attempt.

"You would have us forgive all that spilled blood. Should we hold hands with those devils and hunt an imaginary demon?" Len declared.

"I say never!" Pivane interjected again, more forcefully this time. Other young warriors murmured assent, almost jumping to their feet in angry agreement. Len saw that his words had found their mark. He sat back down.

Ahote continued to stand, feeling both hostility and contempt from the younger warriors now. It felt like ice pelting his skin. He wondered if they were right. He could feel the pain of loss rising inside him, even as the death of his friends still seemed unreal. Seeds of doubt and guilt were splitting open. Was he wrong about Choovio and his motives? Was he foolish to trust the Morning Crows? Ahote felt that he would hate them more tomorrow. In a certain room of his heart, he even hoped for it.

Istaqa looked at Kotori. His eyebrow hiked into a silent question. The room wanted revenge. It burned in their faces. Istaqa wanted it too. His own anger had stabilized but not dissipated. Unseen by all but Istaqa, Kotori shrugged. The room was hot and close. The shaman had removed his cloak to cool himself and looked out of place among the younger warriors. Complex shadows played over the throng of bodies. Istaqa nodded once.

"How can we not avenge the fallen?" Kotori asked. It was the first time he had spoken. All faces turned toward him. He remained seated, staring into the fire at the center of the room.

151

Its hot coals danced with heat. Like the breathing heart of the room, slowly transmuted to sacred ash. His red-streaked hair held the dark hue of blood in the dim light. "Who has hurt us more? The enemy stranger or the Morning Crows?"

Istaqa rose to his feet and pressed his hands together. Decision. "Nalnish and Ahote risked danger to bring us the story they have told. We must continue to respect their voices. But how can I lead if these murders provoke no answer?" he asked. He paused before he continued. "Ash Owls listen to me. We must make true war against the Morning Crows," Istaqa said. He did not raise his voice. He felt a trickle of sweat down his back.

Most of the warriors erupted into shouting. Ahote walked to the ladder and quickly left the kiva. Leaving the fire was potentially an act of disrespect. But Istaqa let him go. Only internal strife, and perhaps some broken bones, could result from Ahote pressing his point any further. Istaqa waited, his jaw clenched, for the room to settle. He saw that Nalnish stared silently at the floor.

"We must plan carefully and strike quickly. Tomorrow we retrieve the fallen and tend to their souls. After that we must avenge them. Kwatoko will lead the attack. Tocho has trained him well," Istaqa said.

~ B ~

The vampire heard nothing as he approached the cliff dwelling. No sounds of battle. No murmur of social activity even though the night was still relatively young. He doubted that they had left the safety of their fortress. They were likely on tense alert. However, if he could discern more about them, he could learn how to isolate his prey. He could pick them off. He could finish his fight with Makya. The vampire would, then, hunt the other ferals, but first, he wanted the boy who was biting them.

The vampire crept forward slowly, moving from shadow to shadow and scanning the land for guards. He assumed that they would control the farthest potential line of sight to the village, and before he was even close enough to the fortress to see its facade, he knelt down behind some tall fragrant bushes and waited. Like any good hunter he knew how to wait patiently. He saw that the wiry stems before him bore small yellow flowers. It smelled oddly like the black char of burnt walls.

The wind kicked up even further behind him, the first edge of the coming storm, cool and full of potential. He still smelled the faintest hint of stale blood on the wind. An hour passed. The vampire was finally rewarded for his patience. He saw an older man stand. He was posted well. Only halfway up the hill, concealed with deliberate skill. Dense shrubs sprayed from the slope. He rose from behind them and stared intently down into the valley. The vampire followed his gaze. The man had seen a deer trotting through the dark shade of the canyon, running ahead of the rain perhaps. The old warrior stretched his back and then, with great stiffness, lay back down. "A little too slow for that job," the vampire whispered.

The vampire had looked closely at those bushes, his senses itching. He was nonplussed that he had not seen the sentry sooner. But he still smiled as he collected himself. The decrepit guard would be an easy kill, almost a gift. It was always good to delay his hunger for another night, but even more important, it would allow the vampire an ideal vantage for observing the cliff dwelling: a spot selected by its very own sentry.

~ B ~

Istaqa stopped Kwatoko before he departed the kiva. Since Kwatoko now carried the burden of leading the Ash Owls after a tragic loss, Istaqa gripped his elbow and smiled sadly. The fire burned low now; the red light of dying coals darkened his face.

153

Istaqa watched the last warrior climb the ladder to leave the kiva. Kotori remained, watching them both.

Istaqa finally spoke, even more quiet than usual. "Are you ready?" he asked.

"My anger makes me ready," Kwatoko replied.

"Good. Please tell Ahote and Nalnish that I forbid them to meet Choovio. Tomorrow or ever. I did not wish to shame them before the warriors. But they must understand . . . we cannot trust Hototo. We cannot give him the means to deceive us. That path no longer exists after today."

"Agreed. We must not honor agreements broken by murder, especially when both the agreement and murder were by the same hand," Kwatoko said. "I will speak with Nalnish and Ahote before they sleep."

"And what of the enemy stranger . . . do we still fear this? Do we no longer believe this story?" Kotori asked.

"Just one more enemy," Istaqa said. "Just one more enemy now. Demons . . ." he trailed off. He smiled but only just.

"What is your thought?" Kotori asked.

"They are easier to kill than rumors of demons," Istaqa said. He gestured toward the ladder. Kotori would not bank the coals and offer the last prayer of the night until all others were gone.

~ B ~

The night was two parts gone of three when Honani woke Choovio from fitful sleep. "Choovio. My friend, wake up. Sowingwa is dead. The relief sentries have brought his body. You must see this."

Choovio nodded. He first pressed his palm against the forehead of Pavati, who slept next to him. Her wound, sustained while defending Crow Ledge from the High Rocks Clan, was deep; and the poison was rising in her blood. She was beginning to burn with fever. He felt the damp sheen of sweat in her hair. He slapped his own head to clear the mist of dreams. He would change her poultice when he returned, ask Shuman to provide him more healing plants to draw out the fever. Perhaps she could make a tea. He hoped that Hototo would return soon. He rose, vigorously shaking his head, and hurried to the outer courtyard.

Sowingwa was laid beside a new fire. The Morning Crow elder had volunteered to stand sentry despite his age. He was cold to touch now. They had already closed his eyes, and he wore a contented look on his face. He would never rub his sore knee again. "No blood," Honani whispered to him. The body looked desiccated. His skin looked pale.

"Like he died in the desert," Choovio said. He examined the skin. "Here?" he asked, touching the deep bite wound between shoulder and neck.

"Yes," Shuman said from behind them. "Do not touch it . . . such a powerful curse," she said. She carried a long spear. She walked directly to where the old man lay. Without hesitation, the old woman brought the spear high with both hands. She drove it down through his chest with all the lean force she possessed. The body did not react. It only took the force of the blow and returned to stillness.

"Shuman!" Honani and Choovio both shouted. They jumped back as the spear flashed between them.

"Why?" Choovio exclaimed. Honani held both hands high above his head, eyes wide with disbelief.

"The curse makes the dead as living. Like your brother has become. The enemy stranger is out there. Pull the other guards back into Crow Ledge," she said.

Choovio stared at her in stunned silence. Sowingwa and Shuman had been such close friends. She looked old and worn in the firelight now. The bruise on her jaw looked worse. She had undone her braid, and her dark eyes glared fiercely through the loose locks of gray hair that caught the wind. "We can cry when the sun rises. But the demon will pick off more of our people in the dark if we leave them out there," Shuman insisted.

"Of . . . of course," Choovio forced out. He had not thought of Makya as dead before now. A shiver passed through his heart. He nodded at Honani to give the signal.

~ B ~

Makya had never been to Smoke Ridge before. He had only seen the Oracular Tower while hunting in the canyon below. He knew that other buildings stood atop Smoke Ridge too. However, one did not visit the Smoke Clan. Spirit leaders and acolytes alone were welcomed. Perhaps clan leaders, like his father or Istaqa of the Ash Owls, could have visited. But they mostly did not.

Smoke Ridge was farther to the north. They had to cross the high plateau first. Hototo chose the path and set the quick pace through the night. Makya followed his lead. He sensed the tired labor of the older man but did not share it. He felt strong. Although dark clouds were coming behind them, the night still blazed with moonlight on the high plateau. The endless light of stars filled the sky. Makya had never seen them so bright. He could see the sagebrush around him distinctly. He could see depth among its leaves.

"I can see like the wolf now," Makya said.

"I know," Hototo replied tersely. "So warn me before I step in a gopher hole," he added to sound a warmer note. Within his bag, sewn from rare beaver leather, precious stones and distant seashells from the Morning Crow treasury clanked out the rhythm of their pace. The sibyl would require payment. Hototo also carried a second bag filled halfway with crystals of salt. He hoped not to spend them.

"What is the sibyl like?" Makya asked.

"We do not speak of this," Hototo said. "The sibyl will flare the bristles of your soul."

"Is the sibyl old?" Makya persisted. Hototo shook his head slowly.

"None speak of this," he insisted.

"What, then, will you ask? I wish to prepare myself. Will you ask the sibyl to lift this curse?"

"We do not ask. We tell your story. Then we wait for the sibyl to speak. This I learned when I trained as an acolyte: *you must not grab at smoke if you wish to see it clearly*," he said.

~ B ~

Jerome sat stiffly on the high cliff. He huddled under a tattered blanket, both for warmth and so that no metal might glint in the moonlight. He cradled his crossbow but doubted he would dare the long shot. Even if he could draw the prod undetected. Jerome had hoped the scourge would come to inspect the carnage in the canyon below. There had clearly been a battle after he had killed those two local boys, and Jerome had counted approximately ten dead natives as he hiked to his current location. He felt disappointed. Black streaks of dry blood across limbs and torsos and pooled in the sand beneath them: any vampire could smell that blood, would know that violence was near.

But now the night was ending, and rain was beginning to spatter around him. Lightning flashed angrily in the dark clouds above him. "Nobody knows you here, old Jove," Jerome muttered. "Time to get some sleep," he added, rubbing his sore back. He would return to his daytime camp to escape the rain. Jerome wanted to track the vampire to his hiding hole. His best chance was to corner the monster with the sun defending his back, but he would have little luck and lots of misery if he tried to find anything during a rainstorm.

He trotted back across the canyon floor, blanket now wrapped loosely around his gear. He passed the same dead warriors. He was surprised to find the bodies unmoved, especially since someone had born away the two warriors he had killed that morning. "These must be the losers," he shrugged.

"Or maybe this tribe just lets the buzzards take them . . . never thought I would see it. At least they all cover their manhood," he added.

When he reached the shelter of the rocky outcropping, still dry and hard to see into from any distance, Jerome tucked himself directly behind one of the rocks that obscured the entrance. He kept his hand against his sword and hoped that fatigue would take him into darkness, the coming daylight and storm guarding his back.

However, his mind drifted through the painful inventory of past failures instead. The debacle with the hounds. The pit trap that had killed three of their own. The brothel in Constantinople. The ambush in Angora; the *Fahreddin* had even helped that time. "Damn turbans!" he breathed. And the plains of Pagan continued to haunt him. Jerome had been so close. He could still hear the terrified shriek of that huge monkey. The vampire had grabbed it from the altar where it slept and swung it by both feet, a writhing mace. Jerome had parried the blow with his sword, his blade ripping into the torso. Blood had spattered his face as the vampire struck another blow. It had been a momentary shock, all the vampire needed to kick Jerome hard and pass his blockade.

Jerome shifted his back against the rock and adjusted his scabbard, shifting it on his belt. He needed sleep. He began to whisper the lyrics to remembered songs. It often helped him move his mind away from painful memories and into sleep. He finally drifted off, the ballad of a bawdy rooster falling from his sun-burnt lips.

~ B ~

Makya and Hototo neared the crest of Smoke Ridge in the gray light before dawn, made darker by the roof of storm clouds now fully overhead and filled with lightning. The first drops of rain spattered the hillside as they picked their way up the rocky trail. Small terraces of crops dotted the slopes. The corn looked withered and thin here. It needed the rain badly.

Hototo panted from the ascent as they finally reached the top. He had pushed himself all night to reach Smoke Ridge before morning. Makya could tell that the strength in his own legs had started to wane too. An urge to sleep pulled at his whole body now. It signaled the coming dawn. Across the ridge a number of smaller individual buildings fanned out around one central edifice and an adjoining courtyard. This primary cluster of rooms rose several levels at one end. In the gloom, it reminded Makya of one more storm cloud gathering itself atop the ridge, only made all of straight lines. Fires lit up several windows. The light danced there like the flashes of lightning that glowered truly in the sky above them.

As they moved closer, Makya also felt that it looked very exposed. It was built under the sky. Smoke Ridge, not constrained by the contour of living stone around it, reminded him of cactus clusters. Only sprung from stone and mortar. He noted with surprise that most of its walls were not plastered.

Hototo pointed past these buildings. "There," he said.

Their line of site had finally shifted to reveal a circular tower, isolated from the other buildings and slightly taller than anything else at Smoke Ridge. Constructed on the very edge of the ridge, it overlooked the steep cliff below and would soon offer an unimpeded view of the rising sun. The famed Oracular Tower. No longer seeing it from the canyon where he had spied it when he was younger, Makya thought it looked shorter than he had expected. The curved walls had narrow slits in the masonry, placed at varying heights, but Makya only saw several true windows from his current perspective. High on the top floor. Also very narrow.

Acrid smoke from several dying fires mixed with the fetid, sour smell of untended trash, unwashed pottery. Animal bones and broken pots were discarded along the path. "So dirty!" Makya whispered. Hototo nodded.

"They seek the unseen world where spirits reside. Perhaps one of their long ceremonies has just ended," he said. He wondered if the drought had hurt the Smoke Clan more deeply than he had realized.

"No walls. No security in the cliffs . . . houses on the ground. How do they defend themselves?"

"The Smoke Clan is powerful. But not like the Morning Crows. All clans know them. None would dare anger the spirits," Hototo said.

"They serve *all* the clans?" Makya asked.

"All who care to seek their wisdom. But there are other places of spiritual power as well among the Southern and Eastern clans. It has been too long since the last Great Meeting," Hototo said.

"Except the High Rocks Clan. They reject the spirits. Chayton respects nothing—"

"Do not speak of him here," Hototo interrupted. His face grew dark. The violence of the night before was too fresh.

"I apologize," Makya said. He hung his head respectfully.

As they entered the village, Makya saw the carcass of a large rattlesnake coiled on a roasting spit, over the ashes of a dying fire. Smoke hissed from it as the rain began to increase. Makya could smell the meat. He fought down the urge to gag. Two gaunt men, their eyes bloodshot, squatted near the fire. Their clothes were ragged. Makya recalled the beggars that came from Low Nest when he was young. Before Chayton had brought them out of squalor.

The sky was still dark, but Makya knew that dawn approached quickly. His strength continued to ebb. He was feeling the true magnitude of his new reality once again. "I must get under some roof soon," he said.

"I am aware," Hototo said. "The clouds might protect. But I am not sure of that. Now listen . . . you must not speak again unless prompted. Only spirit leaders may address the Smoke Clan as equals."

The two men watched Hototo and Makya approach but they did not stir. They gazed out with baleful disinterest. "Like they are dreaming awake," Makya whispered.

"Shhhh," Hototo insisted. A small stone bowl sat between them. Sacred leaves smoked over a hot coal. Hototo held out his bag and shook it. "I bring payment to see the sibyl. And for lodging before the sun rises. We must have it quickly," he said.

CHAPTER 12

A Nest Reclaimed

RAIN DANCED AGAINST the rocks. It flowed from above and tumbled past Low Nest, whose walls were safely recessed in the cliff, like tendrils of water falling and falling. Most of the High Rocks Clan still slept. The morning light, gray as flint, did not call them to rise. They were grateful for the sleep. Exhausted. Dreams both soothed and troubled by thunder.

Old Chu'Si walked with silent care across the terrace. She passed doorways where others still slept. She was always among the first to rise. She would not have stirred attention even if eyes had drowsily opened to see her pass. Her face was rigid, tight with determination. Her breath came quick, her body preparing to fight. She had heard the restless groans from the ritual kiva and kept her own vigil last night.

She clutched the sacred spear of the White Bat Clan. She had kept it hidden from Chayton for many years. He would have surely snapped it across his knee, defiled her people even further. It had not been enough that Chayton had killed their spirit leader, Cha'Akmongwi, and stolen his leadership of the White Bat Clan. Not enough that Chayton had soured her own authority. Not enough that a stranger had stripped the clan of its totem and forbid new spirit leaders. Chayton had also destroyed their emblems of spiritual power.

Much to her dismay, the High Rocks Clan had flourished anyway. They had grown from the ashes of the White Bats, Chayton somehow managing to bury the embers of resentment along the way. He had stolen the very soul of her people. Still, the matriarch had hidden this emblem of power from him, the great spear of the White Bat. She had tricked Chayton into burning a fake. And now she would call upon its power.

With the dawn, even obscured by the rain, silence had fallen inside the ritual kiva. She hoped to find the stricken warriors asleep. She hoped to use the lethargy that befell the undead at sunrise to her advantage. As she climbed down through the opening, the light of red coals bathed the walls. The morning added its own ashen light below the ladder. She saw them in the shadows. Her fingers trembled as she moved from rung to rung. Nuk lay on his back with eyes closed. Wik lay on his stomach near the fire pit. She saw the burns across his back.

And Sik sat on the low stone bench that circled the wall, eyes open but glassy. He stared at the sipapu near his feet, unblinking. He looked dead, as though he had waited in vain for the healing spirits to rise from the lower world and cure his affliction, as though he had watched his own spirit flow down the hole in the night. All three looked drained and ill, too much gray in their color. Barely touched cakes of corn lay near the fire pit. Clay pots littered the open floor. Some held water, some the tea she had prepared, others the undigested vomit produced from their hunger and thirst. The spattered mess around those pots testified to the violent reaction. Two were overturned. The old woman took a slow breath and held it.

She gripped the sacred spear tightly and walked slowly toward Sik. He was the strongest of the three. She thought she needed to kill him first to have any chance of success. The fact that his eyes were not closed made him an even more urgent target. Old Chu'Si was old but not frail. Her arms were lean from pounding corn, butchering game. She bent her knees and, hands level with her hips, prepared to thrust the spear at his heart.

However, as she took one last step forward, her toes kicked a plate. It made a muted *clink* against the dirt floor. She saw the glazed eyes come into sudden focus. She also saw the folly of her errand. She felt the terror of those dead eyes and knew that her mistake could not be unmade. She felt her limbs turn to clay. Even so, she saw no path but forward. Fear and acceptance were suddenly cords in a single braid.

She turned her hips into the blow and thrust the spear with all her strength. Sik had just an instant to react. He twisted his body to avoid the blow. While the spear still landed, biting deep into his flesh, it missed the heart. It found his shoulder joint instead. Fangs bared and eyes instantly lit with rage, the cursed warrior grabbed the shaft of the spear with both hands. He simultaneously kicked the old woman hard across the hip. The painful blow broke her grip.

Old Chu'Si stumbled sideways. Some storage baskets filled with corn confounded her steps. Pitching forward, the matriarch struck her head against the stone wall of the kiva. Dry corn spilled across the floor. Like sharp gravel under her knees. "Unh!" she gasped. She was able to stifle her pain. However, she could not stop the tang of her blood, dark and stubborn, from finding the air.

The others awoke. They did not understand, but instinct consumed them; they felt the powerful drive to feed that ruled the newly undead. They saw Sik injured against the wall, the White Bat spear jutting from his shoulder. Charms and beads swung from its shaft. They smelled the trickle of blood forming on the forehead of the old woman. Old Chu'Si staggered to her feet. She saw no hope for escape but still moved. Pain contorted her mouth. "No! Stop! You know me!" she begged quickly.

Hunger transmuted into violence, the demons launched across the room with blind animal ferocity. She took several quick strides, the wading gait of an old woman, but could not reach the ladder. She managed only to bark "Chayton!" as they reached her. A desperate cry to a lesser enemy.

~ B ~

Chayton still kept his long vigil as sentry but had moved to the eastern corner of Low Nest before dawn. He looked out toward Seven Sisters Canyon now, believing any danger would surely come from Crow Ledge, perhaps at first light. He also watched the rivulets of falling water, a bowl of stewed beans half eaten beside him. He thought back many years and far to the east, recalling his former home among the curving hills of tall grass. The grass danced differently when the rain fell. It bounced like children pleased with a gift. He recalled how hues of green would deepen, become almost bright, with the arrival of storms. He missed that un-crowded horizon, land meeting sky with a gentle and unbroken line.

"Chayton!"

Despite the clamor of rain and the thick walls of the kiva, the hoarse cry from Old Chu'Si still punctured his thoughts like a needle. Panic filled her voice. He was used to hearing only scorn. The hair rose up across the back of his neck. He grabbed his war club, longer than his thigh and curved toward the target, handle wrapped in worn bison hide. He was on his feet, running and cursing to himself. "That crazy old," he growled. Chayton immediately intuited that the old woman had done something rash.

The clan leader hurled his feet past the ladder. His hands barely brushed the rungs, but he landed well, knees bent to react. He spun to survey the room. He first saw an ornate spear lying at the edge of the dying coals. He knew it instantly as a ceremonial weapon, an instrument of authority. Chayton had not seen it for many years. He had dropped it into the fire himself. He had watched it burn.

Motion quickly changed his focus. For one frozen moment, Chayton could not understand the scene before him. Three warriors on their knees, arms braced against the lifeless body of Old Chu'Si, their heads pressed and working against her neck and face. Sik, the strongest of his warriors and almost as tall as Chayton himself, turned and looked at Chayton. His mouth was

165

smeared with gore and fanged like a coyote. Chayton saw liquid blood pooled in his mouth. Nuk and Wik also glanced up like surprised animals. Chayton saw the visage of the old woman as they pulled away, now mangled and bloody. Clearly dead. "No!" he said. Shock and horror sapped all emotion from his voice. He understood instantly what he had rejected the previous morning.

He lunged at them and swung his war club. Its heavy stone head struck Sik directly across the nose with an ugly sound, bone snapping beneath the *thwump* of impact. Sik rolled backwards. Chayton felt the transfer of lethal force from his wrist. A killing blow for certain. He preserved the momentum of his club and let it carry his hands above his head through one fluid motion, ready to bring it down against the skull of Nuk, now nearest him. Both Wik and Nuk lunged at him. Although the dawn limited their immortal strength, hot blood still surged fresh in their veins. But Chayton was quick. His club still caught Nuk in the back as he dove forward. He knocked the cursed warrior onto his hands and knees.

"Nooo!" Chayton barked again. No time to say or think more. Wik uncoiled into his ribs, lifting Chayton off the ground and slamming him violently against the floor of the kiva. Pain exploded across the back of his head. Chayton gasped for wind. Wik grabbed his wrists and, pushing them away, rose up with bared fangs. The clan leader, still the better fighter, twisted and arched, using the momentum of his attacker to throw Wik forward and over his head, into the hearth shield. Chayton rolled to his feet, clutching his club, and bolted for the ladder. Just a few desperate steps away.

Chayton jumped, landing several rungs from the floor, and began to climb. But Nuk had regained his feet. He jerked the bottom of the heavy ladder loose from where it had settled and dragged it, in one violent motion, down into the kiva, bringing the leader of Low Nest down with it. *Thwack!* The ladder slapped hard against the dirt floor. Chayton spun to land on his feet. He stumbled back against the stone wall of the kiva as Nuk charged after him. Chayton swung his club past the blocking hand, caught his attacker hard in the ribcage. Nuk crumpled but grabbed Chayton around the ankles as he fell. And then Wik was upon Chayton, catching him from the left before he could clear his club to swing again. The two of them twisted the leader of Low Nest to the ground. Chayton looked across the room, still trying to break their strong grip. He saw Sik rise to his feet, his nose utterly destroyed, the whole center of his fractured face bashed in. He did not bleed, save a few smeared drops. He bared his fangs and hissed, all his pain channeled into rage now. "How dare you attack us?" Sik hissed. "We will cut that long hair at last."

"I serve Low Nest! Stop this–" Chayton gasped. But Sik leaped across the fire pit and closed on the struggling leader, dead eyes shining, even as he put the dim light to his back.

~ B ~

Tocho grimaced. He smeared the rough paste of clay and mesquite sap across the gash in his thigh. He had wetted it with rain and worked the mixture together on a flat stone. He had seen Kotori prepare wounds in this way. More or less. He had escaped yesterday, in the chaos of killing, from the Morning Crows that pursued him.

One of his men had fallen behind him and distracted the Crows in their savage work; and at that moment, Tocho had veered left and escaped their line of sight. He had spotted an eroded ravine and tumbled to the bottom. Dense brush choked the bottom. Panting hard, he had dragged himself into the tangle of stalks and limbs. He had trembled all over. And then, as his breath slowed, he had finally heard the enemy trail away. Time vanished into the monotony of pain after that. Hot sweat yielded to cold chills. He had felt the dirt meld into the sticky gore beneath him. The gash was deep. Only terror had kept him moving before. The surge of battle. He pressed both hands hard against his eyes.

"Why . . . why would they?" he whispered softly.

Tocho had eventually realized that he needed to move. He had needed to bind his wound. Predators would smell the drying blood, the fresh blood when night came. The war leader used his breechcloth to bind his thigh and then, with slow effort, crawled to the top of the ravine at its other end. He scanned the ground, spying an abandoned den at the base of the nearest cliff, really nothing more than a slit in the rocks. It was clean enough and shaded, obscured by some stunted trees. He saw several mesquites.

Tocho had waited until the sun began its descent. He had struggled to his feet and then, fighting down the intense pain that jarred him with every step, hopped toward the hole on his good leg. Halfway across, he washed himself with his own urine—too amber already—and with handfuls of sandy dirt. To kill the smell of blood. And then Tocho finally slipped inside. He pulled loose brush across the entrance. He had collapsed there. He had passed the night slowly in feverish cold and muddy time.

Tocho dressed his wound carefully now. He watched the rain fall outside. It answered his need for water. But he did not believe he could walk. Not far enough. He did not dare drag himself into the daylight and chance discovery by the Morning Crows yet. Such an ambush before. So many warriors. He could only guess what insanity had motivated such a vicious attack, why they would run down the stragglers who fled. "Murder!" he spat with disgust. He chose to wait. He watched the sluice of muddy water, the shallow wash only two spears away. Istaqa would send warriors to gather the dead. Many warriors this time. They would not find his body at the scene of the battle. And then he could hope for rescue. They would search for him then.

~ B ~

"What happened? Are you alright?" someone called out from above.

"Stay out . . . tell everybody to stay away. Just a disagreement. Have to explain later!" Nuk shouted up to the crowd. His voice shook a little despite his best efforts. He stood far from the mouth of the kiva. Blood still smeared his lips.

"Do you need another ladder?" another young warrior shouted. He stood right at the mouth of the kiva.

"We will explain later. Just go back to your work."

"But is somebody hurt?" the young man insisted.

"We need privacy! We will explain later!" Wik shouted.

"This is Sik. Please just give us time to talk alone. We have important matters to discuss today. And replace Chayton as sentry. His time is over." He sounded calm, more reasonable. After a moment of uncertainty, the concerned murmur started to drift away. While the other two were respected warriors, they did not wield the authority that Sik, as war leader for the High Rocks Clan, could bring to bear. His assurance had done the trick.

Nuk nodded to Sik. "Now what?" he asked softly.

"He came from over the mountains. Not true blood of our clan," Wik said. He stood with Nuk and Sik in the dark shadows of the kiva. Broken pottery littered the floor now. The mangled body of Chayton lay at their feet. They had drained his blood and healed their own wounds. That healing fire had been enough for Nuk. He had stepped away and gaped at what he had just done. He had wiped the blood from his lips.

But the other two had gone further. They had been betrayed, attacked by both clan leader and matriarch. And even as the gush of blood had fallen slack, the anger of battle had not. Rage had rushed into their bloody thirst. Taken it over. The urge to defile Chayton, to answer his betrayal even in death, had blinded them. They had torn chunks of his flesh with their teeth and swallowed them. And it had not sickened them as the earlier food had done. No meat had ever tasted better.

"Old Chu'Si though . . ." Nuk trailed off. None of them dared bring forth the words. None of them looked toward her body either. They did not want to see the carnage. Their fathers had danced and sang in sacred rituals in this space many years ago; and now those memories, dormant but full of childhood wonder, felt both fresh and irrevocably marred by what they had done. It was almost too much for them. They could not understand their own actions, even as the blood sang in their veins.

Sik shook his head and spoke quietly. "She tried to kill us. We defended ourselves. Chayton wanted to kill us too." He tipped his head and lifted his hand, calling attention to his smashed face.

"But the blood," Nuk whispered.

"We are changed. We have the power of the enemy stranger now. Do you not remember the old stories?" Sik said.

"Barely . . . we have not heard such tales for many years. Chayton insisted that they were lies!" Wik replied. He saw now that Chayton had lied. The old woman had spoken the truth about Chayton after all.

"How do the Morning Crows have such a powerful curse? Does Hototo have such potent magic?" Nuk asked.

"It was the bite from Makya. Like snake poison," Wik added.

"It makes us strong. No matter how Makya came by it. That club should have killed me. We can turn the curse of our enemies against them!" Sik said excitedly. His shoulder had healed completely, but the center of his face was still badly disfigured. He did not understand why. He only knew that it no longer hurt.

"But we will thirst for blood. Is that not the way of the enemy stranger?" Nuk asked.

"The power to spill the blood of the Morning Crows . . . we have wanted that for as long as I can remember. Is this any curse at all?" Sik replied.

They regarded each other silently now. Wik strode across the room and picked up the Spear of the White Bat. He waved it toward Chayton's defiled body. "This is the work of the sacred spirits then. How dare this man, this stranger from another land, ask us to renounce the spirits, the totems of our ancestors? How could we exist without them? See this?" he waved the spear at them. "Old Chu'Si sacrificed herself to save us all, to bring this back to us and remind us who we really are. Do you not see? She brought the return of the White Bat Clan."

~ B ~

Choovio stood at the base of Crow Ledge. Mud oozed around his toes. Harder rain now. He licked the cold water that ran across his lips. He thought of his pledge to meet Ahote, but the bloody battle with the Ash Owls had intruded. It swirled behind his eyes like dead leaves churning in the wind.

"I think you are clean enough," Honani said, stepping down the ladder to join him.

"What?"

"The rain . . . I think it has washed you clean," Honani repeated.

"Has it? I am not sure that I feel clean. I was supposed to meet Ahote today. The rain disagrees. I will have to wait until tomorrow," Choovio said.

"You should not go. The Ash Owls attacked us yesterday, even in our own territory. We had to fight back. If we had fewer warriors there . . . who knows what might have happened?" Honani said.

"Ahote was not there," Choovio said.

"What does that mean?" Honani shrugged. "He left us early. He had time to reach Firetown and tell Istaqa your plan.

Maybe that . . . maybe that was why he wanted to talk with you. To learn our plan. Pretty clever if you thin–"

"No!" Choovio interrupted, suddenly angry. He turned and jabbed his finger toward the nose of his friend. "No. He did not trick me."

Honani slapped the finger away. He could not match Choovio if they fought. But no warrior could allow that affront. Especially from a friend. "Well . . . then maybe he got lost on the way home. Maybe the enemy stranger ate him. Or maybe Ahote has no influence." Honani offered a forced smile. Rain dripped from the tip of his nose.

The anger faded quickly. "Perhaps. But would Istaqa really dishonor the pledge that Ahote made on behalf of the Ash Owls?" Choovio asked. He stepped back beside Honani, an unspoken apology of sorts.

"These . . . these . . . these Ash Owls . . . they are not like us. Honor does not matter to them like it does to the Morning Crows," Honani said.

Choovio nodded. He said nothing. Honani pressed him. "You know this. These are the same wicked men that killed Saya. Snakes breed snakes."

"Ahote did not kill my father," Choovio said. Quietly.

"He sleeps with those that did. Hears their words."

"But my gut says that he spoke true when we met," Choovio said.

"We cannot trust the Ash Owls. Especially now. Even if Ahote had good intentions before, they will lust for revenge no matter what. Such buzzards always do. And how can they not after what we did yesterday?" Honani said.

Choovio said nothing. But the memory of Saya, his father, the late leader of the Morning Crow Clan, filled the back of his eyes now. His hate for the Ash Owls kindled easily enough. He recalled the cool touch of his father's arm as his body lay across the sipapu. He recalled the dark bruises, the blood thickly matted in his hair. And somehow worst of all, he recalled two broken fingers that dangled crookedly from the hand. "My father had strong hands," he said into the rain.

"I will leave you to think," Honani said. "We will bury Lusio and Ayawamat when the rain stops. And Sowingwa," he added.

~ B ~

So unwilling for so many years, the rain now tumbled down the rocks and gathered into improvised torrents. Like the grinning trickster, it puddled the fields and slicked climbing paths with mud. Prayers for rain answered with mayhem. It hid the sun, set the deep colors of the land against the dark sky.

Silent and grim like shadows cut loose from the hills, the Ash Owls appeared quickly below Black Roof, many of them. They swiftly gathered the dead. Four men per fallen warrior, they lifted them, now stiff and muddy, with a long loop of braided yucca fibers. They twisted it beneath the body so that two strands crossed below the back, forming two linked circles, one on each side of the body. Each cold arm was then looped, strands rising over the armpit and back down under the shoulder next to the neck. Each cold thigh was then looped in the same fashion, strap brought across the top of the thigh and down over the groin.

The four warriors then pulled the cord up at each limb, four short loops emerging above the shoulders and hips. They inserted their spears through these loops and lifted to their own shoulders. This was the ritual binding and carrying of the soul. It would hold the soul, ensure that it stayed with the flesh, until the spirit leader could open the sipapu and allow its return to the lower world. It was also an assertion that many remained alive, that many would carry on for the fallen. Kotori sprinkled a quick toss of sacred ash where each man had lain.

The Ash Owls vanished back into the rain. Still silent. Unseen by all. They saw that Tocho was missing. But the rain had erased all trace of his flight from the scene. They would scout again, get high and survey the canyons, when the weather allowed. But they could do nothing else now. The rain persisted, even after their return to Firetown.

And then, one more trick, it ceased as the night returned.

CHAPTER 13

Supplicant

"'THE SIBYL WILL hear you now," the woman whispered, an emissary from the leader of Smoke Clan, who refused to greet them himself. She looked old and gaunt, her hair almost white, bones sharp below her neck, as she squatted in the doorway. Many strings of pink shells clanked on her wrists and across her breasts as she gestured for them to depart. She did not look at Hototo and Makya. In her other hand she cupped a jar made of clay. A wick burned out the top. It smoked heavily.

They had been given refuge in a small storage shelter away from the primary dwelling. Rough mats were laid across the dirt. They had slept there for much of the day. The same woman had brought them stew in the afternoon, mostly chunks of fresh squash and some roasted chiles. Makya had not even put the bowl to his lips. He had watched Hototo devour both servings, even adding a sprinkle of salt from his bag.

Makya had rejected the food quietly and shown little emotion. But it had strained his tangled emotions. He wanted to share a meal with his family once again. He wanted Sihu to accept him. And he knew that the simple act of eating again would restore her confidence. But all desire for food had vanished; he could find its memory but not the thing itself. It had disgusted him to watch the spirit leader chewing the squash, slurping the last of the broth. Makya wanted the sibyl to cure him. He knew that he did. He wanted her to return his appetite to normal, but the thought of it also turned his stomach.

They rose now and stepped out into the fresh moonlight. Their feet sank in mud. More snakes hung over the spit now in the courtyard. Wet wood hissed and smoked beneath them.

Members of the Smoke Clan now gathered near the flames, not as many as Makya would have expected, but he saw that a few hung back beyond the firelight as well, perhaps sentries around the ceremonial space. Within the lighted area, several young men wore large masks, colorful and unfamiliar to Makya. One of the younger women, wearing nothing but many strings of beads, held a crude effigy made from bound branches, tied with ragged strips of red cloth. "Will they burn it?" Makya whispered. He sought to distract himself from his own rising anxiety. Hototo did not answer. The men and women around the fire stopped silent as the two strangers crossed the yard.

They finally reached the opposite edge of the Smoke Ridge buildings. The woman nodded toward the entrance to the Oracular Tower and handed Makya the lamp. "Up the stairs," she said.

"Prepare yourself," Hototo whispered. "And do not avert your eyes," he added.

~ B ~

Pavati shivered as Sihu dabbed a wet rag across her head. The injured wife of Choovio had just vomited into a small bowl. "The night makes it worse. Your fever is definitely climbing," Sihu said. She creased the corners of her mouth with concern.

"Where is Kaya?" Pavati whispered. Her daughter had left a small doll by her blanket, constructed from corn husks and decorated with strips of blue cloth. Pavati motioned toward the doll as she spoke.

"She is helping Shuman make more tea for you."

"Good. Where are your little boys?"

"The same."

"Tea sounds a little scary then. Should I drink it?" Pavati joked. Her teeth chattered slightly. She offered a weak smile.

"I know my boys. I will check for rocks and bugs before I let you take a sip," Sihu assured her. The two women silently exchanged a long searching look.

"I'm sure the Smoke Clan can help Makya. Hototo will not give them any other choice," Pavati said

"I am sorry. If Makya had not left Crow Ledge the other day . . ."

"I saw the man who stabbed me. Such hatred in his eyes. Just like all those High Rocks men. I blame them for this, Si-Si. Not your husband," Pavati insisted.

Sihu nodded and gently adjusted the plain blanket. However, she had seen Shuman stab the body of Sowingwa the night before. It danced on the back of her eyes. She had seen the gory blade of the spear pulled free from his chest. Shuman had pinned her bare heel against his shoulder to remove it cleanly. Sihu had feared Makya before he departed, but if the curse was not lifted, she also feared what Shuman, thinking as both grandmother and matriarch, might ask her to do. "I will empty this bowl before it fouls the air in here," she said.

~ B ~

Tocho hobbled, as night settled across the land, slowly away from his alcove in the rocks. He felt partially restored from drinking the plentiful rain. His fever, not really gone, did not rage at least. He wanted to return to Greedy Crow Canyon, the main path in the area, and thought that, even if he could not make it back to Firetown tonight, he could find another place to hide, closer and with a better vantage point. Making slow progress across the muddy ground, he took small, careful steps.

Some water still flowed down the center of the streambed, a comforting sound. He had time to take in the beauty of the moon behind the clearing remnants of cloud. Now that the rain had stopped, its fresh smell filled the gentle wind. But he briefly smelled another odor as well, the faint trace of a pungent stench.

However, he had left Firetown before Ahote had returned from his meeting with Choovio. He thought little of the strange smell, only wondering what wet animal could stink like that.

He had lost his best spear when he fled. He would need to make a new one when he returned. He tried to think about that, how he wanted it to look, how he would shape the point, what length he would choose: instead of the nauseating pain that pulsed up his leg and filled his bowels with each step. A patient man, he liked making things, not only pottery but also tools and weapons. He wondered whether a spear with points at both ends would still fly true. Beads of sweat gathered on his face as he forced his injured leg forward. Tocho wondered if you could feather a spear like a giant arrow. "Maybe with turkey fea- feathers," he winced.

~ B ~

From his hiding place, Jerome saw the lone native limp slowly out into the clearing. Clearly no vampire. He could see his injured leg in the moonlight. It was wrapped in a bloody cloth. "Is this guy bait?" he whispered. The knight watched cautiously and scanned the hills. He could detect no trap. No excessive quiet in the shadows. He watched the wounded man for a while. His progress was painfully slow. He wondered if the vampire was close and how he might turn this scene to his advantage.

He saw that the injured local would soon pass below a rocky ledge, about as high as a tall roof, with irregular boulders sloping up the hill around and behind. It looked big enough to conceal his position. Jerome thought the ledge might give him tactical advantage and defensive position, even against the great strength and speed of the vampire. If only he could get the monster to stand below it.

The knight closed his eyes. He thought again of how close they had come in that whorehouse in the worst corner of

Constantinople. Walls dark with smoke and grime. The stench of intercourse and disease barely cut by the smell of perfumes and spices. "Third room down that hall," the man had told them, festering sores on his mouth and hands. He had demanded payment and jingled the coins as they rushed past him.

They had caught the vampire feeding: teeth sank deep into the neck, blood surging through his veins, line of sight focused on his naked victim. He was distracted. But at that moment of revelation, an attacker had exploded into them from across the hallway. Jerome had sprawled headlong across the filthy room, another knight crashing into him, his sword pinned against the wall. The dim lamp had overturned, starting a blaze. "If that pus-ridden fool had warned us. If we had only known about the acolyte," Jerome shook his head.

"Well . . . maybe bait is what I need," he said. He surveyed the scene one last time, moved stiffly to his feet and trotted toward the injured warrior, weapons in hand.

~ B ~

Tocho heard the muffled clanking sound and turned. He saw a bizarre stranger hurrying toward the dry wash that lay between them, dangerous intensity written into his every movement. A long blade of some sort banged at his side. He wore a strange hat that looked hard and caught the moonlight. He also wore a shirt of the same material. It looked like fish scales and seemed heavy in the way it moved against the stranger's body. "Not now . . . not this," Tocho muttered. Unlike most of the Ash Owls, he had actually seen enemy strangers when he was very young. Two of them watching the village one night. However, the alarm had been raised, and those particular demons had vanished into the night. That had been far to the north, back at Coyote Bluff. That had been before the drought had begun to choke his birth clan with its brittle hands, desiccated and relentless, before his family arrived as refugees to Firetown. Other refugees had arrived too. The leaders of the Ash Owls, even before Istaqa, had wisely put them all to work. They had built new quarters, extended the irrigation trenches. The fall of the Laughing Coyotes had made the Ash Owls even stronger.

He did not speak of those early years at Coyote Bluff. Few remembered that he had come to Firetown as a refugee child, and he did not wish to remind them. However, he had never forgotten the look of the enemy strangers: the long blades, the strange clothes, hair the color of sand. And while this man looked the same in some respects, he also looked different. He had spent many days in the sun. Tocho recalled the skin of the enemy strangers most of all. It had been white like distant mountain peaks. "No," he thought. "Like larvae dug from the dirt."

Tocho turned to the man running toward him, now splashing through the water. He knew he could not run. His body felt like a jar full of dirt. His heart pounded and his breath came quick with fear. Even so, the shaggy beard amazed him as the man came closer. And Tocho saw that he carried some sort of bow with a long handle. He saw the short arrow sitting against the string. He had seen nothing like it but quickly guessed how it worked.

Although Tocho could tell that the man was a threat, he still sensed none of the empty terror that he associated with enemy strangers. This man smiled and spoke to him as he approached. "Stand right where you are," the man said, his teeth bared.

He could not understand the approaching stranger, although he suddenly understood the odor he had caught a few moments before. Tocho held out his hands. He showed his palms and then gestured toward Firetown.

~ B ~

"I need help. Please help me. My home is over there. But my leg is injured," the wounded warrior said.

Jerome guessed close enough at the hand gestures but he did not understand the words. He also saw that the young man balanced well on one leg. He did not need to hop or correct his stance. The knight kept walking quickly toward him. He removed his metal helmet from his head and gripped it tightly on the side, the short neck guard of chain mail clinking against the base of the cap as it hung.

"Just tell me every last detail. I am surely quite interested. Who did this to you?" Jerome replied with soothing calm. He closed the last few steps with confident purpose, intending to release the smell of fresh blood into the air.

~ B ~

"Wait. Sto—" Tocho begged. The stranger reached his range and swung his hat as hard as he could. He swung around the supplicant posture that Tocho had struck. Pain exploded across Tocho's face. He shut his eyes; the dark swam with crimson and purple. Tocho crumpled with the first blow, but the man smashed the hat into his face three more times. First across the cheek. Then directly across the nose. Then the man feinted left and smashed his nose again. Its hollow clunk sounded the force of each blow. Tocho's ears rang like never before. He just laid there, head buried in his hands. Warm blood gushed from his nose.

And yet no more blows came. He heard the stranger walking away from him. Now he heard scree on the hillside. The man was climbing nearby. He spit blood into the dirt as it ran down the back of his throat. He still had no desire to open his eyes. His skull felt like a jug poured full of sloshing pain, but he had nothing left to lose. He felt sure that the man was toying with him sadistically. He yelled into the dirt, heedless of the spray of blood from his mouth. "All those weapons . . . and you just smash my face with your hat?"

"Good boy! Make some noise too!" the man whispered loudly from the ledge above. Tocho drifted into a fog of rising pain. He had little energy left for such abuse, his reservoir already depleted.

~ B ~

Narrow stone stairs curved up the interior wall of the Oracular Tower. Smooth and hewn with uniform precision, they continued through the portal to the second story. An attendant stood along the steps. She wore a brown tunic and several strings of pink shells. She looked strong and vibrant. Makya saw her clearly in the dark. Like an ideal Morning Crow wife if she had braided her long hair properly. But she did not smile or greet them, and as she turned her head fully toward them, Makya saw that one eye looked off and did not track them.

"The sibyl is ready," she said. She gestured toward the hole in the ceiling. Hototo nodded. He thanked her softly and, although the Smoke Clan had already received payment, he gave her several shells from his depleted purse. Small but prized, they were narrow and shaped like a twisted needle. She still frowned.

Makya looked around in the meantime. He sought signs of magic and power from which to draw assurance. The first story was surprisingly empty, especially for the size of the room. Far from the entrance he saw a sleeping mat and several folded blankets. Some plates and bowls were stacked on a stone ledge nearby. He saw some sewing bones and cloth, some sandals half constructed, some finished pairs piled next to them. A heap of slender yucca leaves. Makya also noted that the tower smelled of constant habitation, a sour undercurrent hanging in the air.

They climbed, leaving the attendant below them, to the second story. Moonlight cut through the slits in the wall. Makya saw that it was crowded, only used for storage. Many clay vessels. A large and attractive platter of Ash Owl design leaned against the wall. Stacks of kindling wood. Herbs and medicinal plants in neat piles. Some he did not recognize. Rows of dried meat hung across several poles. A large cloak of vivid feathers, mostly red and green, hung from the end of one of the poles, and two large spotted furs were laid across another long storage ledge. The hides partially draped the wall. Gems and shells were piled across them, many more than the Morning Crows possessed. Makya had never seen such riches. "Are those from jaguars?" Makya whispered. He had seen that animal only once from a great distance.

"Ssshh," Hototo hissed. They continued to the top level. Pots and jars were crowded near the landing. Three large vessels adorned with White Bat designs screened the first glance across the room. Looking over them, Makya could see the high windows, one for each of the four horizons. The night stars shone bright in the frame of shadows. He also saw that drawings adorned the walls all around. He saw the spirits of the harvest and rain, animals and men from the lower world, symbols of power that he did not understand. Five thin figures, arms concealed beneath shrouds, thin slits for eyes, haunted the wall near the stairs, unnerving stillness in their form. His breath quickened with anticipation.

And then as Hototo stepped away from the stairs, allowing Makya to step full into the room, the small lamp reached across the room with light from its erratic flame. It moved his eyes to the sibyl. At that moment, Makya could not understand what he saw.

He inhaled sharply and looked at the ground when finally he did. The sibyl spoke. Two voices together. "Do you dare look away from what the spirits dare do?" Not harsh but not kind, loud in the silence of the stone room.

"We ask your pardon," Hototo said meekly. Makya forced himself to return his gaze. He saw two women sitting close together, heads fused together along the side the skull, hair parted where one head joined the other. His own head felt light and far away. He had never seen or even imagined that such a thing was possible. Both pairs of eyes burned into him, the same look twice. Twins. Each woman contorted to meet the endless union between them, the left twin more twisted than the right. Both atrophy and muscular rigidity marred their frames. Makya thought of crooked trees clinging stubbornly to an eroded cliff. The two women were naked above the waist. Animal skins were draped across their legs. One large necklace spanned both necks, a web of turquoise and amber that dangled between them. Makya saw insects trapped in the amber.

"Step closer," the two voices said.

"Thank you. Sibyl of the Smoke Clan . . . we would hear what you see from this high place," Hototo said. A formal greeting of respect. Makya thought it strange to hear Hototo defer to anybody.

"We accept your audience," the two voices said in perfect unison.

"On your knees now," Hototo whispered softly. Both men knelt as they might for kiva rituals. They were perhaps one body length from the stone bench, matted like a large bed, where the sibyl sat. Makya rested the smoky lamp on the floor before him. Long silence fell across the room.

The dim flame, driving back the light of the moon, lit their faces now. Four keen eyes bored into him. The twins had sallow skin but only a few strands of gray in their hair. Makya could not tell their age. Maybe old but maybe only ravaged by their fate. Makya thought that perhaps the sibyl could not physically leave this room. And yet still his heart chilled. He felt the blood pulsing through both bodies. He felt hunger stir in his veins. His soul protested.

The left twin broke the silence. "Hototo . . . you have brought an enemy stranger before us. His eyes glint in the moonlight. Show your teeth," she said. Makya bared his new fangs. To his horror, it further stirred his hunger to bring them forth.

"This boy leads warriors with honor and tends well his home. He is Morning Crow . . . and so truly not enemy or stranger to us. I have brought him before you because I seek wisdom. What must we do?" Hototo said. He bowed his head.

The left twin replied. "The curse passes by bite. Join the night or die then. An enemy stranger found your neck, did he not?" she asked. Both twins shifted forward.

Makya nodded.

Both voices again. "Tell us your story and bring no lies. We must hear the truth here. Nothing else matters," the sibyl said. An angry edge in the words.

"You may speak now," Hototo breathed, still looking at the floor. Makya nodded once more and began. He was relieved to turn his gaze inward and recite. He was relieved to tell his story too. To lay his uncertain future at the feet of an arbiter. He told the sibyl everything. But he did not tell the twins that he could feel the blood in their veins. The right twin said nothing. The left twin occasionally asked questions. She asked about the taste of blood.

"Like animal blood filled with fire," Makya said. She stopped him again when he spoke of the battle at Crow Ledge.

"Did you feel the curse passing when you ripped the necks of those White Bats?"

"They call themselves the High Rocks Clan now," Hototo interjected.

"Do you steal the bat from its cave by forgetting its name?" the left twin snapped sharply. Both heads turned as she shifted to stare at him more fully.

"No . . . pardon my words," Hototo said.

"Please tell us this. Did you feel the curse impart?" the left twin repeated.

Makya shook his head. "I did not. Do you think that I changed those warriors when I bit them?" That idea had not occurred to Makya. It scared him. He thought of Sihu and his sons unguarded in the claws of the night. Both twins nodded slightly by dipping their heads in unison.

"Do you feel that you are the enemy?" the left twin asked.

"Never," Makya replied. He saw the right twin smile at the corner of her mouth. Her eyes looked sad. Less glaring than before. She shifted her hand, adjusting the place where she braced against the bench. The left twin showed no emotion, her lips pressed tightly together.

Both twins spoke now. "Very well. Now leave this tower. Hoard this encounter in your heart. Speak nothing of the sibyl and never shall your secrets leave this chamber," the two voices said in unison.

Makya looked at Hototo. He raised his eyebrows in silent query. Hototo understood. "Only spirit leaders may hear the counsel of the sibyl. Please go down and wait for me at the head of the trail. I will learn what we wish to know," he said softly.

CHAPTER 14

Cruel Choices

THE VAMPIRE WATCHED from the shadows. The sight and smell of blood tugged. However, they did not move his feet. "Discipline thine appetite," he repeated softly. He saw the wounded warrior struggle back to his feet, badly favoring one leg. His eye had closed with sudden swelling. His nose looked bad too. He yelled up the cliff. "Kill me then!" The Knight of St. John instantly poked his head over the rocks.

"Sit down! Need you right there!" Jerome hissed from under his blanket. He whispered, but his voice still sounded imprudently loud to the vampire. Jerome motioned at the ground, stained with blood, beneath the feet of the young warrior.

The injured man gestured, probably a sign of insult among his people. He took two hobbled steps away from the scene. "Going home! Die of thirst!" he shouted back over his shoulder. The crossbow fired. The quarrel hit him in the calf. It sliced into the muscle and gashed the skin. However, only skimming the inside of the calf, the quarrel kept moving. It stuck in the ground. The man still dropped, clutching the wound, shallow but excruciating.

"Like I said . . . need you right there," Jerome said. He sank back behind his rock. The vampire wondered why the knights still so underestimated his hearing.

"Good evening, Jerome, you stinking pig," he breathed to himself. The night was young. The vampire stood still as death and waited, studying the chessboard. He did not know if any other knights had survived the desert. Were they tucked behind other rocks and waiting for the vampire to move against Jerome?

He listened for motion in all directions. The vampire did not wish to leave this fight for another night. He imagined Jerome ripping the stone away from his hiding place, the bright sun consuming him.

The vampire was greatly disappointed to see that the wicked crossbow still survived. He knew that a good shot could penetrate even his cloak, making any sort of frontal attack on Jerome dangerous. "Bad invention," he whispered.

~ B ~

"Can you lift this curse from Makya?" Hototo asked.

The right twin spoke softly. "Such a powerful curse. We have no such magic. He walks and speaks. But he has departed from the living," she said.

"Bane to the living now," the left twin added. She kept her voice down as well. No person outside the Smoke Clan knew their names. Or even if they had distinct names. Hototo pressed the conversation.

"Chayton seeks to destroy us. And the High Ro . . . White Bats have joined with Istaqa. We cannot stand against their combined aggression. If the Ash Owls attack us too . . . you will see Crow Ledge fall." He paused. But the sibyl only shifted uncomfortably on the bench and continued to stare into him. Hototo continued. "We did not seek this fight. We need Makya. His new power can stave off the enemy. We must shatter their spears. Only the Morning Crows properly honor the spi—"

"You bring an abomination before us and ask for our blessing? You must kill him," the right twin said. She clenched her teeth angrily and spoke quickly. But she did not raise her voice.

"But I have treated Makya like my son. His future is the future of the Morning Crows."

"Enemy strangers have no future. Kill him," the right twin repeated. She struck each word with authority.

"Son he might have been. And loyal to memory for a while. But hunger will soon enough defile that. You must slay him and quickly," the left twin added.

"How can I defeat him?" Hototo said.

"Pierce the heart. Take the head. Burn the whole. These are the ways," the right twin said.

"But how can I defeat the strongest and fastest among his equals? And now his power is multiplied. What chance do I have?" Hototo insisted. He held out his arms to plead his case. As though to show his own advancing age.

"The boy must sleep. But is that enough? Shall we offer more?" the left twin asked of her sister.

"Yes. I think we must," the right twin answered. Both worked with difficulty to the side of the bench. The amber beads rattled between them. Hototo cringed inwardly to watch. The right twin reached awkwardly back while her sister rose to her feet and braced to manage the turn. Wilted flowers were heaped in the corner, dark in the weak light. He guessed that they were purple. She brushed them aside. "Rise and step forward," she said. From behind the blooms she brought forth a finely wrought jar. She cupped it heavily in her hands as her sister sat back down. The jar was ornate with spirit art. But Hototo did not recognize the designs; they were none he had ever learned.

Hototo left the lamp on the floor and stepped forward. The sibyl looked more pallid yet in the closer light. Not well. Hototo saw that the jar formed a perfect sphere. He could see no mouth. Like a bubble of clay. "What must I do?" he said.

"Lay your hands across this orb!" both twins said. Louder like an invocation. Hototo did. It felt hot against his palms. The heat rose as he left them there. The eyes of the sibyl were closed now in intense concentration. They whispered some hurried words back and forth that he could not catch. Or did not know. His hands began to tingle and then burn. He wanted to pull away but fought against the impulse. Just as he thought his hands were surely burning, he heard a scraping motion inside the sphere, even though the sphere did not move. Then the flutter and wicked buzz of a rattlesnake tail. He felt it vibrate through the clay. The heat began to die away. Hototo pulled his hands away slowly. The sibyl carefully set the sphere aside.

"Take this," the right twin said. She pressed into his hand the ordinary tail of a rattlesnake, bony segments smooth and cold against his hand. He felt her long nails across the palm of his hand. "Sound the rattle to invoke the strength and speed that you require. Only once you may call upon it," she whispered.

"What will th–" Hototo said, but the left twin grabbed his hand with her right hand and folded his fist around the rattle. She spoke with quiet urgency. Both twins leaned back awkwardly to meet his standing gaze.

"Destroy him during the day. His power wanes then. Clean your house first. Purify the Morning Crows. And then embrace the enemy of your enemy. Embrace Istaqa. Clasp the spear together and clean all houses. If many among the White Bats are now cursed, and no spirit leader leads them . . . we must not allow such demons to walk among us. Do you understand?"

Hototo had visited the sibyl many times. The twins had often spoken in riddles and circles. They gave questions as answers. Such blunt orders sent chills down his spine. He nodded. "Thank you for your audience. Thank you for your words. I will carry them from here and into the sunlight," he said. A formal valediction.

"Make those words into deeds. Hototo . . . heed us well this time."

Hototo paused. The sibyl had not spoken the formal reply. *And may those words leave a shadow* normally closed the interview. However, the shaman nodded again and turned, scooping up his lamp. He stepped quickly down the stairs. As he reached the lower room he slipped the talisman, the dormant rattle, into his treasury purse. He heard the faint murmur of conversation through the floor above him. But he did not listen. His heart ached. He wanted to stare into the endless night sky. He wanted to dissolve into the stars. Hototo wanted to move far from that room, far from Smoke Ridge. He vowed never to return.

~ B ~

The vampire crouched among the rocks now, his cloak pulled carefully around him. The air thrummed with the presence of blood, more than before. Other men had moved into the vicinity. However, he still saw only Jerome and his unwilling bait. He watched and waited, every muscle ready to move.

Twang! Twang! Twang! The vampire heard the sound of bowstrings snapping. He startled but held his position. He saw an arrow find its mark. Others clattered against the boulder. Jerome stood from behind his hiding place, an arrow stuck from his hip and another caught in the ringlets of mail across his shoulders.

"Curse you!" Jerome roared as he looked roughly about.

The vampire followed his gaze. He saw warriors suddenly moving in all directions. Some leaped from behind boulders further up the slope. Others rose from the brush that lined the canyon. They threw off cloaks skillfully smeared with the ochres of the canyon as they sprinted forward. Two . . . three . . . seven . . . he quickly counted a dozen men. They seemed to have come, more or less, from the other end of the canyon. Several fired more arrows at the knight. Near misses as Jerome ducked. Others sprinted toward the knight. They held their spears for throwing. "Oooooowls!" they screamed. The vampire glanced about nervously to see if he was also a target. But the warriors were fiercely focused on the knight.

He saw Jerome empty his crossbow into the screaming mouth of the closest warrior on the slope. The head snapped back. The knees collapsed. And momentum threw the unfortunate attacker forward. He rolled limp to the canyon floor. "Great shot," the vampire said softly. He saw that they each had two braids. "Like the two with the deer," he added.

More warriors were quickly closing the distance. The vampire saw Jerome thrust his boot through the stirrup at the front of the crossbow stock and strain with both arms to reset the trigger. The fire of desperation showed in the quickness of his pull. The latch caught. The knight reached for his quarrel now. However, Jerome felt the hail of scree on his head. He turned to see two more warriors leap from above. "Jesus!" he barked. He swung the crossbow like a club, catching one of them hard across the ribs. The crossbow fired dry as it connected. At the same moment, the other man caught Jerome around the waist and wrenched him down from the outcropping with a fierce tackle. They tumbled down the steep slope and landed hard in the mud.

The vampire saw the warrior stab Jerome with his knife, but the stone knife faltered against the chain mail. Jerome stabbed back with the quarrel he had intended for the crossbow. Three blows. Hard and quick. He rolled away and stumbled to his feet. He grabbed for his sword. He was a full head taller than most of his attackers. But they were too quick, and their spears reached him first. They skillfully avoided the chain mail this time. "Good riddance," the vampire whispered.

~ B ~

Hototo and Makya walked silently beside each other for a long time. Insects, elated by the recent rain, filled the night with noisy music. However, the two Morning Crows did not hear it. They moved quickly away from Smoke Ridge, their feet cool against the wet earth. Less quickly, they traversed their private thoughts. They were each troubled by what they had seen and heard.

Hototo felt age and exhaustion in his limbs. His heart felt even worse. Makya felt the blood pumping through the veins of the older man. He did not crave it. But Makya knew it was there. He knew he could take it, and the thought scared him. He also feared that the sibyl had disliked him, perhaps distrusted him. He feared that Hototo might banish him. He wanted the spirit leader to speak. He needed to know where he stood. He wanted to scream his need for answers. But he sensed no beginning in the space between them.

"What did the sibyl tell you?" Makya finally ventured as they crossed the high plateau and skirted a stand of prickly pears. His tongue felt awkward in his mouth. His words were jarring after so much quiet. Hototo stopped short. He turned and stared at Makya with sharp eyes. He looked unexpectedly fierce. Makya faced him, his muscles tense. "Can you tell me what she . . . what they said?" he repeated.

Hototo took a deep breath. "I have only been waiting for you to ask. I am surprised that you waited so long." He forced himself to smile. "The sibyl offers her blessing. You must help the Morning Crows turn back the threats against us."

"I was not sure that . . ." Makya trailed off.

"I understand. The sisters often speak in puzzles."

"I have heard that before. But they seemed to speak directly when they questioned me. Did they offer you such a puzzle after I left the tower?" Makya asked. He was genuinely surprised. Standing close with the night all around them, both men only whispered to one another now.

"When they asked if you dared look away from the work of the spirits . . ." Hototo said.

"I should not have looked away," Makya said.

"Yes. But they did not speak only of themselves. They were also telling us to accept your new power. We should not look away from what the spirits dare to bring us. We must embrace what has happened," Hototo said with assurance.

Makya looked hard into his face. "How?" he asked.

"You are called upon, Makya, as you sensed from the beginning. You are called upon to repel our foes and destroy the enemy stranger. This the sibyl commands." Hototo poked his fist in the air for emphasis.

"So the sibyl cannot cure me?" Makya said. He felt a lump of disappointment tighten in his chest. But also relief. Like finding unexpected shade from the desert sun. Hototo would not banish him. The sibyl had granted him time and opportunity to prove his heart. He glanced away from the spirit leader now. He saw the shadow of a hawk drift across the rocky ground. Its pulse was like a wordless whisper far overheard. He knew that Hototo could not see it with his ordinary eyes.

"Higher purpose requires no cure. That is the meaning," the shaman replied. "Now . . . I am too old and battered to reach Crow Ledge by sunrise. You must run ahead and take shelter for the day."

"And just leave you here?"

"I will follow quickly. But I cannot keep your pace for another night, and you must hurry now. We will defend the Morning Crows together when next we meet."

"I think . . . that I understand," Makya said. Hototo clasped Makya by the arm to bid him farewell. He startled at the cold of his undead skin. He slapped Makya gently on the arm to hide his reaction. As though it were his prompt to move quickly. Makya nodded. He turned, thankful for the bodily distraction, and trotted quickly over the hill.

Hototo sat back onto an outcropping of rock. The stars seemed very bright, more present than usual, as Hototo stared into the sky. The fresh smell of rain still permeated the cool night air. He wanted to cry, but no tears would flow. Nothing even close. His heart felt like infertile dust. "To whom have I lied tonight?" he asked himself.

~ B ~

The vampire still watched, his keen eyes allowing him to observe from far across canyon floor as the warriors retrieved their dead and wounded. He was fascinated as four men folded a long loop of rope around the dead warrior and lifted him with their spears. Blood still dripped from the head. The vampire smelled it. He saw the droplets fall. Carrying a heavy burden, the four men departed immediately. The vampire saw a thin man, older than the rest, scatter ashes where the body had fallen. "Local shaman?" he guessed.

Another man, the warrior that Jerome had stabbed with the quarrel, was bleeding badly. He needed help standing, hand pressed tight against his punctured ribs. Two more holes bled unchecked on his arm. "Hurry back with him!" the scrawny shaman instructed before dropping to his knees next to Jerome. He examined the body closely. He even pulled back the lips to inspect the teeth. "What are you looking for?" the vampire whispered. He feared what such an examination might mean. However, it also kindled an ember of hope. If these men knew his kind, then perhaps others had come this way. The rumors of the lost vampire lords might prove true after all.

The shaman finally stepped away as others took the sword and roughly removed the chain mail from Jerome. His head fell back against the dirt, lifeless, as they freed the vest. The men briefly examined the strange garment, fingers exploring the tiny steel rings. It was sticky with blood now, but they still decided to take it.

Two more warriors lifted the last badly injured man to his feet, the one that Jerome had tried to use for bait. Both legs were injured now. They wrapped his arms across their shoulders and took his weight. One of his eyes was swollen shut, but the man began to twist and gesture. "Wait . . . stop! I must bring this to Istaqa!" he groaned. He braced against them. He grimaced with pain as he bent forward. The vampire watched closely. He saw the gritty warrior carefully lift the crossbow from where it had fallen. He shook it. "This must go back to Firetown. Please carry this back!" he said. He then limped doggedly back to Jerome and fished the extra quarrels from his belt. He clutched them as the troop began to retreat.

"Grind my fangs," the vampire murmured. He decided to follow. Much of the night still remained, and these men had pricked his curiosity. He wanted to know what motivated them. And he wanted to break the crossbow if he got the chance.

CHAPTER 15

Nocturnal

LENMANA, STILL MARKED with the dark ashes and white paint of mourning, still aching from the murder of her husband, stood under the newly lit moon, before the sacred cave of the White Bat Clan, far to the north of Low Nest. No fire burned. She shook a sistrum, sacred and very old. It too had remained hidden while Chayton had ruled over Low Nest. However, the story that Chayton had finally killed Old Chu'Si had raced through Low Nest like a shallow stream charged with sudden power, churning and muddy, after the rain. It had served to tragically validate the animus long expressed by Old Chu'Si. It had affirmed their worst fears about the outsider and fueled fresh speculation about his origins. It had also given shape to an unformed desire. And the High Rocks Clan, without regard for the success they had seen under Chayton, without regard for finding the truth, now rushed to reclaim what they had once been. They would become the White Bats once more. Wik and Nuk stood sentry at either edge of the box canyon, staring far into the shadows, amazed at their own bright senses.

Lenmana rattled the sistrum louder. Louder. She closed her eyes and shook her head. The sound clacked louder, an echo of the wings that exploded from the cave at dusk. And then Lenmana abruptly stopped. Tense silence remained as most of the clan stood before her. She let it build as Cha'Akmongwi had many years ago when he led ceremonies. She watched the stillness, the expectant shift in their stances. Finally, she whirled toward the mouth of the cave.

"Spirit of the White Bat," she screamed with anguish, "deliver your leader to your people!" More silence followed. All eyes watched the narrow mouth of the cave, its dark interior demarcated by the silver moonlight on its rocky flanks. "White Bat . . ." she shouted again, ". . . bring forth your leader!" And then a tall figure stepped from the blackness. Sik emerged. Like a soundless scream. He held the sacred spear of the White Bat. His eyes shone in the moonlight. His ears had elongated and sharpened at the tip. All the hair had vanished from his head, even his eyebrows. And two large slits formed his nostrils.

They did not understand it, but the consumption of human flesh had perverted the faces of both Wik and Sik. It had pulled their noses back into snouts and raised ridges along their brow and across the center line of their skulls. Their limbs had started to elongate, fingers and toes as well. The process had also lengthened their jaws and quickly turned their skin the color of ash. However, Sik was even further deformed where Chayton had struck him. It had healed imperfectly. Or perhaps would require even more blood. His nostrils were crooked, without symmetry. Several lightning forks of bruise-blue scarring cut into the rough concavity.

"The bat . . . like a bat . . . he walks among us," rippled in nervous amazement among the White Bat Clan. The stance of the gathered crowd drew back, even as none dared to actually move their feet in fear. Several children whimpered and pressed their eyes under the arms of their parents.

Chayton had kept the cursed warriors isolated after the attack on Crow Ledge. Few had seen them after they had returned to Low Nest. And the three enemy strangers, after killing Chayton, had reacted quickly. They had called for Lenmana to come to the mouth of the kiva. Her friendship with the old matriarch, and the recent death of her husband, made her the perfect choice. After all, Chayton had insisted on only the most basic burial practices, allowing no spirit leader to participate. That fact undoubtedly mingled with her grief. "How can I help?" Lenmana had asked with a loud whisper as she peered down into the kiva. A dim circle of light lit the sand beneath the ladder. Nuk had stood just beyond it. Having only consumed the blood, his visage had not changed. Hiding his fangs, only the light in his eyes, its ineffable absence, marked his transformation. But Lenmana could not see it.

"Sister . . . look now. Chayton has killed Old Chu'Si. He struck against her memory of the White Bat spirit when she showed him the Spear of the White Bat. The bastard always hated her. We should have expected it. But we have avenged her!" Nuk had lied. He had waved his hand at the victims behind him. Sik and Wik had waited along the back wall.

And now their ascent to power was complete. Lenmana shook the sistrum once more, hushing the whispers among the crowd. "Have you come to lead us?" she shouted, still rattling the instrument. Sik strode forward. "Have you come to lead us?" she asked again, more plaintive this time. She stopped the sistrum as Sik stopped before her. A moment of silence hung once more. Her heart fluttered fearfully as she made herself look into his shining eyes. But she held her ground before his fierce visage. Lenmana saw that Sik could truly avenge the death of Lapu. "Have *you* come to lead *us*?" she asked again in a hoarse whisper, one that the crowd could hear.

"I have," growled Sik roughly. He waited and let the silence settle once more. "I have come to lead!" he shouted. His voice echoed from the rocks. The tension among the people fractured like cracks racing across the ice.

"And we will no longer struggle and toil and suffer in the snares of our foes! No more will they dare to kill our families. The White Bats will once again rise. We will once again heed the spirit powers and call upon them. We will once again thrive! Brothers and sisters . . . will you follow?" he roared.

The crowd murmured assent. "Yes. We will. Yes. Lead us," rippled through the nervous gathering. Sik stared them down. Many looked away.

"Brothers and sisters. We have grown strong. We will grind our heel against the neck of our enemy," he said softly. He paused once more and then exploded. "We will . . . rule this land at last!" he yelled forcefully. He raised the sacred spear and shook it, a potent symbol unseen for many years. The ice shattered. The White Bat Clan screamed in response. Lenmana shook the sistrum hard. She felt the absence of Old Chu'Si in the crowd. It stung her heart; her friend had yearned to see this re-birth. Lenmana howled into the night sky, fueled by both fear and grief, the death of Lapu still raw inside her; and by the surge of collective power.

Sik felt that power too. The gathered crowd acted strongly upon his senses. He could feel the rush of blood in their veins, their pulses quickened and pressed close together. He felt his hunger awaken. The war leader looked forward to letting it grow. His lust for blood could only sweeten his next encounter with the Morning Crows. He would, soon enough, break the fever upon their necks.

~ *B* ~

As the rescue party brought its own wounded, and their fallen comrade, close to home, the vampire stalked close behind. He still hugged the shadows, making little noise and leaving few tracks. His own mentors had taught him well, and the ages had offered practice and more practice, endless variation on simple themes. Like stones in the river.

The warriors paused. One put his hands to his mouth. A trilling *hoohoohoot* rolled up the cliffs. Moments later another owl loosed a longer reply. Full throated and slower. It rolled down the cliffs. And then the rescue party moved onward.

The vampire stood still as the stones around him. He had tracked the sound to his right and up the hill. Brush darkened the reddish slope, dense stands of shrubs that seemed to spray from between a disbursed litter of massive rocks. It reminded him of waves breaking onto jagged coastal cliffs. He watched intently but fixed his eyes on no single point.

He finally saw motion, an arm and leg shifting through the tangled branches. The guard was hidden just below three lumpy boulders that stood in close proximity. Particularly large and embedded at an awkward angle, the rocks seemed to cling to the slope with stubborn intent. The vampire continued to scan the terrain. He judged how much night remained.

Enough remained. Hunger did not stalk him tonight, but he had learned to eat when he could. And this night was special. The vampire knew that none of the other knights would have allowed Jerome to act alone. None of them would have watched him die. The manner of Jerome's death could only mean one thing. The knights—the Order of St. John—had failed. The vampire would feed to celebrate tonight. He would raise one final humiliation to Heaven in their honor. "Jerome . . . you smelly bastard . . . I raise my glass to you tonight," the vampire said softly. He did not smile.

Moments later, he sprinted back toward an erosion trail that would take him high up into the rocks. It would allow him to descend and hunt from above. He knew that the sentry would, almost certainly, have focused all his senses on the canyon below.

~ B ~

"You did well tonight," Sik said. They both stood inside the defiled kiva after the ceremony. Only the red glow of dying coals lit the room. Wik and Nuk worked digging sticks behind her. An expedient burial of the dead. They had already rolled the bodies of Chayton and Old Chu'Si into blankets to conceal them.

"Thank you," Lenmana replied. She smiled. The demonic faces of Sik and Wik still scared her. And the deep shadows in the kiva only made it worse. But she was still ready to serve them. She believed that they had served justice to Chayton and avenged the murder of her friend. And she believed that they could avenge the death of Lapu many times over.

"And yet the White Bats must have a true spirit leader. Chayton destroyed our memory of the spirit traditions. Little remains of the secret knowledge. We crave new magic," he said. He still clutched the great spear.

"I remember too well," Lenmana said. She nodded and closed her eyes. Could any of them ever forget the public execution of Cha'Akmongwi? They had let it happen. It seemed more like dream than memory now. How had they allowed it? They had jeered and shouted, cheered Chayton as the new leader. And then Chayton had smashed the ceremonial masks. He had made the White Bat acolyte, an unfortunate child, walk to Firetown alone, the trail still deep with ice and snow. No rain had come from the spirits that year, only one cruel snow. "And Kotori . . . he let that poor boy die of fever in Firetown," she added. The coals warmed her shins.

"They care only for themselves. As they always have. We will not beg acolytes from the Ash Owls. We will train our own. Will you serve?" Sik asked.

"I will," she said. Her eyes blazed. "But I know so little. How shall I learn?" she added.

"Much of the night remains. Leave now. Nuk will take you to Smoke Clan. Head north and then east; there are many places to find shelter along that path. You will demand that they teach you at Smoke Ridge. How could they deny such a request? Spend a few nights there while we ready the attack against Crow Ledge," he said.

"But acolytes study for years," she said.

"Learn enough. Learn enough so that the people will follow. Just begin your training. Memorize the blessings for battle. We had none the other night and paid for it. You may train further later. You could even choose your own acolyte to join you. But your husband will be avenged. We must make Crow Ledge into an empty shell."

"What if Smoke Ridge only sees Nuk as an enemy stranger? They might reject us because of that. Do you think they will accept us?" Lenmana asked. Nuk looked up from his digging. He raised his eyebrows as he waited for Sik to answer.

"Explain to them that the White Bat has touched us . . . blessed our physical form. His sanction of the curse is etched upon my body. We wish to follow a spirit leader once again. How could they not heed that wish?"

"Then why is Nuk not transformed as well? I mean . . . what if they ask me that in response?" Lenmana persisted.

"He may still walk among men with little notice. We have determined that the White Bat has called him to a different purpose," Wik offered.

"To escort me to Smoke Ridge."

"Exactly right. What else could explain?" Sik replied. The heaped embers throbbed at Lenmana's feet. Wik and Nuk began to cover one of the corpses; Lenmana heard the soil falling into the shallow hole. She did not look behind her. Her sistrum lay upon the shelf now with proper respect. No longer hidden.

~ B ~

As the night faded into the gray light of morning, telling of the coming dawn, Makya arrived at Crow Ledge. He was panting. His feet and calves protested. However, nothing like true fatigue confronted him. He felt refreshed the moment he stopped. He was amazed.

He saw multiple Morning Crows awake and visibly standing guard along the front wall of Crow Ledge. He whistled at Kele with a quick warbling sound. "Any danger?"

"All clear," Kele quickly warbled back. Makya trotted quickly to the rocky pediment of Crow Ledge. The ladders were stowed for safety. He still climbed nimbly to the courtyard, using the sequence of toeholds that his fathers had carved into the living rock. Turkeys were beginning to stir in their pen as he passed. Makya noted that Kele stayed at his post and offered no further greeting. However, Honani climbed down from the roof where he had stood watch. He looked very tired and handled the rungs of the ladder stiffly. His arm was badly bruised from the fight below the Cave of Visions.

Makya spoke first. "Lots of people awake. How are you?"

"Where is Hototo?" Honani whispered, trying not to sound alarmed. A chill climbed the back of his neck. They had not seen each other since Makya had been bitten by the enemy stranger. Sihu had told Honani what to expect. However, the fact that Makya looked and sounded no different, but was transformed by what seemed absent, still briefly jarred Honani.

"He follows. He sent me ahead. What happened to your arm?" Makya replied. Honani stared hard for a moment but decided to believe him. Makya felt his strength clearly ebbing. The coming sunrise. He thought how lucky he had been to confront the enemy stranger while the sun hung high in the sky. He felt relieved to stand with his friend once more.

"The Ash Owls attacked us near the Cave of Visions. But we smashed them, mostly thanks to my great skill. Choovio waits for you and Hototo in the family kiva. He can tell you more. We expect the Ash Owls to respond."

Makya thanked Honani and moved briskly toward the opening. He felt annoyed by the approaching dawn and the limits it would soon impose.

CHAPTER 16

Seeds, Blessed and Planted

"HE WAS JUST a man," Kotori said.

"Are you sure of that?" Istaqa asked.

"The two men stood in the sunlight. They stood on a level field a short walk from Firetown. The practice field. Istaqa lifted the long blade, taken from the body of the man they had killed, testing its balance. He wondered at the sharp edge. He slashed the air. Back and forth. Back and forth. He saw that an inlay of wood, thin and dark, ran down the middle of the blade. Both sides. Broken in three or four places.

"Yes. He bled. I think that he would have killed Tocho if he were an enemy stranger. He would have drunk his blood instead of beating him," Kotori responded, standing a good distance from Istaqa. He wore a necklace of blue feathers today.

"Is this weapon not what demons would carry? See how it shines."

"I do not know where the enemy strangers come from. But men live there too, and I believe they make such objects," Kotori said.

"How do they?" Istaqa asked.

"I do not know. Perhaps the spirits have not seen fit to teach us," Kotori said.

"Why . . . not?" Istaqa pressed him. He jabbed the blade forward like a spear, both hands on the handle.

"I know what I know . . . but the rest hides from me," Kotori shrugged.

"Is this weapon cursed? Will we anger the spirits by using it?"

"It did not help the man last night. Nor did it harm an Ash Owl in the fight. Still . . . I will perform a ritual to cleanse it."

"Bring me that spear shaft," Istaqa said to Alo. The acolyte quickly rose from the herbs he was grinding, fresh salve for Tocho's wounds. He ran to the flat rocks nearby. The warriors crafted many spear heads and arrows there, blades for axes and scraping knives too. Some poles lay unfinished, passed over for one reason or another. Flakes of stone littered the ground nearby. The boy brought the shaft quickly and held it out before Istaqa.

"Hold the spear up and out in both hands. As though to block a blow," Istaqa said. The acolyte did as instructed. Istaqa raised the strange weapon above his head.

"Aaaahhh!" Alo gasped. He dropped to the ground.

"Boy! Get off your knees," Kotori barked. But Istaqa laughed.

"Alo, I will not strike you. I only wish to strike the wood. Hold it strong and tight. Show me your mettle now," he said. Istaqa motioned for Alo to stand.

The boy nodded. He braced the spear shaft, holding it straight out from his shoulders. Istaqa raised the blade again. He saw that Alo did not flinch this time. He measured the stroke carefully. And then the blade slashed down, flashing in the sunlight, motion exploding from stillness. It sliced the wood cleanly. No sound but a *snick*. Alo still held his hands high, halved shaft trembling in each hand. Another moment passed before he could exhale. He smiled with relief. Istaqa and Kotori looked at each other and nodded.

~ B ~

"What did the sibyl say?" Choovio asked.

They stood in the dim shadows of the small family kiva. Only the two of them. A few twigs blazed yellow across the red hue of stirred coals. The room seemed strangely vacant. It felt like an empty room despite the clutter of living: firewood and cooking pots, bracelets and combs on the shelf, the small flute that Muna had carved for Choovio as a child. Several bright necklaces hung from pegs. Makya saw dirty clothes behind the ladder, smelled the taint of stale blood in them.

"That I can help the Morning Crows. That the spirits have smiled on us!" Makya replied. He smiled. He looked for acceptance in the face of his brother. But the two brothers stood far apart, the fire between them.

"How so? Has not the curse of the enemy stranger passed into you?" Choovio asked.

"It has. But the sibyl told Hototo . . . that I should accept it as a gift. It brings us power that will help us prevail," Makya said.

"Against the enemy stranger?"

"Against all of them. The power I have at night . . . we can finally crush the bastards that have brought years of grief. I have the power to truly avenge our father now," Makya said.

"Hototo retaliated many years ago for that. He repaid the Ash Owls five to one. You know what he did at Gathering Rock," Choovio said softly.

"Saya was the leader of our clan. Only . . . only Istaqa can answer," Makya said.

Choovio nodded slowly. "I hear you," he said. He let silence fall across the room. He would not defend Istaqa. He stared uneasily into the dark eyes of his brother. They shone too bright for the deep shadows.

"This is what the sibyl told Hototo. Are you not glad to hear it?" Makya said, his tone respectful and concerned.

"Of course," Choovio said. He walked to the loom that hung from the ceiling and anchored across the clay floor. He plucked at the unfinished blanket. He liked his design but had no time to finish it. The border was intricate, weaving three different colors into the pattern.

"That looks good so far. Maybe one of your best," Makya added, tipping his head toward the loom.

"But are you dead? Should I listen to Shuman?" Choovio asked. He ignored the compliment, even as he continued to stare at his design. "Do I still hear your spirit when you speak? Or only an empty husk that does not wilt? Am I talking to my brother right now or do you wander still below the Cave of Visions?"

"Choovio . . . it *is* me. I feel changed but I am still Makya. I remain loyal to the Morning Crows. I will still protect my family. I will make Shuman understand. I feel no change in my heart!" he insisted. He had forced his blood-hunger to the back of his mind. Makya smiled. Choovio smiled back warily and nodded. Honani leaned his head down into the kiva then. He looked grim.

"Pavati wants to see both of you. She is worse," he said.

"Can you bring some thick blankets?" Makya asked. "I must block the sun to cross the terrace."

~ B ~

Several warriors came over the hill. They carried a slain coyote between them. Its wounds were still wet. "Here they are!" Istaqa said. He stabbed the long blade into the dirt and lifted the shirt of small rings that lay behind him. He spoke softly to Alo, "Dress that coyote with this shirt of rings. We must see how it works."

Alo nodded, thankful that Istaqa had not asked him to wear it himself. He carried it clumsily forward to meet the warriors. Some parts were still slightly discolored, but the Ash Owls had mostly scrubbed it free of blood when they arrived at Firetown.

Kwatoko and Pivane dropped the carcass for Alo. They kept walking to meet Istaqa, faces grim. "One of the guards was killed last night. After the sentry change. He was thrown off the cliff near Three Fat Hens. And the coyotes found his body before we did," Kwatoko said. Heavy silence filled the air.

"*After* the stranger was killed that attacked Tocho?" Istaqa finally said. The warriors nodded.

"Was the stranger not alone after all?" Kotori asked.

Istaqa shook his head. "Tocho saw nobody else."

Kotori frowned uneasily. "Perhaps an enemy stranger still hunts here after all. It might help explain the man last night. Why was he here?" he said.

"I disagree," Kwatoko said. Staring into the dirt, he spoke softly but with conviction. "The Morning Crows killed our men just two days ago. And it was not the first time or the second time or the tenth. So if another Ash Owl has been killed . . . we should look first to Crow Ledge," he added.

"Well said," Istaqa said.

~ B ~

Choovio knelt next to his wife as Makya looked over his shoulder. Pavati still lay on the floor of their sleeping quarters, all jewelry removed from her neck and arms. A bowl of water lay untouched by her shoulder. The morning added only a gray light to the room, dim and indirect. Choovio lifted her poultice. The putrid smell of infection, already lingering in the room, filled the air. They saw the red lines of poison creeping far from the oozing wounds, two ragged slices near the hip. One angry line snaked up her torso. It had nearly climbed to her heart. Choovio touched the inflamed flesh, a full hand away from where the weapon had entered. Pavati still gasped. "Ahhhh. No . . . do not touch me," she moaned weakly. Her skin burned with fever, even hotter than before. A blanket lay across her knees.

Pavati looked utterly spent. As though she could sweat no more. And although he did not quite understand it, Makya felt she was nearing death. Beyond the foul smell in the room, he could smell the rising taint in her veins. Choovio gently lowered the poultice back across the wound. Pavati still winced.

"What can we do?" Choovio whispered, clasping her too-hot hand between his own. "Hototo has not yet returned," he added. Her eyes were glassy from the fever, but she focused her gaze determinedly. She looked at Choovio and shifted her head slowly back and forth, deep sadness in the set of her mouth.

"Shuman examined my wounds a little while ago. She says the poison is winning. That even Hototo cannot heal me now."

"He will return soon. He will heal you to prove Shuman wrong," Choovio said. He tried to smile but failed.

Pavati looked to Makya. "Is it true what they told me . . . has the curse of the enemy stranger passed into you?"

"Yes. But Hototo says that the sibyl has blessed me."

"Tell me. What did Hototo say?"

"He said the power of the enemy stranger can help us. That we should consider it an unexpected gift from the spirits," Makya said. Pavati closed her eyes. She paused for a long time. Both men waited.

"Then you . . . are you changed as the stories say?" she finally asked.

"I am. But my heart is still Morning Crow. I did not change behind my eyes," he said.

Against pain that made her legs tremble, Pavati pushed herself up onto her elbow. She panted, her face growing ashen. "Do you swear that? Will you swear that your heart remains? Even loud enough for the highest spirit to hear you?"

"Why do you ask him this?" Choovio said, moving his head to intercept her gaze.

"Swear it!" she hissed through gritted teeth, looking around Choovio once more. The skin around her lips turned sallow with the effort.

"Of course," Makya said. "I do swear. My loyalty and my heart . . . that demon did not change them."

Pavati closed her eyes once again, her face set with rigid resolve. She returned her gaze to Choovio. "I must not leave

Kaya. Still just a child. I refuse to abandon her in such difficult times."

"I know you will keep fighting. Hototo will help when he returns," Choovio sought to assure her.

"No. I do not . . ." she grimaced, ". . . have much time left. Do you understand?" she asked.

"You must hang on just a little longer," Choovio said. His voice trembled.

Pavati looked once more to Makya. "Better to have a mother at night than none at all. You brothers know that better than most," she said, her breath coming short now.

"What? Pavati . . . how can you ask him that?" Choovio said, fully grasping her thinking for the first time. He fought the urge to drop her hand. She still persisted.

"No, you must listen. I will not leave Kaya. And I will not leave you. Makya, take my blood and pass your curse to me. Do it quickly. Please," she pleaded, her eyes fixed on the younger brother. A mix of terror and resolve burned behind the fever glaze.

~ B ~

Many rods of juniper wood lay on the floor in an unused room at the back of Low Nest. Varied lengths. Holes were bored in each end, the fruit of tedious work. Two had stones mounted at the end and looked like axes with four heads. Lengths of braided rope lay in a heap nearby.

"Can you finish this? Did Chayton tell you what he planned?" Sik asked.

"Yes. They will help us clear the ledge and keep the enemy away from our siege poles," Badger said. "We have the new siege poles completed. Some of the men hid them near Crow Ledge," he added.

"Excellent work," Sik said. "They were exhausting to carry last time."

Badger rarely left Low Nest. His arms and legs were short, not in proportion; and climbing the rocks posed a challenge. The ladders also proved difficult. However, his limbs were sturdy. He did many things for his clan, offering long days of quiet labor. He had even invented a new knot last winter, one quickly adopted for carrying water vessels. "Touched by the spirit of Brother Badger," the shaman had told him many years before, and the nickname had stuck. In fact, the young at Low Nest knew him by no other name. However, he had earned the trust of Chayton with his ingenuity, a trust that Sik accepted as well.

Wik kicked one of the rods. "Just a bunch of sticks. Mostly too short for spears," he said. Badger nodded.

"Let me show you," he said. "These poles will tie together with these braids of rope. End to end. You will hold this longer one. Leverage to get the whole chain moving. And maybe ten shorter rods linked from that one. We will try some different numbers. And then this one will go on the end." He nudged the pole with the stone head. A hint of eager pride flashed across his long face.

"And then what?" Wik said flatly. Badger picked up some of the braided rope.

"Do you . . . do you still feel pain?" he asked, his expression grave once again.

"Yes. We are stronger but not so changed," Sik answered. He smiled. His flattened snout and sharp ears had unnerved many. And his arms and legs were longer now and full of sinew. Badger smiled back. He believed. And although he had served Chayton well, he rejoiced to embrace his beliefs once more. Badger, no taller than the hips of his new leader, took one of the cords and spun it in a circle. He then whipped Wik sideways across the arm with it, lightly but enough to sting. Wik snarled and bared his fangs. He closed on Badger, who stumbled back several quick steps.

"Do you dare stri–"

"Stop," Sik said. "Let him finish."

"It will work just like that. It should work the same way. Except that it should reach further and strike harder. They should reach Crow Ledge from the ground. This end should knock warriors down. Kill them!" Badger said. He smiled again. He was pleased to see the idea come together. "Unless they prove too heavy," he added with a look of concern.

"Excellent," Sik nodded, understanding more quickly than Wik. "We will call them *Striking Snakes*. And we will teach the Morning Crows why," he said.

~ B ~

Makya lay in the darkest corner of his sleeping room, his hands folded across his chest. He was alone. Sihu had taken refuge in another corner of Crow Ledge along with both of his sons. He did not blame her, but yet again, anger sat in his chest like venom. It seemed that his visit to Smoke Ridge had only pushed her further away. "I am still the same . . . how dare you?" he whispered to console himself. He could still taste blood in his mouth. He could also taste the fever that had raged inside Pavati, the sour tang of something ugly in her veins. But it could not hurt him. He had shaken off her fever as though it were hard sleep.

Makya was immensely troubled now. Loyalty and compassion had moved him to comply with Pavati. Choovio, his poor brother, the fear of loss upon him like a thousand selfish hands, had nodded warily and urged him to hurry. As both husband and father, hope had persuaded Choovio. It had rushed him past every doubt. However, Makya had felt eagerness in his own motives too. When his mouth had touched her neck, when he felt her hot skin, his breath had quickened. His hunger had powerfully stirred, almost like desire. Her blood had tasted good despite its fever.

And when Choovio had slit his palm, let his untainted blood run freely into her mouth to complete the change, Makya had smelled it. It had filled his nose. It had reminded him of the best roasted meat. "But she lives," he muttered. "Bring the night. Her strength will justify," he assured himself. He longed for the return of his own nocturnal strength.

He closed his eyes. What he might say to Sihu, how he might reclaim her affection, began to churn through his brain. "Good friends with Pavati," he murmured. He tried to imagine what he might say to Shuman too. But the ecstatic rush of taking blood intruded even so. He recalled how the vein popped as the fangs entered. How the blood rushed into his mouth with the pounding of her pulse. How the fire of life raced into his limbs. He had not wanted to stop. He shook his head defiantly. "Her family needs her. They need her. And she lives now."

Makya rose. He could return to Pavati without stepping into the sunlight. He would speak to her and tell her all that he knew about the curse, what little he had learned. He told himself that, in this way, he would further share its responsibility.

~ B ~

"I saw seven coyotes pass last night. They were hunting in a pack. I sat on a lonely rock, resting like an old man, and I watched them pass. They trotted silently away as they sniffed the air. I thought their fur looked like dirty moonlight. I could see how the muscle rippled under the skin. How their eyes caught the light. What fine hunters they were," Hototo said. He sat slack against the wall. Exhausted and sore. He sipped some water from his ladle.

Finally returning to Crow Ledge, Hototo had immediately gathered the Morning Crow warriors by the front wall, chasing several women away from their chores in the process. "You can all just wait on dinner then," one of them had grumbled at Choovio as he climbed down the nearest ladder to join the

214

crowd. The sun had only just started its fall toward the horizon, flooding the terrace with bright light and barring Makya from attending.

The warriors waited. Hototo finally spoke again. "What do you think they were hunting?" he asked.

"Dinner," Honani said. Laughter trickled across the courtyard.

"Exactly what I thought," Hototo said. "And then I thought a little more. I recalled that they do not crawl into burrows and dens to get that dinner. I have never seen them with digging sticks," he said.

More quiet laughter. Hototo sipped more water and nodded.

"And that is the meaning. They do not seek prey while it hides in the dirt. They wait for the mouse to crawl from his hole. They know the mouse will feed under the stars. And then the coyote eats as well," Hototo paused. He looked at Choovio. "So we were fools to hunt this demon under the heat of the sun. He prowls the night. We must hunt him then. When he is not hiding."

"I speak with respect . . . but we must not leave Crow Ledge unprotected again," Choovio said firmly. He looked at the floor.

"I do not forget that lesson," Hototo said quickly. No trace of fatigue in his voice now. He stared until Choovio met his gaze. Hototo smiled. But the lines in his face were hard. "However . . . however . . . the coyotes were sent from the spirits. They show us the way. You will form a hunting party of seven to seek the demon. Makya will form another."

"Of course. I did not mean—"

"While the rest of us guard Crow Ledge," Hototo cut him off.

"Of course," Choovio repeated. He had not yet told Hototo about Pavati. He already feared his wrath. In fact, Shuman had come to once again check on his wife earlier in the day. Seeing Pavati healed, the Morning Crow matriarch had stopped mid-stride and then left without making a sound. She had slapped the wall and hurried from the room like a startled bird. Nobody had seen Shuman since. He would need to mend her trust. Even if Hototo readily blessed what Makya had done. Choovio felt regret writhing inside him.

Hototo continued. "You and your brother must return quickly if you see that Chayton or Istaqa moves against us. But if they are quiet, then you lay the head of that demon at my feet. I will hang it from my high window, and then those bastards will see. They will see and they will know," Hototo said with rising intensity.

"What will it tell them?" Honani asked.

"That the spirits stand with *us*!" Hototo replied. He slapped his hand against his chest as he spoke the last word.

~ B ~

Lansa, young warrior for the restored White Bat Clan, trotted toward Firetown with much news to share. Beyond the attack against Crow Ledge and the change of leadership at Low Nest, his cousin and close friend, Kwahu, had also been missing for the last two days. Kwahu had never returned after Chayton had sent him to postpone his wedding. Lansa hoped that the Ash Owls had simply asked, or demanded, that Kwahu stay with them. "Let me run. I am anxious for news," he had told Sik.

"Is it beneath Istaqa to send word to us? Why must we always report to them?" Sik had snapped, his face grotesque in the shadows. But the new clan leader had reluctantly agreed, bending his pride against the need for information.

Lansa was scared of Sik and Wik. Bats had always scared him. He wanted time away from Low Nest. Things were happening too fast there. He had barely slept. He saw the awful sight of Sik emerging from the cave, transformed by the power of the White Bat, every time he closed his eyes. However, the bright sun overhead and the open landscape cheered his spirits, and his sandals gripped the ground well after the recent rain. He looped away from Morning Crow land, taking the long trail west of Black Roof. For safety. The White Bats called it "Mushroom Run" because mushrooms grew in certain spots when the rain was kind. The Ash Owls simply called it "Long Path."

His arm was badly bruised. His ribs also ached. Lansa played the battle at Crow Ledge in his mind. He feared that Sik might hold his poor performance against him. Just as he had gripped the top of the siege pole, an old woman had struck his arm with a large rock. He had tumbled loose and landed hard, the breath slammed out of him. He had not gotten any closer to the fighting. He had only dragged himself back to his feet in time to join the chaotic retreat. He hoped that useful news might help repair his standing.

Lansa stopped abruptly. Another warrior crested the hill before him. His heart jumped. He shifted his feet to find level footing. He gripped his spear tightly. The other came up short as well. But then Lansa saw the double braid of the Ash Owls. He relaxed but not completely. Their alliance was still new.

"Messenger," he yelled.

"Same," the other warrior shouted back.

~ B ~

Hototo sat with legs crossed, his back beneath his small window. He had climbed to his private room on the topmost level of Crow Ledge. He was surprised that Shuman had not yet pressed him for information. However, he was glad for the delay. He needed more time to think. And he needed more time to rest.

The room was small, but the walls were adorned with sacred art, spirits and symbols for instruction and protection. His calendar stones stood on a ledge across from the window, carefully placed to follow the sun from season to season, to mark its changing shadow. Bundles of plants, some sporting wilted flowers, and thin strips of bark were stacked in one corner, next to his grinding stone. A few ceremonial bowls lay nearby.

Tied from the ceiling, three strings of feathers also swayed gently in the breeze. One held turkey feathers. Like a trickling waterfall of black and white pottery. Iridescently black crow feathers hung from another. And the final string held red and blue plumage, costly macaw feathers from the unseen south. Just a few of them. Trade had grown difficult in recent years, the great festivals faltering amid feuds and crop failures. Hototo also cursed the schismatic spirit leaders who had estranged Smoke Ridge with their lies. Despite their ceremonial importance, his supply of feathers had dwindled.

The light had only the first breath of sunset in its glow. He reached into his pouch and pulled free the rattle that the sibyl had provided. It seemed unremarkable. It was old, from a very large rattlesnake. He turned it around in the square of light on the floor before him. The bones were yellowed but just. A clever knot at the base held the nested beads in place. It also gave him a place to grip it. He dared not shake it.

It was unadorned otherwise. Hototo lifted it gently to his ear. He heard nothing. He sensed no more warm magic between his fingers. He thought of Makya resting in his quarters below. He thought of what the sibyl had asked him to do. He wondered if the sibyl could really understand the situation, never seeing beyond the walls of that tower. He hated them for asking him to kill Makya.

His thoughts turned to Makya, his birth so many years ago. "My poor Muna," he whispered. He could still see her birth water spilling into the stream as Muna shuddered in shock. Too far gone. Her ribs gored by his own spear. The empty husk of an enemy stranger thrown just out of reach. "The baby . . . is coming," Muna had whispered.

"Hurry!" Saya had said, panting hard as he knelt beside her. But then Muna had inhaled deeply. Rigidly. The dying breath was coming. "Free the child! Free the child!" Saya had begged.

Hototo had pushed firmly against her stomach, finding the boy inside, making room for his knife. He worked quickly. He could still remember how the skin resisted his knife. The sinew and gore. But so little blood. The demon had taken too much. And then, hurrying in the dark, Hototo had torn her flesh wider with his hands. He could still recall the tearing in his sense of touch. Muna had not moved.

Saya had lifted Makya from her, his skin purple in the moonlight, the blood starving in his veins. Hototo had slashed the mother-child cord as quickly as he could grasp it. Both men had worked the tiny arms and legs. An eternal moment had hung between them. And finally the boy had moved. His arms startled. He took a deep breath, a strong breath. His lungs embraced the air; his color began to lighten. Hototo remembered shaking almost uncontrollably as the boy finally whimpered.

Hototo watched the dust drift in the shaft of sunlight. He heard the feathers rustle softly over his head. He slipped the rattle back into his bag. He tied it around his waist and closed his eyes. He needed to sleep.

~ B ~

"We hope to attack the Morning Crows soon. Although we also wait for our new spirit leader to return from Smoke Ridge," Lansa said. His voice shook a little despite his best effort. He had just learned that Kwahu had died in Greedy Crow Canyon. He held his spear with both hands, leaning the point back over his shoulder.

Moki, the messenger from the Ash Owls, casually leaned on his own spear. "Istaqa may not wish to wait that long. We have much to avenge. Many good men were killed with Kwahu," he said. Moki disliked the short hair of the High Rocks Clan. It made their ears stick out. He did not understand why Chosovi had wanted to marry Kwahu in the first place.

"What of Kwahu's body and soul?" Lansa asked. He stared at the rocky cliff face that flanked Mushroom Run.

"Rituals were observed for both," Moki said. "Kwahu was buried rightly with many brave Ash Owls . . . so that Chosovi might say farewell, might easily visit his grave."

"White Bat souls have not passed through the sipapu properly in many years. Thank you for that. Thank you," Lansa replied.

"Why will you attack at night if Makya, by some dark magic, has the curse of the enemy stranger?" Moki asked.

"We are White Bats once more. We belong to the night. The spirit of the White Bat will protect us," Lansa responded. He told Moki nothing of the changed warriors at Low Nest. Thus were his orders. And since he could barely contain his own fear, Lansa saw how the Ash Owls might react poorly to the news.

"Owls love the night too. But we like to attack when the enemy is weak. Still . . . I will tell Istaqa. He must decide. That the son of Saya has turned enemy stranger . . . this may clarify many things," Moki said.

"And I will tell Sik. He . . . he leads the White Bats now."

"I am glad that Long Path brought us together. We have saved each other a lot of running today by avoiding Greedy Crow Canyon. Perhaps we will talk again soon."

Lansa nodded politely. However, the prospect of returning more quickly to Low Nest did not raise his spirits. He thought of the cold fog that, on rare winter days, would fill the canyons and chill the air. On such days, everything beyond Low Nest would recede into shadows. The fog imbued the slight sound of falling pebbles or flapping wings with vague portent. Lansa felt as though that fog had stolen into his stomach as he turned toward home. He decided to walk most of the way.

~ B ~

"I think he might live," Kotori said. He turned his back to Tocho after applying a paste of ash and fresh medicinal herbs. "I have burnt sacred roots to purge the poison."

"Working then?" Istaqa asked. He had climbed the ladder to check on his injured war leader. Istaqa had seen men survive bad wounds. He had seen men die too. He saw that both life and death pulled hard to claim their prize. Like two starving animals.

"Very tough," Kotori said. Tocho moaned but did not open his eyes. Fever still gripped him. His face was still swollen and dark with bruising from the helmet. Kotori had cleaned his wounds, cutting the spear wound wider to bleed out the infection. He had then salved them with healing plants. "Come. We must let him sleep now. Alo will bring more water and watch his fever tonight," the shaman added.

Moments later, the two men emerged into the open courtyard of Firetown. A group of women sorted produce in the amber light of sunset. "The spirits smile upon the harvest at last," Kotori said. He gestured toward woven baskets stacked with corn. Many ears had already been cleaned, their green husks piled nearby for new bedding. Istaqa picked one up and eyed its deep red kernels.

"Indeed," he said, turning it in his hand. "Good seed. The yellow and blue hybrids look healthy too," he added. At that moment, Moki approached. He greeted them and shared his exchange with the White Bat messenger. The clan leader paused before speaking.

"Is that possible . . . that the son of Saya is an enemy stranger now?" Istaqa finally asked. He kept his voice low and surveyed the failing light. He felt the tremor in his soul but kept his voice calm.

"Perhaps related to the stranger we killed last night," Kotori said. "But this fits poorly with the news that Ahote brought. Did the Morning Crows hunt one of their own in Broken Spine Canyon? They might have concealed that fact out of shame."

Istaqa did not answer right away. He stared off at nothing. He sighed and finally spoke his mind. "But if he fought with them at Crow Ledge . . . no matter. If they are willing to abide the presence of a demon among them, then truly we know the enemy. Such men . . . we can count no lie too great."

"Such men might even seek unholy friends. Like the one that tortured Tocho," Kotori added.

"Who would toy with an enemy like that?" Moki said. He shook his head with grim understanding. He had been among those that had rescued the wounded man.

"We need to act soon," Istaqa said.

"We will have a true ally if the White Bats are now reborn," Kotori added.

"Mmmh," Istaqa grunted. "Will they want your apprentice to become their new spirit leader?"

Kotori clasped his hands. "That would be wond–"

"No," Moki said. "Lansa was very clear. One of the White Bats travels now to Smoke Ridge to seek training. They will accept no acolyte from us."

"That is . . . that is unfortunate," Kotori said, holding back even harsher words. He unclasped his hands in disgust. Moki raised his eyebrows in surprise.

"I agree with Kotori. Cha'Akmongwi was from Smoke Ridge. If that old fool truly listened to the spirits . . . then the spirits were yanking his rattle," Istaqa said quietly.

"I am too young," Moki said.

"Wise men led the White Bats once. Many years ago. But when their last true clan leader coughed himself to death, like so many others that winter, then the White Bat shaman, Cha'Akmongwi, took over. One year, he forbade his people from planting until long after our custom. He misread both the sun and moon. It would displease the spirits, he said. And when the rain stopped, his budding plants paid the price. Those fools came to our granary three times that winter. Three times."

"While the Morning Crows helped none but themselves," Kotori added.

"They turned the White Bats away?" Moki asked.

"And stole game from White Bat territory. Hunters were killed in Seven Sisters Canyon. They fought viciously that winter."

"That winter nearly starved us all. But let us hope that they still remember Chayton wisely around the fire at Low Nest," Istaqa said.

"Still . . . it is better to have allies that do not deny the will of the spirits as Chayton did. Allies that do not bury the traditions that sustain us."

"Of course," Istaqa said without emotion. Uncomfortable silence hung in the air.

"Do you have more questions?" Moki finally asked.

"Thank you, Moki. Well done. Go drink some water," Istaqa said. The clan leader walked to the stone wall that formed the outermost defensive perimeter of Firetown. It also formed the front wall of several kivas below his feet. He looked down over the edge. Kotori stood two steps behind him. "No way . . ." Istaqa finally said. "No way that we let the High Ro–, I mean, White Bats claim Crow Ledge for themselves. That will not happen. We have people for those rooms and crops for that good ground."

"Shall I prepare the war blessing for tonight?" Kotori asked.

"No. Wait until tomorrow morning. Moki was right. We will attack while the cursed Crow is at his weakest. If it is even true," Istaqa said. "Help me find Len and Nalnish. I have another task for them."

CHAPTER 17

Hunters and Prey

"HOW? HOW CAN Smoke Ridge accept such demons among us?" Shuman asked. She hiked both eyebrows with disgust.

"Speak plain, Shuman. Do you doubt me or the Smoke Clan?" Hototo retorted.

"I doubt both if you agree with this so-called wisdom," Shuman scoffed. A reddish glow still painted the sky near the horizon. However, dark shadows already blanketed the field where Shuman stood, the high canyon walls obscuring the remaining light. To further screen herself from Crow Ledge, the matriarch stood behind several bean plots, tall poles lashed together and leafy with climbing vines. Tiny night insects swirled around the vegetation. A lone cicada buzzed loudly in the leaves behind her.

Wishing to speak where Makya and Pavati could not overhear, Shuman had summoned Hototo to this place. Sihu, following the request from her grandmother, had roused Hototo from his deep slumber and forced him to climb down, despite his sore joints, into the canyon where the matriarch waited. It had sharpened his edge before the conversation had even started.

Shuman continued to press her attack. "Would the sibyl bless hungry flames starving for wood? Let those flames wander through Crow Ledge with its wooden beams and ladders? Would you?" she asked.

"The sibyl sees that threats are upon us. I see them too. And recall that we burn fires in every kiva, Shuman. Yes, flames can burn. However, we can also control them. Consider that we could not survive the winter without—"

"Enough!" Shuman interrupted. She clapped her hands for emphasis. "I know the many uses of fire. And I know the dangers we face. I asked you to seek help from Istaqa because I do understand the threat. I asked you before you sent Choovio to the edge of Ash Owl territory. You refused. And now we must weather his certain revenge."

"Morning Crows are dead because of Istaqa. How dare you fault my leadership for his murderous Ash Owls?" Hototo snapped.

Shuman took two steps forward. "You will address me with respect or you will no longer lead the Morning Crows!" she whispered. Cold anger filled her voice. Hototo chewed his lip before he replied. He held both hands behind his back. She had never before threatened a change of leadership.

He finally responded, lowering his voice in kind. "I apologize for my anger and will consider your concerns, Shuman. I beg you to trust me, though. I have walked with Makya for two days. His heart seems no differ—"

"Then he will continue to make trouble? He will still reject our warnings?"

"He has made mistakes. I know that . . . but you also know that Makya would trade his life to protect the Morning Crows. Just as his father did. I promise that we have nothing to fear from either of them. And we have much to fear on all sides right now."

Shuman turned and walked deeper among the crops. Her lean shoulders sagged with concern. Hototo followed slowly. A gentle breeze rustled in the corn. She finally turned back toward him. "I will trust you for now."

Hototo nodded. "Thank you, Shu."

"I have thought about little Kaya many times today. Pavati hungers for blood now. But would it serve Kaya better if she had no mother? Every answer hurts my heart. So follow this path for now. Perhaps the sibyl offers wisdom after all."

Hototo made no reply. A moment of silence passed between them. The anger had gone from the air. A small mouse darted through the leaves by her feet. Shuman startled but hid it well. Hototo gestured toward the cliff dwelling. "Come back to Crow Ledge. We are not safe here under the stars. Not until we have killed the enemy stranger." The tired shaman squeezed the small bag that hung from his waist, nervously checking its contents.

~ B ~

The vampire, now far from his den, no longer disguised his trail. The night had started to bloom. He chose soft earth for his boots, leaving clear prints. Intermittently. He had sensed the presence of men in this vicinity and sought to distract them from his true hiding place. "Careless feet carefully placed," one of his mentors had taught him. He moved erratically like a bee in search of nectar. He also scanned the hills and ravines as he moved, fully aware that the local warriors had shown the ability to blend into the landscape.

He thought about last night. The sentry he had killed. Although his line of sight had not cleared the intervening cliffs, the vampire had seen the dim glow of firelight touching the canyon floor in the distance. The coming sunrise had forced his retreat before he could investigate further. However, he still wanted to know what was worth guarding. He angled back toward where he had taken blood the night before. The cool night air filled his lungs. He thrilled to see the vault of stars above him.

And then he heard the telltale *snap* from the hill above him. He had no time to move. The quarrel bit into the front of his shoulder. Pain exploded down his arm and across his chest. The vampire gasped in surprise and agony. He dared not attack the hill above him. Too much open ground to cover. He turned and ran. Dead sprint. He gritted his teeth in pain and clutched his sword to silence its movement. His cape billowed out behind him, a modicum of protection as he moved away from the crossbow.

~ B ~

Len and Nalnish scrambled down the hill. They moved deftly through the dense brush that thrived in certain parts of the Broken Hills, especially along the flanks of Deer Trail. "Load it again! Load the arrow!" Len whispered. His voice trembled with excitement. Nalnish stopped at the bottom. He fumbled with the strange weapon but finally set the trigger.

"You saw his speed. We should get help," Nalnish panted.

"We got him. We need to finish him," Len panted back.

"Need more warriors."

"Never find him if we go back. Hurry," Len insisted.

"We wounded him!" Nalnish hissed in frustration. He knew Len was right. It would take them too long to return to Firetown. He stamped his foot and took off running again. The demon was taking them deeper into the Broken Hills. Len ran right at his heel, arrow notched in his own bow.

~ B ~

Kele and Cheveyo followed the new plan that Hototo had laid out. Straining their senses against the dark, they stalked quietly through a large ravine in the Broken Hills, not far from Ash Owl territory, one of a handful of ravines that snaked gently down and eventually opened into Seeker Canyon. Maybe two or three arrow flights further down. Erosion had carved shallow dens into the sides of the trench at various points along the descent.

"Nothing," Kele whispered as he jabbed his spear into the shadows, hitting the dirt behind. His bow was slung across his back. They did not expect to find the enemy stranger there, just standing in the shadows, and yet it seemed foolish to pass without checking. Every empty den seemed like progress.

"Wait. What was that?" Cheveyo whispered. Both men heard quick footsteps approaching the ravine. They tensed and pressed back into the concavity of earth that Kele had just stabbed. They waited only an instant. Dark against the starry sky they saw the enemy stranger leap and land in the wide trench, taller than any Morning Crow they had ever seen. His great cloak billowed and then fell heavily against his back. He was only nine or ten lengths away. Cold terror filled the ravine. It felt like stumbling at the edge of a sudden abyss. Even with his back turned. He glanced quickly up and down the fissure. He moved and breathed, and yet, no ephemeral spark of life disturbed the air around him. The demon spun toward them. They saw his pale hands and face, his sunken cheeks and the dark light in his eyes. They did not yet see the stubby arrow buried in his shoulder. Kele knew instantly that he stood in the presence of an ancient ruin, both old and vile in purpose. "Dead," Cheveyo mouthed. But the air to make a sound was stuck in his throat.

The demon saw them too, having already sensed the blood in their veins. He lunged without making a sound. His blade flashed. He covered the ground with incredible speed, even moving uphill. Kele struggled to whistle and alert the five that hunted with them. "Here! Here!" he finally screamed as the enemy stranger closed the distance. "Help us!" Cheveyo shouted. Both warriors waited for him to close the distance and then thrust their spears. They aimed for the heart as Hototo had instructed. However, the demon swept both spears aside with the flat of his blade. The smacking sound filled the ravine.

Kele lost his spear as the demon turned it powerfully aside. He lowered his shoulder to tackle the demon, exploding off the embankment behind him. But the enemy stranger brought the handle of his long knife back and down across his body. He caught Kele across the back of his head, narrowly missing the soft hole in his skull. Kele hit the ground, red pain exploding across his vision, and rolled away, blood springing from his scalp. Dirt smeared the palms of his hands.

~ B ~

Enraged that the crossbow still afflicted him, even after the Order of St. John had met its end, the vampire wanted to kill. But he also needed to feed. The quarrel had struck entirely too close to his heart this time, and his injury was deep. The shaft had penetrated all the way to the fletching. He could not lift his left arm without great pain. Only fresh blood would heal that quickly, and that fact impaired his caution. As one hunter collapsed in the dirt, the vampire stepped past him, easily absorbing a desperate punch from the other. Still holding his sword, the vampire slammed the flat of his hand into the face of his intended victim and twisted to expose his neck in one deft motion.

~ B ~

Cheveyo felt the handle smash into his face and the cold hand that wielded it. The dead chill of the skin sent a special flash of terror through him; and in that same moment, his head hit the wall of earth and roots behind him. Hard. Cheveyo was stunned. The terrible strength of the demon pinned his skull against the wall. He struggled to pry himself loose but could not match the power that held him fast. However, as the fangs found his neck, Cheveyo felt the pain, sharp and hot, and his head cleared.

He heard the carnal slurp of blood. He knew it ran from his neck. He saw the arrow jutting from the shoulder right in front of him. He punched it hard now, driving it deeper into the flesh. He felt it scrape past bone. The vampire loosed his grip and yelled with anger, blood spraying from his lips. Cheveyo felt it spatter his cheek, knowing it was his own. At that moment,

Kele tackled the demon once again, hitting him blind from behind. He took the demon down and slashed at him with his stone knife, cutting him several times.

Blood streaked his neck, and his head swam; but Cheveyo stumbled forward to grab his spear. He had lost it when the enemy stranger had struck his face. His friend could not hold the nocturnal strength of the monster. The demon grabbed Kele by his braid and, even from his back, pitched him into the dirt nearby. Cheveyo stabbed. The demon had lost the sword when Kele tackled him but still parried the blow with his hand. He grabbed the shaft of the spear and knocked Cheveyo off his unsteady feet. The monster scrambled to his feet with flowing speed and kicked Cheveyo hard, striking the groin.

Kele also rose and attacked again. The demon feinted away from both men, toward the other side of the ravine; and as Kele closed the distance, the enemy stranger ripped the quarrel from his shoulder with an angry snarl and snap of ripped flesh. Kele swung his knife hard. But the demon swung his cloak forward with his lame arm and blunted the blow. At that same moment, Kele saw the demon swing his other arm. He felt the already-gory quarrel strike deep between his ribs.

~ *B* ~

The vampire grabbed the scrappy warrior by the neck, tossing him against the bank of the ravine with ease. Lunging after him and swiping the knife from his hand, the vampire once again went for the throat, refusing to leave this battle without healing blood. He felt more fiery warmth flash through his body as he clamped down upon the artery. The pain in his shoulder lessened. The vampire sought to drain the man quickly. He also watched the other warrior, seeing that his kick had taken its toll. He not yet decided whether he would kill the other one by sword or by fang.

However, the vampire heard steps coming from above. "There!" another voice shouted. The vampire spun around, suddenly realizing that, as the immediacy of combat had claimed his focus, he had forgotten about the hunters who chased him. *Snap.* Another shot from the crossbow. The quarrel sank into his upper thigh, just below the hip. An arrow also grazed his cheek. "Damn you!" he hissed.

The vampire jerked the second quarrel from his leg and stabbed the warrior still pinned before him. Narrowly missing the neck, his target, the vampire drove its sharp point deep into the meat of the shoulder. The vampire rolled. In one skilled motion, he reached his sword and rose once more to his feet, cape drawn across him defensively. The two hunters, now landing close in the ravine, stopped short. They had not yet placed new arrows in their weapons. They saw the long blade, felt the unnatural power before them. The vampire lunged. He swung his sword hard at the one who carried the crossbow.

Although the warrior parried the stroke with the heavy crossbow stock, the power of the blow wrenched it from his hands. He charged the vampire to pass the range of his sword. However, the vampire stepped back deftly. He punched the man to the ground with the pommel of his sword, the same efficient move he had used before. The other warrior fired an arrow from his bow. The vampire easily deflected it with his cloak. It clattered lightly into the dirt near his feet. The man slowly backed away in response.

With fresh blood in his veins and now sober to the risk around him, including the sound of more footsteps from another direction, the vampire dared not press the battle further. He took three powerful steps to leap clear of the ravine. He sprinted down the hill and into the shadows. He was grimly silent, even inside his own head.

~ B ~

Choovio scrambled into the ravine a few short breaths later, four warriors with him, arrows notched. He saw Kele slumped against the side of the ravine, Cheveyo on his knees. In the same moment, he saw Nalnish lifting the strange bow from the ground. He saw the double braid hanging forward as he reached down. He saw that Len held his bow at the ready. "Ash Owls!" he shouted.

"Wait!" Nalnish shouted, but it was too late. The Morning Crows had heard the cry for help. The hunt, like setting snares for animal feet, had already pulled the men tight. Bows twanged. Two arrows hit Nalnish, one right in the throat. He dropped upon his knees, shock frozen in his face. Two more arrows clattered in the dirt, further down the slope. Len had felt them pass, one even fanning his cheek. Len had seen the Morning Crows slaughter his friends below Black Roof just days before. He was also badly outnumbered. He ran without hesitation. He scrambled from the ravine, seeing the dark silhouette of the demon vanish into Greedy Crow Canyon ahead of him. Len turned toward Firetown. He kept his head low, but no arrows followed. The Morning Crows had turned to their wounded.

Nalnish was dying quickly. Blood gurgled in his throat. Spasms wracked his arms and legs. The Morning Crow warriors let him lie where he had fallen. "Good shot!" one said. Several others nodded.

Choovio knelt and examined both Cheveyo and Kele. He saw the ragged bites on their necks. Ugly open wounds. "Not much bleeding," he said. He knew what it meant but would not speak it aloud. Both men struggled to stand. "We need to get them back to Crow Ledge. Hototo can help them," Choovio assured, even though he did not believe it.

"He touched me . . . so much older than the pit houses . . . he bit me . . . his teeth were like angry bone needles . . ." Kele murmured. The demon had felt as cold as winter stone. It had felt like the restless spirits that lingered still in certain ruins.

"The enemy stranger . . ." Cheveyo said. Choovio helped him to his feet.

"I know," he said.

". . . the Ash Owls were chasing him!" Cheveyo groaned.

"I know," Choovio said again, frustration in his voice. He went to extract the weapon from beneath Nalnish. Choovio saw that the eyes were already vacant. He gently rolled him over to pull the short arrows from his breech as well. He also gathered the weapons of his injured men. "Let's hurry now," he said. "I will not bet our lives that those two Ash Owls hunted alone."

~ B ~

Makya led his men closer to Low Nest. They walked through Seven Sisters Canyon. Running water chilled the air here, once the sun departed. They wore winter shirts, woven from cotton, to stave off the cold. However, they had rolled these shirts in the dirt to better hide their movements.

Makya had seen the enemy stranger in Seven Sisters Canyon before. On the night the High Rocks Clan had attacked Crow Ledge. He suspected that the demon might hunt there again. In fact, his mind had pulled in that direction while he slept. He had seen the Seven Sisters themselves, burning in the dark. They had crackled and hissed, seven bright fires in the center of some vast cavern. However, they cast no light upon the distant walls. And although Makya could touch the walls and feel strange symbols etched into the rock, he could see nothing but the flames. He had come to Hototo when the dream released him. "I wish to explore Seven Sisters Canyon tonight. Will you allow me to hunt the demon there?"

The shaman had narrowed his eyes. "Why should I allow it? Why do you choose that path?"

"My dream suggested that I look there."

"Tell me the truth . . . do you intend more trouble with the High Rocks Clan?" Hototo had asked.

Makya had sworn that his intentions did not involve Low Nest; and while Hototo had nodded his wary assent, averring that Makya had followed dreams to find the demon twice before, the lack of trust still gnawed at Makya as he walked. His warriors had fanned out now. It was impossible to keep the line of sight. "But stay within easy earshot," he had told them.

He walked with Honani and felt grateful to walk with a friend. He valued any thread of connection to what his life had been before his climb into the Cave of Visions. "Do you think we are getting too close to Low Nest? Or are you trying to smell what they ate for dinner?" Honani asked.

"We owe them nothing," Makya said.

"Why did the—"

"Shhh!" Makya interrupted. He heard running footsteps. Honani heard nothing but froze where he stood.

"What?" he whispered.

"Coming that way . . ." Makya said. He pointed over the high escarpment that divided the ground ahead and to their left. The wall of the canyon dissolved into a wide gap in that direction. You could ultimately follow it into the Broken Hills. ". . . but not very close!" He took off running toward the distant sound. Several of his party had intended to explore in that direction. Makya realized now that they had drifted too far apart. Shouts erupted. Honani could still barely hear them.

"Run!" a voice yelled hoarsely. An animal snarl broke viciously across their screams. Makya heard scuffling feet. He heard the clatter of wood, the dull smack of colliding flesh. And then bones snapping. The muddy quiet that followed made him sick to his stomach. He sprinted harder. He scrambled over rough terrain, ignoring the brush that scraped his shins.

"Ahhhh!" he gasped as he finally crested the final hill. He saw two High Rocks warriors, or so he guessed, running away very quickly. They were already far from where two Morning Crows had fallen. Even at a distance, Makya felt the queer coldness of the runners, and more strangely yet, with his keen nocturnal eyes, he saw sharp ears and hard ridging along their bare spines. He saw their pale skin, the brutal reach of their arms and legs. He felt unclean as he saw them. "What were they?" he breathed.

Honani finally reached the top of the hill behind him, panting hard. He quickly began to slide down toward his fallen comrades. Makya stood there yet, stunned as he contemplated what he had seen. "No-no-no-no!" Honani wailed as he reached the slain. Close enough now to recognize his friends through the veil of night, Honani fell to his knees. He reached out his hands but did not touch either corpse, still warm and gently twitching.

Makya heard the rest of his men scrambling up the hill behind him. His wits returned. "Honani . . . keep your voice down!" he hissed as he shuffled quickly down the hillside.

"What . . . happened here?" Honani gasped.

The two warriors lay in pools of blood. A spear had struck one hard in the ribs. For the other, bloody stripes that looked like claw marks cut across his chest and one of his arms. Makya saw that both their heads were twisted too far, necks broken. But worst of all, their necks, and well into the shoulder, were torn away entirely, flesh ripped out like fawns found by panthers. They were dead, an ashen pallor across the skin.

The wounds had bled quickly and unsparingly; the smell was intoxicating to Makya. Hunger flashed like fire in his veins. He struggled against himself as he looked at the dark blood that had gathered in the dirt beneath his friends. Fear filled his chest.

"Chayton has brought monsters to Low Nest," Makya said.

"Wh-what do we do?" Honani asked. He wiped tears from his eyes.

"We need to carry them back. You four take him. I can carry the other," Makya said. His tongue felt thick in his mouth. It scraped against his fangs.

~ B ~

The vampire smelled bloodshed on the breeze, and his damaged body lusted for it. He stood at the entrance to his hole in the rocks and breathed in deeply. It was not so far away. His feet took several uncertain steps. Then two steps back. He felt the shadow of a vulture glide over him. It smelled the blood as well. He knew that more blood would heal him quickly. It would cool the hot pain in his shoulder and thigh, pain that would not subside until more fresh blood flowed through his dead veins. He took another step into the breeze but stopped. He thought of the Order of St. John, newly deceased.

"And let Jerome have the last laugh from Heaven . . ." the vampire muttered. "Not tonight," he added.

He scanned the hills in every direction, all his senses wide awake. Content that none observed him, he looked at the dirt and rocks all around him, looking for any trail that might betray him in the sunlight: spilled blood, boot marks, torn fabric.

"Clean," he whispered.

One more look to the horizons and then he slipped, like a leopard leaping to a tree branch, into the makeshift burrow. He stifled the pain as his shoulder landed and squeezed past the small entrance. With wounded effort, the vampire positioned some brush and then laid the large rock carefully across the hole. He blocked several cracks with more stones he had stored inside. And finally he closed his eyes and allowed the darkness to engulf him, peace of sorts for one who saw the night with vivid sight. He tucked himself as far from the entrance as possible.

The vampire struggled to adjust his cape to cover him. He had not taken enough blood from those men in the ravine to kill them. He knew they would turn. He had violated the Fifth Precept again, would now have to contend with two more ferals. He could not speak their language. He could not train them or share the secrets of his kind. They could not hear the hard history of his race or commit the Eight Precepts to memory. That meant that he had also technically violated the First Precept again. "What a mess!" he voiced with frustration. He breathed deep. The pain lay there with him, its fangs holding him.

The vampire thought back to the iron maiden so many years ago. He told himself that this pain was nothing. If he could leave that spiked coffin, depart it still sane, he could endure the long day and hunt fresh tomorrow night. He could fix his mess tomorrow. He could wait until his hunters could be surprised once again and then revel in the sensation of healing.

"And this too shall pass. This too shall pass. This too shall pass . . ." he whispered to focus his mind and steer it away from the steady pain. He wondered how many of his kind had chanted a similar mantra in the lonely dark.

~ B ~

Honani clutched the right thigh of his slain friend. Three other Morning Crows lifted the other limbs. They panted from the burden, arms and shoulders aching from the awful task. Makya trailed many steps behind. In the heart of the night, he carried the other limp corpse easily across his shoulder. Blood droplets gathered at the gored neck. Makya caught them in his hand and then, carefully watching the men who walked ahead of him, licked his palm. The wind blew gently against his back.

He did not know how long enemy strangers could go without feeding. He felt very little hunger now. And yet he could feel that its presence would come one day. He told himself that what he did now served to stymie that future day. His thoughts flew to Pavati. Hunger would find her too.

"Do you need help?" Honani called back, looking over his shoulder, hissing the words as loud as he dared. They had moved a good distance from High Rocks land now.

"No. I'll catch up. Hurry ahead if you can," Makya hissed back.

He felt his heart flutter, quickened by the taste of blood. How strange it felt now in his chest. He felt great fear. As though he was falling and could not land. He would destroy the enemy clans with his great power. But what then? He could see only hunger. He saw that perhaps Sihu would never return to his bed. Shuman would never let her fear subside. He saw his children running through sunlit fields while he hid behind walls.

He also saw that true Morning Crows would never drink the blood of fallen comrades, and the shameful act terrified him. And yet he caught another droplet. It was deep red to his eyes, even in the shadowed canyon. He told himself that he needed his strength to defend the living after all, especially from the beasts he had just seen fleeing toward Low Nest. He told himself that the dead had passed beyond such cares. He told himself, and not for the first time since his battle in the Cave of Visions, that the story of his birth surely confirmed his present path, that the spirits had intended him to find the enemy stranger first.

He looked once more at the men who walked ahead, checking their line of sight. He licked more blood furtively from his palm.

CHAPTER 18

What the Sibyl Commanded

C HOSOVI LIFTED A decapitated turkey. She gripped the twitching legs tightly and looped the twine around the pole. At the same time she adjusted the bowl with her bare foot to catch the blood. A few drops spattered her leg. She would let the bird drain, allow the body to fall quiet before plucking its brown and gray feathers.

The sun had just climbed high enough to set the highest cliffs ablaze across from Firetown. The lingering wall of shadow would soon dissipate and restore the harvest ochre to the land. However, the death of Kwahu, her intended husband, numbed Chosovi. The thought of his cold corpse had played across her fingers even as she had wrestled the turkey from its pen. "Kwahu," she sighed. She had endured the ritual of burial, stood over the soil that interred him, and now she felt as though an empty room moved with her at all times. Her hair hung long against her back, an act of mourning.

Chosovi stood back and waited, ensuring that her twine held fast. The bowl filled with dark blood. Tocho had made it for her wedding. He had painted it with careful designs and allowed her to see it in advance. It mocked her now, and she used it with muted rage, knowing the blood would stain it and ruin its beauty. She saw cruel symmetry in the fact that Tocho himself now fought for life.

Her mind drifted to Widow Rock. The wind swirled hard on that high ledge. You stood so close to the sky there. She imagined the smooth stone beneath her feet, nothing else to anchor her. Chosovi saw the distant canyon in her mind. It curled below Widow Rock, tranquil and dissolved of detail, the empty sky above her. She let the image fade from her mind, unwilling to make that long hike, unwilling to take that final step. "Not a widow anyway!" she scoffed to herself. The Morning Crows had denied her even that.

White smoke rose from the nearby kiva now. She heard Kotori begin to incant, and the murmur of the war blessing drifted toward her. It seemed to dissolve with the smoke as it crossed the terrace. She could not hear the words distinctly. She knew that Kotori wore the Ash Owl robe as he tended the fire. He had walked past her several chores ago, its somber feathers and woven hair obscuring his thin frame. Actual owls had once nested in the fissures and alcoves high above. They had shed those feathers. Chosovi had collected many of them as a child, often with Pimne and Chua. They had always been close friends. With regret but no unspent feelings to spare, she realized that she had not mourned them enough.

Kotori would soon finish the blessing. He would then stir sacred ash into the paint, marking each warrior for protection. The wind shifted, carrying the smoke into her face. But Chosovi did not step aside. "Smoked turkey," she said with a hollow smile. She watched the dead bird. It still worked its wings by some deep cadence. She let the acrid smoke sting her eyes.

~ *B* ~

"No. They will kill you," Hototo said flatly. He felt frayed at the edges.

"But they were hunting the demon. We share an enemy," Choovio replied. He faced Hototo and met his gaze. The sun was rising, driving the stars from the sky. His brother had retired to his room, to the safety of shadows. They stood next to the corn, much of it ripe for harvest.

"We cannot trust them. And they are friendly with the High Rocks Clan. Those cowards from Low Nest were killers again last night . . . and so brutal. Did you see what they did?" Hototo insisted.

"I will call for Ahote by name. I will shout that I wish to meet with empty hands. We can trust them to honor that."

"No. They no longer value the customs as we do. And how long will they help us when they find that your brother carries the curse? Or when they find that Pavati, your own wife, hungers for blood like an enemy stranger?"

Choovio winced. He had not told the shaman yet, but Hototo had discovered it just the same. His cheeks flushed hot with shame, but Choovio persisted. "What they faced last night was . . . its strength was terrible. Please. Let me seek help from the Ash Owls."

"You killed many of their clan only days ago. And you killed another tonight. Choovio, they will want revenge. How can they not?"

"I understand that, but if I can off—"

"You say they hunt the demon, that we share this enemy. Yet, Ahote does not come here. Recall that they attacked you *after* you spoke with him!" Hototo said, his voice growing tight with anger. Several moments passed in silence. "They will kill you on sight. Another prize for Istaqa," he added.

"I am willing to take that chance after last night. I will accept the risk," Choovio answered. He spoke softly. Hototo turned abruptly away and looked toward the dawn.

"I am not willing to take that chance. I cannot risk—"

"But if the sibyl told you and Makya that—"

"But nothing," Hototo suddenly snapped. He still looked away. "You . . . your brother did not heed me when he left Crow Ledge. You see the consequences now. Am I not the leader of the Morning Crows?" he snapped.

"You are. You know th—" Choovio replied.

"Then you will obey what I tell you. I will not abide another disloyal act. Do you understand me?"

Choovio did not answer right away. He fought with himself before finally speaking. "Yes," he said softly.

"Yes what?" Hototo pushed. He stepped very close to Choovio now, his eyes wide with intensity. His breath quickened.

"I will obey. I will respect your leadership of the Morning Crows . . . I will not seek help from the Ash Owls," he said. Defeated.

"Get some sleep now," Hototo said. He patted Choovio on the shoulder and forced a smile. "This night has been another hard one for all of us. I must go to the kiva and return two more souls. They press against my chest like heavy stones," he added.

~ B ~

Istaqa spoke now. The clan leader had gathered the Ash Owl warriors on the terrace once the war blessing was complete. Although his face looked hard and full of struggle, he still did not raise his voice. "Nalnish has been killed by the Morning Crows. Last night in the Broken Hills. I know that your anger already flows. That your thirst to avenge the murders in Greedy Crow Canyon runs through every vein. Let his murder add to the torrent as you prepare for . . ."

Ahote stepped backward. It felt like Istaqa had punched him in the chest. The death of his close friend stunned him. Ahote had seen Len slip into the kiva after Kotori had already started. He had worried that Nalnish had not followed, especially as Len had brooded through the ceremony. Still, Ahote had hoped for a logical explanation, a minor injury perhaps. But this news felt like falling from a great height. The pain of real damage beneath a blanket of ringing numbness.

How had the two warriors even come across the Morning Crows in the Broken Hills? Both groups must have hunted the same demon. But whether Choovio had told the truth seemed suddenly irrelevant. Firetown had been betrayed either way; too many Ash Owls had died. Nalnish included. Ahote felt his grief diluted by anger. It promised a kind of relief. He imagined Choovio pinned beneath a spear. Its sharp point drawing blood. He imagined the Morning Crow pleading for mercy.

Ahote looked toward Len once again. However, the outrage that Len had shown at the war council had vanished. His body said something different now. The tired warrior looked isolated. He had opened a small space away from the warriors standing nearby. His eyes were cast down. He did not even glance toward the clan leader. His arms were folded tightly. As though he fought an invisible chill. Ahote suspected that Len and Nalnish must have seen an enemy stranger last night.

In fact, Ahote knew that Len and Nalnish had been sent to hunt for signs of the demon. His friend had shown him the strange bow before departing. Ahote had also heard rumors that an enemy stranger actually hid within Crow Ledge. However, Istaqa said nothing of demons as he spoke to the assembled warriors. Nothing of those rumors. Ahote understood. If the clan leader sought to prepare warriors for battle, it would not help to speak of monsters lurking in the shadows.

As Istaqa finally finished speaking, Ahote realized that he had stopped paying attention many words back. The shouts that followed, the jeers against the Morning Crows, the barking calls for vengeance, all seemed like distant thunder, even as Ahote joined in. He saw that Len barely uttered a sound. And then the noise died away. The time had come to move against Crow Ledge.

Ahote worked his way toward Len now. He wanted to know more about the death of his friend. But he stopped short. Through the crowd of warriors, he saw Kwatoko grab Len by the arm. The war leader whispered something to Len. Several unheard whispers passed back and forth, and then Ahote saw an unspoken moment pass between them. It seemed more than it should have been, something like an objection or disagreement. Len looked uncertain as he stepped back and pulled free his arm. Kwatoko waited there. And then finally Len nodded, giving one short gesture of assent before he removed himself from the crowded terrace. His steps were quick and determined.

~ B ~

A square of sunlight painted the wall opposite the window. Makya watched from the darkest corner of his room. Its bright glare hurt his eyes. The shaft of light also marked a source of danger as it crossed the room. Like a spear constantly flying above his head. The din across Crow Ledge also kept him from sleeping, a result of his enhanced hearing. The clacking percussion of women grinding corn, the frequent rattle of ladders, conversation and laughter, the sudden shrieks of playing children: all floated through the window to torment the young warrior. Every noise sounded like unfettered freedom of movement.

Makya also knew that Sihu and the boys had gone into the canyon, planning to pull weeds and gather beans. He imagined them bathed in radiant light. He decided to move to the very back of Crow Ledge and try sleeping there. He crawled from the room, seeking the narrow space, cool and dark, between the cliff and the rear wall of the dwelling, the relative quiet it might confer.

~ B ~

The Ash Owls marched quickly in the direction of Crow Ledge, holding themselves to a measured pace. Fast enough to loosen muscles. Slow enough to preserve stamina. Many ladders moved with them, each resting across multiple shoulders to distribute the weight. Ahote trudged beneath one such ladder. Outrage against the Morning Crows churned behind his ribs. Fresh questions filled his skull. He could not fully reconcile the two. His stomach hurt as though he had eaten rotten meat.

The death of his friend, Ahote reasoned, could not have been an ambush. The Crows would not have known to wait for Len and Nalnish in the Broken Hills. But if both parties had come there to hunt the enemy stranger, then why did the two groups not stand together when, as Ahote suspected, they had found the demon? Choovio would have shown restraint. He had proven as much that night in the Spine. Nalnish would have shown restraint toward the Morning Crows too. Would Len not have done the same?

Ahote reasoned that, if there was an enemy stranger, then the demon could have actually killed Nalnish. Istaqa could have lied. He would want to protect the focus of the Ash Owls at this crucial moment. Ahote could understand that. But the rumors of an enemy stranger among the Morning Crows puzzled him as well. The story simply did not align with the night he had spent among the Morning Crows. The death of Nalnish and the multiple deaths on Short Path also made little sense from that point of view.

Ahote saw that he could resolve this confusion easily. He only needed to admit that he had been wrong about Choovio. If the Morning Crows had spared his life for the purpose of sowing confusion, it all made sense. It would mean that they were killing Ash Owls by design. The riddle of the enemy stranger would not matter. The idea seemed both difficult and enticing. He wanted to believe it. "No!" he breathed. Ahote seethed with anger, but he refused to accept that Choovio had deceived him.

As they moved toward Broken Spine, Ahote called another warrior to take his place under the rungs. He moved near the head of the column, falling into step just behind Kwatoko. Ahote felt ashamed that he had argued against attacking Crow Ledge. He wanted other warriors to see him at the front of the line. He hoped that it might help restore his standing in the eyes of the younger men. He also felt glad for the spots of white paint that marked his body. The paint separated him from that argument. It proved that he had, like those who marched behind him, taken war as his second skin for today.

"Where is Len?" Ahote ventured to ask.

"I sent him ahead . . . one of the advance scouts."

Ahote paused. "I understand," he finally said. Len had already been awake all night. Even as one of the most trusted scouts, it still seemed cruel to assign Len another running role in advance of the battle. And Kwatoko was not cruel. He was an architect; he planned ahead. It proved that Len had seen the enemy stranger. The war leader had clearly assigned the exhausted warrior a role that would isolate him. It would serve to keep questions to a minimum prior to the attack on Crow Ledge.

Despite his other feelings, Ahote also furtively scanned the floor of the canyon. The ground had been scrubbed clean from the recent rain. His eyes searched for footprints or some sign left behind, etched lines or some rocks suggestively placed, that might tell him whether Choovio had come, even after Greedy Crow Canyon and even after the rain, to honor their agreement.

Ahote saw no such sign. The cursory examination told him nothing for certain. But to imagine that Choovio had not honored their agreement still offered some solace, some additional vindication for his present anger. Even so, the troubled warrior also yearned to find something that might justify his previous faith in the Morning Crow. In truth, if he had seen footprints, even if he had seen Choovio waiting for him, he did not know what he might feel. What actions he might take.

~ B ~

"Hold me," Pavati said. Choovio had just stepped into the room. He saw his wife huddled in the darkest corner. Her eyes reflected the light with a predatory luster. She bore no trace of her injury. In fact, she wore the shade like a veil of thin cloth, and Choovio thought she looked both strong and alluring, even more so than usual. The pang of lust unsettled him. She stared at an empty square of sunlight on the opposite wall.

Choovio sat carefully beside her. "Can we sleep?" he said. She nodded. Pavati curled up against him, folding his arm across her chest. He tensed as her cool skin touched his own. Choovio had carried the dead many times. He had laid them across the sipapu to return their souls. He had lifted them into graves. Only in motion, the ebb and flow of breathing, did Pavati feel distinct from the dead. He struggled to relax. Panic was rising inside him. She sensed his rigid arms.

"Do I scare you too? Kaya will not touch me yet. She slept with Sihu and her boys last night."

"I am not scared of you," Choovio said. The words felt both true and false. "It is just that more warriors were killed last night. And I see the demon when I close my eyes," he added. His body had still not fully relaxed.

"My heart is unchanged. Like Makya," she said. She pressed more tightly.

"I know," he whispered. "Are your teeth sharp?"

"Very," Pavati said. "And the night shines now. I walked down to the stream last night. I could see like the wolf. I could see minnows dart along the bottom . . ." she was excited but trailed off. She turned and looked at her husband. She saw that his eyes were closed.

"Your voice is exactly the same," he said. Her sharp teeth scared him, but sleep crowded his mind. "Your voice is the same," he repeated.

"My *heart* is the same," she insisted.

"I know that too," he said. But he thought of the enemy stranger, its eyes burning through the shadows of the night, easily finding him and his men. "Hototo forbids me to ask the Ash Owls for help," he added.

"How can we trust them? They are dangerous. Liars and killers. They might hurt you," Pavati said. She shifted again.

Her cheek and hand rested against his chest now. Her breath touched him like wind from the mouth of a cave.

~ B ~

Makya leaned against the raw stone of the cliff. His knees were pulled up toward his chest. In the comforting dark, he slept but did not dream. When he had arrived at the back of Crow Ledge, he had still been able to hear the sound of his people attending to daily life. He had still sensed blood moving through their veins. Like swarms of grasshoppers exciting the air. However, it was all muffled now, gently attenuated by the intervening rooms. In the perpetual shade, the rock normally felt cold against his skin. It matched his skin now. Slumber had taken him quickly, the unseen sun still exerting its influence.

And then suddenly he was awake. His eyes were open. An alarm was rising from the canyon: "Ash Owls . . . Ash Owls . . . Ash Owls . . ."

Its refrain was quickly shouted across Crow Ledge. The words unleashed an avalanche of commotion and noise. Makya jumped to his feet. He took two quick steps and then faltered. He was checked by his present condition. He was trapped inside Crow Ledge. He could not reach his family, he could not even defend the wall. He felt the unfamiliar hand of fear and indecision. He stamped his foot in frustration.

Makya finally ran into the heart of Crow Ledge. Morning Crows crowded his path. Some ran toward the battle. Others sought refuge, those designated to care for the children and those who could not fight. Makya simply froze. He scanned the tumult for signs of Sihu and his boys but could venture no closer to where they might enter the dwelling.

~ B ~

Sihu squatted under the late morning sun, deftly snapping bean pods from the lower part of the vine. The soil under the leaves still felt moist. She tossed them into a shallow clay bowl, rough and unadorned for the dirty work of the field. The harvest was better this year. Better rain all season. She snapped one between her teeth and chewed it raw. The sweet, fresh juice dissolved quickly. She worked the stringy parts of the green pod in her mouth long after.

Her children, both still quite young, played in the dirt behind her. They filled her second bowl with dirt then emptied it. Then filled it again. "I make it better," her older son argued.

"No no no," his younger brother replied. But Sihu heard nothing of their squabble. Her mind circled the dark window to their room. She could see it from where she worked. She thought of the sunlight that filled that dark hole, her husband lying far from its intrusion. His form dissolved into lurking shadow inside her mind.

Sihu glanced at the growing pile of beans and measured it with her eyes. "More?" she wondered aloud. And then she clinched her jaw. "No," she whispered. Makya would not eat them, and her appetite was gone. She had more than she needed already. She began to pull a few weeds. Her mind sought in vain for an image of her husband but saw nothing but shades of black in an unlit corner, a malign abstraction of the fear she had felt when last they spoke. And now Pavati had gone into the dark as well.

"Mine!"

"You give it back!"

"Mine!"

"I had it first!"

"I had it!"

Sihu heard her sons now and stood stiffly. She turned to resolve the dispute. Both boys tugged at the bowl. Her older son, stronger, gripped the edge with one hand and slapped at his brother. Her younger son jerked at the bowl with both hands.

Sihu filled her lungs with air to yell at them, but the breath caught in her throat.

At the far edge of the canyon, she saw a young Morning Crow sentry, running and sliding down the brush-choked hill that guarded the southern pass. He pitched forward and stumbled, falling hard, as the ground leveled. Sihu saw his ankle twist hard. He was green, still just a boy actually. All the daylight sentries were too young but had been pressed into service while the demon hunters, the lead warriors, slept. He fought to his feet. Dust smeared his face and chest. He sprinted forward, but the sprain hobbled his stride. Even though Sihu could not see clearly who it was, she could still see the pain. He moved toward her, toward Crow Ledge. She heard nothing, only saw the drama unfold in cold silence.

And then his voice finally broke through the canyon. "Ash Owls . . . Ash Owls . . . Ash Owls . . ." he screamed as he ran. Sihu dropped her bowl. Her beans spilled across the dirt. She said nothing. She leaped forward and scooped both toddlers into her arms. The world slowed as her muscles strained to cover the open ground. She could see the boy running as they both converged on Crow Ledge from different angles. He was running too slowly. She sensed that other women ran behind her. A few warriors finally scrambled out into the light. Her husband did not.

Bearing the extra weight of her boys, her feet pounded hard against the packed earth as she approached. Another ten steps would carry her to the foot of Crow Ledge. Sihu looked beyond the young sentry. She saw that Ash Owl men were already sprinting into view. They were painted for war, white spots stippled across their bare arms and shoulders, and carrying weapons. So many of them. Sihu had not imagined that so many warriors could disgorge from Firetown. Her ten steps seemed eternal. Choovio jumped onto the ladder so that she could hand up her toddlers. Both were crying now, mouths wide open, from their rough ride. "Hurry! Get them away from here!" he said.

She glanced back as she cleared the steps herself. She heard the twang of bows. Arrows snapped past the young sentry. They were running him down. Some of the Crow Ledge warriors notched arrows to reply. But she could not linger. More women and children were scrambling up the cliff behind her. Her boys ran inside. She needed to secure them deep inside Crow Ledge. She needed to get them to the upper levels.

Sihu dipped into the cool shadows behind them. She heard a desperate shout from the canyon. Her heart sank. Several men screamed from the top of the wall. She was pushed roughly aside as more warriors raced past. They were shaking off their belated sleep. Shouts and orders now filled the terrace behind her. "Pull the ladders!" Choovio shouted. Feeling the fear all around them, her toddlers yelled inside the next doorway now. Sihu knew that she had no time to look back.

~ *B* ~

Hototo stood alone on the Hill of Return. After the soul was released, the husk was taken here and returned to the earth. "From you before. To you now. Let loose the flesh quickly. We gratefully return our brothers," he said. Formal words. He stood before two more fresh graves. He felt gritty sweat between his fingers. The digging stick hung loosely in his hand.

He thought uneasily of Shuman. She had lingered after others had departed from the burial site. She was angry because Hototo had forbid Choovio from seeking help in Firetown. He had seen Shuman speak with Choovio in private after they had argued; and then at the Hill of Return, she had found another way to challenge him.

"Too much fresh dirt here," she had said.

He had agreed. But then, without word or warning, she had driven the Morning Crow spear, used for spiritual rites, through the stilled hearts of the two slain warriors. "Shu!" Hototo had gasped.

"You know how these wounds look. We must make sure the dead will rest," she said. Her voice was hard with certainty. She wiped her spear clean in the fresh dirt. "Would you like help now?" she added.

"N-No. It is my burden," Hototo had replied. He had been too surprised to say anything further. Shuman had simply turned and stalked away from the Hill of Return in cold silence. Hototo thought, now, that perhaps he should have chastised her and made her help. Whether she was the matriarch of the clan or not, Morning Crows did not defile their dead; and even if Shuman were right in her precaution with the bodies, which Hototo could admit, it disturbed him that she did not ask. The spirit leader should clearly make such decisions. She had now reproached him as both spirit leader and clan leader.

However, the thread of reflection was quickly snapped. A warning cry rolled through the canyon. "Ash Owls . . . Ash Owls . . . Ash Owls . . ." Many shouts erupted on the heels of that warning. It reached Hototo like an indiscriminate wind of confusion and alarm.

"Istaqa!" he hissed between his teeth. Instinct took over. Still holding the stout digging stick, he grabbed the Morning Crow spear as well and trotted quickly toward Crow Ledge. He did not sprint though. The Hill of Return was its own place, not near his home; and if he arrived winded, his arrival would shortly precede his death.

~ B ~

The ladders of the Ash Owls, taken from Firetown, where they had only offered passage between living areas, had been hastily lashed together in the night for added length. They were easy to push away from the front wall of Crow Ledge. However, the Ash Owls had brought many ladders, and they stretched the defenders thin. Their great numbers quickly tipped the balance. Arrows swarmed the tops of the ladders on cue, and the Ash

Owls gained the courtyard. The Morning Crows were quickly pushed back from the ledge. Choovio and his men fell back. The rooms to his right were not connected to the main complex, currently empty of people and used for storage. Choovio waved his men away. "Let those rooms go!" he shouted.

"Where is Hototo?" Honani shouted. No time to even guess. They retreated back toward several arterial entrances that led into the actual building complex, where the middle terrace terminated. More arrows hummed above them, clattered into the back wall.

"Watch those doorways! Watch the roof!" Choovio screamed. He pointed his spear to his left for emphasis, the tiered apartments and tower rooms where the Morning Crows slept, where they sought refuge now. The number of men climbing over the wall now stunned him. He saw a few Ash Owl warriors drop away from the vanguard, seeking weakly guarded points of entry. Morning Crow spears bristled and stabbed from narrow doorways, but for how long? Older boys and old women hurled rocks from above. The Morning Crows had piled them on every roof for just such an attack. They even dropped jars filled that morning with water. The barrage briefly slowed the intruders from advancing beyond the terrace.

Snap! Choovio heard the sound from the roof. He saw an Ash Owl fall, a stubby arrow driven far into his chest. "Vultures!" Shuman screamed from the high roof. She backed away to reload the strange bow Choovio had taken from the Ash Owls. She had studied its mechanism at first light. Arrows followed her retreat, striking the curving roof of Crow Ledge above her head. Several dropped harmlessly at her feet.

Reaching the rear of the terrace and forced into tighter formation, the Morning Crows stopped to make their stand. No more arrows as the two sides clashed. Choovio ducked his head to avoid an axe. He put his shoulder into the ribs of its owner and slammed him to the ground. As the Ash Owl punched and turned to free himself, Choovio slid his hand forward on his spear, gripped it directly below the stabbing point, and thrust it knife-like. He struck the man under his chin. He rolled free and looked out across the terrace as several comrades fought past him. He saw Ash Owls, so many of them, pulling ladders from the underlying kivas now.

They clearly meant to take the vulnerable roofs near the front while they pinned down the Morning Crow warriors at the back of the terrace. Choovio knew the upper levels were thinly defended. He also knew that the Crows could not lose the high ground. He made an instant decision. "Fall back! Retreat into Crow Ledge!" he shouted. He would draw them inside. He would yield the lower rooms to save the upper floors. He knew with grim clarity that no other course of action was possible. He felt the enemy surge forward as his men hurled themselves through the twin doorways. He felt the dark rooms of Crow Ledge at his back and knew his family waited there. Like an exposed wound.

~ B ~

Makya trembled with comingled fear and anger as he watched the Ash Owls surge forward. He had seen Sihu and his boys reach the relative safety of the upper levels. But he had not seen or heard Hototo. He feared that the shaman had been killed. Now, he stood far from the entrance. He could only watch the battle unfold through its narrow frame. His breath came quickly. He had known that Istaqa could not ignore what Choovio had done. But he had not expected the Ash Owls to retaliate on this scale. Not this kind of direct assault on Crow Ledge. Not so quickly.

Makya felt his anger catch sudden fire toward Choovio. His brother had helped precipitate this battle through his ambush of the Ash Owls. The thought passed quickly. His long hatred of the Ash Owls washed away all other resentments.

In fact, Makya felt the consuming desire to drain the blood from every one of them. But he also understood, despairing, that the enemy would have to plant their feet deep inside the living spaces of Crow Ledge before he could even touch them. That would mean utter defeat for the Crows that now fought in the sunlight.

And then he heard his brother shouting: "Fall back! Retreat into Crow Ledge!" Makya instantly understood that only the threat of being flanked, and the attendant loss of defensive advantage on the rooftops, would force Choovio to issue such dire orders. Makya glanced at the ceiling above his head, quickly considering the layout of his home. He turned to his right and ran for the nearest connecting room. He yelled for Kele and Cheveyo as he reached it. Pavati too. "Where are you? Head for the storage rooms! I have a plan!"

~ B ~

His strategy working well, even better than expected, Kwatoko saw the Morning Crow line disintegrate. He saw them stumble over each other as they retreated, crowding the doorways to get inside. "Follow them! No mercy!" he yelled. He waved the Ash Owls forward. Kwatoko believed that the murdering cowards, lacking the numerical advantage they had enjoyed in Greedy Crow Canyon, were breaking already. He would not give them time to collect their wits. He grabbed Pivane by the arm as they pressed forward. The young warrior was already bleeding from the scalp and breathing hard. Kwatoko leaned close to overcome the din of battle. "Through there first! Kill the head!" he barked. He pointed to where Choovio had entered.

"All of them!" Pivane shouted back. He jerked his head fiercely toward the walls, his anger inflamed by his wounds. He nodded quickly and launched his squad of warriors toward the opening, understanding perfectly that the elder son of Saya was his target.

~ B ~

The Ash Owls took the bait. They shot a volley of arrows at the point of entry. Choovio dodged aside as he leaped across the threshold. His men were forced to feint from the line of fire. And then the Ash Owls crashed the doorway. Warriors clashed at the point of entry. Time slowed. Like the moment before falling. Choovio felt his feet slide back across the floor. Every muscle strained as he fought to hold their position, unable to escape. An incoming spear darted toward him. He deflected it with his free hand and attempted, unsuccessfully, to pull it loose from its owner. He had intended to retreat further. He had hoped to pull them in deeper, stretch them out. But the enemy had caught his men too soon. "No enemy has ever breached this threshold," Choovio thought.

And then time sped up. The man next to him—he could not even see who—slipped or was stabbed. A Morning Crow spear shot past him as he buckled, striking the gut of the Ash Owl warrior before him. The attacker crumpled across the threshold, but another Ash Owl vaulted over his back, knife swinging. He hurled himself through the wide space at the top of the doorway. He gained the room, blood running from his scalp, bright red against the white spots, smeared now, across his face and neck. Limbs and weapons collided, the blur of impact. Choovio staggered backwards and fell, his skull ringing from some hard blow. He fought back to his feet, but the enemy crowded through the opening. More of them. The small room exploded into clots of vicious, close fighting now, the Morning Crows losing ground. No room to swing spears or launch arrows. Hands grappled against knives. Knees and elbows swung wildly. Snarled grunts and formless shouts crowded the room. Still more men pushed in from the terrace. Choovio heard a voice yelling behind him.

"Brother! Brother! Bring them back into the dark!" Makya screamed. Choovio understood instantly.

"Fall back! Give more ground! Fall back hard!" he shouted. His voice was hoarse, quick with desperation. Some of the men around him could not break free. But Choovio was very quick and twisted loose with a violent burst of speed; others threw themselves after him, his departure creating the slight moment, and the physical path, they needed to escape. The new retreat was unexpected. It gave them a single breath of separation now as they ducked through several successive rooms, retreating in several directions. The Ash Owls pursued. They roared as they sensed Morning Crow panic. The sound reverberated through every chamber of Crow Ledge. They had gained the other nearby entrance as well. Choovio could feel the Morning Crow retreat washing across Crow Ledge, flowing through multiple rooms. A child screamed through the nearest wall. Confused shouts from the women raced across the upper levels.

With some small measure of relief, he saw that his people had drawn up the interior ladders as he sprinted forward. They would pelt the attackers from above. It also told him that the Morning Crows still held the upper floors. Even so, cold panic filled him.

He reached the back wall of the cliff and veered right. He stopped abruptly and waved his warriors past. Turning to follow them, Choovio toppled a stack of heavy jars across the path behind him. One of the jars disgorged a treasure of dried beans as it shattered. They had been good vessels, already stocked and sealed for winter, but it could not be helped. He heard several Ash Owls stumble almost immediately and the sound of more pottery shattering. But other warriors surged past the blockade, leaping easily over those who had fallen.

Choovio and his warriors raced through two larger communal rooms. They would soon be cornered. "Where . . .

are you?" he shouted. And then, as the Morning Crows cleared the next threshold, a simple storage room, Makya and Pavati hit the intruders, fangs bared. Makya had understood the need to stretch out the intruders as well. Choovio felt a wind of terror and pride sweep through him as he saw his wife throw herself against the foe with wild abandon, with animal strength. Chaos swept through the dark room.

Several rooms over, Cheveyo and Kele sprung the same surprise, new thirst strong upon them. The coordinated ambush arrested the leading edge of the Ash Owl charge. The first warriors across the threshold were brought down easily. And then the undead touch of the enemy stranger. Cold and strong. The bitten Ash Owls thrashed in panic. They howled and clawed back toward the exit, courage shattered by the sudden shock, by the nature of the reversal. They lurched and dove from the room. And the next wave of Ash Owls, close on the heels of the first, crashed into their retreat. The enemy strangers leaped after them, biting and tearing, fresh blood further fueling their ferocity. They attacked with indiscriminate fury. Choovio and his warriors reversed their own momentum. They turned and pushed back through behind Makya, who moved even faster than Choovio.

"Get out!" Choovio barked as he lunged forward. He slashed with his knife and sliced his foe below the ribs. As the wounded Ash Owl recoiled, Pavati tackled him. Choovio flinched as he saw her seek the abdominal gash with her teeth as they rolled. The battle swept quickly back into the larger communal room. Ash Owl warriors shouted, "Enemy strangers! Demons!" The alarm rippled across the lower level. For five long breaths the balance teetered; some fled while others still charged, spilling into the room. On the sixth breath, panic ruled. Ash Owls, many bleeding and bitten, ran to escape the dark. The violent insanity of fear drove some into adjacent rooms of rallying Crows. Others burst into the sunlight, terror in their eyes. The Ash Owl rearguard stuttered and stopped, bloody confusion spilling back toward them.

~ B ~

Hototo, finally reaching Crow Ledge and moving across a nearby outcropping, was able to survey the scene from relatively high ground. He saw wounded Ash Owls stumbling, running from the interior of Crow Ledge. He saw many more standing on the terrace, suddenly wavering as the Morning Crows had turned back the first wave. Several bloody Ash Owls continued fleeing through their own ranks, determined to abandon Crow Ledge. "Cowards," Hototo muttered. His heart danced.

He stalked forward now. Quick and low. Dropping into the canyon, he heard Choovio and his warriors burst back onto the terrace moments later; but without the ferocity of their undead, without the power to wield their weapon of fear, they quickly stalled. The Ash Owls on the sunlit terrace still had courage. And greater numbers. They recovered almost immediately. Hototo had seen that the Crows still held the roof. But most had nothing left to throw; many Owls flanked right to renew their attack in that direction. Hototo knew that, beyond the stone walls, many of his friends and family were bleeding or worse. He reached a small stand of corn, only a few quick strides behind the ladders. He saw three guards. But they were focused fully on the violence above them, shouting up bloody encouragement.

Never had Hototo seen his home in such jeopardy; never had so many Ash Owls stood upon Crow Ledge. His heart boiled with the anger and fear of the last few days. His hands shook with rage. Once again, Istaqa sought to take everything from the Morning Crows and give it to these vultures. Did the Ash Owls hope to kill them all? Hototo could see no honor in such destruction; curses swirled inside his head. He thought of Saya's death so many years ago. Hototo clutched both the

Morning Crow spear and his digging stick in his right hand. His left hand, shaking with battle nerves, reached for the bag at his waist. His fingers closed on the rattle, his talisman from the sibyl. He drew it quickly forth. He held it there for a long moment of indecision, or its likeness. And as the Crows stumbled back toward their doorway once again, Hototo, betraying his charge, shook the rattle.

Its sound was slight. Just the loose, dusty click of a dead tail, barely audible over the din of battle. He stared with consternation. He had expected more. But then, in the next full breath, he felt the hair rise across the back of his neck. Intense heat washed across his hands; it shot through his veins. His arms and legs felt like newly strung bows. His chest filled with roaring fire. And he did not waste time. Slipping the rattle back into his pouch, he took the digging stick, and the Morning Crow spear, and sprinted at the nearest Ash Owl guard.

Feeling as though he moved through a powerful dream, Hototo made no sound as he struck down the hapless guard and leaped to the ladder. He scaled it, and as the nearest man caught sight of him, Hototo swept him from the terrace with a deadly swing of the digging stick. He caught the next man turning. The force of the thick Morning Crow spear, coming down, drove the surprised man to the ground. And even as the man crumpled, the stick was falling toward the next Ash Owl warrior. Hototo felt as though he stood apart from himself, amazed at the strength and speed at his command. But years of focus and training allowed him to control it. He quickly disarmed the next warrior, discarding his digging stick for another spear.

The warriors in the rear were young, most of them more green than those that pressed the wedge of the attack. They spun toward the unexpected assault and then stumbled back, unable to reconcile the ferocity of the onslaught with the wizened body before them. Hototo still whirled forward in unnerving silence.

Commotion and confusion rippled forward now. To Choovio and his exhausted warriors, it felt like a wave suddenly running out. The attack went slack; and sensing their chance, the Morning Crows drove toward the front of the terrace with violent abandon. "Take back Crow Ledge! No mercy!" Choovio shouted.

~ B ~

Kwatoko stood in the middle of the Ash Owls, now suddenly on their heels from two directions. He was already rattled by the ambush from inside. He could not understand why the victory was suddenly slipping away. And now he saw Ahote, one of his better warriors, close on Hototo. He saw Ahote swing his axe. The shaman slipped under the blow and stabbed with his spear. Ahote, in control of his body, spun away. The spear only grazed him. But then Hototo, dropping the extra spear as quickly as he had stolen it, grabbed Ahote by one of his braids. He was rattlesnake quick. Before Ahote could even react, Hototo hurled him backwards against the front rampart. Ahote barely caught himself from going over the edge. Kwatoko could not fathom what he had seen. But he understood his role. "Kill him! Kill Hototo!" Kwatoko shouted.

~ B ~

Choovio saw Ahote hit the wall hard. He recognized him from their meeting at Broken Spine, even beneath the mask of white spots. One glance, full of questions, passed between them; but the violence allowed nothing more. Choovio pressed forward, and only then did he see that it was Hototo, and only him, that had turned the tide and thrown Ahote. He was confused. But many strong warriors were closing on Hototo now. They threatened to choke the swing of his spear, smother his room to maneuver.

"Help him . . . help Hototo!" Choovio screamed. The Morning Crows pushed forward once again. Old men, strong

261

women jumped from the roof to join the fight. They saw Hototo wield the Morning Crow spear and surged forward. The Ash Owl ranks strained but still held despite the shift in momentum.

Choovio saw Hototo fight back against the far wall, Ash Owls trying to tackle him and tie up his deadly weapon. "Hototo needs help!" he screamed again. But the Morning Crows were panting desperately now and wounded several times over. They could not yet break through. Choovio felt his heart sink. "No!" he gasped, swinging a discarded axe himself. Many weapons were dropped or broken now.

But then he saw Hototo hurl one of his attackers cleanly over the wall. The Morning Crow leader spun away from the wall. He caught the closest Ash Owl across the jaw with his spear handle. Another Ash Owl dove for his knees. Hototo saw him coming and thrust his spear down into the back of the man, a looping swing of his arm executed with incredible speed. The body smacked against the stone floor with surprising authority, the spear planted deep in his back. The blow caused several Ash Owl warriors to pull up short. Hototo still said nothing. "Now! Now! Now!" Choovio repeated. And with that the Ash Owl ranks finally shattered.

"Fall back! Clear out!" Kwatoko shouted in disbelief. Ash Owl warriors, eager to retreat, began climbing, jumping to the ground, even as the Morning Crows rushed to throw off the ladders.

The breathless Morning Crows were too tired to follow the Ash Owl retreat. Still, they saw their shaman hurl himself over the wall. Jumping onto the rungs below, Hototo ripped loose a stunned Ash Owl with impunity and slid quickly to the bottom. Choovio watched in stunned disbelief as the shaman gave chase alone. It seemed like a dream. Slicing between the stands of corn, he ran down two of his enemy from behind, slitting their throats with the edge of his spear.

~ *B* ~

As he let the second man fall and as he saw the Ash Owls scatter, Hototo felt the fire leaving his veins. A third warrior limped ahead and should have been easy to overtake. However, the spirit leader felt his limbs turning abruptly to sand. His breath came hard. Nothing left but dregs. He had never felt so drained. Legs folding under him, he sat straight down.

With a determined effort he pulled forth the rattle. He saw that it had crumbled into broken segments. Its power had departed. He had not done what the sibyl commanded. He let the pieces fall from his trembling fingers, and as they landed in the dirt, an avalanche of regret washed over the shaman. Tears swam in his exhausted eyes.

But he heard the Morning Crows coming to his aid; they were cheering for him now, shouting his name. He quickly scattered the innocuous tail fragments. He also wiped aside his tears with a shaky hand.

CHAPTER 19

Bloodlust

MAKYA AND PAVATI stood at the feet of an injured Ash Owl warrior, deep in the heart of Crow Ledge. His wounds were deep. Sweat and dirt, sticky blood, smeared the ritual paint across his face and body. His bleeding had stopped. "Murder me and Istaqa will avenge me," he coughed. The base of his neck stung like fire. Most of the Morning Crows had run outside, jeering as the Ash Owls fled. But isolated sobs of lament also penetrated the shadows as one family or another found its dead.

"We need to finish the wounded. I have instructed Kele and Cheveyo to do the same in the other room," Makya said softly. As the first to have been bitten, and especially since he had bitten Pavati himself, he felt obliged to lead them. To help them walk this new path. Blood streaked his face and arms. Although he had been stabbed twice in the battle, his injuries were almost healed now.

"Curse—" the Ash Owl spat. But Makya kicked him sharply across the jaw.

"I feel no more hunger," Pavati whispered, her appearance equally gory. She lifted a nearby spear to deliver the final blow. Dark blood already painted its tip. It was an Ash Owl spear. A pair of owl feathers dangled from the shaft. She ripped them loose, letting them fall to the floor, one last insult, before she raised the weapon.

Makya gently checked her. He laid two fingers softly across the spear. "Many days might pass before we take revenge. And the thirst will return," he said. He had licked Morning Crow blood from his fingers last night. He felt ashamed. He was determined to spare his friends such indiscretions. He glanced both ways and then tipped his head toward the battered Ash Owl. "Go ahead. Drain him. Take blood when you can. We will only sustain ourselves in the presence of our enemies."

~ B ~

"Istaqa wants Crow Ledge for himself! He would steal it for the Ash Owls!" Sik exclaimed. He stood in the dark, uneven space between the cliff itself and the back wall of Low Nest. Since water had recently started to flow again, the sacred spring generously filling the stone basin for the first time in years, he felt that passing the day there would bolster his authority while keeping him safe from the sun. And he had already determined that, if he started the morning in one of the kivas, he was trapped there until dusk. From his current location, he could at least move safely among the interior rooms.

Lansa had just returned from witnessing the Ash Owl attack. The young warrior stood before Sik now. Even here in the dark, where only a little ambient light penetrated the shadows, Lansa was unnerved. Sik had continued to change. His ears and limbs had further elongated. His fangs were viciously long. Even his fingers and toes had grown longer, his nails becoming sharp and thick like claws.

Lansa glanced down at his own feet. Sik knew that his smashed nose looked even more inhuman. More like the bat. In fact, Sik hated the destruction of his nose. He had probed the scarred space repeatedly in private. He had traced its contours. He also disliked the increasing pallor of his skin. It was growing white like old hair.

However, Sik watched with interest as the young warrior cowered before him. Height and strength had always given the war leader the power to intimidate, and he could easily intuit the advantage his new form might impart. He saw more clearly than ever that he was imbued with the power to terrify. He regarded this with satisfaction.

"Th-they did not succeed," Lansa said. "They lost many men . . . as did the Morning Crows. Their spirit leader killed many," he added.

"Who . . . Hototo? He is a withered old husk!" Sik said with contempt.

"I saw him throw warriors with one hand," Lansa insisted. Lansa felt as though he were staring into a cold tunnel, no light past its mouth.

"No matter. If the Ash Owls think they can steal Crow Ledge from us . . . then we can't afford to wait until Nuk and Lenmana return. We will attack tonight while the Crows are weak and tired. I will lead the raid myself. Spread the word."

"I will. Right away," Lansa said. He was eager to leave the dark room and get back into the sunlight. He walked quickly to the exit. But Sik spoke again.

"One more thing," the White Bat leader said. Lansa stopped at the doorway.

"Of course," he replied. He glanced back but not where Sik stood.

"Fear . . ." Sik began, ". . . we cannot see it among the White Bat warriors. You will look into my eyes before you leave this room. Show me that you are worthy of the White Bat," he said. Lansa froze and then turned back to the monster, more than a full head taller than himself. His heart pounded. Sik could feel his racing pulse, and he knew it. Lansa had no choice. He feared that refusing to comply would put him in grave danger.

Lansa was thankful for the shadows that filled the room. Clinching his fists for the task, he looked for a moment; and while he saw the cold, dead eyes of an enemy stranger, he also saw something else. A shiny spark of madness swam there as well. He let his eyes fall back to the ground, more terrified than ever. "Only an enemy should fear me. You are not my enemy are you, Lansa?"

"N-no," the young messenger replied. "I apologize. It is only . . . your power is so much greater. My weakness frightens me," Lansa did not know whether his words were true. He only hoped they would flatter. His heart pounded as Sik allowed a long pause to follow.

"Hmm. Could I change that?" he finally said. He felt an idea forming. "Yes . . . I could change that. And I will," he repeated slowly. "Why should the White Bats have many weak warriors among us? A leader must strengthen his followers."

And now Lansa looked full in his eyes. Too stunned to speak. The demon stepped closer and dragged the tip of his claw lightly down the young man's neck.

Sik continued. "You have given me an idea. Tell the warriors. Tell them they may choose to wield this power for themselves," he said. He gestured toward his gruesome face. "Tell them. And I will wait for them here." He nodded toward the exit. Lansa backed through it as quickly as he dared.

~ B ~

"They are huddled in the empty storage area. The sun burns their skin. They cry for water but cannot drink it. They take food and cannot swallow it," Kwatoko said. He stood, dirty and exhausted, cut and bruised, before Istaqa and Kotori.

"Because they thirst for blood. Nothing else will suffice," Kotori said. Istaqa said nothing. He clinched his jaw. They stood inside his private kiva. Close together.

"Have you no rite to heal them? Will the spirits not help them?" Kwatoko asked. Kotori shook his head sadly. The tired shaman wore no necklace at all tonight. He had tended many wounds since the Ash Owls had returned. Dry blood still rimmed his fingernails.

"Then are those six men enemy strangers now?" Kwatoko continued.

"Soon enough if my lore is true. Other demons beset this land in years past. The fangs pass the curse," Kotori answered.

"What will happen to them then?" Kwatoko said.

"We must kill them," Kotori said softly. "Enemy strangers cannot live among us."

"But they are brave Ash Owl warriors. Loyal and good men. Not our enemy. Not strangers," Kwatoko said.

"How well would you sleep while demons breathe nearby? They will lay just steps from your wife and children, Kwatoko. Just steps away," Kotori waved his hand toward the sleeping quarters past the wall.

"I spoke with them again before I came here. They are still the friends and brothers of mine. How can we kill our own wounded?"

Istaqa nodded slowly. "I do not desire this. I only know what must not happen," he said.

"Banish them then. They have done nothing wrong. So only send them away at dusk and have them swear. Have them swear to travel far away and not harm their people. They will keep their word," Kwatoko blurted out suddenly. Istaqa looked closely at Kotori now. Kotori frowned. He shook his head with uncertain disapproval.

"But they will want blood," Istaqa said. He was interested even so. He did not wish to execute warriors that served well, warriors whose wives and families served well still. He was not even sure his people would accept such an order. Especially after the deaths at Crow Ledge. Although Mansi trusted him with all decisions in recent years, he suddenly wished that her shoulders too carried the weight.

"They can spill all the Morning Crow blood they want," Kwatoko said.

~ B ~

"I was troubled beyond my wisdom after the attack today. I decided to smoke and fall into dreams. I saw two rows of sharp teeth there, closing and opening, the mouth of an awful pit. I could feel its hot breath against my skin. However, my good sister, the noble spider, held me over the hole by just one sticky thread," Hototo said. Squinting into the afternoon sun, the shaman held up one crooked finger for emphasis. Most of the clan had gathered before him to listen, all but the children and the weary scouts who watched the canyon. And all but the cursed, who listened from the back rooms of Crow Ledge. The crowd listened with sacred attention. Even their shadows leaned forward. They felt awe tinged with fear after witnessing his prowess in battle.

Some had only just hurried back from burying the dead. Hototo, still spent beyond measure, had spoken the final rites at Crow Ledge and sent them to inter the bodies on his behalf, a breach of custom but necessary. The spirit leader still clutched the Morning Crow spear, partially to hold himself up. He wore only his breechcloth, inviting them to notice his many cuts and bruises.

Shuman stood back away from the crowd. Her hands and arms were stained from caring for the wounded, dried blood and herbal salves crusted beneath her fingernails, but she wore a clean skirt. She had thrown the last one, smeared with blood, into the fire. The ferocity of the Ash Owl attack had rattled her. In fact, she felt certain that Istaqa would try again. She kept Sihu close now and clutched her elbow. Her tired eyes moved warily between the floor of the canyon and Hototo. After seeing the shaman repel the Ash Owls, she guessed more than most regarding what might have really transpired at Smoke Ridge. It had probably saved them today. Still, he had not told her everything. "More talk of dreams!" she spat to herself.

"Grandmother," Sihu whispered.

Hototo continued. "I could hear Sister Spider laughing as I dangled there. I cried out that I did not wish to fall. I called for her to hoist me up. I cried out and then, as I started to cry out again, I found myself awake. I laid there for a while, watching thin curls of smoke rise toward the ceiling without a sound. I saw it drift along the strong beams above me and climb past the ladder . . . but I chose not to follow it any further."

The crowd smiled and waited, its tension still unrequited. Hototo knew that, even as they were tired and injured, many of them grieving, he needed to ready the Morning Crows for drastic action. He saw many tearful eyes.

"I told myself that I was alive. That I had not fallen into that maw. That those teeth had not devoured me. But still, I know that we have suffered great violence these past few days. Brothers and sisters have been stolen from us, and even so, the storm has not yet passed. Our enemies have joined against us. They will attack us again. I am quite sure of that."

Hototo watched his words play across the faces of the Morning Crows. He watched their sad eyes form into certain knowledge that he was right. He needed them to understand the necessity of further effort. He needed them to look ahead. He avoided meeting the gaze of Shuman.

"Yes, our enemies will attack again. However, what did my dream really mean? I realized that those teeth did not want me . . . that Sister Spider did not let me fall. And despite all that we have lost, I realized that those teeth do not want the Morning Crows. No. Those sharp teeth hunger for the wicked. They hunger for our enemies. That was the meaning. And I have a plan."

~ B ~

Lansa arrived at Firetown in the leftover light before dusk. He had run more quickly as the sun had begun to fade, and now he finally caught his breath as the sentry brought him before Istaqa. Lansa was grateful to walk past the dancing light of the perpetual fires. The scale and beauty of Firetown always impressed him. But somber quiet hung in the air. No songs or drums, no eager discussions. Like winter fog. Lansa had expected as much after observing the retreat of the Ash Owls from Crow Ledge. Warriors milled about on various levels. One group sat with legs crossed, patiently fletching new arrows. Who could say when the Morning Crows might retaliate? Many grim faces turned to survey Lansa as he passed. His short hair made him feel suddenly uncomfortable.

Istaqa brooded on the upper balcony as Lansa approached. He could hear that wives and mothers wept beyond the walls behind him, and hatred of the Morning Crows burned along the walls of his mind. They were wicked, keepers of demons now. He refused to do the same. But how could he kill his own men? They were victims of the Morning Crows. What guilt did they have? He would send his cursed warriors away. He would release enemy strangers into the world to purify his home.

He looked balefully at Lansa. "What brings you here?" he said.

"Asylum," Lansa said. "I beg for your protection."

"From who?" Istaqa asked. He felt genuinely surprised. His heart skipped. Had the Morning Crows possessed the strength to destroy Low Nest?

"From my own," Lansa replied. The young man explained the changes that had swept the White Bats. He estimated that more than twenty warriors had voluntarily agreed to take the curse of the enemy stranger upon themselves. "They waited in line. Some of them were scared. But some were eager. They wanted the White Bat to touch them."

"How could . . ." Istaqa trailed off. He clasped both hands behind his head and took an unsteady step back.

"Badger begged them to stop or it would have been worse. He said that . . . he told them some warriors needed to guard the day. Or it would have been worse."

Istaqa felt as though he stood before an approaching panther. His legs felt like too-wet clay. He believed the boy. He heard the tremor of terror in his voice. "To tell such lies would have no purpose," Istaqa said, trying to reason with himself.

"Please," Lansa finished. "I cannot go back there again. Sik will kill me. I was standing guard and then . . . I just ran away."

Istaqa answered right away. Quiet but still strong. "You are welcomed here. The news that you bring me . . . we will need every good man. Start growing out your hair this very night. What is your name?"

Lansa fell to his knees. "Thank you. Thank you. I will swear any oath to you. To the Ash Owls," he said. "Lansa . . . they call me Lansa," he added.

"Lansa, you had no other place to run. Just serve well for now. An oath must simmer longer," Istaqa said softly. He dismissed the frightened boy to find sleeping quarters and then hurried to where Kwatoko tended his own wounds. Kotori had provided an herbal paste but not enough. His supply was stretched thin.

"Orders?" Kwatoko asked.

"We need eyes on Low Nest right now. They must hurry," he said.

"Low Nest?" Kwatoko asked, bemused and alarmed.

CHAPTER 20

Spiders Spinning Webs

THE SUN HAD just slipped below the horizon. And as night settled across the land, two large fires were lit on the forward edge of the terrace to illuminate the work, an extravagant use of wood for the Morning Crows. "Tear out those beams," Hototo directed. He sat on the hard stone sill of the doorway. He motioned with his right hand. He had been unable to lift his left hand since the power of the Smoke Clan had departed. The light from the fire played across his face. He took another sip of tea from a small bowl, hoping to restore his strength.

Before him, Morning Crow men and women, sweat breaking across their backs, had used digging sticks and sturdy poles to pry loose the packed clay and sticks that, comprising the back portion of the terrace, had also formed the roof of the largest kiva, the primary ritual kiva. They piled baskets of dirt nearby. Loose material rained into the kiva as they pulled larger twigs free, finally exposing the timbers upon which the ceiling rested.

Others, working at the front of the courtyard, hewed poles and staves to lengths that Hototo had specified, many cannibalized from weapons and ladders newly abandoned by their enemies. They sharpened the ends of many, blistering their hands against stone axes. The clamor, beating against the stone around them, sounded like hail. "Expose the stone walls. Hurry!" Hototo whispered loudly. The full effort of the clan had made quick work of the demolition. They swarmed the task as one.

Hototo continued. He spoke to motivate his tired brothers and sisters. "Istaqa would have slaughtered us all today. The spirits moved to defend us though. What kind of devil seeks to destroy an entire clan, even the women and children? What kind of devil is that? I saw gnashing teeth in my dream. We will prepare those teeth for Istaqa," he exhorted.

He saw that the Morning Crows were inspired to work even harder. They had seen his ferocity today. They knew that Crow Ledge was in his hands.

~ *B* ~

The vampire emerged from his hole. He kicked away the rock that guarded his improvised coffin and twisted free of its constraints in one swift push, using his good arm to propel him forward. As he did so he pulled the cloak across his chest for added protection. Pain seared through his injured shoulder as he moved. But only fools attenuated such moments of weakness to spare discomfort, and their immortality did not last long. Hand on his sword, he rolled quickly to his feet. He stifled the pain that lanced through his thigh. He sensed no danger. The vampire breathed in the cool air of dusk and felt reborn, free for another night.

He heard a faint and distant clamor. Although the canyons directed the sound, making it difficult to track the source, the vampire guessed that it came from the settlement where he had first seen Makya. The noise seemed too regular for battle. Too gentle. It sounded more like the syncopated pulse of many people chopping wood. It sounded like work. And even though the vampire was curious, he would not go that way. Too many were awake. They were active. He needed to find a more isolated target.

He also smelled blood on the wind, faint and stale from the day. It seemed present from multiple directions. It reminded him of the horrors of Adrianople. The smell of stale blood had hung like fog. All had been lost before his small, undead detachment, the *Praetoriani Strix,* could even join the battle.

However, seeking to buy enough time to ensure his own escape, Emperor Valens had still sent them forward at dusk, sent them into the teeth of overwhelming numbers. He had set them against the chaos of a total rout. The vampire sighed. Most of his brethren had been slaughtered. And the Goths, not understanding his nature, had left him for dead too. He could still recall to his fingers the sensation as he held back his own wet intestines.

Abandoned to the dark, the vampire had crawled among the dead in search of the dying, listening for a moan or a ragged breath, healing himself one faint pulse after another. He had seen such carnage there. Like a cemetery disgorged. The memory returned his grim mood. Well, he would heal tonight. He would pay back his injuries. He would assert once more that he was the hunter and not the prey.

~ B ~

"I have brought some food. Grandmother is cooking as fast as she can," Sihu said, standing on the ladder. She held a plate of roasted corn, fresh from the stalk, up to the roof where Choovio and Honani worked. They sat near their own small fire, repairing spears and arrows by firelight. Hototo had asked the children to scour the canyon floor for used arrows in the late afternoon.

"Thanks. That looks great!" Honani said. Hototo had excused them from the kivas. His plan required weapons too. It also required rested warriors.

"Your wife and brother patrol the canyon tonight," she added. Choovio looked up, climbing out of his private reverie.

"Thank you. Thank you for tending Kaya as well," he said.

"They no longer need food, but the clan must find time to hunt again soon. We need more cured meat before the winter. More of our crops also wait in the field," she replied. Sihu saw several hot welts on his arms, a scabbed gash high above his ear.

She reflected that both Makya and Pavati had looked untouched after the Ash Owl retreat.

"I agree with you," Choovio said. "Thank you for this."

"We will need to trade for salt soon too."

"I understand," Choovio nodded. He did not wish to provoke Sihu. He did not have the energy to defend himself. He felt sure that she blamed him, as well as his brother, for allowing the curse to pass into Pavati. For tainting her friend. But her anger only stirred his private concerns.

Sihu stared a moment longer and then climbed down briskly. Choovio and Honani continued to work in silence. Clatter and labor filled the air around them, the resonant clack of stone axes, the stew of hushed exchange. Poles were stacked or fixed into place. The fires crackled and painted the walls with yellow light, the commotion of many shadows.

"That was fun. Should we go trade for salt right now?" Honani asked.

"She will not accept Makya or Pavati. She thinks that I should not either. Can you hand me some feathers?"

"And do you . . . accept the change?" Honani asked carefully.

"We might have lost Crow Ledge if not for their ambush. I think the Ash Owls would have killed us all," Choovio said.

"I cannot argue with that. Did Kele tell you that the hole in his skull has healed?" Honani asked.

"I think he told everybody." Choovio dropped his voice to a whisper after a short pause. "But what do you think about Hototo? Where did that come from today? What strong magic does he hide?"

"You heard him. The spirits come to his dreams. They filled his veins with fire today. They prize the faith of our clan. What else?" Honani asked.

"I think he says less than he knows."

"They scold me for saying more than I know."

"It feels like the spirits have handed us angry snakes. In order to secure our salvation, they demand that we hold their tails and wield them like weapons," Choovio said.

"You think that applies to Hototo too?"

"That exceeds my wisdom. But perhaps you are right. Our victory today demands gratitude. I hope the spirits have more fire to share," Choovio said.

"And maybe sooner next time," Honani added. He pushed his stack of arrows aside. He lifted an ear of corn from the platter. He began to carefully peel its charred green husk, steam rising from the blue-white mosaic of kernels. Choovio continued to work.

~ B ~

Makya and Pavati walked in Seven Sisters Canyon. Still closer to Crow Ledge, they moved in the direction of Low Nest. Hototo had sent them to watch the approach, reasoning that Istaqa would not dare another attack so soon, especially in the dark He had also reasoned that, as Chayton had dared one night attack, he might try another. Especially after the two grisly murders last night. "They have cursed warriors now too."

"And if we see them coming?" Makya had asked.

"Take no chances. Sprint back to Crow Ledge. My plan requires it."

Makya watched now as Pavati dropped to her hands and knees, her face near the dirt and her braid falling to one side, as she examined several dark spots amid the pebbles. She inhaled deeply. "This is human blood. I can still smell it." She inhaled again. "But it has lost its savor. It smells . . . dead." She stepped into a crouch and looked ahead. "I can see the trail too. The droplets shine as bright as quartz in the moonlight. I see where sandals left their mark too. This is . . . your hunting party followed this path as you returned last night. Am I right?"

Makya nodded. Her enthusiasm concerned him. She had scented the blood of two slain Morning Crows, but he heard no sobriety in her voice, only delight in her new sense of power. "Yes. We carried the dead along this very path."

Pavati stood. She walked to a shock of bushes that crowded their tracks. She knelt again. She carried a spear tonight and braced against it as she leaned forward, drawing another long breath. Her nose almost touched the leaves. She closed her eyes. "I can still smell it! The scent of our warriors still clings to these branches. Barely but just enough." She jumped back to her feet and looked at Makya. "We are like wolves now!" she whispered.

"I made a grave mistake when I bit the High Rocks warriors. They have wolves of their own now. Or something even worse. They tore the flesh of my friends like rabid animals last night."

Pavati looked down. She shook her head as though trying to clear the sleep from her mind. "The attack on Crow Ledge makes it seems so long ago. But I should have spoken of last night with more respect. I apologize."

"I understand. I am beginning to see that the curse is not only . . ." Makya struggled for the words, ". . . the curse tempts more than it denies."

"The thirst for blood."

"And maybe even more."

"Then why does Smoke Ridge still approve?" Pavati coaxed.

"They bless our ability to serve Crow Ledge. But we are like flames, I think. The blessing depends upon what we burn."

"Speaking of . . . we should move closer. We might hear them coming before they even leave Low Nest," Pavati suggested.

Makya pointed ahead, choosing not to press the conversation further. His own remorse made him uneasy. Even though Pavati had done nothing wrong.

~ B ~

Sik stood on the rocky ledge on which Low Nest was constructed. He stared at the ground below him. Wik stepped quietly to his side. "Are we ready to attack? Thirst has begun to torment our new converts. And they are eager to avenge our last battle," Wik said. Light rose from several kivas behind them. It danced softly across the ladders.

"Look at the ground. Pretend that we are talking," Sik said softly.

"We are talking. I'm asking you a question," Wik said. He looked at the canyon floor as requested. His reply was also quiet.

"Now look around casually. Let your eyes pass the rocks where Mushroom Run begins. We are not alone," Sik said. He clicked his long nails. "I can smell them too. Such power that Makya passed to us . . . the fool," he added.

"I see them. The night hides nothing now. See those ugly pairs of braids. They spy for the Ash Owls," Wik said.

"And these are the allies that Chayton made?" Sik snorted with disdain.

"He did not belong here at Low Nest. We gave that stranger what he deserved," Wik scoffed.

"We will attack soon. But I would like to confront our Ash Owl friends down there first." Sik swept his bald head gently toward Mushroom Run. "They must be told that the White Bats will not tolerate such prying eyes. I would hear what reasons they offer. Ten arrows say this comes from Lansa running off. What a trembling runt!"

"You want to talk with them? Why not let me teach them some manners instead?" Wik replied. Both men continued staring idly into the canyon below them.

"Do you think it wise?"

"They must learn to fear the White Bats now. You know this. You feel the power in your limbs. We deal from strength. From this night forward . . . we must deal from strength," Wik said.

"No more servility to the larger clans. No more building the walls of Firetown for Istaqa. Never again," Sik said. He shook his head.

"We agree then," Wik nodded. "We will take Crow Ledge this night. But we must also teach Istaqa respect. Do you know when men learn respect?"

"When?" Sik asked softly.

"When they are taught with claws. Let me teach them a lesson tonight," Wik said. He flexed his own sharp claws for emphasis. Sik brooded for several moments.

"Alright. Ready the warriors. And when we leave Low Nest . . . you split off with three others. Take men who need fresh blood. Teach Istaqa some manners and then catch up."

~ B ~

One thick timber, taken from the demolished roof, stood upright in the center of the hole. Where the kiva fire had once burned. All vessels and sacred objects had been removed from the space. Hototo had sealed the sipapu with ash from the hearth.

Using every tumpline and lashing they could find, many hands had braided leather and fiber together into a thick rope, long and sturdy. They tied one end at the top of the central pole and pulled it gently across the hole and over the threshold into Crow Ledge itself, securing the loose end with a heavy masonry rock, broken from the top of the kiva when they had demolished the roof.

"Good. Very good," Hototo nodded. Two strong poles, the length of legs, were then lashed atop the central pole in a crossed configuration. Then shorter sticks were tied to span those and form a rough platform over the middle of the hole. Almost level with the terrace.

All across the bare floor below, around the central pole, halved spears and freshly fashioned spikes were now planted in the clay like a cactus thicket, sharp points reaching skyward. Many of the staves had been scavenged from recent attacks. Some were stained with blood. Some were digging sticks, quickly sharpened to a point. Only the hearth shield, the thin stone that shielded the fire from the vent, sharp in its own right, remained among them.

"What next?" Cheveyo asked. His nocturnal strength had proved invaluable as they removed the heavy beams. However, he still felt no fatigue. Amazed by his new stamina, the young warrior refused to rest. Fear pushed him to set an example. He had seen too much these past few days. And he still fought to earn back the trust of the clan as well. He could sense their unease as they moved around him.

"Now we lay the web that Sister Spider showed me. Careful around that hole!" Hototo warned.

Twelve sturdy poles, mostly the stiles of broken ladders, were placed from the sides of the hole to the central platform, their length only just spanning the gap. Their weight and symmetry served to stabilize the central column. Thinner sticks were then laid, very close together now, between each pair of radial poles. As though the spider worked from the outside in. A few were lashed to their supports but most were not. Soon, the hole was roughly covered.

"Corn husks and dirt now. Make the floor. Conceal the sticks completely," Hototo urged. He clapped his hands at the exhausted Crows and anxiously scanned the dark. His instincts told him to hurry.

~ B ~

Wik assembled the White Bat warriors on the floor of the canyon. Like Sik, his physical form had changed, his waist emaciating, his arms and legs growing longer and more severe, echoing the line of his jaw. The color of his skin had died away as well. And all who watched could see that Wik savored his grotesque transformation, his vague resemblance to the White Bat and the power it conferred.

Sik stood above them. He balanced on the lower wall, his elongated toes gripping the edge of the stone. He had no need for light but brandished a torch for dramatic impact. The flame threw his ashen skin into bright relief, and the shadows danced behind him as he gestured, his long limbs drawn even longer against the walls of Low Nest. His other hand clutched both the Striking Snake, its end hanging down the wall of the cliff, and the White Bat spear.

"The Morning Crows have been the thorn that ever afflicts us . . . we will pluck it out tonight! They are like dry leaves before us now!" he shouted as he shook his torch. His vicious fangs were clearly visible. The White Bat warriors cheered.

"Look at them. What dark magic is this?" Moki said softly, watching Low Nest from the terminus of Long Path.

"He looks like their bat spirit. Like an awful nightmare," Ahote whispered back. He assumed that the events unfolding related to the enemy strangers they had faced at Crow Ledge, but he could not account for the physical change. He felt sick to his stomach once again. "Shhh," he added as the shouting died.

"All will know that the White Bat has blessed this clan! That he has breathed great power into us!" More shouts. And then, Sik jumped from the ledge, four full lengths high, and landed cleanly before his men, cinders scattering from his torch. A powerful leap. Another shout burst from the warriors. And then they turned, Sik himself at the lead, and ran quickly toward Seven Sisters, the path to Crow Ledge.

"Did you . . . did you see that?" Moki whispered.

"Shhh. Stay down. He glanced this way when he jumped!" Ahote breathed excitedly. "I think he saw us. He saw us before. I knew it. We need to get out of here."

Moki pointed down the path. "We should follow them and see—"

"Sssshhh! I saw the other monster turn aside with some men. We need to leave now!" Ahote hissed. He scrambled to his feet and ran. Moki rose and followed. However, he ran more slowly. He was young and did not know Ahote well. He wondered if the older scout was overreacting. He wondered if Ahote was showing some battle nerves after the defeat at Crow Ledge.

Ahote, looking back, motioned again for Moki to hurry. Ahote pushed his pace even harder. Perhaps harder than he could even sustain. He wished Istaqa had not sent such a young scout to accompany him. He wished Nalnish ran with him. However, Nalnish was gone. Kotori had returned his spirit into the heart of the earth.

~ *B* ~

The vampire cautiously picked his way back toward the men with two braids. He had not yet found their home. His mind dwelled upon the undead locals, the scourge he had unleashed, but he dared not face them in his current state. He needed to drink mortal blood, let the fire heal him. The vampire carefully passed the ravine where he had fought the night before. He scanned the land even more carefully now. He imagined that the crossbow surely watched the night from somewhere.

He wrapped his cloak tight around him. He sought the cover of trees at first, but they were too sparse. He moved into the uneven amalgam of boulders and talus that rose along the periphery of the canyon floor, the slow tribute that every cliff paid for its throne. Despite his injuries, he recalled his own mortal boyhood and smiled at the notion that scaling rocks was truly an eternal pleasure, one that immortality could not dim. "Perhaps," he whispered. He needed such moments. Time could offer nothing but hunger without them, nothing but an endless wheel of satiety and hunger.

With his inhuman ears he heard the faint murmur of shouting in the far distance behind him. "... like dry leaves..." He knew none of the words, but the vampire knew the tone even so. He could hear the hunger in that mob. He could hear the bloodlust and anger.

"Another attack?" he whispered. "Or they are coming for me?" he added. The vampire guessed that the shouting was still quite far away. He turned his attention back to his present landscape. He assumed, from long years of experience, that sentry positions were regular affairs in violent times; and with all possible stealth, he approached the very same location where he had celebrated the death of Jerome two nights prior.

He stared into the dense brush where he had sighted the sentry before. He saw nothing. "Curse my roof," he breathed. However, the vampire, his wounds still hot with pain, did not change his position. He doubted that the sentry had moved far. Guarding an approach dictated proximity. It limited options. He worked his gaze slowly up and down the hill, his body bent with the contour of the massive rock that hid him. He waited.

"There . . . clever move," he finally whispered. The new sentry was also well concealed, lying among some piled scree much farther up the slope. A small cliff rose vertically behind the man this time, clearly chosen to protect him from behind. The vampire guessed that the cliff was about two stories tall. The warrior had shifted to stave off stiffness.

The vampire looped back. He reached the blind side of the hill and climbed all the way to the top. He picked carefully up the incline, working to achieve as much silence as possible. He found an old path. It was steep but forgiving enough to his injured shoulder and thigh. Mindful of his silhouette against the night sky, the vampire kept low and away from the side of the cliff until he reached the sheer edge where he knew the sentry waited below. Well short of the precipice, the vampire stood tall to survey the land and take advantage of his ascent. He stood in front of an emaciated tree to hide his presence against the moon.

He guessed juniper by the smell. But it had been tortured by the wind. Its spare branches provided imperfect cover. He would not stay there long.

He finally glimpsed the settlement that he had sought in the distance. Although he could only see part of the structure, it looked even larger and more complex than the first one he had encountered, a true fortress beneath the vault of rock. Small fires burned on the balcony despite the late hour, lighting a flame motif across the walls.

He judged the distance and guessed that at least one more checkpoint was guarded between where he stood and that impressive dwelling. He also saw that several other major paths led away from the city as well. "More points of entry means more guards." Patient but greedy to repay the pain inflicted on him, the vampire mapped an approximate mental image of those other paths. He would hunt there next. But he would keep his distance from the fortress itself.

And then he was ready. He took his sword gently from its scabbard. He crept to the ledge and, looking up and down its ragged rim, quickly found the warrior he had seen. The man still lay on his stomach, between some jumbled rocks and behind some scraggly weeds. The vampire stepped to the precipice. He gripped his sword with his good arm and pointed it down, fist above his head.

The vampire stepped off silently. He disturbed some loose gravel as he stepped. The warrior below had time to jerk his body on its side and look up. He had time to see the demon falling toward him in silence, cloak flowing out behind him, blade like water falling in the moonlight, like a nightmare. But nothing more.

The vampire, focusing all his strength and speed, landed on his feet and then, even as the pain of impact exploded through his injured leg, the vampire let his momentum carry the blade down into his victim. Deadly accurate. He felt the blade snap twice through the skull. It sank into the earth and pinned his twitching victim to the ground. He left the sword where it stood and dropped instantly to his task.

~ *B* ~

In the corner of his eye, Ahote saw motion to his left, the White Bats bearing down. They were closing the angle toward Long Path, despite the difficult terrain. He pointed his spear toward them—he carried no bow when he scouted—and shouted back toward Moki, who lagged well behind him, more than a spear throw down the hill. "Hurry! They come!" he yelled with all the wind he had. Moki said nothing in reply. He only ran harder, fully sensing the danger now.

But the White Bats had broken into a dead sprint, the gruesome Wik pulling ahead by many lengths. They closed steadily and angled toward the slower man. Like all true predators, the scent of prey drove them, the promise of violence before them. Moki and Ahote sprinted too. But with only mortal strength. The land inclined before them. Their calves burned. Their lungs strained for air. In another moment Moki saw that the race was lost. The devils had almost reached him. "Go! Warn!" he gasped. And he turned, bracing his spear with both hands to meet the charge.

Ahote turned. He slowed and stumbled as Wik leaped at Moki. "Run!" he gasped. But he saw the demon slap away the leveled spear and smash the young Ash Owl to the ground. Momentum carried Wik past where Moki fell. But the others arrived before he could regain his feet, accursed thirst driving them. Ahote could say nothing more. He dared not challenge multiple enemy strangers in the night, even as they pinned Moki down, fangs bared. Ahote turned, and pushed by fear and revulsion, willed his feet to move again, to sprint over the hill and out of sight.

The enemy did not immediately follow. The blood surged into them, filling their veins with fire for the first time; and as they worked their teeth into the shuddering body of Moki, they thought of nothing else.

"Good. Feel your strength grow. See what *White Bat* means now," Wik said. He only stood guard. He was already more than sated from the changes wrought that afternoon; he had refused to let Sik claim them all.

~ B ~

The vampire sat with his back to the cliff. All pain had vanished from his body. The blood of three guards had washed it away. Strength and heat throbbed in every limb. He carefully and quietly cleaned the blade of his sword as he scanned the hills and ravines around him. But worry clouded his mind as he returned the scrap of cloth to its pouch.

He needed to kill the young man that had escaped his grasp. He also knew that multiple warriors had crossed over during the battle he had witnessed at the other settlement. He needed to kill them too. And two more had escaped him the night before. However, he sensed that more changes were afoot. He had heard the clatter and shouts in the distance. And even more disconcerting, his ineffable ability to feel the presence of others of his kind, like a whisper in glass, was more intense tonight.

In fact, now that the vampire had fed and cleared the pain from his mind, it gnawed more deeply than he could recall for many years. He recalled his descent beneath the hills of Rome. He had fought there with his brethren to clear ferals from the catacombs. His service had helped to establish the pact so many years ago. The vampire sighed. Incompetent predation could get out of control so quickly. "Never again an immortal horde!" he chastised, reciting the last of the Eight Precepts.

He sheathed his sword slowly now and furrowed his brow. He heard shouts from the nearby dwelling. "Istaqa! Come face your ally and learn respect!" And yet he sensed the undead presence, the silent cacophony of unfamiliar minds, more strongly in the opposite direction. He was also still curious about the sounds of toil he had heard at dusk.

Hours of night still remained. The vampire emptied several rocks from his boot and then rose. He trotted quickly away from the shouting. He was headed back to the place where Makya lived. He tried to assure himself. "Only a local argument back there." But he grew more wary with each step forward.

~ B ~

"Istaqa!" Wik shouted. "Come face your ally and learn respect!" He stood in the deep shadows. Fire crackled on the balcony above him. However, he stood well beyond its dim apron of light. His three warriors flanked him. They had drained the blood from the spy, leaving his body along the trail, and power surged through their veins now. They felt the hot strength of immortality for the first time. It made them bold, full of the greed that only new pleasures can inspire. "Come out and greet us!" he shouted again. His voice was harsh, full of contempt. It slashed across Firetown like a lightning strike.

They had walked right to the heart of Ash Owl territory. No sentry had sent warning. As he considered what that meant, Istaqa felt his stomach turn to stone, even as warriors jumped down the ladder to hear his orders. His heart trembled for the many good men that the Ash Owls had lost already. He thought of the warriors he had banished into the night.

"You must not go out there. Let them scream until the sun rises. They are enemy strangers and worse. Let the dawn finish them," Ahote said. Sweat dripped from his fingers. His hands shook. He had only just briefed the Ash Owl leader moments before and had not even truly caught his breath. Long Path had never seemed longer.

"And let them abuse us in our home? We will not!" Pivane scoffed. The promising young warrior had fought well at Crow Ledge. He knew it too.

"I only count four of them," Kwatoko added.

"I know. But do you understand what they are capable of? They will—"

"I fought at Crow Ledge today. Just like you. We should not allow th—" Pivane said.

"These demons are stronger in the night," Ahote insisted. And then Istaqa raised his hand. All his warriors fell silent.

"Pivane is right. We cannot allow the White Bats to intimidate us. Especially if they have tapped into this dark power," Istaqa said with finality.

"If we just—"

"Do I still lead this clan?" Istaqa snapped. His eyes bored into Ahote. "Do I still lead?" he snapped again with uncharacteristic fury. Ahote struggled with his tongue.

"Yes," he finally whispered. He still breathed heavily.

Another shout echoed from outside the kiva. "Istaqa! Come out and greet us! The new White Bats have brought you a present!" Wik taunted.

~ B ~

"Everything eats. What then?" Sihu whispered to Shuman. She often confided in her grandmother, and she could no longer trust Pavati. They watched over many children who had been brought to sleep on the upper levels of Crow Ledge tonight. These were the most secure rooms. The rooms of last resort. Only the night, framed by one isolated window, tempered the darkness around them. They sat close together, and the work of time could not hide their kinship. It was clearly etched in their posture. The same probing look inhabited their eyes. They sipped a cup of warm beer to relax, passing it back and forth.

"I told Hototo that many fear Makya. Even though they bite their tongues," Shuman said. Both women wore only simple work tunics, the color of sand, still dirty from the labors of the evening. They had set all jewelry aside after Hototo had shared his plan. They had cached it carefully in one of the walls and fitted the stone back into place.

"I do fear him now. His teeth are sharp. His flesh is cold. I know that he will crave blood. What does Hototo say?"

"He says only that your husband is Morning Crow. That he will not betray us. Hototo says we need the power that Makya wields. The same for Pavati and the others. And perhaps we do right now."

"But what happens after that?" Sihu asked.

Shuman sighed. She sipped the beer slowly. She finally answered. "Every path looks slippery and full of tears. But one way or another, I think the marriage must end. You must not sleep with him again. Do you agree?"

"Grandmother, do you wish to kill him?" Sihu asked. She lowered her voice even further. "I do not know if I can help you."

Shuman bowed her head. Her mouth felt suddenly dry. "I would . . . I will never ask that of you," she assured. She thought for a moment. "We will hunt together for the best path forward. I promise. But let us survive the night first. Finish the rest of this?" Shuman asked. She held out the black and white cup. Sihu declined.

"I think the spirits have abandoned us. Has he . . . has Hototo failed to please them?" she said. She felt Shuman stiffen in response.

"No, Sihu. We live still. Hototo fought like the Morning Crow himself today. That shows that the spirits stand with him. That they reside with us still."

Sihu heard reproach in her voice. She had dared too much. For reasons that the younger woman did not fully understand, Shuman would not allow others to malign the spirit leader. "Of course. I am probably just too tired to think," Sihu explained.

Shuman smiled and bid Sihu sleep while she watched the children on the several platforms around them. She heard little Kaya moan in her sleep. Looking over the children, crowded together on woven mats, Shuman considered again what Sihu had told her. "The mouth of an awful pit," she whispered.

CHAPTER 21

Everything Falling

ISTAQA APPROACHED THE White Bats, flanked by six good warriors. They toted long spears. He gripped the long knife, taken from the body of the stranger, and truly itched to use it. Istaqa also wore the shirt of rings under a loose shirt. The armor had no sleeves but still protected his body. It clanked loosely as he walked. Kotori followed close behind. "Keep your distance," Kotori whispered.

Heeding his holy man, Istaqa stopped his men short. Maybe eight lengths. He said nothing as he waited for the shadows to resolve. As his eyes adjusted, Istaqa felt the hair rise on his neck. He saw that Wik had been transformed, the wicked severity of his arms and legs, the sharp ears and visible fangs. "This is not . . ." he whispered. The words caught in his throat. The others showed no such physical changes, but their eyes were still wrong. Too bright for the darkness. Istaqa knew now that Ahote had warned him well. Even the gentle breeze seemed to scream in formless protest. Four enemy strangers had walked into the heart of his land. They had probably killed his lookouts. And now they stood before him unafraid. He wondered once more if he had erred by sending his own cursed warriors away at dusk. He wished they flanked him now.

Istaqa saw that Wik held his left hand behind his back. In his right hand, he held what looked like the long shaft of a spear. It was tied to another stick, a third hanging from the second. More sticks trailed on the ground behind Wik. The experienced leader had seen nothing like it. He also saw that the other Bats all stood to the left of Wik. Despite the cooler night air, they did not wear shirts. However, they did wear an oval of leather strapped tightly across their chest. Istaqa tugged the hem of his own shirt.

"Why so shy? Are you scared of your friends?" Wik sneered.

"Does an ally demand audience in the dark with angry shouting?" Istaqa said. He made his voice calm and steady. Wik fired back immediately.

"You spy on us. You call us your friends but set eyes in the hills against us!"

"Why did you attack the Morning Crows without warning us?" Istaqa said. "We wish to underst–" he added.

"As did you this very day!" Wik interrupted. Spit flew from his mouth. He had drunk much blood in the last two days. Consumed too much of the flesh. The taste still lingered. He had little practice at channeling that fire. Pulses pounded hard before him. He could sense the blood in hundreds of bodies here. Like the sound of bees inside his veins. It felt like a raging fever. "I have come to bring you a message," he growled.

Istaqa said nothing.

~ B ~

The smell of festering flesh tainted the air. Tocho smelled it. He knew that it rose from his own injured legs. And it made the dark too present, almost corporal in its putrid embrace. The war leader had seen many wounds over the years. He knew the smell of poison in the blood. He knew what it looked like when the poison was winning. And he knew that he was about to die. He struggled to breath.

Tocho had heard distant shouts below Firetown. The timbre of hostile voices. He had heard "Istaqa!" and ". . . learn respect!" clearly. But he had not caught the source.

"This way! Out through the crevice!" Pivane hissed from the other side of the wall. Tocho heard the firm footsteps of warriors at his heels. Many people were awake and moving within the dwelling. The clatter of ladders. The murmur of quick conversations.

"Mama . . . I want . . ." the voices of quickly hushed children. And then tense silence like the air rushing out of every room.

Tocho had heard the Ash Owls leave that morning. He had heard them preparing for war, voices full of anger and enthusiasm. A sense of quiet had fallen across Firetown as they had left the canyon then too. But this was different, more pregnant and full of fear. Tocho had wished, with the morning sun, that he still led the attack. But he wanted none of it now. Was this Morning Crow retaliation? Had relations soured with Low Nest? Tocho did not care. The conflict was no longer his own.

The war leader imagined the succor of starlight instead, the comfort and immense silence of the open sky. However, he dared not lift his legs or try to move. He bit into his lower lip and determined to stare into the suffocating dark. He would not distract his clan as they faced the trouble outside. He would not call for help from Kotori. The shaman could do no more.

Tocho ran his fingers across the corn husks that lay beneath his sleeping mat. He welcomed the texture, the gentle rasp against his skin. It helped turn his mind away from the dark and draw his focus from the pain. Cool air chilled the floor around him and heralded the deepening desert night. But it could not touch the fire beneath his skin. Tocho had thrown off his blankets. He had stopped shivering.

Tocho heard voices rising once again. ". . . or face us as enemies!" He heard those words clearly. Several women stifled screams.

"Now! Now! Now!" Istaqa barked. The sound of chaos erupted after that. Tocho knew well the sound of battle. Like the discord of many hungry coyotes. It splintered the night.

The war leader reached farther and ran his fingers across the earthen floor now. He wished only that he might make another piece of pottery. He saw the design in his mind. A vessel for water, he would make its neck long and graceful, like the very act of pouring He would etch its body with stars. The Seven Sisters at the center. It would have been like nothing he had made before.

~ B ~

"You will . . . you *will* respect the White Bats from this night forward. We will take Crow Ledge for our own this night. And you . . . and you . . . and you . . ." Wik could hardly concentrate. He wanted so badly to tear the flesh of those that stood before him. He craved it.

"Madness," Kotori murmured. Istaqa waved him to silence with a short sweep of his hand, slow and subtle.

"And you will please us as friends or *face us as enemies!*" Wik shouted, finally remembering the words he had rehearsed in his mind. "And here is a present to help you remember!" he added. He pulled his hand from behind his back and threw something dark toward Istaqa.

It bounced less than one length from the clan leader. It struck the rocky soil with a wet thump and rolled awkwardly back against some weeds. Istaqa and his men pulled back sharply. The head of Moki. His eyes were open but vacant. Blood, black in the moonlight, smeared his ragged neck and face. "Spirits preserve us!" Kotori gasped in terror, his breath stolen from his chest.

"Now! Now! Now!" Istaqa barked. Two groups of warriors led by Kwatoko and Pivane had quietly flanked the White Bats on both sides. One exit from Firetown was hidden, a secret path, a thin crevice where the rock had fractured from the cliff but not fallen. They had slipped out behind that massive shard and then angled toward the intruders from behind, arrows notched, as Istaqa had slowly climbed down the slope. Now they pulled the bowstrings and fired. Arrows closed from two directions.

"Down!" Wik snapped. The enemy strangers ducked and rolled but they were not quite quick enough. Some arrows hissed overhead. But others hit their mark. Some only grazed arms and legs. Others sank into soft torsos or pierced thick muscles. Kwatoko saw one arrow fly true under the armpit of the hindmost demon as he stepped forward, piercing the heart. The monster crumpled like a desiccated spider.

"Yes!" Kwatoko hissed, but his celebration did not last. The other three enemy strangers roared but instantly rolled back to their feet. Multiple arrows jutted from their flesh. "Shoot them again!" Kwatoko yelled. His fingers trembled as he struggled to notch the next arrow.

~ B ~

The vampire knelt behind some shrubs dotted with red berries, twiggy but tall enough to hide him. He had taken a position high enough on the slope to preserve his options for escape and offer him a clear view of the courtyard where he had first seen Makya. Several large fires had died down across the main level, only a few blue flames still writhing in their deep orange embers, not enough to cut the shadows. But the vampire saw that guards watched in the dark. He counted four and judged that their overlapping view of the canyon was comprehensive.

A tiny lizard darted past his boot. He plucked it from the dirt with his own reptilian dexterity. He held it gently and allowed it to wriggle between his fingers. Its erratic contortions made him smile. "Have you been following me?" he breathed in its ear.

But shouts exploded to his left. From the terminus of the adjoining canyon. He saw Makya and a woman sprinting toward the settlement. Their long shirts mottled with the red dust of the canyon, they both moved along the banks of the small stream with animal quickness. "High Rocks warriors! They are coming!" they shouted. The vampire froze. The lizard still squirmed silently in his hand as he watched them pass. The sight of the attractive female stole his attention. He could tell she had been bitten. He wondered how it might have happened, whether by accident or choice. He watched her bare legs stretch gracefully as she ran. It stirred his longing. However, his thoughts soon turned. He both heard and felt the rival clan as they bore down in pursuit. Like a wave of bloodlust racing through his chest.

"So many of them?" he murmured in dismay. He set his tiny prisoner loose. He heard the lizard scuttle away beneath the shrub but did not let his eyes stray from the canyon. As the attackers moved into his field of vision, carrying more of their spiked siege ladders, the vampire felt anxiety rising in his chest. They had all strapped some sort of leather armor across their hearts. And he estimated that nearly half were cursed. Perhaps twenty. He could see it in the way they moved, forced to wait on the slower humans. Even worse, the vampire saw that a deformed monster led them. "Not a ghoul!" he hissed. He was dumbfounded. The situation was even worse than he thought. How could a ghoul lead the attackers, one of the vile ones that dared consume the flesh of the dead? The vampire had not seen one for many years and had wished never to see another.

His mind flashed back to clearing the Roman catacombs so long ago. They had already cleared the ferals by that time. However, a ghoul had taken shelter in the dark tunnels and grown monstrous there. The emperor had sent the *Praetoriani Strix* to destroy it. The vampire recalled how he had confidently descended the stairs, not understanding what lay ahead. But the ghoul had heard his soldiers open the gate. He had heard their footsteps in the shallow water. And with an insane laugh, hoarse and rumbling through the fetid tunnels, the abomination had dared his brethren to come further.

The vampire recalled passing the endless rows of alcoves, some sealed and many more waiting for the dead, and since not even his kind could see in total darkness, he recalled smoky torches as the line of soldiers hurried through one tight passage after another, descending ever further into the labyrinth.

Deep below the crowded streets of Rome, the flames had revealed larger rooms at intervals, some for worship and some for the benefit of wealthy families. The air smelled like mushrooms, like the earth reclaiming all. One such family crypt had been defiled by the ghoul, the bones torn from their recesses and thrown across the floor. They were forced to wade through discolored remains to continue. "Only madness in the flesh," the first centurion had told them, reciting the Fourth Precept, respectfully sweeping a ribcage from the entrance with the blade of his spear.

Taller than any man, even more distorted in form after months among the dead, the ghoul had lured them deep into the tunnels. It scratched at their minds with unclean madness. It was an affront to both humanity and his kind. Its presence at the back of his brain felt like gazing upon an incomplete skull.

The ghoul had gotten behind them in the maze of tunnels—the vampire did not understand how—and waited for them to enter a large circular vault lined with burial alcoves. Some of the mummified bodies had been dragged into the floor and torn apart. The ghoul had even stood the upper half of one corpse upright in the middle of room; and its appearance there, its black mouth gaping in the dusty grip of decay, had cost his brethren a crucial moment of attention.

The monster had hit them from the rear with a hiss that came from deep in its throat. Some torches dropped to the floor while others spun wildly to meet the sound, flinging shadows across the vault. Its talons had slashed like knives. It had hurled the undead soldiers against the wall as though they were children, plucking off the nearest head with impunity. The vampire could still hear the sickening *pop* of that sudden decapitation, even over the clatter of shields and lances. They had finally destroyed the demented beast, driving a spear through its mouth, and then two more through its heart; but the vampire cringed at the memory. He pushed the names of slain friends from his mind as the attackers closed on the settlement. "White Bats!" they screamed.

~ *B* ~

The ladders had already been pulled from the canyon floor when Makya and Pavati reached Crow Ledge. Makya used the toeholds carved into the rock. He knew each notch by heart and climbed quickly toward the terrace. Hoisting himself over the front wall, he glanced back toward Pavati. She lagged some steps behind but still ran well ahead of the approaching enemy. "Hurry!" he urged. The attackers were calling themselves the White Bats now. Makya realized that it could only mean one thing; Chayton was ousted and probably dead.

Jumping clear of the wall, still looking back toward the canyon, Makya tripped over a heavy clay vessel that sat on the other side. The jar rattled thickly. It caused him to stumble, and although he caught himself, annoying pain shot through his toes. He cursed. Filled to its seal with beans for the next spring planting, it had been left behind, temporarily shifted as Hototo prepared his plan. "They are coming! Clear these things away from wall!" Makya barked. He snatched the jar from the ground and held it easily in one hand.

He saw hesitation among those around him. He saw that they feared the anger in his voice, his ability to lift the vessel so easily. It stung like rejection. He had loved these beans, the hint of sweetness when they were roasted or boiled. And now they tasted like dust. The vessel was useless to him.

Surprising even himself, Makya hurled the jar against the nearest wall with unnatural force. It caught the corner of the roof to his left and shattered, sending an explosion of white and red beans in all directions. They rained to the ground. Some beans skittered into a nearby kiva. They bounced off the lower rungs of the ladder before striking the floor. Many people startled at the crash, freezing in place as they saw its source. Makya felt immediate regret. Even as the coming violence required an unbinding of his anger, the young warrior knew that such rage did not reflect his heart.

A chunk of plaster was broken away where the vessel had struck, exposing the stones beneath like an open sore. It only added to the damage from the recent battles. However, the White Bats were coming close now. Pavati reached the top of the wall behind him. "Stick to the plan! Eyes on the canyon!" Hototo shouted. He watched Makya with a deep frown.

Shuman stood on the highest roof. And although none saw it, her eyes bore through Hototo with the same expression.

~ B ~

"Shoot for the heart," Choovio yelled. They fired in unison, many arrows flying true despite the limited light from the moon. However, the attackers had recalled the old lore too. They had stitched together layers of leather and padded the middle with flint chips and animal grease, sticky enough to hold the shards of rock in place. They had tied this improvised armor tightly across their hearts, front and back. And each of them wore it, making it more difficult to target the cursed. The attackers tore through stands of corn for extra cover, trampling stalks and vines as they advanced. Like a dry storm.

While many arrows found exposed skin, these did nothing to arrest the attack. Not even an arrow in the eye socket could turn their bloodlust for long. Choovio felt his men falter at the site of Sik especially. At least, he assumed it was Sik. "See the power of the White Bats now!" the monster shouted.

"Follow the plan!" Choovio exhorted. He forced hollow calm into his voice. His heart trembled, though. He wondered if Pavati might also transform in such hideous fashion. Or Makya. He did not understand what he saw, did not understand how such magic could occur. After all, Chayton had executed the White Bat spirit leader many years ago.

White Bat warriors shot their own arrows back toward Crow Ledge and momentarily pushed the Morning Crows away from the rampart. The siege ladders came forward, dull slaps echoing across the courtyard as the poles struck the front wall. "Another volley!" Choovio yelled. His men popped back up and fired arrows straight down over the wall, but it was not enough to drive them back. The enemy strangers were undeterred and very fast. Choovio saw one of them swat his arrow from the air.

The Morning Crows had more defenders now than before, and they pushed the first poles away more readily. Now reaching the talus slope, Sik shouted at them: "Come and meet my Striking Snake!" Giving the weapon several tight whirls, like the motion of a dust devil, to build its speed, he loosed the weapon with ferocity. Its first strike ripped one defender from the wall as its segments coiled about him. Its second strike caught another warrior squarely with the axe. It whirred with intimidating power as he swung it. Where Sik stood, the Morning Crows ducked away from the wall to avoid its indiscriminate bite.

~ *B* ~

The vampire stood straight up to watch the weapon in action. Nobody would look to his position now. "Tie me to the roof! Not possible," he murmured. Despite his long years and long journey of exile, he was still impressed by new weapons. He was always amazed to learn that he had not yet seen or imagined them all. The ghoul swung it again, brutally knocking another defender away from the ladder. He had clearly practiced to control its motion. Designed specifically to combat the high rampart, the weapon curled forward like the tail of a scorpion as it struck the top of the wall. It found its ducking victim on the other side. "Clever men . . . how long have they planned this?"

the vampire asked. He felt sure that the defenders would quickly suffer an awful defeat.

~ B ~

Makya shoved several enemy strangers backwards as they topped the wall. Kele and Cheveyo defended others part of the wall. However, Pavati lacked the same level of martial training, and although she had protested, she had already retreated into Crow Ledge as Hototo had previously ordered. However, the cursed Morning Crows held no special advantage against the enemy strangers that leaped up the ladders now. They could not terrify this foe. And the numbers were against them. The enemy jumped the wall easily in other locations. Some climbed the siege poles with inhuman speed. Others scaled the naked cliff, new strength amplifying their natural skill. The fact that this renewed White Bat Clan had stolen his nocturnal advantage made Makya hate them even more. His complicity made no difference. The young warrior saw mortal friends hurled powerfully backwards across the terrace. The night added more confusion and fear for the Morning Crows. "Keep them against the wall," Makya shouted. He needed to let the enemy fully arrive atop Crow Ledge.

Snap. Shuman fired the long-handled bow from atop the lower roof, but it only grazed Sik along the ribs as he cleared the wall. She retreated to load it again. The last of the stubby arrows. Led by Honani, many defenders guarded the upper levels, more than in the prior battle. Hototo had used detritus from the dismantled kiva roofs to blockade key entrances. Discarded roof beams. Spare ladders. What little firewood they had not spent. It freed them to better control the roof levels. But they stood back warily. They spared their arrows, hurled rocks instead. Some crouched in silence, as though they only intended to watch, even as weltering shouts filled the courtyard just beneath them, even as more enemy strangers vaulted over the wall and Morning Crow warriors stumbled back on their heels. Like some horrific dream, recurrent and painted with shadows and moonlight. But their only task was to keep the White Bats on the main level at all costs.

Despite superior numbers, the Morning Crow ranks crumbled quickly. Faster than expected. Makya glanced upward over his shoulder. Sihu guarded his sons and an entire room full of children there. Just behind where Shuman stood. He looked back toward the two unblocked Crow Ledge points of entry. He feared the complexity of the plan. The stability of the trap. Hototo stood before the threshold and watched closely. He was still far too spent for combat but led nonetheless. "Lizard! Lizard! Lizard!" Hototo screamed hoarsely as their eyes met. Pavati waited behind Hototo in the dark.

"Lizard!" Makya shouted into the fray.

"Lizard!" Choovio echoed in refrain. The Morning Crows collapsed toward Hototo on command. Makya and his kind dropped into the rearguard to draw the attack forward in a controlled manner, leading the White Bats toward the upper terrace that divided the main structure from its smaller annex, that until recently had formed the roof of the largest kiva. Choovio rolled and reached the hot coals of one of the dying bonfires. Their reddish glow smeared across the terrace but added little light. He scooped the hot embers into his bare hands, hurled them into the eyes of his attackers to gain his own moment of retreat.

Sik stood fully on Crow Ledge now. His men surged forward before him. An obvious target, several arrows struck him from above. One pierced his shoulder. Another sank deep into his thigh. "Maggots!" the White Bat screamed as he plucked the arrows out of his flesh. He felt blind anger as the pain contradicted his sense of great power. He looped the Striking Snake high above him with all his fury. It slashed down toward the Morning Crows. The air hummed. The axe head struck Kele square on the skull as he turned. Even that terrible blow could not really kill the cursed Morning Crow, but the pain buckled his knees and blinded his vision.

An advancing spear found his heart after that. The blow twisted Kele backward over his ankles. Hototo saw his corpse trampled as the enemy advanced. He kicked his heel against the threshold with rage. "Get behind me. Get inside!" Hototo hissed as the Morning Crows retreated past him.

The shaman saw the newly constructed floor shake and jostle before him. He feared it might collapse too soon. Errant steps pushed twigs apart and opened small gaps into the dark hole beneath, covered so recently. He saw several Morning Crows stumble but right themselves as they crossed the shifting floor. They traversed the fake floor at his insistence. And as the violent clamor filled the courtyard and amplified off the stone arcade that sheltered Crow Ledge, even so the spirit leader could hear the cracking wood, the rain of dirt beneath those pounding feet.

~ B ~

"Hit them again!" Istaqa shouted. Wik lunged swiftly forward, two long and powerful steps toward Firetown. He seemed impervious to the arrow stuck in his hip. He looped the Striking Snake overhead to gather its momentum and then slashed down across his body. It hummed through the air. The weapon, as Badger had feared, was too heavy for the men of Low Nest to wield well, too hard to set in motion. It should have failed. However, the unnatural power of the enemy stranger allowed Wik to swing it with ferocity. One wooden segment, hard to track across the dark canyon, caught the warrior farthest to the left across the scalp. The last segment, axe mounted at the end, curved past him, smashed the wrist of another man. Wik yanked the weapon back for another strike.

Istaqa saw instantly how it worked. He charged to close the distance and render the weapon useless. Five warriors followed him, one with his hand broken. Kotori dropped back. He had brought no weapon. The three remaining White Bats charged. A few more arrows fired from the flanks. They missed as the demons sprinted suddenly forward. And then the two groups reached each other. Kwatoko and Pivane dared not fire more arrows so close to their own warriors. "Knives!" Pivane yelled. Both flanking groups ran hard to where Istaqa and Wik clashed.

Istaqa brandished the long blade but had little practice with it. He thrust it toward Wik like a spear. However, he could not use both hands to steady it. It only had one point of control. Wik slapped it aside as he lunged for the Ash Owl leader, taking only a minor slash across the left arm as he passed its blade. Istaqa was thick and powerful among his people. But the strength of the demon was inexorable. Like the weight of a falling tree. Wik drove him backwards and into the dirt, his claws slashing straight for the heart. Istaqa dropped his blade as his back smacked the rocky ground. However, the hard interlocking rings under his shirt stayed the knife-sharp talons.

Wik had not yet learned to control his fierce power. He had overcommitted as he tackled the Ash Owl leader. Istaqa used that forward momentum against him, throwing Wik past his head. The White Bat demon was lighter than he expected.

Istaqa rolled quickly to gain his feet. The demon was upon him before he could fully gain his balance. The clan leader landed on his back once again, even harder than before. It knocked the wind from his chest. Time slowed for an instant. Istaqa saw one of the other enemy strangers catch one of his Ash Owls by the neck. The demon threw the flailing warrior easily aside. It seemed as though he tossed away the carcass of a fox.

And then searing pain. Wik slashed Istaqa across the face with his long claw, a quick blow that tore his cheek open to the bone. Rage overwhelming his fear, Istaqa swung blindly with his fists, connecting hard with the jaw of the demon, and then tried desperately to roll free. But as he rolled, the demon slammed his face into the dirt and dropped across Istaqa. Sharp flames of pain shot into his neck. Istaqa felt the fangs tear into his flesh.

~ B ~

Makya and Cheveyo retreated as the spirit leader had instructed, swinging their spears with little purpose aside from preserving the gap until the Morning Crows could dive through the designated doorways. As the enemy surged forward, Makya saw one of the White Bat warriors approach Kele. His body. The warrior slammed his foot across the cheek of the fallen Morning Crow. He yanked the spear from the contorted body. Almost drowning in anger, Makya fought hard against the temptation to charge back into the White Bat ranks. To kill that warrior at all cost. To rip open every one of their necks.

Choovio pushed his men roughly through the entrance. He had felt the floor tremble and shift as he crossed it. He did not know how long the makeshift platforms would last. And no other plan existed. "Hurry!" Hototo shouted over the rising din.

"No more time!" Makya shouted. The White Bats pressed forward with exultant bloodlust, feeling that the Morning Crows were fleeing in terror, paying no heed to the shaky ground beneath their feet. Those who did notice were eager to interpret it as poor construction, a deficiency of the Morning Crows. Still the defenders on the upper levels hung back, only stepping forward or letting loose arrows as attempts were made to breach the rooftops. However, momentum enticed most of the White Bats to follow the Morning Crow retreat as Hototo intended.

"Destroy the cowards! No place to hide!" Sik roared. He pushed his men forward before him. And as he saw the Morning Crows falling back, he dropped the Striking Snake, determined to use his talons in close quarters.

Cheveyo stumbled, his foot twisting between the loose poles. He regained his feet instantly. But the breath of opportunity was enough. The White Bats closed the small gap.

The battle compressed against the back of the terrace. Makya and Cheveyo grappled and were slammed backwards into the few Morning Crows still not through the openings. Men were knocked down, falling across the raised threshold and choking the portal. Enemy strangers folded around Makya and Cheveyo and grabbed at the stragglers with fangs bared. Hototo had just slipped inside. He heard them scream.

One of the demons rushed Choovio like a snarling predator. Only upright. But Choovio stepped aside to gain an extra step and brought his spear down from over his head. Its stone point found the nape of the neck and plunged down into the heart. Even so the force of the attack hurled Choovio back against the wall, snapping his spear and smashing the plaster behind him. The corpse slumped against his legs. Another enemy stranger instantly leaped forward over his fallen comrade. The elder son of Saya took the splintered shaft and stabbed blindly with the desperate speed of reflex. Some of the White Bat armor had shifted or broken straps in the heat of battle, and by skill and good fortune, Choovio found the heart once again.

"Spider! Spider! Spider!" Hototo barked. His voice cracked with alarm. All was lost if his plan failed at this moment. The long rope that ran beneath the false floor snapped taut, the Morning Crows pulling hard from inside. The floor lurched upward as the braided rope strained beneath it.

Choovio struggled toward that same doorway, only an arm's length away, as the second foe rolled to the ground. Makya had been forced back against the doorframe beside him. Several demons pinned him there as he strained to hold the portal. Cheveyo fared no better at the other point of entry. Sik was little more than two lengths away from them now. "They are weak! The–" the White Bat leader shouted. But Choovio saw him glance suddenly down.

"Hrrraaa!" the Morning Crows groaned. For an instant they strained in vain, even as Pavati added her dark strength. And then, the strong center pole toppled with the sudden force of friction released. The Morning Crows tumbled back through several dark rooms as the rope snapped slack. And a great pop resounded beneath the White Bats. They felt the floor fail beneath them, the chaotic dissolution of poles, limbs and loose dirt under the weight of many men. The shudder and clatter of everything falling. And before they could even process the strange upheaval, they felt the sharp spikes that lined the kiva floor.

Sik lunged forward, climbing across the backs of his own men as the ground failed, as Crow Ledge seemed to lurch into the air all around him. But his body was already pitching forward into the hole. His cruel fingers sliced toward the kiva wall in one last desperate bid. They landed where Choovio fought to keep his balance at the edge of the trap.

Choovio felt the sharp claws of the demon slash down his shin and flay open the skin. Sik tumbled past him into the trap and landed, face first and arms outstretched, across the sharp stakes. Choovio heard the stakes rip into meat. He was slowly falling forward now himself. However, cold fingers powerfully gripped his shoulder as Makya pulled him back from the edge and into the doorway, even as agony exploded across his leg.

~ B ~

Makya had gently warned Pavati earlier in the night, but the number of enemy strangers among the White Bat Clan still shocked her, and even more so the monster that led them. Squeezing the braided rope, her hands trembled with a mixture of fear and intensity. She had already fought twice in defense of Crow Ledge, almost dying in the process, but the scene unfolding now was more like a dream.

She watched in terror as Hototo called "Lizard! Lizard! Lizard!" If the cursed warriors failed to take the bait, if they turned aside to attack the rooftops instead of crossing the upper terrace, they might easily reach Kaya before she could intervene.

She was prepared to drop the rope and hurl herself toward the upper levels. She had placed herself near one of the interior doorways accordingly. The frame also allowed Pavati to brace her feet and use her nocturnal strength more fully.

She felt hearts racing all around her. Like a crowd of voices through a fevered haze. And even though they pulled together, bound up in the same task, Pavati felt the person behind her jostle backward. Giving the cursed mother a wider berth. She wondered, for no particular reason, if it might have been old Sowingwa behind her. But then she recalled that he had died several days before. She did not look back.

The Morning Crow retreat brought the enemy into position. The moment of culmination. But time seemed to slow as Pavati saw the last defenders, including her husband, falter at the doorway. It was suddenly slipping away. She had lost sight of Choovio. She saw the pale demon advancing. Even so, Hototo waited there. He waited. "Doooo it!" Pavati yelled in desperation.

And then Hototo was shouting, even before her words were finished, "Spider! Spider! Spider!"

Pavati screamed as she pulled. She let both fear and anger find full expression in her arms. The rope snapped taught, but the weight of the High Rocks Clan momentarily held the center pole fast. She felt the fibers of the rope beginning to snap under the strain. Strand by strand. She channeled even more effort into her thighs and back. The stones she braced against began to shift beneath her sandals.

Without warning, the entire room lurched forward. The rope snapped slack in her hands. Pavati felt her feet leave the ground. She smashed into the person behind her as they both hit the floor. Others that strained against the rope crashed as well. And the calamitous noise that boomed through the corridor told her that the trap had been released.

The Morning Crow beneath Pavati began to scramble now. Pavati could feel the panic as knees jostled against her spine in quick succession, as she felt warm hands touch her shoulders and pull away. But no matter. Without another look, Pavati curled back to her feet and leaped through the narrow interior passage. She would reach the upper levels and exit onto the roof. She had done what the shaman had asked from her. She had played her part. But she would wait no longer to join the fray.

~ B ~

Hototo screamed with angry elation as he watched the floor collapse. He pressed back toward the terrace. "Spirits devour you!" he spat. His words broke the sudden moment of shocked silence. And then he recalled his plan. "Hawk! Hawk! Hawk!" the shaman cried. Morning Crows atop the roof rushed forward, sending arrows and spears, conserved for that command, into the stunned White Bats that still stood on the far side of the trap and on its periphery.

The White Bats had just watched their brothers fall. As though the night had simply swallowed them. Consumed with hunger—reckless in their mastery of the night—the cursed had filled those front ranks. Mostly mortals survived now.

Honani leaped into the midst of his enemy now. "My home! My family!" he raged as he swung his axe wildly. Other able fighters followed, trusting the instincts of the skilled warrior. Many more raced through the interior rooms of Crow Ledge to reach the roof exits and engage the White Bats once more. Pavati emerged first. She sprinted across the roof and dove from its edge. She was briefly framed against the night sky. Choovio saw her crash into an unready warrior. She grabbed his short hair and pulled back his chin as they hit the ground. Choovio winced hard and struggled to climb inside Crow Ledge. He felt the blood running warm across the top of his foot. Once the wall hid him, he bowed his head in silent lament, pain and regret coming together in a sudden gust of nausea.

Chaos quickly broke among the attackers as they realized the demise of their leader. The resurrected White Bat himself had fallen. And it felt as though the clay vessel had shattered, leaving no form for the water inside. They had carried the promise of immortal strength into battle, but Hototo had suddenly negated that promise and turned their courage to lies. Three or four more White Bats were toppled into the pit as Honani led the charge. Others fled, the night making their retreat even more ragged; the Morning Crows pursued them into the canyon below. They saw the White Bats crash back through the corn as they fled, more stalks trampled beneath their feet.

Hototo howled after them. "We will not return these bodies. We will burn your dead for this. We defy every enemy!" he screamed.

"They live!" Shuman shouted with alarm. She still stood on the tower roof and gestured toward the pit. Motion now stirred from the black shadows. Groans and shouts of tortured pain. Many impaled enemy strangers, fallen but still alive, fought now to extricate themselves from the trap below. A few snapped off staves and rose to their feet. Some of the remaining Morning Crows sent arrows down after them.

"Light a torch. Not for long. Scoop those coals into the pit. Throw down more wood," Hototo said.

The shaman did not yet see that more Crows were bitten. One stood alone by the fading coals of the bonfire, pressing the palm of his hand against his neck. Its red glow painted his bruised and scraped shins. Another cradled his mangled arm and leaned unsteadily against the front wall of Crow Ledge. A third man met the eyes of his wife with knowing looks of puzzled alarm as she stepped down from the roof and surveyed him under the moonlight. The man felt the patch of raw flesh where his shoulder met his spine; he pressed the smear of tacky blood between his fingers. Less than he expected.

CHAPTER 22

Slipping Away

PIVANE WAS YOUNGER than Kwatoko, and sprinting hard, he reached Istaqa first. He drove his knife directly into the ghastly ear of the ghoul. The force of his blow ripped Wik from atop Istaqa and threw him onto his back. Both rolled. Pivane sprang to his feet. But Wik rose with him. The knife jutted from his ear. He screamed with inarticulate rage and slashed at Pivane with his nails. The swift warrior lunged back to avoid the blow but still caught the sweep of claws across his chest. And then the demon turned. He heard the other Ash Owls arriving. Most came with knives drawn, but Kwatoko had kept his bow. Little more than the length of a spear from his target, he fired his arrow in full stride. Before Wik could spin fully around, he hit the demon beneath his arm, finding his heart through the unprotected flank. The arrow penetrated all the way to the fletching, tip erupting from the other side. The demon collapsed into the dirt with an awful, rattling gasp. His brutal face, smeared with blood, seemed to wither immediately. His limbs looked vacant and contorted with pain. His body, almost immediately, looked more dead, more bereft of life, than any corpse Kwatoko had ever seen.

The other two White Bats were also quickly overwhelmed by the many Ash Owls that Istaqa had ordered to flank them. But at great cost. One warrior dropped to his knees as the clash ended. He cupped his hand against his neck. Bitten. Another, ear mangled and wrist punctured, stood alone. He gazed at his injured wrist as though it were far below him. As though his own arm had jumped from Widow Rock.

More Ash Owls lay unmoving in the dust. Blood pooled around the head of one. The other looked behind him, his neck snapped. Many stared at the gruesome corpse of Wik before them. And then Istaqa pulled himself to his feet. His neck was gashed but barely bleeding. No blood flowed now from his mangled cheek. Disbelief filled his eyes. Awkward silence gripped the group. None of the Ash Owls stepped toward him, standing well away out of both deference and fear. After the battle at Crow Ledge, they all knew what it meant.

Something rattled against the rocky ground. The scuffle of quick footsteps. The warriors turned to see Kotori sprint between them. He had scooped the long blade from the dirt and now raised it high over his head, charging Istaqa. "This must not—" he shouted. He swung it down with all his force as he yelled. Istaqa reacted. He stepped aside from the wild swing and punched Kotori hard. The blow knocked the old spirit leader to his knees with a painful skid and ended his words.

Kotori was undeterred. "Wait!" Istaqa barked. The spirit leader, spinning back to his feet, swung the weapon again. Its former owner had passed many nights under strange stars, and its edge was sharp from boredom. Even though the blow lacked power, it hacked deep into the forearm of the Ash Owl leader. Istaqa twisted away from the hot pain, drawing his knife in a sudden rage. "What is wrong with you?" he winced. The stunned warriors finally reacted. They lunged forward to intercede. But Kotori had already gathered the next strike.

Istaqa narrowly dodged him, the weapon slicing just over his scalp as he dipped under its stroke. "Help me! Kill him! Abomina—" Kotori gasped as he swung. But Istaqa defended himself now. He brought his stone knife straight up. He caught Kotori under the chin. The old spirit leader buckled at the knees. The long blade tumbled from his hands and clattered to the ground beside him. Its surface reflected like deep water in the moonlight. Istaqa had dealt a killing blow and knew it.

His warriors pulled up short with gasps and wordless shouts. Kwatoko reached them first as Kotori hit the ground. "What are . . . we need to stop the bleeding!" he gasped. He pressed his hand against the ragged hole. Years of battle experience told Kwatoko that Kotori could not be saved. However, the war leader also sensed that accepting that fact too readily would only deepen the crisis. He felt the pulse fade under his fingers.

Istaqa breathed hard. His war instincts slowly retracted. Kotori twitched before his feet. The Ash Owl leader sank to his knees. "Of all the wretched . . . what have you done? What have you done? What have you done?" Istaqa said. He was stunned with grief.

~ B ~

Alo gasped and covered his mouth, unable to speak. His cheeks were pallid in the firelight. The young apprentice stood on the high balcony of Firetown as the death of Kotori unfolded. He backed away from the ledge and gagged. In his sixth year of training, he loved Kotori like his father.

He started for the ladder as tears welled up. But he was checked by the grip of strong fingers on his shoulder. "Alo . . . wait. Stay here," Ahote spoke to him. It was an order but gently stated. Ahote had watched from the balcony as well. Istaqa, seeing that Ahote was exhausted from his race along Long Path and knowing that Ahote disliked his plan, had asked him to stay behind when the attack party was chosen.

"Did you see . . . what happened?" Alo sputtered as tears filled his eyes.

Ahote nodded. "We need to leave. Gather what you most value. What you need. Bring your mother and meet me on the other side of the cornstalks just before sunrise. I will speak to some others," Ahote said. The boy stared at him with fear and confusion. He wiped away tears with the back of his hand.

"But I must . . . I must take his place. I become spirit leader now," Alo said. His voice trembled, but he squared his shoulders.

"No," Ahote shook his head. "You must not serve demons," he said. The boy stared at his feet and thought.

"But who will seek blessings from the spirits. We've not performed the harvest rituals yet. And . . . and who will help the dead return to the spirits? Who will help Kotori pass through the sipapu?" Alo waved his hand toward the kiva below him.

"Your sense of duty would make him proud. But he would tell you what I am telling you now. Why else would he attack Istaqa?" Ahote whispered kindly.

"But if I leave th—"

"Shhh . . . we need to leave or die. Let what follows fall to others," Ahote said.

"But their souls," the boy persisted. He pulled toward the ladder. Ahote held his shoulder fast. He breathed out slowly and took the moment to think.

"We can return later . . ." he lied, ". . . but this is no safe place for young spirit leaders right now. Trust me. The violence has only started here."

"Where will we go?" Alo murmured.

"First to Smoke Ridge. Perhaps our northern brothers and sisters can help you with necessary rituals," Ahote said. He took his hand from Alo. He sensed that the boy understood. "Before sunrise. Ready to travel light," he repeated.

The boy gave a tentative nod. Ahote went to slip down the ladder. As he climbed down he stopped. He pointed his finger sharply at Alo. "Tell only your mother. Nobody else. Not even the matriarch. Or I will kill you myself," he whispered. He hiked one eyebrow and tilted his head, asking for assent. Alo gave him another quick nod.

~ B ~

The vampire watched the retreat unfold. He saw that a few of the ferals had not fallen into the pit. He was determined to intercept them as they fled. "Never again an immortal horde!"

he declared once more as he scrambled quickly down the slope. But he had already breathed a great sigh of relief. He had seen the ghoul die. He felt relieved that he would not have to face that monster, even though it had only eaten human flesh for several days.

As he angled into the canyon to intersect the fleeing warriors, he wondered with amazement and dread at what he had just seen. That those poorly armed and nearly naked men had killed the ghoul and many undead warriors, even without the benefit of metal blades, rattled his confidence. The improvised leather armor troubled him as well. "They know too much. And not enough," the vampire said with consternation.

The shouts and footsteps grew closer, many sandals pounding the earth. The vampire gripped his sword, crouched behind a boulder, thankful that he had fed fully before returning to this canyon. He waited with military discipline. "Wait for them." And finally the footsteps were right there. Mostly on his side of the stream.

He exploded from behind the rock with forward momentum. The closest warrior, stunned beyond words, struggled to change direction. His feet slipped in the dirt as he saw the vampire rise before him. Like nothing he had ever seen. He saw the arc of the sword. He saw its strange hue in the moonlight. But he could not avoid it.

The vampire removed the head in one deft stroke. He clutched its short hair and charged toward the next victim, one of the cursed warriors. He brandished the gaping head before him. The vampire understood how to sow fear. It required no translation, no common language. The warrior before him cried out and stumbled as he sought to run away. He angled away but could not elude the sword, and the vampire claimed his second head.

As the bulk of the retreat moved past him, none of them offered anything like real resistance. They were already routed, and the vampire soon plucked his third head from the dirt. He waited as the next wave moved toward him, mortal stragglers with the opposing clan running close at their heels. Like angry wasps. And he saw that Makya led them, now wearing only a breechcloth. The vampire held his grisly trophies high above him. "I am ready for you!" the vampire shouted.

~ B ~

Makya sprinted ahead of the rest. He hurtled toward an injured White Bat. He craved the blood he smelled and felt the frenetic pulse. He clutched the Striking Snake that Sik had discarded in one hand, but easily closed the gap without calling on it. He held a bloody spear in the other. Pavati and Cheveyo ran behind him but could not match his speed. Behind them, some of the mortal Morning Crows followed as well. Lagging behind, the heat of revenge still pushed them forward despite deep exhaustion.

But only steps away from his panting prey, Makya sensed the presence of the enemy stranger that he had faced in the Cave of Visions. He felt that empty scream and veered away from the suddenly fortunate White Bat. Makya urgently swept his eyes across Seven Sisters and quickly sighted the pale demon, an arrow or more away. The enemy stranger shouted at him and brandished three heads. Makya saw how cleanly they were severed. He saw that fresh blood dripped from one of them, but only one. Even fully imbued with nocturnal power, fear stirred inside Makya. He considered waiting for Cheveyo. He even wondered if he might call upon the fleeing warriors to help him. However, he felt called to this moment, the opportunity to redeem his prior failure; and his fear was quickly subsumed. He wanted that blade for his own.

"Yaaaaah!" he screamed. As he bolted toward the demon, Makya recalled how Sihu recoiled from him now. How she had instructed his sons to avoid him. He recalled again what Hototo had told of his own birth and the death of his mother. He saw once more his narrow defeat inside the Cave of Visions. And his hatred for the enemy stranger burst into flames. He dropped the end of the Striking Snake and let it stretch behind him as he ran.

~ B ~

The vampire flung his trophy heads across the ground as Makya approached. He saw the young warrior twirl the strange whip to life. It sliced three complete loops through the air and clipped, as it whirred past, twigs and leaves that hung from several trees along the stream. The vampire heard its hum as it parted the air. He judged its distance and rolled skillfully under its path as Makya stopped at ideal range and aimed for the head.

However, as the vampire reached his feet, the whip was already coming back around and moving very fast. He rolled again but saw that Makya had adjusted the angle and stepped with his own lateral motion. The head of the whip was almost upon him.

The vampire, coming up onto one knee, could only duck his head and lift his cloak to blunt the blow. The heavy mace struck his hand through his cloak. The metal ringlets sewn into the leather offered little cushion. He felt bones shatter in his wrist.

He snarled like a wolf and stepped toward Makya. The blow had arrested the momentum of the weapon, sent it bouncing into the air. Makya lost precious time as he jerked it back toward him and swung again. The vampire had dared not risk his sword against the initial strike. He could more easily heal himself than repair a broken blade. But now he had stepped inside the range of the weighted head. Its arc had lost considerable speed too as Makya sought to bring it through another rotation. The vampire severed the whip cleanly across one of its braided joints. The top three segments clattered harmlessly across the rocks behind him.

~ B ~

Makya threw away the decapitated Striking Snake and shifted the spear to his other hand. The demon now stalked forward with brisk purpose, the corners of his mouth tight with pain. He let his long blade glide just above the ground. Passing some dense brush he angrily slashed across its tangled branches. Makya circled away and to his own right, establishing movement away from the blade and toward the stream.

He held the spear as he had in the cave, bending his right arm just higher than shoulder level, hand over spear and poised for stabbing. He wanted to wait now, knowing that Cheveyo and Pavati would arrive soon, knowing that his ranged weapon was severed. The demon could easily slice through his single spear. He had learned that already. Makya eyed the sturdy handle of the Striking Snake even as he moved away from its landing place. He had discarded it too quickly.

And then Makya sensed fresh movement along the opposite bank of the stream. He snapped his head to the left and looked back over his shoulder. He saw the blur of motion just before two arrows hit him. One only sliced his arm near the left elbow. The other pierced his left calf. He felt the wind from two more as they passed. For an instant he did not understand. The unexpected nature of the wounds only intensified the pain. And then he saw four White Bats with their bows still raised. Several were already reaching for more arrows.

"The demon kills for Low Nest . . . the White Bat lives!" they yelled.

~ B ~

The vampire stopped abruptly. He saw the approaching warriors, clearly mortal, and was puzzled by their jubilant yells in the midst of retreat. "Enemy of my enemy?" he murmured. The fleeing men clearly saw him. However, they shot another volley at Makya instead, who threw himself into the dirt and rolled to avoid the arrows. As the four assailants approached, two braided figures also sprinted into view, a man and woman, lips already smeared with blood. They ran with unnatural speed. But prior success had slowed their arrival.

"Stop those bows!" the man shouted as he splashed across the shallow stream. He carried only his knife and, like Makya, wore only his breech despite the night air. The woman, totally fixated on her intended victim, carried no weapon at all, her shirt ripped badly in several places. Two of the men who wielded bows spun back away from the water, trying to buy enough time to fire another arrow. However, they were quickly dragged to the ground. The other two ran hopefully toward the vampire and crossed the stream in his direction.

"Why?" the vampire asked. But Makya had regained his feet. He jerked the arrow from his calf and lunged after the closest warrior. Pain fueled his rage now. Even as he limped, Makya still caught the man easily, his short pursuit carrying him further from the vampire. Makya tackled the local around the knees and, using that forward momentum, leaped quickly across his neck. The vampire knew too well the throbbing allure of that thick vein, the power it promised.

"Help m—" the victim screamed. The other short-haired warrior did not stop. Afraid to help his fallen friend, he jogged uncertainly toward the vampire, his stance more hopeful than aggressive. The vampire had seen worship before. He had known men willing to serve his kind. The desire for immortality could motivate zealous fealty. The ancient kingdom of Nyx had once thrived upon such promises.

Seeing his chance, the vampire took several quick steps toward Makya. He hoped the confused man would join him. But the vampire soon stopped short. Additional mortal warriors were arriving. He saw that the cursed man and woman would soon rise to join them as well. Even more alarming, the vampire saw that Makya, kneeling over his new victim, still watched from the corner of his eye, one hand on his spear. The young warrior, far from being distracted, was waiting for the vampire to approach. Makya was clearly hoping to lure the vampire into a hasty charge, impale him as he sought to pounce. "Clever move," the vampire whispered.

The vampire also saw that thin gray light was supplanting the darkness. Too much of the night had passed. The voice of prudence had started to whisper inside his head. "Only the patient man returns night after night. Should I be patient?" he muttered, quickly reciting a famous aphorism. And then like his own shadow, dim in the moonlight, racing untouched over the rocky soil it traversed, he fled the canyon in silence. Dead sprint.

~ B ~

Makya was disappointed to see the enemy stranger retreat. He had hoped to tempt another fight at close quarters and surprise the demon with his ready spear. But he watched now as the demon sprinted away. He moved with impressive speed. His legs were very long. Makya knew that he could not give chase until his leg fully healed. He sucked hard against the neck of his victim. He could taste the sweat of the man against his lips. Pinning the wrist of his victim, he could also feel the fading pulse. It kept time with the blood that surged into his mouth. The pain eased quickly through his arm and leg.

The demon climbed a steep slope that twisted away from the canyon floor and quickly vanished from view. However, the other White Bat warrior had continued to follow, still carrying his bow but taking no shot. Makya wondered if Low Nest had been allied with the demon from the beginning. Makya started to rise. For a few moments longer, the White Bat warrior would still allow Makya to extrapolate the position of the enemy stranger from his direction and line of sight. "I am faster!" he said.

But even as he reached one knee and wiped the blood from his lips, the young Morning Crow stopped. "Foolish!" he spat. He saw that Pavati and Cheveyo were behind him, and that the retreating White Bats continued to move toward Low Nest. He returned to the neck of his victim. He had learned, all too well, the cost of an unfinished bloodletting. Makya told himself that he could still find the demon tomorrow night. He told himself that dawn was coming soon. And with both anger and satisfaction, he told himself that the warrior beneath his fangs was no better than an enemy stranger.

~ B ~

The vampire finally stopped far from the action. He ducked behind a large outcropping of rock. Pain still throbbed in his wrist. It had recoiled up his arm with every step. The vampire licked a smear of blood from his blade. It was not enough to quell the pain. He heard panting behind him, farther down the slope, a mortal struggling to follow. He dared a quick glance. It was the poor warrior who believed, or so it seemed, that they fought together. His short hair bounced as he ran. Spittle flew from his mouth.

The vampire was surprised that the man had followed him with such tenacity. "All the better for my wrist," the vampire shrugged. He quickly slipped his sword back into its scabbard. He would clean it more carefully later. He stepped back around the obstructing rock and motioned for the tired warrior to keep climbing. He kept his face stern even as he encouraged. Men wanted to be intimidated by their gods. The vampire knew that well enough. Gods in need of friends were no gods at all.

The vampire surveyed the land in front of him. He could not see Makya or hear that others followed. And as he waited for the hapless man to deliver himself, the vampire knew with sudden certainty that he intended to leave these canyons far behind. He would run while the dregs of the night remained.

He told himself that he could always return. He could come back and clean up his mess later.

However, he was no longer willing to fight the fire he had started. He was injured once again. There were still too many ferals, and a ghoul had been brought forth. He was not sure what scared him more: that such a monster had arisen or that the local warriors had destroyed it so quickly. "And armor over their hearts," he mused. It was time to move on.

CHAPTER 23

The Ruins

L ITTLE OF THE morning now remained. Ahote saw the smoke before anybody else. His keen eyes made him an excellent scout. And the smoke looked wrong to him. Not ritual or celebratory. Too much and too messy for cooking fires. Multiple plumes streaked the morning sky. But he said nothing yet, only urged his followers to hurry. He wanted to reach Smoke Ridge before the sun was brutally high in the afternoon sky.

Alo and his mother both limped footsore behind. More than a dozen others had also followed. He had also wanted to bring Chosovi. Ahote had always liked her. In fact, after the attack on Firetown, he had stood uncertainly before her. But the words had stuck on his lips. She was too close to Istaqa. He had been unwilling to reveal his plan. Len, the only leading warrior that Ahote had trusted, moved into step beside him now. "This is not a festival day," he said quietly. He had seen the smoke too. He wore his slung bow over his shoulder.

Kwatoko had looked for Len when the White Bats had come to Firetown to challenge Istaqa. But Len had already seen enough, and Kwatoko had not found him. "No reason for the Morning Crows to attack Smoke Ridge. Or the White Bats," Ahote said. Len only nodded before dropping back into rearguard. Ahote had seen Smoke Ridge years before from a waiting distance. He had not been very impressed. However, he hoped for the chance to consult with them now. Or even to seek temporary refuge. He had no illusion that he would be permitted to see the sibyl. Only spirit leaders earned that privilege. But even an audience with the clan leader or his proxy might help him gather information.

Ahote climbed paces ahead of the others now. The Oracular Tower came into full view. He stopped in horror. Half of the top floor had collapsed, leaving a ragged crown of bricks against the summer sky. "You should wait here," he called back to the others. "Alo . . . you come with me," he added. He hoped that even an acolyte might help him gain more credible access to the spiritual site.

As they finally crested Smoke Ridge, high above the surrounding landscape, the two Ash Owls saw that smoke drifted from multiple windows and doorways within the main complex. Too much. It smelled awful, a little sickening, not the clean smell of wood. It also smoldered in several outlying huts. Nobody stirred.

Smoke Clan men and women littered the central courtyard or lay across the roofs of the main complex. Some were burnt. Others showed signs of predation. Two women, skin painted with strange swirls and designs, had collapsed dead nearby. They lay inside a circle of polished stones, one fallen across the other. They still wore ornate spirit masks, the embodiment of fierce spirits that Ahote had never seen before. He saw no visible sign of harm. Two charred warriors lay just outside the stones. Their limbs curled in mute agony.

Ahote tapped the body with the point of his spear. "The skin is like ash." He leaned closer and then winced in grim recognition. He saw pairs of braids still visible, not fully burnt. He also recognized some of the jewelry. "I know these warriors. Istaqa banished them," Ahote said. He stared into the empty sky. It was stained with the diffusion of smoke.

"Do not step across that ring of stones," Alo said.

"Wise advice. Do you recognize this magic?" Ahote asked.

The acolyte shook his head. "Almost none of it," he said.

They picked their path toward the Oracular Tower now. They passed the corpse of another Ash Owl warrior. Face down in the dirt, two ceremonial spears jutted from his back. Feathers and talismans hung from the shafts and clanked slightly in the breeze. His corpse, although desiccated, was not charred like the others. "Only three," Ahote muttered.

Stone and debris stretched away from the shadow of the tower. It looked as though the wall had exploded away from the structure across half its circumference. Like a sealed bladder left too long over the flames. Ahote saw sacred marks on some chunks of stone, markings from the interior walls, staring figures not meant for his eyes.

He also saw that Alo did not wish to go further. It did not surprise him. Kotori had sometimes spoken critically of the Smoke Clan. "Just wait over there. Away from the buildings," he said. Ahote trusted the main dwelling less with each passing moment. He felt the unease of eyes upon him. And yet it felt too empty. Like panic in the eyes of a captured lizard. "Stay away from there," Ahote added, gesturing at the building with the tip of his spear. The boy nodded.

Ahote felt a tinge of trespass as he stepped through the dark entrance to the Oracular Tower. He braced his spear against his hip and let his eyes adjust. He saw the living quarters in disarray. Yucca fiber lay everywhere. Bowls were shattered. The body of a woman lay prostrate against the far wall, her neck clearly broken, arms splayed out, knife still in her hand.

He took a deep breath and listened. Intense silence filled the air. Birds had stopped singing across Smoke Ridge. He heard nothing else, only the hiss and crackle of dying fires. Ahote stepped over stones that had tumbled down the steps and carefully took the first few stairs. Shells and beads littered the steps.

He trotted quickly to the third floor. He could smell the first odor of death as he closed upon the portal. Ahote did not breathe as he climbed the last few steps and emerged beneath the open sky. The floor shivered and creaked as he stepped off the stone staircase. He caught himself and then saw two more charred figures, one of them female. He judged them White Bat by their short hair. Both looked as though they had been hurled into the several layers of stones that remained where the wall was destroyed, every muscle contorted with pain.

And then he saw the sibyl. Or so he guessed. Dead like the rest. Two gaunt twins sprawled across the floor behind some toppled jars. Ceiling timbers and fallen bricks lay across the hips and legs of the left twin. Their vacant eyes stared into different quadrants of the sky. Their mouths were closed in rigid resolve. Flies already gathered around them. He saw that their skulls were joined into one. "This cannot . . ." Ahote breathed.

He saw their necklace. Its amber gleaming under the sun, captive insects dark and still within, mocked by those that buzzed the air. An orb of pottery had shattered just beyond the reach of the right twin. The bones of a very large rattlesnake lay jumbled among the shards. Ahote felt suddenly dizzy and starved for air. He felt both defiled and profane.

"Stay down there. Just . . . we are leaving," he called down to Alo as he looked down over the broken wall. His tight voice violated the silence. He saw the boy bite his lip as he stared past the edge of the cliff, eyes growing glassy with tears, clearly agitated by all that he had seen. By the unclean sense of presence within the main dwelling.

"We are leaving right now," Ahote repeated as he reached the bottom. "We do not speak of this," he added. His own voice shook a little despite his best effort.

Alo nodded silently. He looked anxious to depart.

"We will not speak of this," Ahote said once more. This time with resolve. He spoke the words to Alo but said them to himself.

~ B ~

The Morning Crows, all those not cursed, had retreated to the canyon when the morning sun had cleared the cliffs. They had moved in hurried silence from the dark rooms of Crow Ledge and sought refuge in the bright light. They had acted in concert by some secret sign, taken only what they could readily carry. While the cursed Crows slept.

"I must . . . follow them!" Pavati insisted. Makya gripped both of her wrists. She fought to free herself, loose hair obscuring her face, the neck of her tunic badly ripped. But her nocturnal strength was more than matched by his own. "Please let me go. I must follow Kaya! I need—"

"Stop fighting me!" Makya barked. He could feel the fangs in his mouth. Although he felt Pavati relax her arms in response, he could still see the tension in her stance. Her intentions. She met his gaze now. Her tears were defiant. Makya released one wrist in response but still held tightly to the other. He understood both her anger and her desire. The last measure of blue light was fading from the canyon, and he wanted to leave Crow Ledge too. He wanted to attain the plateau and track the Morning Crows. He wanted to chase after his family and demand they speak with him. Demand they accept him. "But then what? What happens after you catch them? Will you let me speak?" he asked.

She nodded, breathing hard. Makya loosed his grip and quickly transitioned to holding her hand, firmly but not harshly.

"Come with me. Please," the young warrior told her. He walked Pavati slowly to the dark hole where the upper terrace had once stood. Her steps were reluctant, and he understood that too. The Morning Crows had removed the burnt remains, and Hototo had supervised their burial in a secret place. However, the pit still emanated suffering. Hototo had left Crow Ledge without cleansing the site. And perhaps such purification was not even within his power.

Makya did not like to confront what he felt as he stood before the pit. Still, the two cursed Crows stood at the rim now and gazed into the empty hole. They saw an uneven welter of cinders and the charred stumps of staves; the bodies of victims had enveloped the bottom portions, sparing the wood from the flames. The sides of the pit were scorched with black soot. And the smell of ash still filled their noses.

"This memory is fresh. What should I see here?"

"I fought against a skilled warrior named Sik several times last winter. He dodged my arrows well. But I think he was one of the warriors that I bit . . . when the High Rocks Clan first attacked us."

"I have heard of him. Why does he matter to you?" Pavati asked. Looking uncomfortably away from the hole, she gazed up at the cloud of soot that had stained the rock ceiling, marking the path of the dirty fire.

"The awful demon that we destroyed here . . . they called him by that name. They called him Sik before he tumbled onto our spears."

"You think they were one and the same. Do you . . . do you think you caused that beast?" Pavati asked, her interest suddenly flaring. Makya saw the first light of fear, like the first spark of dawn, climb across her face. He barely nodded.

"I don't know."

"No, Makya. Do not tell me this!" Pavati protested. She tried to pull away her hand, but Makya did not break his grip. His voice was etched with sorrow as he continued.

"The curse afflicts us but explains nothing. I have asked myself every night what caused him to change. Is that disfigured demon my future? Is it yours? How can we follow the Morning Crows if we do not know? And if Hototo does not know . . . how could he allow them to stay?"

Pavati drew a sharp breath. She strained to look back toward the canyon as though she wished to devour the last bitter dregs of daylight. Makya saw her posture change. He felt the urgency drain from her hand. And he sensed that she understood. The young warrior released her hand and allowed her to face the canyon. "I accepted the curse of the enemy stranger for nothing. For less than nothing. My daughter still has no mother!" Pavati said. She struck both fists against her thighs as she said it.

"We have to prove them wrong. Prove that our hearts are still true by letting them depart," Makya said. His own brother had left with those cowards. His temper felt like a bed of hot coals in his chest. He did not want to stir it. Makya still forced himself to speak with quiet assurance. "They are not safe if we follow them," he added. He hated every word and despised the calm in his voice. But he was determined to mean them.

Pavati walked slowly toward the front wall of Crow Ledge once again, moving away from the unsettling pit. Makya followed one step behind, unsure of what she planned. However, when she reached the wall, the young mother only watched the small stream below. She allowed the dusk to deepen. Makya knew that he must wait there. That he must wait for her thoughts to settle. The breeze rustled through what remained of the corn, now untended. And when the gloom had consumed the shadows, Pavati finally spoke.

"Hototo has betrayed us," she said with quiet conviction.

"Yes."

"If I ever see him again, I will snap his neck and leave his blood untouched," Pavati added softly.

"Yes," Makya agreed.

~ B ~

The vampire had run for three solid nights. Mostly moving east again, the mountain peaks rising higher each night. He wished to put those locals far behind him, but they lingered in his mind. So did the chafing sense of failure. "More cats than mice now." He regretted leaving his mess unresolved, his breach of the Eight Precepts. Not all of them but enough. His mentors would have scolded him for running away. They would have told him to confront Makya again and hunt down the others. "But those mentors have been forcibly returned to dust and ash," the vampire thought. In truth, he counted himself lucky to have escaped.

A small fire burned before him. He fed twigs into it. He watched embers rise in the updraft and then vanish as bits of ash. He did not need to make fire. It was not prudent to advertise his presence. However, the vampire felt certain that he was alone. The Knights of St. John no longer hunted him after all. For the first time in years. And he could watch the land all around from the rocky outcrop where he camped. He had lit the fire to watch it dance, to enjoy its company.

After a while the vampire took a small, weathered box from the bag that held his few possessions. He had carved it from a single piece of black wood. He untied the string that held fast its lid, set the lid carefully aside, and folded back the tattered silk inside. He lifted a small sundial into his palm. The rich verdigris of old copper looked even darker against his pale skin. He stared down into the disc for a long while.

He watched as the fire marked a thin shadow across its green face, a false prophet of time, staying its passage as long as willing hands might feed the flames. The vampire finally looked off into the stars, the mocking suns of other worlds, or so an old man had told him once. He cupped the sundial in his hand and stroked its gnomon with his thumb, now rounded from wear and darkened from contact, an artifact of the day.

And then he ended the ritual without a word, carefully packing the box, tying down the lid, closing his bag with care. He thought, not for the first time, that he might like to watch the sunrise, that he might revel in its blinding ascent, even as it consumed him, finally. But he also thought that he might turn south. In his travels, he had gathered rumors of endless jungles, uncharted beyond the vast ocean. He had not yet found these jungles but felt certain that he might find them further south. Those rumors breathed in his memory. He had once heard that the vampire lords still ruled there, that some of his defeated brethren had risen to power again, and the idea stirred hope within him.

~ B ~

The relentless sun of late summer beat down on the Morning Crows. They pressed doggedly forward across the desert plateau, moving south and gently west. They had raced the setting sun for many days, leaving at dawn and hoping to move far before dusk, not knowing whether an enemy stranger might seek to follow, fearing the thought of both friend and foe. Some pulled makeshift litters to transport men and women still wounded. A few walked behind to disguise the trail. Other litters held what food and possessions time had allowed, a poor heap of vessels and baskets settled among blankets and winter cloaks. Some good axes and spears. So much left behind. So much abandoned. Pumpkins would rot on the vine.

Choovio walked alone at the tail of the group. He balanced his spear loosely across his fingers. He had not slept last night. He watched Kaya far ahead, knowing that she did not grasp the purpose of this trek, knowing that she expected to see Pavati again. He knew that Sihu carefully watched his daughter too. Even as she struggled to keep her own small boys on the path. They jumped on and off the nearest litter. Honani still dragged it forward without complaint. He knew the game kept them moving.

Choovio would keep Kaya close tonight as they slept. He feared what the instincts of an abandoned mother might provoke. In fact, he feared Pavati more than Makya. He hated that fact. However, his hatred made it no less true. He recalled her return to Crow Ledge after Hototo had sprung his trap. Black smoke from the pit had fouled the air. Choovio had smelled the burning hair, heard the crackle and hiss of baking flesh. As gray light gathered before the dawn, Pavati had stood before him nearly naked, her bare chest and chin stained with blood, her arms smeared with it, every limb and every finger exultant. "I could heal that leg. Would you like me too?" she had asked serenely.

Choovio pushed away the memory with a chill. He glanced down. His shin was wrapped where Sik had cut him. He felt dull pain in every step, but the bleeding had finally stopped. Although Hototo had cleaned and dressed the wound well, the deep gash would take time to fully heal. Like the start of a hard winter.

Hototo himself limped at the front of the ragged line, his left arm still lame and his hips aching more than ever. Shuman walked beside him. She used her own spear like a staff. Their lips were parched, and both looked like bones discarded by the fire, their eyes glazed with exhaustion and sorrow.

"Where do we head again?" asked one of the older children.

"We will find the southern clans and rebuild there. They will welcome us and come to respect the Morning Crows," Hototo said with an encouraging smile. The boy dropped back among his peers. Shuman had not spoken for a long while.

"When we join them . . . you will not lead," she said finally.

Hototo stopped in his tracks. He faced her. "Shu . . . how can you say that? We have faced so much together. The spirits may yet call upon—"

"Do not argue this, Hototo. I have made my decision. The spirit leader will serve a new clan leader in the south."

"This is rash. I have led the Morning Crows through trials that—"

"You shall not lead!" Shuman screamed. The matriarch flicked her spear upward to grasp the lower end. Holding it like an axe now, she sliced it through a looping arc and struck the shaft across his shoulder. Just away from the base of the neck. She struck him hard, and the shaman fell to his knees, felled by her words even more than the blow. He trembled in pain but made no sound, save hard breathing. "You shall not," she repeated sternly. Her voice trembled with defiant anger. She still gripped the spear tightly.

The clan froze behind them. Hototo did not rise. He did not answer. And then finally, Shuman turned back to the path and marched defiantly forward. "We need to keep moving, Crows!" she barked. Hushed into burning silence, unsure of the altercation and unwilling to defy Shuman, the Morning Crows moved around Hototo and followed her. Several small children began to cry as they passed. Choovio paused, his heart pounding with indecision and grief, but then without uttering a word, the elder son of Saya kept walking.

Hototo knelt there for a while. Until his people had walked far beyond him. Pain gripped his right shoulder like a cruel hand. And he could not lift his left hand to soothe it. His hands shook. His gaze did not stray from the parched desert soil before him. He did not see that many of the Morning Crows looked back and hesitated, concern written in their faces.

"Too many enemies," Hototo whispered at last. And he knew that he spoke the truth.

~

CHARACTER KEY

The Morning Crow Clan

Choovio	War leader, older brother of Makya, husband to Pavati.	*Warriors of the Clan*
Hototo	Spirit leader and clan leader.	Ayawamat Cheveyo
Kaya	Daughter of Choovio and Pavati	Honani Kele
Makya	War leader, younger brother of Choovio, husband to Sihu	Lusio
Muna	Mother of Makya and Choovio	
Pavati	Wife to Choovio, mother of Kaya	
Saya		
	Father of Makya and Choovio, former clan leader	
Shuman		
	Matriarch of Crow Ledge, Sihu's grandmother.	
Sihu		
	Wife to Makya	
Sowingwa		
	Clan elder	

The Ash Owl Clan

Chosovi	To marry Kwahu	*Warriors of the Clan*
Alo	Apprentice of Kotori	Ahote
Istaqa	Clan leader, brother to Chosovi	Len Moki
Kotori	Spirit leader	Nalnish Nayavu
Kwatoko	Second war leader	Pivane
Mansi	Matriarch of Firetown	
Pimne & Chua	Friends of Chosovi	
Tocho	War leader	

The High Rocks / White Bat Clan

Cha'Akmongwi	Former spirit leader and former clan leader	
Chayton	Clan leader	
Kwahu	To marry Chosovi	
Lapu	Husband to Lenmana	
Lenmana	Wife to Lapu	
Old Chu'Si	Matriarch of Low Nest	
Sik	War leader	

Warriors of the Clan

Badger
Lansa
Nuk
Wik

Other

The Vampire	Hunted by the Knights of St. John
Allain	Knight of St. John
Jerome	Knight of St. John
The Sibyl	From the Smoke Clan

ACKNOWLEDGEMENTS

Special thanks to Laura for her quiet encouragement, graceful companionship, and patience through many drafts. And to Taryn and Colin, who constantly motivate and inspire me. And thanks to my Hohenbary readers for your valuable advice on the very first and roughest of drafts: Laura Hohenbary, Jean Hohenbary, Joshua Hohenbary, and Josey Strong.

Thanks also to my non-Hohenbary readers for your insightful comments and generous interest: Elizabeth Dodd, Bill Lansdowne, Daralyn Arata, Stephanie Woods, and Steve Dandaneau. Additional thanks to Daralyn Arata, Rebecca Crowley, and Amity Thompson for taking the time to share your understanding of the publishing process.

I would also like to express my appreciation to Chris and Ben at Blueberry Lane Books for their support, guidance, and willingness to give this story a chance. And I am grateful for the valuable work of Rebecca Fontenot, whose editing advice and intelligent reading helped *Before the Ruins* find its final form.

And finally, I want to give a shout out to the National Park Service, who maintain and protect many of the major Puebloan ruins, and whose interpretive guides were unfailingly professional, informed, and engaging as I toured various sites across the Southwest.

Made in the USA
Middletown, DE
08 February 2021